The fiery brilliance of the Zebra Hologram Heart which you see on the cover is created by "laser holography." This is the revolutionary process in which a powerful laser beam records light waves in diamond-like facets so tiny that 9,000,000 fit in a square inch. No print or photograph can match the vibrant colors and radiant glow of a hologram.

So look for the Zebra Hologram Heart whenever you buy a historical romance. It is a shimmering reflection of our guarantee that you'll find consistent quality between the covers!

Sensual Spell

"What spell have you cast upon me?" Jarred's voice was a harsh whisper. His hand glided down the silky fabric that clung to her curvaceous figure, aching to mold her bare flesh to his. "I know what you are, but when I touch you I can think of nothing but holding you . . . loving you. . . ."

A mischievous smile lifted the corners of her lips as Chelsie leaned back to meet his all-consuming gaze. "I am what I have become," she taunted him as she traced the cleft in his chin. "And you will become what I make of you. . . ."

Jarred's voice was raspy with desire. "And just what is your intention, witch?"

Wantonly, Chelsie slid her body against his and whispered, "I will turn you into a human torch."

"Feed the flame," he groaned in tormented pleasure. "God help me but I want you the way I've never wanted any other woman. . . ."

Captive Enchantress

GINA ROBINS

ZEBRA BOOKS
KENSINGTON PUBLISHING CORP.

ZEBRA BOOKS

are published by

Kensington Publishing Corp.
475 Park Avenue South
New York, NY 10016

First printing: June, 1989

Printed in the United States of America

This book is dedicated to my husband Ed, for the assistance, encouragement, and support. Love you . . . And to Jeanette Stotts for her valuable help. Thanks, Mom. . . .

Part One

Voyager upon life's sea:
To yourself be true,
And whate'er your lot may be,
Paddle your own canoe.
Edward Philpots

Chapter 1

A lump of fear constricted Chelsie's throat as she pushed her way through the congested crowd that swarmed along the wharf. One backward glance prompted her to quicken her already frantic pace and run for her life.

Isaac Latham's whiskered face was puckered in a scowl. The familiar curses that had erupted from his mouth the past six weeks were flying from his lips once more. The mere sight of Isaac giving chase caused Chelsie to grimace in fear. Her wild green eyes scanned the unfamiliar city, searching for a place to hide, to end the horrifying nightmare that had held her captive for more than a month.

Praying nonstop, Chelsie burst through the throng of people who milled around the auction blocks. With her fists clutched in the folds of her tattered gown, she lifted up the ragged hem and dashed toward the row of wood-and-brick buildings that lined the streets. Another hasty glance over her shoulder had her swearing all the salty curses she had learned from Isaac and the rest of his ruthless shipmates. Isaac was still hot on her heels, and Chelsie swore she'd run until she dropped, if need be. Isaac wasn't going to put her in chains again. Curse his black soul!

Isaac's gruff voice shattered her thoughts. Chelsie bowed her neck, determined to outrun the wiry sailor who was as hell-bent on catching her as she was on eluding him. Chelsie darted into the alley the instant Isaac stumbled through the crowd in quick pursuit. Like a runaway stallion, she charged through the narrow passageway cluttered with garbage cans and discarded crates. The sound of echoing footsteps caused her to rush toward the first door within reach. A muffled curse escaped her lips when she tugged on the portal only to find it locked. Wasting no time, she scurried to the next door and murmured a prayer of thanks when the portal creaked open.

One glance around the lantern-lit room brought a smile to her heart-shaped lips — the first smile to settle on her smudged face in six agonizing weeks. A bathhouse! A bathhouse situated on the lowermost floor of an elegant hotel! Her guardian angel must have heard her pleas. Chelsie had found sanctuary and a bath, both in the same moment. She had vowed at least once a day to sacrifice anything for a long-awaited bath or freedom — or both!

The creak of the door on the opposite side of the bathhouse jolted Chelsie to her senses. She sailed across the vacant room and dived into the huge tub that was a mass of fragrant bubbles and warm water.

Never again would she take bathing for granted, Chelsie promised herself. It was a luxury as much as a necessity. The tepid water soothed her taut muscles, and the scented bubbles washed away the offensive aroma that reminded Chelsie of her recent nightmare in the musty hull of the ship.

When the sounds of footsteps — two sets of them — echoed in the bathhouse, Chelsie sucked in a deep breath and scrunched down in the steamy vat, concealing herself in the sparkling bubbles. If her prediction proved correct (and she was sure it would), the rattle at the back exit would be Isaac Latham coming to drag her back to the docks and punish her for escaping. Chelsie didn't have the foggiest notion who had inadvertently entered the bathhouse in the normal fashion — through the hotel. And she really didn't care. Her only concern was eluding Isaac and forgetting the tormenting chain of events that had landed her in the New World Colonies — the very last place she had ever expected to be — at least in this lifetime.

A weary sigh escaped Jarred McAlister's lips as he stepped from the dressing room into the bathhouse. Garbed in nothing but a fluffy towel, he ambled toward one of the waiting tubs, anxious to soak away his exhaustion.

The past few months had been a long and frustrating ordeal for

Jarred. As an illustrious member of the Maryland Assembly and a commander in the colonial militia, he had ventured west with soldiers from both Maryland and Virginia to confront the French. From their well-established settlements in Canada, the French had swarmed south to take control of the English frontier in the fertile valleys along the Ohio and Monongahela Rivers.

The area had previously been granted to the colonies of Pennsylvania, Maryland, and Virginia, but the French seemed determined to restrict the English colonists to the seaboard and claim the interior of the continent for themselves. They had established Fort Duquesne and tramped around the valley as if they owned the place. Naturally, the English colonists were outraged when their lifelong enemies began crowding in on them.

Jarred had assumed command of the volunteer militia and had joined forces with George Washington and his troop of Virginians. When they politely asked the French to abandon areas that rightfully belonged to the English, the intruders refused to budge. The first confrontation found the colonial militias the victors. But the French called in their well-drilled army of regulars and overwhelmed their natural-born enemy—the English. The conflict at Great Meadows found the colonists outmanned and in the throes of battle with not only the French, but their cunning Indian allies.

Although Jarred was no stranger to the backwoods and had been taught the skills of survival in the wilds by the legendary Christopher Gist, he recognized defeat when it stared him in the face. The militia had been forced to withdraw from the hastily constructed palisade they had named Fort Necessity, to await reinforcements from England.

Jarred dreaded reporting to the Assembly when it convened the following day. Although the English and their colonies were supposedly at peace with France, the shots fired in Great Meadow would be heard around the world. Trouble was brewing again, and the third war against the French and their Indian allies was about to escalate. The colonists were outraged by French infiltration and France seemed determined to colonize the west—especially on land with disputed boundaries.

From what Jarred had seen, he was sure Marquis Duquesne, the French governor of Canada, had planned to assume complete control of the West and confine the English between the Atlantic and the Appalachians.

Shrugging away his troubled thoughts, Jarred plunked down into the huge vat of steamy water and bubbles. His alert blue eyes swung to the back door when a scraggly sailor abruptly burst into the bathhouse to stand on the steps, staring in all directions.

Isaac muttered a string of unrepeatable curses when he found no trace of the sassy blond wench he had been trailing for a quarter of an hour. There was no one in the room except the powerfully built, raven-haired rogue who was glaring back at him for making an improper entrance into the bathhouse.

Grumbling, Isaac backed toward the door. After combing his fingers through his mousy brown hair, Isaac performed a bow that was far more ridiculing than apologetic. " 'Scuse me, I wuz lookin' for somebody."

Jarred's sapphire eyes narrowed at the mocking gesture and he coolly dismissed the grimy little man by scooping up a sponge and bar of soap and glancing the other way. As the portal banged shut, Jarred stretched out his long legs and eased his head back against the rim of the large wooden tub. When his foot struck an unidentified object, Jarred jerked upright so quickly he splashed water onto the brick floor.

"What the hell . . . ?" he growled.

After his disconcerting encounter with the Indians who swarmed the dense forests near Fort Duquesne, Jarred was as jumpy as a grasshopper. With his knees bent up beside his shoulders and both fists doubled, he glowered at the floating bubbles that seemed to come to life before his very eyes. Lo and behold, a face that was embedded with wide green pools arose from his bath like a magical genie materializing from a bottle!

Chelsie couldn't hold her breath a second longer for fear her lungs would burst. Jarred's misdirected foot had accidentally rammed into her chest, knocking out her last ounce of air. Like a spouting whale, she burst to the surface, blowing the soap bubbles from her face and gasping for breath.

For a moment Jarred sat still as a statue. He stared amazed at the exquisite features and the most fascinating pair of eyes he could recall seeing in all his thirty-two years. They were like an ever-changing kaleidoscope that sparkled with expression. They looked haunted and yet lively, wary and yet brimming with remarkable spirit.

Those rounded pools were as wide and colorful as the Emerald Isle. Long thick eyelashes that glistened with droplets fanned out from those eyes that dominated the woman's pixielike face. The mystifying radiance that lay within the confines of her eyes held Jarred spellbound. Never in his life had he been stricken by such odd sensations, ones caused by merely peering into a woman's eyes. There was something about them that seemed to reach out and touch him. Although the chit's delicately carved features were smeared with grime, and although she appeared gaunt and frail, those crystal-clear eyes more than compensated for it.

Chelsie's cheeks flamed with color when she realized the uncomfortable situation she confronted. She was sharing a bathtub with a naked man, for crying out loud! After her six-week nightmare, she thought she had endured everything. But even after all the enlightening experiences she'd tolerated on the ship, she was only partially prepared for this embarrassing encounter. She found herself staring into twinkling blue eyes that were fringed with curly dark lashes.

Hair as black as a raven's wing capped his head and glistened in the lantern light. His mouth was rimmed with full, sensuous lips pursed in a rakish smile. One heavy brow quirked in curious amusement as he scrutinized his bathing partner. His jaw bespoke strength and self-assurance, and all his features were commanding. There was a certain unflappable confidence in that tanned face that appealed to Chelsie. Having never been the shy, retiring type, she admired strong, forceful vitality . . . unless the man who possessed it clashed with her own willful personality. Little did she know this swarthy, domineering rake was about to!

Although she tried not to be obvious with her all-consuming assessment, her unblinking gaze left his alert eyes to focus on his aquiline nose and inviting lips. Her attention shifted to the cleft in his stubbled chin and then dropped to the broad, bronzed chest that was covered with a crisp matting of dark hair. The man had shoulders like a bull, and sleek muscles bulged on his arms as he leisurely propped himself up against the tub. That incredibly masculine chest expanded as the rugged stranger inhaled deeply and proceeded to give her the once-over twice.

Chelsie, who had never possessed the ladylike habit of fainting

13

in shocking circumstances, felt oddly light-headed. She was embarrassed no end, weak from the lack of proper nourishment and shocked by the indecent amount of masculine flesh the waning bubbles couldn't conceal. The last thing she expected when she dived into the tub to take cover from Isaac was a lesson in male anatomy! My oh my, she was getting an eyeful!

Calmly Jarred wiped the spray of water from his face and regarded the misplaced elf who had somehow wound up in his tub. "Fancy meeting you here, love." A skirl of bright, ringing laughter rumbled in his massive chest as he watched the lovely sprite push upright and lean back as far as the wooden vat would allow. "Is this one of those fairy tales in which a genie appears to grant me three wishes?"

Chelsie's jaw sagged on its hinges. She couldn't believe this dashing rake was so cavalier about their situation and his nudity. She certainly wasn't! Seeing a man in all his naked splendor was thoroughly embarrassing, especially since the bubbles were evaporating with each passing second, exposing more than she needed to see!

"I wish you would kindly take your leave," Chelsie bleated, her voice an octave higher than usual.

Another rakish grin crossed Jarred's face. "I thought I was the one who was to be granted wishes." Those laughing blue eyes slid over her flushed face to dwell on the fabric that clung to her heaving bosom like a second skin. "Are you sure you want me to rise? Or is it the moment you have been waiting, for, little leprechaun?"

It took a second for the taunt to filter through Chelsie's daze. When it did, she turned all the colors of the sunset. And when Jarred braced his hands on the rim of the tub to hoist himself up, revealing even more bare flesh, Chelsie squawked like a chicken.

"Don't you dare stand up!" Now her voice was two octaves higher than usual.

"I thought you wanted me out," Jarred teased mercilessly. "Make up your mind, genie."

When Jarred sank back into the tub, Chelsie struggled with her heavy petticoats, which were saturated with water. Finally she gained her feet. She stood glaring down at the raven-haired rogue, silently consigning him to hell for taunting her.

"Just you wait until my father gets here!" Chelsie threatened with a furious hiss. "He will see to it that you pay dearly for mocking me in my state of duress!"

Jarred's assessing gaze wandered over the battered garment that clung to Chelsie's voluptuous curves. The torn fabric hugged her high-thrusting breasts, outlining the tempting peaks that lay beneath it. The gown accented her trim waist and the tantalizing curve of her hips. Her oval face was framed with wild silver-blond tendrils that had become matted because of weeks without proper care. But there were no two ways about it . . . this saucy sprite was what a man's dreams were made of, and Jarred was having one at this very moment.

How this wench could look madder than a wet hen and still be as appealing as the most fashionable belle, Jarred didn't know. But he was attracted to her. It was as simple as that.

The only flaw he could detect was the lack of meat on her bones and the hollowness around her eyes and cheeks. The chit was a mite too thin for his tastes, but she most definitely had plenty of curves in just the right places. In fact, her enchanting face and figure had such an arousing effect on him that he wasn't sure he wanted to rise from the tub. The chit was offended by the sight of bare flesh, and she would be shocked out of her soggy clothes if she were to see the full extent of his arousal.

"Damned bloody colonials anyway," Chelsie muttered bitterly. Flashing Jarred a glare that was as hot as the hinges on hell's door, Chelsie flung a leg over the tub and drew herself up to her full stature. "I wish I were home sick in bed. *Anywhere* would be better than sharing a bath with the likes of you."

"And I wish I were there with you," Jarred drawled in a low husky voice that oozed with seduction. His eyes roamed over her titillating figure, and it was a long, fanciful moment before he could muster the will to meet her condescending glare.

"When my father hears about your crude insinuations, you will be eternally sorry!" she sputtered, outraged.

How dare he fling suggestive innuendoes at her! She'd had enough of that the past six weeks, and she'd had enough of men to last her a lifetime! Damn men everywhere. They were a lusty, disgusting species that should have been confined to another planet, far far away.

15

Another throaty chuckle reverberated in Jarred's chest as the wench flounced over to snatch his towel to mop the water from her face. "Would you mind telling me what you were doing in my bath, minx?"

" 'Tis none of your business," Chelsie bit off, then squealed in shock when Jarred had the audacity to rise from the tub—stark naked—and yank his towel from her hands. Before he could wrap the towel around his lean hips, Chelsie was granted an unhindered view of whipcord muscle, not to mention another quick lesson in anatomy. If this rogue didn't stop embarrassing her she *was* going to faint!

Jarred was amused by the startled expression on her animated features and by the astonished attention he was receiving. He had never been with a woman who was unnerved by the sight of a naked man. Obviously this termagant didn't know all that much about men, judging by her wild-eyed reaction. Even Jarred's fiancée was aware of what a man looked like in the altogether.

Abigail Shaw was a young widow of twenty-five, and one of these days, Jarred was going to have to marry Abi. He couldn't procrastinate forever, he mused as memories of the past sent a stab of pain down his spine. He owed Abi a debt, and he had vowed to repay it by giving her his name and what security he could provide.

Shaking off these thoughts, Jarred tied the towel around his hips and peered down into Chelsie's flushed face. "This towel is mine. Fetch your own if you are in need of one."

Chelsie was so flustered that she simply stood there. She couldn't speak, not when she had swallowed her tongue and her heart was thumping in her throat. It was a full thirty seconds before she regained command of her voice. By that time Jarred had swaggered toward the door that led to the dressing room.

Frantically Chelsie darted a glance toward the back door, wondering if Isaac was lurking there, waiting to pounce on her. Chelsie was desperate. She needed assistance and she was in no position to be particular.

"A . . . er . . . about those three wishes you expect me to grant you," she called after him.

Jarred half-turned, his blue eyes remeasuring Chelsie's arresting assets. His naughty look said it all, and Chelsie gnashed her teeth, wondering if she hadn't just waded in deeper. She knew what he wanted, but by damned, he wasn't going to get it. At least not from her!

Chelsie had learned to read lust on a man's face. Her nightmarish experiences had embittered her toward the male of the species. Jarred's rakish leer wasn't helping matters one whit. She detested this cocky philanderer, but she needed a place to hide until Isaac abandoned his search for her.

"I will grant you three wishes if, in exchange, you will aid me in my hour of need," she bargained.

One thick black brow rose and a taunting smile spread across Jarred's sensuous lips. "No stipulations, little leprechaun?" he mocked. "When this father of yours gets here, will I be expected to pay the full price for what I want from you?"

The teasing rejoinder poked fun at her reference to her father's arrival. Apparently the dashing scoundrel didn't take her seriously. But then, intuition assured Chelsie that this stranger wasn't in the habit of taking *any* woman seriously. He, like all other men, chose to look upon women as objects to appease their sexual appetite, chattels who waited on them hand and foot. Jarred's male arrogance earned him Chelsie's immediate dislike. After her recent degrading experiences with Isaac Latham and, after watching Meredith Holt—the resident harlot on board the schooner—roll and tumble with the sailors, Chelsie had resolved to hate all men and their disgusting whores, now and forevermore.

"I need funds for my return voyage to England, suitable clothes, and money to pay my living expenses," she announced in a businesslike tone. When her betraying eyes began to rove at will, Chelsie focused her attention on the wall, even though Jarred's striking physique was what her eyes kept coming back to. Damn him for making her so vividly aware of him!

His eyebrows rose in response to her outrageous demands. "Is that all?" he scoffed sarcastically. "A new wardrobe, cash, and traveling expenses? Doesn't a regal princess like you require a coach, drawn by six strapping white stallions, to cart her back to the docks?"

Her chin tilted a notch higher and she counted to ten, hoping to control her temper, one that had been sorely put upon. But counting didn't help a smidgen. "I have asked for no more than necessity dictates, sir. And you will be justly rewarded for your trouble with my gratitude and monetary compensation. My father will see to that."

His scrutinizing gaze made another deliberate sweep of her thin but appetizing figure. Chelsie had the unshakable feeling this rogue knew exactly what lay beneath her battered garments, and that infuriated her all the more. Never in all her twenty years had she been forced to tolerate such suggestive glances without delivering a sound whack on the cheek — which was exactly what this lout deserved for being so obvious in his appraisal of her physique! But Chelsie's back was to the wall. She needed assistance, and she had to call a truce with this blue-eyed devil. He was her salvation, though he left a lot to be desired as a good samaritan.

"What is your first wish, sir? I will do my best to see it done." Chelsie declared, hoping he would be reasonable, but doubting that. He was a man, after all. To her knowledge, they were not reasonable creatures. Men were crude, lusty animals governed by their more primitive instincts.

Jarred studied the proud elevation of her chin, her sophisticated pose. There was something unique about this sassy hellion. He couldn't quite put his finger on what drew him to her like a kite against the wind. But she appealed to him, physically and emotionally. She challenged him with those bright, intelligent green eyes and her quick wit.

The wench was obviously a pauper who put on airs and played at nobility, but she was fascinating nonetheless. Unless Jarred missed his guess (and he was sure he hadn't), this virago was probably a lady's maid who had learned the manners of sophistication by rubbing shoulders with gentry. She was trying to pass herself off as nobility and elicit his assistance to only God knew what sort of wily scheme.

"I think you know what my first wish will be," he murmured as his gaze drifted over her shapely curves, not missing one detail. He extended his hand. "Come along, princess." He snorted in amusement when Chelsie stiffened her back, offended by his suggestive remark. "We shall first see what we can do about getting me into my clothes and you into something dry."

Chelsie stared at his tanned hand as if he had offered her a dead fish. She knew what he wanted from her, but he was a fool if he

18

thought she would grant that wish! Did all men think that by just snapping their fingers, they'd get women to throw themselves on the nearest bed to appease their lusts?

Reluctantly Chelsie accepted his assistance up the steps. The large hand that folded around hers was warm and confident. But what really rattled Chelsie was the way her heart leaped in her chest the instant she made physical contact with this blue-eyed rake. There was no reason why his touch should alter her heartbeat, no reason why faint tingles should ripple down her backbone. Absolutely no reason at all!

Jarred stared down at the bedraggled bundle of beauty, amazed at the odd chill that overcame him when he made contact with Chelsie. She reminded him of a pint-sized elf who had walked out of some long-forgotten fairy-tale. The electric jolt he received from their innocent touch left Jarred wondering if she truly *was* a misplaced leprechaun with magic powers. She certainly had cast an unexplainable spell over him!

"What's your name, little sprite?" he queried as he led her down the narrow passage to the dressing room.

"Chelsie Channing," she replied smoothly. "I hail from Chessfield."

A quiet rumble resounded in Jarred's chest as he paused to glance down at the soggy little imp. "Chelsie Channing from Chessfield? And a duchess, no doubt," he smirked.

His tone implied he didn't believe her for a minute (which he didn't). Chelsie stared up at the six-foot-two-inch package of bronzed flesh and rippling muscle, wishing she had a stepladder so she could glare straight into his smug expression.

"As a matter of fact, I am," she declared haughtily.

"Of course you are," Jarred snickered as he dropped her hand and stepped behind the dressing screen.

Chelsie squared her shoulders and put out her chin. "I am exactly who I say I am," she said in a defensive tone. "I was kidnapped from our estate north of London. I was bound, gagged, and hauled aboard a ship, where I have spent the past several weeks being treated like an animal. The men who abducted me plan to sell me to the highest bidder. But when my father gets . . . "

" . . . here, he'll corroborate this fantastic story," Jarred finished for her with a ridiculing snicker. "How soon can we expect the Duke of Nottingham?"

"Chessfield," Chelsie corrected.

"Ah, yes, how could I have forgotten," he sighed in mock innocence.

Chelsie stamped her foot in frustration, and water squirted from the soles of her tattered shoes, forming another puddle. "You are going to be sorry you have mocked me."

"I'm sure I will, Miss Chelsie Channing from Chessfield," Jarred chuckled as he shoved a bare leg into his breeches. After thrusting both arms into his white linen shirt, he swaggered back beside the dripping bundle of femininity.

Chelsie ground her teeth. She was not accustomed to being patronized. When Jarred tried to grasp her elbow to usher her up the steps, she jerked away as if she'd been stung by a wasp.

"I can walk by myself, thank you very much," she snapped.

"As you wish, Chelsie," Jarred murmured with a teasing smile that infuriated her no end.

"As I wish? How gracious of you. I have been dragged from my home by crimps and spirits, forced to humble myself to a lowly colonial, and you have the audacity to say—as you wish." Chelsie expelled a disgusted sniff. "Nothing has been as I wished since I woke up to find myself a prisoner in a dreadful nightmare!"

For the sake of argument—something that came easily when he confronted this haughty firebrand who seemed to be determined to play this ridiculous charade—Jarred clamped down on the intimidating rejoinder that darted to the tip of his tongue. In silence, Jarred led the way up the back staircase. Without uttering another word to provoke the fuming beauty, Jarred proceeded up the second flight of steps to return to the suite he had rented in Annapolis.

All the way to his room, Jarred asked himself why he had bothered with this lying minx. She was bound to cause him trouble. Chelsie Channing looked like trouble, Jarred decided, unable to bite back the amused grin that twitched his lips. Although this green-eyed leprechaun stood barely five feet tall, she behaved as if she were twice that height. In fact, Miss Chelsie Channing from Chessfield (or whoever she really was) was so caught up in her charade, she honestly believed she was who she said she was!

Perhaps it was curiosity that motivated Jarred. It wasn't every day that a man found a genie in his bathtub. Why she was there was a question that hadn't been satisfactorily answered. Aye, curiosity was what lured him to this sassy vixen, Jarred convinced himself.

A wry smile dangled on his lips when a thought crossed his mind. There was this business about three wishes . . . a man couldn't overlook the possibility of stumbling onto a bona fide leprechaun, now could he? And being a normal man with normal yearnings, Jarred wasn't about to cast this blond-haired sprite aside. They had made a bargain, and Miss Chelsie Channing from Chessfield would fulfill his wishes . . . Just see if she didn't.

Chapter 2

When Jarred opened the door to his room, Eli Thompson stumbled to his feet. Bewilderedly, he stared at his master and at the dripping wench who flounced into the room, leaving puddles everywhere she stepped.

"We haven't time for you to dally with a doxie," Eli grumbled disdainfully. "Your father and brothers are expecting you to join them at the auction. You know how excitable Kyle becomes when he has the chance to purchase fresh blood for his racing stock. Need I remind you that the auction is to begin in a little over two hours?"

Eli Thompson was the world's most devoted servant, and Jarred dearly loved the man. But Eli had one noticeable flaw: ordinarily, he said exactly what was on his mind, whether his master wanted to hear it or not.

Jarred ignored his valet's lecture and grinned to himself when he spied Chelsie's reaction. She was silently fuming. "My lady, I am Jarred McAlister and this is Eli Thompson, the personification of my conscience," he introduced.

"I'm sure you need all the help you can get, Master McAlister." Chelsie cooed so sweetly that it took a moment for the sting of insult to inflict its wound. "And since you are in a bit of a rush, if you will keep your end of the bargain, I will be on my way to fetch decent clothes. We can settle later." If things went well, she wouldn't have to settle at all. In fact, Chelsie was counting on never laying eyes on this handsome rake again. She intended to be long gone when he looked her up to repay him for the loan.

"Settle what later?" Eli wanted to know. There was something fishy going on here, and Eli wasn't sure he liked it.

A wry smile pursed Jarred's lips as he strode over to shave. This minx's hauteur beat anything he'd ever seen. She was certainly playing the part of regal duchess to the hilt. But he had made his wish, and this feisty leprechaun would grant it.

"Chelsie and I have struck a bargain, Eli. But I think 'tis wise if I went to fetch new garments for the lady while you rifle through my belongings to retrieve a hairbrush. It will take a half hour to tug the rattails from her tangled mass of hair."

Eli glanced back and forth between Jarred and Chelsie, wondering what the blazes was going on.

"I can attend to the matter myself," Chelsie insisted. " 'Tis not a man's place to select a woman's apparel."

After wiping his chin clean, Jarred pivoted to face Chelsie's snapping eyes and rigid stance. His gaze ran the full length of her shapely physique, estimating her size and mentally listing all the paraphernalia needed to properly outfit this chit. "You and Eli can become better acquainted while I fetch you suitable clothes," he suggested. "If you are seen on the street in these rags, the good citizens of Annapolis might mistake you for a witch."

"Well, thank you very much," Chelsie sniffed in offended dignity. She knew she looked like hell, but the infuriating Jarred McAlister need not remind her!

"You are very welcome," Jarred replied with another mocking grin that Chelsie itched to smear all over his handsome features.

After strolling toward the door, Jarred paused to glance meaningfully at his huffy servant. "See that Miss Chelsie Channing from Chessfield doesn't flit away in my absence. I expect her to uphold her end of our bargain. There is the matter of my three wishes with which she must contend."

"What three wishes?" Eli let out his breath in a rush when Jarred departed without answering the question. "What the devil is going on here?" he demanded gruffly.

Chelsie sized up the stocky servant, who was a bundle of unappeased curiosity. Eli was regarding her as if she were some cheap trollop who had wandered in off the street. Never in her life had she been forced to tolerate having someone look down his nose at her. But in Eli's defense, she realized she had made a miserable first impression. Eli didn't want her here, and she suddenly wasn't sure she wanted Jarred McAlister's assistance. He was expecting physical compensation, and Chelsie would prefer to die before she surrendered her body to that lusty philanderer! Surely she could lose herself in the thick crowd that was roaming Annapolis, anticipating a fair and auction and only God knew what else. Surely there was one good samaritan in the lot, one who didn't expect her body in exchange for traveling money.

Chelsie met Eli's disgruntled stare. "I have reconsidered the bargain," she announced. "I will manage on my own. When Jarred returns, thank him kindly for his assistance."

As Chelsie sailed toward the door, Eli darted across the room. With surprising agility he blocked her path. "I don't know what the devil is between you and Jarred, and I probably won't like it when I find out what it is. But if Jarred said you were to stay here, then that's what you will do, whether you and I like it or not . . . which I don't!"

Two flashing green eyes narrowed on Eli's leathery features. "Remove yourself from my path," Chelsie gritted out between clenched teeth. Her good disposition had been preyed upon far too often this past month, and Eli's blind devotion to his master was playing havoc with her temper.

Eli puffed up like an indignant toad when Chelsie flung him a menacing glare. "I said you were staying, wench," he growled at her.

"I am getting very tired of being told what to do," she snapped back. "I was abducted from my home in England and held captive by two unscrupulous men on board a ship. I escaped their clutches before they tried to sell me as an indentured servant." Her voice was growing wilder by the second. "And I will not be dictated to by some pompous colonial and his obedient guard dragon!"

When Chelsie tried to uproot Eli from his spot, he wrestled for position. Muttering at the defiant chit's refusal to obey Jarred's command, Eli clamped his arms around Chelsie's waist. Chelsie clawed for freedom. Expelling a yelp, Eli set her back on her feet, but not before the fiery wench bit a chuck out of his forearm. Eli was still fussing over his bites and scratches when a dull thud clanked against his skull. The marble statue that once sat upon the nightstand became Chelsie's improvised weapon.

Eli's gray eyes rolled around in his head as he toppled back against the nightstand, setting off a chain reaction of crashing furniture. By the time he hit the floor in a limp heap, the nightstand had collided against the chair, which had slammed against the table, and the lantern shattered amidst the pile of debris.

Chelsie surveyed the room, which now lay in a shambles, and the cold-cocked manservant, who lay sprawled spread-eagled on the floor. Satisfied that Jarred and Eli would cause her no further distress, Chelsie rummaged through the luggage to collect a small purse of coins. Taking only enough money to provide her with the barest of necessities, Chelsie dumped the rest of the coins in Jarred's satchel, snatched up the pouch, and breezed out the door.

Wouldn't that cocky, blue-eyed rake be surprised when he returned? It served him right for doubting her, for patronizing her with that annoying grin of his. If she never laid eyes on Jarred McAlister again, it would be all too soon!

Of all the rotten luck! Chelsie muttered as a pair of arms clamped around her midsection. She had taken but one step outside the hotel and she was pounced upon. Her captor had seen her bound down the stairs and had sneaked outside to await her exit.

Chelsie didn't have to see who had sneaked up on her. She could smell the offensive varmint. His foul aroma prompted a vivid picture. Chelsie cringed in disgust. The good Lord hadn't wasted much time when he molded Isaac Latham's pitiful face. Isaac had a nose like a bird's beak and tiny little deeply-embedded hazel eyes that flickered with a sinister gleam. But the thing Chelsie hated most about the coarse, ugly heathen was that he had clamped his arms around her.

"Yer askin' for another throttlin', wench," Isaac sneered as he shoved her down the street. "Cap'n Hutton don't like it when his indentured servants go trottin' off before they're sold. Yer due on the auction block any minute, and you'll turn a tidy bundle for me and the cap'n."

"Take your filthy hands off me!" Chelsie hissed furiously, wiggling to escape. "I'll scream this town down around us."

"It won't do you no good," Isaac snorted. "You signed the redemption papers."

25

"You drugged me," Chelsie spat into his homely face. "I would *never* have put my name on that paper if I had been in command of my senses."

"But yer name is on that paper and you've got an obligation to me and the cap'n. . . . "

Isaac glanced up when a dark shadow eclipsed the sun. Cold blue eyes glittered down on him, and the threatening expression on the man's face caused Isaac to flinch. It was the same face he had spied when he'd barged into the bathhouse. What Isaac did not need was interference. This feisty minx was enough trouble all by herself.

"The lady is a friend of mine." Jarred rapped out the words in staccato.

He had stepped from the boutique just in time to see the scrawny sailor whisk Chelsie down the boardwalk. Jarred was annoyed with Eli for allowing Chelsie to leave against his wishes and agitated with this blond-haired hellion for getting away before he'd satisfied his curiosity about why she was hiding in a tub in a bathhouse.

"The wench ain't a friend of nobody's yet," Isaac scoffed as his hazel eyes raked the fashionably dressed aristocrat with scornful mockery. "She's an indentured servant who ran away from the auction block before she was to be sold. If you want her, you'll have to pay for her friendship."

Jarred wasn't surprised by the announcement. He hadn't believed that tall tale about Chelsie being a duchess from Chessfield. But what shocked him was the illogical possessiveness that overcame him when he saw this undernourished chit being toted off by this scalawag. Chelsie may have been an amateur liar. But Jarred felt a certain sense of responsibility and compassion for her plight—just as he did for underdogs, lost causes, and stray cats.

"Now if you'll 'scuse me sir, my cap'n is waitin'," Isaac muttered impatiently.

When Chelsie opened her mouth to protest, Isaac twisted her arm halfway up her back, causing her to shriek out in pain.

"You needn't abuse her," Jarred scowled, his dark brows puckering over his icy blue eyes. "She won't bring a fair price with a broken arm."

It was easy to see why the poor chit would lie through her teeth

26

about her identity, Jarred realized. Judging by this blackguard's rough treatment, Chelsie had every reason to attempt escape. Jarred honestly couldn't blame her for running. He would have been tempted to do the same thing if he had to tolerate the likes of this foul-smelling hooligan.

"I intend to accompany you to the wharf to ensure the lady arrives in one piece," Jarred announced as he pinched Isaac's arm, forcing him to slacken his grip on Chelsie.

Grimacing, Isaac loosed his grasp and begrudgingly permitted Jarred to walk beside him, since he seemed to have little choice in the matter.

"Damned troublesome wench," Isaac muttered. "You kept the rest of the redemptioners astir durin' the voyage and picked fights with Meredith. I'll be glad to have you sold. I hope some stern master buys yer papers and whips you until you lose that snippy disposition of yers."

"And I hope you roast in hell," Chelsie fumed, rubbing the numbness from her arm. "You lay another hand on me and I'll chew it off at the elbow."

When Isaac cocked his arm to backhand her for her daring remarks, Jarred caught his wrist in midair. "If you strike her, *I'll* cut off your other arm," Jarred snarled.

Isaac heard and believed. He didn't like being threatened by this ominous-looking man. The powerfully built aristocrat looked as if he could do as he promised. Isaac clamped his mouth shut and stomped toward the dock, never taking his eyes off the annoying chit who had given him scores of headaches the past six weeks.

Whenever the passengers on the schooner had complained about conditions or food, Chelsie had been in the midst of the uproar—a rabble-rouser looking for a cause. She constantly antagonized Meredith Holt, and more than once Isaac had pried the fighting women apart. Only when he had beaten Chelsie and drugged her with his potion had she become subdued. Damn, what a troublemaker she was. Isaac couldn't wait to be rid of her!

When the threesome reached the string of indentured servants who waited to find their masters and a new home in the colonies, Jarred sought out Captain Hutton. Although he strode toward Cyrus Hutton, his eyes never strayed from Chelsie and the abusive first mate.

"The young lady who escaped from you insists she is a woman of quality," Jarred began, gauging the captain's reaction with a critical eye. "She protests her mistreatment. Has she a justifiable complaint?"

Cyrus Hutton chuckled nonchalantly as his gaze circled to the fuming blond who'd been nudged into the line of unfortunate souls who'd sold themselves for four years of labor in the colonies. "I've heard that same fantastic story scores of times before," Cyrus told Jarred. "These poor British citizens sign their agreements when the 'spirits' come to town to enlist workers who want to make a new start in the colonies. They promise to labor for a few years in exchange for their passage by ship. They seek a better life across the Atlantic. But during the voyage, some of the passengers become seasick and homesick and decide they don't want to find greener pastures. Half of them invent farfetched tales about how they've been abducted and forcefully marched aboard ship."

Captain Hutton sighed and shook his dark head. "The wench is just like so many of the travelers I've brought to the colonies. As I recall, there was a chit who passed herself off as Princess Susanna Carolina Matilda, Marchioness of Waldegrove. Philadelphia society was in for a surprise when the indentured servant, who claimed she'd been kidnaped, turned out to be just plain Sarah Wilson, who'd been deported from England for stealing the royal jewels. I could cite countless other examples, sir," he assured Jarred, who was pensively surveying the bedraggled blond. "But if Chelsie something-or-other is a lady of quality, I'm a crown prince. I'm immune to those stories. I've heard them hundreds of times at sea."

Still frowning, Jarred fished into his pocket for his coins. "How much will it cost me to buy Chelsie's indentureship?" he asked quietly.

Cyrus Hutton stroked his fuzzy beard. "Of course, you realize she'll bring a fine price on the block. She's a bit of trouble, but she's pleasing to the eye. I won't have difficulty selling that one." Soberly, Cyrus regarded the tall, swarthy rake. "I'd give several pounds for her myself if I had an itching to drop anchor and put down roots, instead of returning to the sea. I'd say twelve pounds would satisfy. . . ."

Twelve pounds clinked into Cyrus' hand and he broke into a bucktoothed smile. "I bet she'll be a firecracker in bed," he said with a roguish wink.

Jarred wondered if that very thought was what prompted him to purchase Chelsie's indentureship. Although Jarred needed a female servant like he needed a hole in the head, he plunked down the money without batting an eye. "I'd like to see Chelsie's redemption papers, if you please," Jarred requested.

"Of course." Cyrus dug into his pocket to sort through the stack. "Here is her agreement," he announced, producing the parchment.

While Cyrus marched over to fetch Chelsie, Jarred unfolded the document to see Chelsie's signature etched at the bottom. So she had signed the paper of her own accord, had she? But when the time came for the transaction, Chelsie protested and invented ways to escape four years of labor.

When Cyrus returned with Chelsie in tow, he retrieved the parchment from Jarred. "This gentleman has paid your passage to the colonies." He tore the agreement in two, as was the custom, and handed half of the document to each of them. "You must sign your names on your half. At the end of the four-year term, Chelsie will be given both halves as proof of her freedom from all debts. Until that time, each of you will be entrusted with half the agreement."

Chelsie said nothing. She didn't have to. The look she flung at Cyrus and Jarred was worth a thousand words, none of which could be translated without weaving a tapestry of obscenities that would have hung over Chesapeake Bay like a black cloud. She was *that* furious! And this was yet another of the many humiliations Chelsie had been forced to endure since she'd been uprooted from Chessfield and transplanted on this godforsaken continent with these arrogant colonials who seemed to have forgotten where they'd come from in the first place! Who would have thought Chelsie Channing, heiress to a fortune, would wind up sold to a colonial bumpkin? Damn it all! She had never been so mortified in all her life.

As Jarred led her away, Chelsie was forced to quicken her step to keep up with his agile, catlike strides. Silently she cursed her predicament and the man who refused to take her word over that of Cyrus and Isaac. "Surely you don't expect me to honor this ridiculous agreement," she grumbled sourly.

"Surely I do," Jarred growled, then mentally kicked himself for buying a redemptioner he didn't need. Abi would be appalled by the insinuation, and Chelsie was already mad as hell, even if she had no right to be. How could Jarred explain to his fiancée why he needed a comely wench in his home when there were already more indentured servants at the plantation than a man could shake a stick at?

"You should have shot Cyrus Hutton instead of paying him. The man is a scoundrel who sends his spirits and crimps ashore to abduct innocent victims who have no desire to sail to the colonies. I did not come of my own accord. I was kidnaped!" she very nearly yelled in his face.

Jarred waved the redemptioner paper in front of her. "If that is so, why did you sign this document?" he interrogated her.

"I barely remember signing it, because I had been drugged," Chelsie fumed. "But I do remember having my arm twisted up my back when I refused to sign the first time. I very nearly lost the use of my arm because of my resistance. You witnessed Isaac's tactics. He is an abusive cur!"

It would have been so easy to believe the tattered imp when he met those incredible green eyes. They dominated her gaunt face. But Jarred had made a point to converse with Captain Hutton. Cyrus swore the story was a ruse, and Chelsie hardly looked like a duchess in her pitiful rags. And she certainly didn't have the temperament of any duchess he had ever met. Obviously, she was relying on her natural beauty to persuade him to believe her wild story and gain her freedom. But Jarred was no one's fool. He tended to side with Cyrus Hutton. The man had hauled indentured servants from England for years, and he ought to know who had marched on board his schooner. If Isaac Latham and the rest of his shipmates were abusive, Chelsie was probably using their mistreatment as part of her defense and attempting to prey on Jarred's sympathy.

And, as Cyrus had said, Chelsie wasn't the first homesick peasant to invent a story that might convince a compassionate colonial to grant her freedom. The chit probably didn't even have a father, and most likely she pulled the name Chelsie Channing off the top of her head. If she truly *did* have a father, the man probably hadn't claimed his illegitimate offspring. The closest she had probably ever come to nobility was when some aristocrat hired her as a house servant. That was where Chelsie had learned the haughty airs and proper speech, Jarred imagined. No doubt she had mimicked her employers until she could pass herself off as a noblewoman. But Jarred wasn't so gullible as to believe her tale. Aye, he was physically attracted to this misplaced beauty, but if she was royalty, he would eat his hat, brim and all!

The firm set of Jarred's jaw assured Chelsie she might as well plead her case to a stone. Jarred was not receptive. "You don't believe me, do you?" She questioned resentfully.

"Quite frankly, I do not." He spied the familiar pouch clutched in her knotted fist. "How did you get hold of that?" he scowled in disbelief.

Chelsie gulped hard when she realized what had drawn Jarred's attention. His expression changed from skepticism to anger in less than a heartbeat. She was staring at a far different man than the sexy rake who had confronted her in the bathhouse. His irritation spurred her temper and Chelsie responded with sarcasm. If she had allowed herself a moment to consider a better technique of dealing with Jarred McAlister, she might not have been so hasty with her mocking rejoinder. But she didn't; she reacted on impulse.

"You consider yourself an intelligent man," she smirked as she slammed the coin purse into his hand. "You figure out how I got hold of it."

Jarred stared first at the pouch and then at the firebrand who had somehow snatched the coins from his room. How she had sneaked past Eli baffled him. Shaking off these curious thoughts, he set his penetrating gaze on Chelsie.

"Do you know what happens to indentured servants who are found guilty of theft?"

Chelsie didn't look as if she wanted to know, but Jarred made it a point to tell her anyway. "A redemptioner by the name of Mary Reed stole some goods, including nothing more significant or costly than a nightgown and a few supplies, before she ran away from her master." Jarred paused for effect, waiting for Chelsie to lift her gaze to his stern frown. "They hanged her."

31

The words dropped like stones in the silence.

"I didn't exactly steal your money," Chelsie hedged, averting her eyes from his probing stare. "I was taking out a loan, but you weren't there to complete the transaction. Rest assured, when my father gets here . . ."

"I won't hold my breath waiting until the Duke of Nottingham comes to fetch you and pay the debt," Jarred derided her.

"Chessfield," she spewed in correction.

"Whatever," he muttered disinterestedly. With an impatient tug he dragged Chelsie along quickly. "If we don't hurry, *my* father will be chewing me up one side and down the other."

"I hope he does. I would enjoy seeing you in bite-sized pieces."

Jarred controlled his temper and detoured into the boutique to retrieve the garments he had left behind in his haste to intercept Isaac. With the packages in one arm and Chelsie's elbow in the other, he dodged passersby to reach the hotel in record time. He couldn't fathom how this blond wildcat had escaped Eli and swiped the coin purse, but he was eager to find out. And when he had time to sit himself down, he was going to ask himself why he had bought this bundle of trouble in the first place.

Jarred had the unshakable feeling he was asking for it by tying this sassy spitfire to him for the next four years. What could he be thinking of? Leprechaun? He scoffed at his foolishness. Chelsie Channing from Chessfield (or wherever she really was from) was a witch who had cast some peculiar spell over him. And if she hadn't been so confounded attractive, he wouldn't be dragging her back to his room a second time. Damn, for a man who prided himself on being logical, sensible, and reasonable, he was certainly behaving impulsively. This wasn't at all like him.

Another hazard of fraternizing with a witch, Jarred supposed. Those three wishes Chelsie had offered him would most likely turn out to be curses! He should have left this minx on the auction block and never spared her another thought. Now what the sweet loving hell was he going to do with her . . . other than what he wanted to do with her from the moment she rose from his tub to bedevil him? Jarred had never had any trouble finding a woman when he wanted one. But he had certainly gone out of his way, and to considerable expense, for this wench. She had better be worth it!

It was those mysterious emerald eyes that caused him to go to such incredible extremes, he decided. He had peered into those alert, sparkling pools and lost the good sense he had been born with. He had wanted that saucy sprite and he hadn't behaved rationally since he was stung by this fierce obsession.

Jarred shook his head in wonderment. Was he the same man he had been yesterday? He certainly didn't feel like it!

Sweet mercy. He wanted this blond-haired hellion in a way he had never wanted another woman. She challenged him, defied him, treated him as if their roles were reversed. She touched off conflicting emotions. He had stared into that hauntingly lovely face and those bright green eyes and poof! He had been bewitched by a pint-sized elf. Jarred hoped he never had to explain himself to anyone else, because he wasn't sure he could.

Chapter 3

The moment Jarred stepped into his room, his eyes bulged in their sockets. The chamber was in a shambles, and Eli was abed with a cold cloth draped over his head.

"You should have let her go," Eli groaned as he propped himself up on one elbow and glared at the disheveled beauty. "She's more trouble than she could ever be worth."

Jarred had found himself thinking the same thing a few moments earlier, and he did not need to hear his thoughts vocalized. Heaving a sigh, Jarred motioned for Chelsie to take the packages and step behind the dressing screen to change.

"Are you all right?" Jarred questioned as he peered down at his peaked valet.

Eli sat up and glowered at the dressing screen. "Considering that I just had a stone implanted in my skull, I'm fine," Eli grumbled. "When are you going to tell me what is going on? What is that chit doing here? She is a walking terror."

"I bought her indentureship," Jarred reluctantly explained. Purposely avoiding Eli's gaze, Jarred flicked an imaginary piece of lint from his black velvet breeches.

"A female servant?" Eli croaked. "I don't think Miss Abigail is going to be pleased about that. She's going to be wondering the same thing I'm wondering." His gray eyes riveted on Jarred, who had the good sense to stare at the far wall. "What is this wench supposed to be? Your mistress?"

"Even if that is what she is to be, 'tis no one's business but my own," Jarred reminded him curtly. "I can name more than a few of my friends and associates who have mistresses as well as wives."

Eli was shocked all the way to his socks. Jarred had a way with the ladies, it was true. They took to him like bees to honey. Though Abigail Shaw had been Jarred's fiancée for almost two years, Jarred went elsewhere to appease his needs, and he never had to look far to find a willing young woman. His engagement wasn't a love match, but rather the fulfillment of an obligation Jarred felt compelled to honor once he finally decided to settle down. But bringing a mistress into the house, right under his father's nose? Now *that* was crazy! The wild witch had obviously cast a spell on this usually sensible aristocrat.

"You seem to forget the Shaws are friends of your father's. He isn't going to take kindly to having one of your harlots underfoot."

Eli absently rubbed his aching head and glanced sideways at the stunning beauty who emerged in her finery. His thoughts dispersed when he peered at the fiery female who had cracked his head wide open in her fit of temper. Suddenly Eli understood why Jarred was so drawn to this saucy minx. There was something compelling about her. She drew a man's eyes, even when he didn't want to like what he saw. Although Eli hated to admit it, Chelsie was the loveliest creature he had ever seen, especially when dressed in elegant clothes.

For a moment Jarred lost his train of thought. Chelsie's transformation was staggering. Her natural beauty and undaunted spirit enhanced the garments. Her tantalizing figure filled out the chartreuse gown as if the dress had been tailored just for her. The low décolletage exposed the creamy swells of her breasts, and she took his breath away. Chelsie had combed the rattails from her hair and tied the silky tendrils with a matching satin ribbon Jarred had purchased for her. The lustrous strands no longer resembled a bird's nest. They glistened in the sunlight that filtered through the window.

Jarred knew why Chelsie clung to her story about being a misplaced duchess: she truly fit the part, even if her temperament was nothing like that of a well-bred lady. Her unrivaled beauty and refined features lent credence to her allusion to royal ancestry. Her petite stature and poised carriage complemented her bewitching appearance. If this pauper-turned-princess was well-fed, to fill out the hollowness around her eyes and cheeks, she would have a line of suitors forming behind her, Jarred predicted.

Chelsie might have been flattered by the rapt attention she was receiving if she wasn't in such a snit. But in her present mood, being stared at as if she were on display rubbed her the wrong way. "Are you quite finished assessing your creation, or would you prefer to have me sit for a portrait?" she questioned causticly.

Eli frowned as he surveyed her. "You know, Jarred, this chit might just be what your older brother needs," he murmured, while Jarred floundered for a suitably sarcastic rejoinder to Chelsie. "Neil has been moping around so much lately, it worries me. You already have a fiancée, but Neil doesn't. He spends far too much time doctoring his patients, and he won't take time out for courting."

When Jarred didn't immediately pounce on the suggestion, Eli smiled wryly. "You always said you would do anything for your older brother, and you have also contended that he needs a woman in his life." His gaze swung back to the pert vixen. "As pretty as Chelsie is, we could pass her off as the duchess she keeps claiming to be. No one would ever have to know the truth."

Chelsie's hackles rose. She was outraged that Eli was discussing what to do with her as if she wasn't even there. Men! How she detested all of them. Isaac had herded her aboard ship like a stupid lamb. Jarred had bought her the way a man would purchase a plow horse. And Eli was scheming to match her with some doctor who had buried himself in his work for only God knew what reason. Chelsie had never been treated so disrespectfully in all her life, and she proceeded to tell Jarred and Eli what she thought of the ridiculous suggestion.

"I will not play the simpering twit to attract some forelorn doctor. If he is Jarred's brother, he is no friend of mine!"

Chelsie may as well have been spouting to a brick wall. Neither man paid one tittle of attention to her protest.

"Well?" Eli prodded. "Shall we have a go at it? As spirited and high-strung as Chelsie is, she might breathe a little life back into Neil. He damned sure needs *something*. He's been sullen and somber for so long that I've about forgotten what a vivacious, carefree lad he used to be." Eli nodded pensively. "Aye, I think Chelsie is just what he needs. She could be just the right prescription for the good doctor."

Jarred said nothing. He simply sat on the edge of the bed, regarding this vibrant bundle of unmatched beauty, miffed by the unexplainable feeling of possessiveness that overcame him when he visualized Chelsie and Neil together. It was true that Neil had drawn into himself of late and definitely needed a diversion. It was also true that Jarred would do most anything for his older brother, as well as for his two younger brothers. But there was something unique and compelling about this lying little thief of an indentured servant. She warmed his blood and made him want her, even when he could list a million reasons why he shouldn't have her, even when he could pick and choose the women who came to his bed.

"Your father wouldn't be annoyed, even if he did eventually discover Chelsie wasn't really a duchess," Eli went on to say, dragging Jarred from his silent reverie. "Hell, Kyle came to Maryland as an indentured servant himself thirty-eight years ago, just like I did. He's been hiring me and other redemptioners for years, just to give his fellow countrymen the same chance he had to make a fresh new start in the colonies. Now I work for your family because I choose to.

"If we manage to pull this off and no one is the wiser, we can tear up the indenture paper and this pretty pauper really can be a princess." Eli's gray eyes wandered over Chelsie's stunning figure. "She's got it all, Jarred. The delicate bone structure, the ladylike poise, that hint of refinement. I'll bet Chelsie could pass herself off as a real live duchess if she wanted to." A disconcerted frown puckered his brows. "That is . . . if we can break her of that bad habit of beating men on the skull with any weapon at her disposal. But for her freedom and the chance to marry a Maryland aristocrat, she might be willing to play the role of a genteel lady."

"I won't do it," Chelsie contested, stamping her dainty foot. She wasn't beneath slamming a few doors or throwing things, either, when her temper got the better of her. At the moment she felt like stomping about and throwing things—starting with Jarred and his wily manservant.

"You couldn't hope to do better than to marry a doctor," Eli declared with conviction.

"I wouldn't marry God's gift to women, if it meant I had to be

37

anywhere near the two of you!" Chelsie sputtered, furious. "I won't do it and that is that!"

Her chin lifted to that stubborn angle Jarred had come to know. Not sure what he was feeling, he was suddenly set off by Chelsie's blatant defiance. "You will do whatever I decide you will do," he assured her in a tone that squelched all argument. "If you don't you might find yourself hanged for stealing my coins and clubbing Eli over the head. For your information, Miss High-and-Mighty, I am not only an assemblyman, but also a practicing lawyer, and I will personally see to it that you receive proper punishment for your various and sundry crimes."

Chelsie snapped her mouth shut so quickly she nearly bit off her tongue. Jarred's piercing blue eyes no longer twinkled with roguish playfulness. He was dead serious. Although she had known this rascal for barely three hours, it wasn't difficult to determine when he was displeased. His swarthy features turned to granite when he was annoyed.

Indeed, there were several personalities housed in that virile physique of his. Jarred could probably charm a woman out of her slippers if it was his want. He could also stare down Satan himself if he had a mind to. The firm set of his jaw and the probing intensity of his sapphire eyes forced Chelsie to remain silent, even when she felt like screaming and pulling out her hair in exasperation.

"Well, what is it going to be?" Eli demanded as he dug into his pocket to retrieve his watch. "Kyle and your brothers are waiting at the auction. Is Chelsie going to be your temporary mistress until you marry Abi, or is she going to become the woman Neil desperately needs in his life? You know Chelsie could light a fire under your older brother and get his blood circulating again. I would bet my right arm on it." He stared at Jarred long and hard. "And if you seek satisfaction, there is always Carla Dayton to accommodate you. She has never turned you away. Carla is only a hop, skip, and a jump away."

Jarred's attention swung from Eli's leathery features to Chelsie's flawless face with its peaches-and-cream complexion. She hated him. Contempt was written on that bewitching face. Eli hadn't elevated Chelsie's opinion of Jarred with that careless remark about the voluptuous redhead. Obviously Eli was trying to throw obstacles between Jarred and this saucy beauty. Lord, there were enough already!

Jarred had saved Chelsie from uncertainty at the auction block, and he had yet to hear so much as an insincere thank-you from those heart-shaped lips. This sassy virago could have wound up with a cruel, molesting master who forced himself on her each night. Jarred had offered Chelsie hope for a better future than she could ever expect as an indentured servant, and far far better than she could anticipate in the rigid caste system of English society.

If Chelsie was allowed to portray the regal duchess, as she had been prone to do since the moment they met, Jarred would see to it that she had the finest wardrobe for her role. She would be living in the lap of luxury, instead of facing another nightmare. Damn it, she could have been a little more appreciative of the trouble and expense he'd gone to on her behalf.

And Eli was right, Jarred reminded himself sensibly. Neil *did* need a woman in his life. Jarred was *never* without female companionship when he wanted it. He could pick and choose his lovers. Just because this green-eyed leprechaun was the most dynamic young woman he'd ever encountered was no reason for him to drag his feet. Jarred had to control his lust for this lively nymph. He had to be reasonable.

Chelsie would be good for Neil. With her undaunted spirit and keen wit, she could woo Neil out of his unexplainable depression. And Chelsie was fairly innocent of men—to what extent, Jarred couldn't say for certain. But after their encounter at the bathhouse, he knew she was not so experienced. She may not have been a virgin, but she wasn't a hardened harlot, either.

Finally Jarred nodded agreeably. "Very well, Eli, we will give Chelsie the opportunity to play the charade she is determined to portray. We will see if she passes the test with my father. If she pulls it off, we'll let her turn her charms on Neil."

" 'Tis a pity Neil didn't accompany your family to Annapolis," Eli sighed disappointedly. "I'm anxious for him to get a look at Chelsie."

"This is not a charade, and I do not want to turn my charms on a depressed doctor," Chelsie spluttered, unable to control her tongue. How dare these arrogant louts sit here and formulate her future! She was her own woman and she wouldn't be dictated to by a couple of colonial bumpkins! "Just you wait until my father gets here. When I tell him of your scheme, he will have you drawn, quartered, and roasting over the hottest fire in hell!"

Her outburst brought Jarred to his feet. "You are my servant and I am your master." His voice rolled over her like thunder, angry and threatening. "You will do exactly what I tell you, when I tell you."

Chelsie could control her temper for just so long before it exploded. She was frustrated to no end, and she had been for six tormenting weeks. She had been whisked from her home and stowed in the cabin of a ship with dozens of other passengers. She had been deprived of food, antagonized, beaten, and drugged. Now, to top off a perfectly miserable month-and-a-half, she had been sold to this pompous, overbearing aristocrat who had been persuaded to groom her for his older brother! Her! An heiress who had her pick of scores of eligible men in England! Chelsie couldn't help but wonder if this was her punishment for rejecting so many marriage proposals. Now she found herself with no choice. Jarred and Eli were planning her future without her consent, and she was fit to be tied.

"You may have bought my body, but you have no control over my soul," Chelsie all but shouted at him. "I will not be a party to this ludicrous scheme!"

Impulsively, she sought out a weapon to crack Jarred's rock-hard frown and shatter his iron will. She whirled about to snatch up the lantern Eli had replaced after the first one was smashed to bits. Her fingers curled about the lantern, wishing it was Jarred's head. Cocking her arm, she hurled the projectile at the source of her exasperation.

Jarred and Eli sprawled flat on the floor before they were assailed by splinters of glass and whale oil. The lantern had just sailed over their heads when Chelsie scooped up a nearby chair and put it to flight, catching Jarred in the shoulder. And before he could untangle himself from the legs of the chair, his neatly folded garments were in Chelsie's clenched fists. Suddenly he and Eli were bombarded with knee breeches, silk stocking, black leather buckled shoes—anything and everything Chelsie could get her hands on to heave at them in her fit of temper.

With a wordless scowl, Jarred vaulted to his feet and pounced

40

on the hellion, who was throwing everything within reach and spewing curses that would have burned the ears off a priest. Fighting the French and Indians at Great Meadows had been child's play compared to dealing with this one-woman war party! And Chelsie was no lady, even if she pretended to be. The salty curses flying from her lips would never have tripped off a true blueblood's tongue!

Chelsie sputtered furiously when Jarred wrapped her in his arms. Although she fought him with every ounce of strength she could muster, he stifled her attempt to plant her doubled fist in his mutinous frown.

"Find my father and tell him I'll join him as soon as possible," Jarred ordered Eli. "Chelsie and I will be along as soon as she regains control of her fiery temper."

Eli gladly scurried across the ransacked room, snatching up crumpled garments and setting them aside as he cut through the maze of upturned furniture. "Aye, sir," he chuckled as he watched Jarred manhandle the feisty wildcat, who writhed in vain for freedom. "But if you aren't coming until Chelsie composes herself, we might all be in for a long wait."

When the door eased shut behind Eli, Jarred glared down at the restrained Chelsie. Her green eyes were throwing hot sparks, and her hollow face was puckered in a murderous glare. In all his liaisons with women, Jarred had never ever found himself in such a knock-down-drag-out fight. Damn, this minx was in a class by herself! How could one petite young lady be so destructive? She had turned his suite upside down in a matter of minutes . . .

"Will you hold still, for God's sake!" Jarred muttered when Chelsie arched her back and tried to throw herself away from him in another burst of fury.

"Take your hands off me!" She railed in exasperation. "I hate you, Jarred McAlister! I hate your arrogance, your male domination! I will not be treated like a chattel, and I will not play up to your father or your depressed brother or anyone else. I'll make your life and theirs a veritable hell if you persist in forcing me to . . ."

For the life of him, Jarred didn't now why he selected kissing as a technique to shut Chelsie up. He was, after all, as furious as she was. But the instant he stared at those soft, tempting lips, he had to have them. Maybe it was because he had been stung by the instant urge to kiss this sassy elf since the moment her enchanting face appeared above the bubbles of his bath. Or maybe it was because he knew this might be his first and last chance to appease his curiosity and cure the illogical lure this blond hellion held over him. Or perhaps it was a natural reaction to having her curvaceous body pressed intimately against his while she wriggled for freedom. Whatever the reason, his warm lips swooped down to devour hers, stealing her breath and muffling her protest.

Something very strange happened in that moment of anger and frustration. Jarred had managed to shut this firebrand up before she shouted the walls down around them. But he wasn't prepared for the internal explosion of sensations that vibrated through his body. His composure was shattered by the taste, feel, and scent of the woman in his arms. It was as if he had plugged himself into the limitless supply of energy and spirit Chelsie possessed.

Jarred could feel the electrical charges sensitizing every inch of his body. Sparks were flying—leaping from her body to his and back again like an ever-constant current. Angry with Chelsie though he was, she ignited sensual fires within him, making him want her in the most incredible way. Desire burgeoned in him like a blossom opening its petals to the bright midday sunshine, and Jarred found himself craving more.

Chelsie didn't want Jarred's skillful kiss. She didn't need to be reminded of his sleek, powerful body. She had seen far too much of his masculine physique already, and she didn't really want to have his hard contours meshed familiarly to her feminine curves. She detested this domineering man with a passion, yet his masterful kiss unleashed a peculiar gnawing she had never before experienced.

Oh, she had been kissed before, by a number of rakes, coxcombs, fortune hunters, and foppish aristocrats . . . or at least she *thought* she had. She had suffered through dozens of bungling embraces, a few mildly arousing kisses, and several abusive maulings, thanks to Isaac Latham. But none of her other encounters had been anything like this!

Never had *any* man come remotely close to buckling her defenses. But Jarred had melted them completely. This impossible, infuriating rogue was literally kissing her senseless. Chelsie couldn't remember her own name, couldn't see past the haze of unexpected desire that clouded her senses.

Kisses weren't supposed to be like this . . . were they? She wasn't supposed to enjoy the embrace of a man she had her heart set on hating . . . was she? The world wasn't supposed to shrink, filling no more space than Jarred occupied.

Chelsie couldn't fathom why, but suddenly she was kissing Jarred back, instead of slapping him silly, as she should have done. All the pent-up frustration that had sustained her these long, harrowing weeks had transformed into a peculiar hunger that demanded appeasement. She was no longer exasperated and annoyed. A wild sense of urgency compelled her to return Jarred's heart-stopping kisses, to absorb his steel-honed strength, to satisfy a need that made her ache all over.

Maybe she simply needed to feel needed, for whatever reason. She had suffered the worst upheaval of emotions since she was kidnaped and subjected to countless humiliations. No one could possibly imagine what it was like to be whisked from a secure world and treated like a slave, to be ordered about, ridiculed, and sold. For the first time in weeks, Chelsie let her guard down and reacted to the feel of Jarred's warm lips moving sensuously over hers. He had aroused a need Chelsie couldn't identify.

She had been strong and courageous during her voyage under the most adverse conditions imaginable. But she was dangerously close to the end of her rope. Jarred's encircling arms offered protection. She needed a sturdy shoulder to lean on, a man who had the knack of chasing her fears and frustrations away with his kisses.

It was totally unlike Isaac's prodding and shoving, his hateful scoldings, and the harsh blows she had received when she dared to verbally attack the scoundrel or his deceitful whore, Meredith Holt. Chelsie needed Jarred's embrace to erase the tormenting memories of what she had seen and felt and heard on board the schooner. Jarred supplied something that had been missing from her life, something that provoked her to respond impulsively.

It was a mere physical reaction, Chelsie assured herself. There was nothing between her and this brawny giant. But they seemed to satisfy some unexplainable need in one another. Chelsie had needed to be soundly kissed to quell her outburst of temper, and

Jarred needed to kiss her to smother his irritation with her.

The theory sounded strange, even to Chelsie, who had conjured it up. But it made perfect sense to her. And so she yielded to the feel of Jarred's moist lips pressing gently against hers. When his questing tongue guided her lips apart, she felt a tantalizing tingle down her spine. He explored the recesses of her mouth while his hands drifted down her ribs on an arousing journey of discovery, and Chelsie felt her resistance slip another notch.

Ever so slowly, Jarred raised his head. From beneath the thick fringe of velvet lashes, his sapphire eyes limned her kiss-swollen lips. She tasted as good as she looked, and Jarred hungered for more. Gently he pressed his hips to hers, letting her feel his desire, teaching her things she had never known about passion. His body shuddered when he felt her curvaceous contours molded intimately against his. Jarred forgot he had a fiancée several miles away and a family he hadn't seen in three months. All he could recall was the honeyed taste of kisses that were as potent and addicting as wine.

"You kiss as well as you fight, little nymph," Jarred rasped, his voice husky with passion.

"You're not so bad yourself, even if I detest the ground you walk on," Chelsie replied.

His tanned fingers glided along her ribcage, brushing provocatively against the side of her breast before ascending to her flushed face. Tenderly he cupped her chin, tilting her head back to meet his rakish grin.

"Do you suppose I could kiss your hatred for me away, Chelsie?" he murmured, focusing on her petal-soft lips, studying them as if they were the first he had ever seen.

"I'm comfortable hating you," Chelsie insisted, though her voice was too thick with desire to sound convincing. "I think 'tis safer this way. I'm not sure I even want to like you."

A low rumble of laughter rattled in his chest. The impish grin that surfaced on her exquisite face was contagious. Suddenly Jarred was laughing and smiling just like this green-eyed leprechaun. Chelsie struck a chord of pleasure inside him. There was no rhyme or reason to the fierce attraction he felt for this spitfire. It was simply there, like the moon glowing in the night, or the sun beaming down at midday.

"To tell the truth, I don't know why I want you to like me," he whispered as his lips slanted over hers.

Chelsie couldn't explain why she permitted another kiss. She had been too startled to resist the first two embraces. And she was too startled by her strange reaction to protest the third. She surrendered to the feel of his full lips playing provocatively against hers. It was like quenching her thirst with a long-awaited drink. Her naïve body quivered uncontrollably as Jarred lifted her off the floor and pulled her against him.

Involuntarily her arms slid over his broad shoulders to toy with the thick black hair that lay at the nape of his neck. Sweet mercy, Jarred was delightful to kiss. Chelsie couldn't seem to get enough of him. She was like a starved peasant who had been invited to a succulent feast. Each nibble left her wanting more.

Warning signals were flashing. Her eager response made no sense at all, but Chelsie was too caught up in the titillating sensations to question her reaction. She merely melted against Jarred's solid strength and practiced his expert techniques on him. Whatever power he held over her was the same power she seemed to hold over him. Chelsie reveled in making Jarred shudder in response to her inquiring caresses.

When Chelsie thoroughly kissed Jarred back, he swore his knees would fold beneath him. Her tongue darted into his mouth, teasing and tempting him until he teetered on the brink of insanity. Her hands wandered to and fro, making him groan in unholy torment.

As if his hands possessed a will of their own, they migrated to the taut peaks that brushed seductively against his laboring chest. God, she felt good in his arms! He ached to touch what his eyes had beheld, to peel away the hindering garments and caress her to his heart's content. He needed to hold her, to kiss her. Jarred swore he would burn himself into frustrated ashes if he didn't relieve this monstrous craving that made his temperature rise a quick twenty degrees.

Jarred had defended himself against the French and Indians who had swarmed the forest and attacked the militia. He had no fear in battle. His instinct took command of his senses, bringing them to life. But he couldn't seem to defend himself against this mystical pixie with hair spun from silver and gold, and eyes like polished emeralds.

He couldn't fight this fierce, uncontrollable attraction, even if his life depended on it. This sweet hypnotic witch had weaved a spell around him. Her lips held delicious surprises Jarred couldn't resist. Her shapely body fit so perfectly to his that he had the strange feeling Chelsie belonged there—like the other half of a living puzzle, the half that had been missing from his life. And for that space in time, Jarred closed his eyes and mind to all except the pleasure this green-eyed leprechaun bestowed on him.

After several minutes Jarred found enough self-control to withdraw. It wasn't an easy task; he was drawn to this saucy sprite like metal to a magnet. But he had obligations to fulfill. As much as he'd have preferred to lay this dazzling beauty down and make wild, sweet love to her, he had an appointment with his father and his younger brothers. And he needed time to cool off, to remind himself he was grooming this charading duchess for his older brother.

Chelsie Channing from Chessfield would certainly light a fire under Neil. Look what she had done to Jarred! He was an engaged man, but that hadn't stopped him from wanting her, from buying her indentureship, from aching for her from head to toe. Aye, Neil would respond to Chelsie Channing, because it was impossible for a man not to. But damn, it was going to be hard to give her up to his brother when Jarred wanted to expend all three of the wishes Chelsie had promised him by taking her to his bed.

When Jarred turned toward the door, Chelsie studied the broad expanse of his back. "Do you think just because you kissed me and I liked it, that I will play this little charade for your family?"

Jarred half-turned. His blue eyes measured her rebellious stance, the defiant tilt of her chin. Damn, she was a pretty little thing—all that dazzling beauty. She was like fire personified. A sly smile pursed his lips as his gaze roamed over the curves he had dared to touch.

"I wish you would," he murmured without realizing he had wasted his first wish, instead of saving it for what he wanted most. But Chelsie was well aware that he had uttered his whim, and she didn't intend to let him forget it.

"You assured me several times that this was no charade, that you were a real live duchess," he reminded her. "If you are what you claim to be, you won't be playing at anything, will you, Miss Chelsie Channing from Chessfield?" His eyes twinkled with deviltry when he caught the spark of irritation that flickered across her features. "In fact, duchess, I challenge you to prove you are a lady, instead of the persnickety ragamuffin who laid this room in shambles."

Challenge her, would he? Well, she would teach this pompous colonial a thing or two about English aristocrats! If Jarred McAlister wanted to see a genuine blueblood in action, he had better stand aside. She would give him a taste of nobility that nothing could match—the real thing! His father and brothers would believe she was who she said she was, even if Jarred muleheaded McAlister didn't.

Just because on occasion her temper got the better of her and she lowered herself to cursing didn't mean she wasn't a full-fledged lady of quality and breeding. Jarred would have backslid a ways himself if he had been subjected to the degradation she had suffered at Isaac's hands. Chelsie would show him, but good!

If only she had the locket and emerald ring Isaac had stolen from her, she mused wistfully. The engraving of her family crest and the inscription from her father would have been proof enough. But she didn't have them, and Jarred refused to believe her. But when her father arrived to save her from this ridiculous indentureship, Jarred would be more than sorry he'd doubted her. He was going to realize he was a first-class fool. That should put a sizable dent in his inflated male pride.

With a haughty nod of consent, Chelsie sashayed across the room. Her head was held high, her shoulders thrown back. "Very well, Squire McAlister, you may accompany me to the auction to meet your father and brothers," she announced airily.

One brow quirked in amusement. Chelsie had thrown herself into the role of the regal heiress. "And I am most grateful for the honor, duchess," Jarred assured her before dropping into an exaggerated bow. "Your wish, Miss Chelsie Channing from Chessfield, is my command."

With a flair for the dramatic, Chelsie swept toward the door. A sugar-coated smile glazed her lips as she tossed Jarred a fleeting glance—the way a queen glances at a servant on her way to meet the crowned heads of state. "On the contrary, Jarred," she cooed pretentiously. "I am here to grant you three wishes. Your first is that I portray the well-bred lady for your family. I will see to it that you receive even more than a scoundrel like you deserves."

Jarred muttered sourly when reminded that he had wasted his first wish on a carelessly worded request.

Arrogantly, Chelsie outstretched her hand and curled her fingers in the crook of his arm. "And when I'm finished with you, your second wish will be that you have never laid eyes on me. That will leave you with only one wish. Make sure you spend it wisely, sir."

Chelsie breezed down the hall beside Jarred like a princess on her way to court. He began to have serious misgivings about this charade and his involvement. Knowing this feisty minx (and he was beginning to know her quite well), he *was* going to wish they had never met. Maybe his reckless slip of the tongue had cost him his first wish, but there was still something he wanted from Chelsie, something that had nothing to do with this masquerade. Perhaps her prediction would come true, perhaps he would soon wish they had never met. But at the moment he just wanted to finish what they had begun a few minutes earlier.

One glance at Chelsie had Jarred grumbling under his breath. He had the uneasy feeling that he and this ornery leprechaun were on a collision course with trouble. She had that mischievous look about her, one that spelled catastrophe.

Duchess indeed, he sniffed skeptically. For all her pretension, she was just a commoner attempting to pull a fast one on her master. And she had better watch her step. If she made trouble for him, she would find herself wading neck-deep in it herself! Jarred could give as good as he got, and Chelsie Channing from Chessfield would be wise to remember that!

Chapter 4

Kyle McAlister shifted his weight from one foot to the other. Still fidgeting, he readjusted his wire-rimmed glasses and impatiently searched the crowd for his second son. Although Eli had arrived to inform the patriarch that Jarred was on his way, Kyle was anxious to see him. Jarred's trek across the wilderness had worried Kyle. The French and Indians were spoiling for a fight, and Kyle didn't relish losing his son. He had four of them, and each one was precious to him. They were the living symbol of the love he and his wife had shared before she had been stricken with typhus while she was recovering from the birth of their fourth son.

Absently Kyle glanced down at his wife's wedding ring, which encircled his little finger. For a moment he wandered through the haze of gone but not forgotten memories they had made together. Sighing, he tucked the sentimental thoughts away and scanned the fairgrounds, hoping to catch sight of Jarred.

"I thought you said Jarred would be along shortly," Kyle muttered to Eli.

"Something came up that needed his immediate attention," Eli replied with a cryptic smile. Something had come up, all right — Cyclone Chelsie!

"Be more specific," Kyle grumbled as he turned toward the auction block.

"I think 'tis best for Jarred to explain when he arrives," Eli hedged, striding along behind Kyle, whose pace was swift.

"I hope the lady who needed my brother's attention was worth

49

keeping Papa and the rest of us waiting," Grant McAlister snickered confidentially. When Eli shot him a silencing frown, Grant grinned wryly. "I know my brother well. He may be engaged, but he attracts women like flies."

"Well, this time it was the other way around," Eli assured Grant. "And when you get a look at this one . . ."

His voice trailed off when he caught sight of Jarred's dark head above the crowd. Taller than average and undeniably handsome, Jarred stood out in the congregation that gathered around the auction block.

"Ah, there are your brother and his companion. You can decide whether she was worth your wait." Eli chuckled as Grant stretched his neck to get a good look at the lady on his older brother's arm. "You will probably be wishing you had found her first."

As Jarred pushed his way through the throng that converged at the auction block, Grant's mouth gaped. There beside his elder brother, who had the luck of the Irish, was a vision of exquisite beauty. Her regal carriage, ladylike poise, and angelic smile melted Grant's composure. And Daniel, the youngest McAlister, who had just celebrated his seventeenth birthday, was also drooling like a teething infant.

"Lawd, she's the prettiest thing I've ever seen," Daniel breathed in awe. "She's like a vision out of a fairy-tale."

"Just what Jarred needs when he already has a fiancée," Grant commented resentfully.

Jarred's bronzed features had been puckered in a scowl since the moment he stepped into the hotel lobby with Chelsie on his arm. Men's heads had turned when she sashayed past them with poise and grace. Jarred's acquaintances had greeted him on the street, but not one of his friends whom he hadn't seen in three months paid him any mind. They rushed to him just to get a closer look at the "duchess."

All the rapt attention Chelsie was receiving hadn't sweetened Jarred's disposition. But seeing his two younger brothers standing there with their tongues hanging out turned Jarred as sour as curdled milk. If Chelsie announced she was the Queen of England come to acquaint herself with her subjects, Daniel and Grant would believe her! They'd believe anything this sorceress said! She was lively, flamboyant and one-hundred-percent distracting. Daniel and Grant were bewitched.

Well, that was what he wanted, wasn't it? Of course it was, damn it! He and Eli were going to use Chelsie as a cure for his older brother's melancholy. Chelsie had already passed the first test. The younger McAlisters' faces lit up when Chelsie walked in and filled up their world. They were impressed and, for the life of him, Jarred didn't know why that disturbed him so much.

"Good looks obviously run in your family," Chelsie observed as the two men scurried toward her. "You must be Jarred's brothers."

Her gaze wandered flirtatiously over Grant's straight blond hair and sparkling blue eyes, which matched his older brother's in intensity. At twenty-eight, Grant had every ounce of Jarred's sensual charm. And when Grant burst into a roguish smile, becoming dimples gave his tanned cheeks an endearing, boyish quality that Chelsie had also noticed in Jarred.

Daniel was a miniature version of Jarred, with jet-black hair, a cleft in his chin, and the same twinkling blue eyes as the ones that were already beginning to haunt Chelsie.

"Chelsie Channing, Duchess of Chessfield, I would like you to meet my brothers, Grant and Daniel," Jarred mumbled in introduction, although why he bothered, he didn't know. His brothers stopped listening the instant they learned her name.

Grant and Daniel fumbled all over themselves to take the delicate hand Chelsie offered to them, and they proceeded to slobber all over it. Confound it, Chelsie was playing this duchess role for all it was worth, Jarred thought. Chelsie had turned her irritation toward him to more profitable avenues, and she had set out to charm the breeches off the two youngest McAlisters (and with great success.) She had accepted the challenge like a seasoned trooper. What this wily minx didn't know about being a wealthy duchess she compensated for by batting those green eyes and breaking loose with a succession of radiant smiles.

Jarred found himself crowded from the limelight while Grant and Daniel fawned all over Chelsie, plying her with flattery and devouring her with their leering gazes. Damn! Jarred had narrowly escaped disaster when the militia was hopelessly outnumbered in the wilderness. But did his younger brothers care that he had very nearly lost his scalp to marauding Indians? Nay, they were too busy hovering around Chelsie to bother welcoming their

51

older brother back to civilization.

Kyle cleared his throat when he saw all the commotion behind him. "Am I to be allowed a proper introduction to the duchess?" he questioned his second son.

His own father, for God's sake! Jarred fumed. One would have thought at least the patriarch of Easthaven could have spared his prodigal son a greeting or inquired about his journey from the backwoods of the Ohio Valley. Apparently none of his family cared a whit what he had been doing for the past three months. All they wanted was for him to make the proper introductions to Chelsie.

"Forgive me, Papa," Jarred replied, his tone nowhere near apologetic. "Kyle McAlister, may I present Chelsie Channing from Chessfield, heiress to a duchy."

Chelsie dropped into a graceful curtsy that granted the McAlisters an enticing display of bosom. Jarred cursed himself for yielding to the temptation of purchasing such a seductive gown for this nymph. The garment called attention to her distracting assets (of which there were plenty), and Jarred's brothers were again watering at the mouth, damn them.

"I am most honored, squire," Chelsie murmured with genuine sincerity. "And I am forever in the debt of your family."

Her sparkling eyes shifted to the sour-faced Jarred. Chelsie relished watching the rascal get what he deserved. The rest of the McAlisters had accepted her without question. Jarred obviously resented her ability to charm his family, but that was his wish, even if he didn't think she could do it. Serves him right, Chelsie thought spitefully.

"Your dear, sweet son came to my rescue when I was in dire straits," Chelsie explained to the gray-haired man, who was at least an inch shorter than his youngest son. "If not for Jarred's compassion, I would be wandering about these bustling streets like a lost soul." A rueful smile quivered on Chelsie's lips. "I arrived only today to learn that my ailing aunt has departed this world before I could pay her a visit. Now I find myself to grieve her passing and await my father, who isn't due to arrive until after he attends to some unfinished business in London."

Her hand folded around Jarred's, giving it a squeeze and digging in her nails just for spite. "Jarred befriended me and invited me to join you. His consideration and chivalry has helped to ease my loss and the discomfort of finding myself in an unfamiliar country with no one to call my friend."

Her soft voice and angelic expression almost had Jarred believing that concocted crock of lies. And he knew better! A poor, deceased aunt and a helpless duchess? This wench was an accomplished liar—either that, or she possessed remarkable theatrical abilities. Chelsie was getting better with her stories as the day wore on. Hell, if she kept this up, she'd have *herself* believing she was a forlorn duchess!

Discreetly, Jarred glanced at Eli, who was doing his damnedest to keep from grinning in amusement. One look at the manservant assured Jarred that Eli was pleased with himself for dreaming up this crazed scheme and delighted with the way Chelsie had entranced the McAlisters with her disarming smiles. And Eli was! He preferred the spirited duchess to the feisty termagant who had pounded him flat and left the hotel suite in shambles.

With elegant poise, Chelsie drew herself up and graced Kyle with another blinding smile. "I envy your family, squire. All I have is my father. Your home is blessed with an abundance of fine, upstanding men. I would have given most anything for a passel of brothers and sisters."

"I'm willing to be adopted," Daniel eagerly inserted.

While Daniel was grinning like an idiotic fool and Grant was giving her the once-over, Kyle stood quietly admiring Chelsie. This stunning blond had bewitched him as well. Chelsie was like a breath of springtime. For years he had harped to his sons about taking wives and filling their plantation home with dozens of grandchildren. Although Jarred had finally taken a fiancée, he was no closer to the altar than he'd been two years ago. Even with Kyle's constant harassment, Jarred hadn't tied the matrimonial knot. He seemed reluctant to settle down. Kyle often wondered if the engagement was merely a token vow offered only as an attempt to pacify his needling father.

This dazzling duchess would be a fine addition to the McAlister family, and she would certainly compliment Easthaven, Kyle mused as his brown eyes assessed Chelsie from behind his wire-rimmed spectacles. Neil and Grant could both use a wife, and Kyle craved a daughter-in-law. If he could pick and choose, this enchanting heiress would be married to any one of his eligible sons by nightfall!

Kyle extended his hand, drawing Chelsie to his side. "Are you fond of thoroughbreds, Chelsie?" he questioned as he led her to the auction block.

"Indeed I am," she enthused. "My father and I raise racing champions, and I was riding before I could walk. My father has a penchant for hunting and racing, and I share his interest in breeding quality stock."

"A woman after my own heart," Kyle sighed appreciatively. "Come along, duchess. You can help me select new blood for my stable."

"My father and I raise racers . . ." Jarred mimicked sarcastically when he was left standing all alone. Damn, Chelsie had picked up on Kyle's love of racing and prize horses, and she already had him wrapped around her little finger. Blast it, some homecoming this had turned out to be! Thus far no one had paid him a smidgen of attention. If he decided to throw himself into Chesapeake Bay, he doubted his family would notice. They were too busy drooling over the charading duchess.

Casting the grinning Eli a mutinous glare, Jarred stomped toward the benches near the auction block. Since Chelsie was surrounded, Jarred plopped down on the end of the bench beside his manservant.

"Things seem to be going splendidly," Eli remarked. "Kyle and your brothers took an instant liking to the duchess."

"She's not a real duchess," Jarred scowled.

Resounding laughter reverberated in Eli's thick chest. "You'll never convince the rest of the McAlisters of that. Chelsie walked right into their hearts. She'll never let them see the fiery side of her nature." A muddled frown crossed his brow. "By the way, how did you convince her to play along? When I left, she was taking the place apart with her temper tantrum."

Suddenly the image of this bewitching blond materialized in Jarred's mind. The memory triggered a rash of warm tremors that had Jarred aching. He wanted to forget he had agreed to Eli's crazed scheme. He yearned to tote Chelsie back to the room so he could help himself to another taste of her intoxicating kisses. . . .

"Don't ask," Jarred snapped when the memory of their embrace caused his temperature to shoot up.

Eli surveyed the frown on Jarred's handsome features. For the most part, Jarred was an even-tempered, good-humored and well-educated individual who let nothing get under his skin. But all of a sudden, he had dragged a wet wench back to his room and the fireworks had begun. And come to think of it, Eli never *did* discover how Jarred and Chelsie had met.

After Chelsie breezed into his life, Jarred was as gruff as a grizzly. Eli wondered if Jarred was feeling slighted because his family had overlooked his homecoming to flutter around the dazzling duchess. Or was it Jarred's fierce attraction to this sassy minx that was the root of his disposition?

For a long moment Eli contemplated Jarred. He couldn't recall seeing the man so flustered over a woman. Rather strange behavior for a rogue who had scores of women at his beck and call, not to mention a fiancée waiting in the wings. A wry smile hovered on Eli's lips. Unless he missed his guess, Jarred had been bewitched by this saucy hellcat. But Eli had the inescapable feeling Chelsie was one of those feisty females who held a grudge. She would never let Jarred forget he had used her for this scheme. She might brighten Neil's life when the eldest McAlister son got a look at her, but in the meantime, she would make Jarred's life hell.

Maybe this wasn't such a good idea, Eli thought in retrospect. He hadn't meant to enrich Neil's life at Jarred's expense. But it appeared that in attempting to solve one problem, Eli had created another. Squirming on the hard bench, he shot forth a glance at Chelsie, who had captivated the bystanders, who were peering at her, unable to take their eyes away.

Jarred was in serious trouble, Eli predicted grimly. And before Cyclone Chelsie was through with the McAlisters, the whole brood might be in a tailspin. Damn, next time Eli was going to keep his mouth shut and resist scheming and matchmaking. But then, this had to be better than permitting Jarred to make Chelsie his private harlot, he consoled himself. That would have been infinitely worse!

Had Chelsie been able to read Eli's thoughts at that moment, she would have heartily agreed with him. She was having enough difficulty dealing with the memory of Jarred's masterful kisses, even while she conversed with Kyle. Chelsie had no desire to

55

become Jarred's lover. She wasn't even sure she liked him! And she was not about to suffer any more humiliations. She had endured enough the past six weeks. If Jarred McAlister planned to use one of his wishes to get her in his bed to appease his lusts, he had better wish again. That was one whim she refused to grant him. She had her pride, after all, and very little else at the moment, and she clung fiercely to it.

For the first time in a long while, Chelsie relaxed. Kyle, Grant, and Daniel were delightful company. Chelsie was relieved to have Jarred sitting at the far end of the bench. The man disturbed her in ways that were unfamiliar to her. She detested being bought and sold as if she were a brood mare. She despised Jarred's highhanded manner and his refusal to believe her story about being abducted from her estate. But what rankled her to no end was her involuntary response to his skillful embrace.

Lord-a-mercy, she had never let a man get so close in all her twenty years. True, she had been aggressively courted since her season in London. But Chelsie had grown up a mite too independent for the tastes of most of the gentry in England. They expected her to bat her eyes and agree with whatever prattle poured from their mouths. Chelsie, however, had not conformed to their expectations. She refused to play the game. She had flatly rejected each marriage proposal, vowing she would never marry until she found a man who treated her as his equal, not as a possession to be displayed in court or planted in his manor like some imported stick of furniture.

Chelsie was the first to admit her father had spoiled her. She was both his son and his daughter. When she voiced a whim, Evan Channing saw it done. If Chelsie was inclined to hunt or race, her father permitted it. Evan had never excluded his vivacious daughter simply because she was one of the feminine persuasion. He had seen to it that she was versatile, adaptable, and rarely out of her element. She was constantly at his side as he toured his estate and attended court. Chelsie had been properly educated by the finest tutors in England and raised by a governess who tried to be the mother she had never known.

Because of Evan Channing's indulgence, Chelsie had been allowed to run wild and free, chasing every rainbow, wanting for nothing. When she encountered stolid young men who believed women to be second-class citizens, her hackles went up. She proceeded to tell her narrow-minded suitors what she thought of them, and most of them had enough sense to take a wide berth around her thereafter.

Although Jarred McAlister persisted in treating her like a chattel who could be ordered about and who should dutifully obey, Chelsie was attracted to him. The mere fact that she was aroused by a man she wasn't sure she liked baffled her. But there was something about Jarred that fascinated her, something that lured her to him when she should have backed away.

A pensive frown knitted her brow. She paused to ask herself just what it was about that blue-eyed rake that intrigued her so. It wasn't just because he was attractive. Chelsie had been courted by the most dashing rakes in Europe, and she knew good looks made a charming wrapper but could never compensate for what was inside. In Jarred's case there was something besides a striking physique and bronzed features. It was that hint of wild nobility beneath a veneer of sophistication and his rough sensuality that intrigued her.

She didn't like Jarred, of course. There were too many conflicting elements in their personalities. Jarred was every inch a man, and Chelsie was her own woman. But Jarred didn't quite fit the mold of the run-of-the-mill aristocrat, and that was what piqued her curiosity and attracted her against her will.

The problem was that they set off sparks in each other, some of which Chelsie would have preferred not to experience. Well, at least Kyle and his other two sons would provide a buffer, Chelsie mused as she squirmed uncomfortably on the hard bench. It was wise for her to keep her distance from Jarred. That rake knocked her off-balance. He aroused her slumbering passions, and Chelsie wasn't accustomed to dealing with a Pandora's box of desire. Jarred made her want things she didn't even understand. How did he do that? He was only a man.

Chelsie glanced in Jarred's direction. The intensity of his probing gaze made her jump. He actually looked angry with her. *Her*, mind you! *She* was the one who was outraged, and *he* looked put out with her. Men! Who could understand them? Jarred challenged her to behave like a full-fledged lady and a dignified heiress. When she did, he glared malignantly at her. Damn that infuriating man. She wished he would make up his mind what he wanted . . .

Chelsie's attention caught on the colt that was being led forward by Isaac Latham. In disbelief, Chelsie gaped at the handsome steed. What was Trumpeter doing here? The answer to that question boiled Chelsie's blood. Her fuming gaze swung past the thoroughbred colt to the elegant brood mare that waited her turn on the auction block.

Those thieving bastards! Not only had they abducted her, but they had stolen two of Chessfield's most valuable horses. Chelsie wondered if perhaps she had been strolling too near the meadow where the horses had been grazing. Maybe that was why she had been abducted. Apparently Captain Hutton and Isaac Latham had been more interested in swiping the prize steeds to sell for one hundred per cent profit in the colonies, and she had been just an afterthought. Damn that Isaac, he was going to pay for his thieving one day! She would see to that!

After scrutinizing the two horses, Chelsie came to the conclusion that the steeds had fared better than she had during the voyage. Where they had been stashed was anybody's guess, but the horses had been groomed and fed while she had practically starved to death. Neither the three-year-old colt nor the ten-year-old brood mare looked the slightest bit undernourished. Their coats were as silky and shiny as they'd been before the abduction.

A wordless growl hovered on Chelsie's lips when she saw Isaac raise his whip and whack Trumpeter, who protested being led to the auction block. Her fingers clenched in the folds of her skirt, wishing she could bolt to her feet and fly at that bastard's throat. Trumpeter was a temperamental colt who responded to kindness, not beatings. But Isaac knew nothing about kindness.

The moment Captain Hutton strode over to gesture toward Trumpeter, boasting his credentials and breeding — all of which was a concocted lie — Chelsie tugged on Kyle's arm. Although Trumpeter was priceless and had been bred to race, he didn't belong to the imaginary aristocrat whose name Cyrus rattled off to impress buyers.

"If you seek quality horseflesh, bid on the colt and the bay mare," Chelsie insisted. "Both steeds came from my father's stock. The colt has shown great promise, and the mare is legendary for producing enduring champions. They are both descendants of Darley Arabian, who was shipped to England from the Orient to be bred with thoroughbreds."

When Kyle raised a hand to open the bidding, Jarred nearly fell through his seat. For God's sake, that spiteful minx was going to see to it that Kyle wasted his money on some fly-by-night steed that had legs like a stork! True, the steeds appeared to show signs of good breeding. But the animals were probably some Englishman's rejects, and Cyrus Hutton had purchased them for little or nothing. The colt was most likely injured and unable to run, and the mare was probably infertile.

And why was Kyle paying the least attention to Chelsie's suggestions? He prided himself in being an excellent judge of horseflesh. Damn it, he didn't need the advice of this pretentious chit. Hell's bells, all Chelsie had learned about horses was probably no more than she'd discovered when she'd accidentally stepped in a pile of manure! Kyle had been blinded by Chelsie's beauty and she was preying on his weakness. And the worst part of it was that Jarred and Eli had put her up to this!

When Chelsie glanced sideways, Jarred was glowering at her. Muttering, Jarred bounded to his feet, but Eli yanked him back down before he made a scene. While Jarred silently cursed her, Chelsie displayed an ornery smile and primly adjusted her full skirts about her.

"Thank you so much for inviting me to the auction, Jarred," she purred. "Your family is marvelous company, and I am having the time of my life."

"At my expense," Jarred grumbled under his breath. His lean fingers contracted—a gesture that assured Chelsie she was fortunate she wasn't within his reach. He most certainly would have pinched her head off if he could have gotten his hands on her. "You and your bright ideas," he muttered at his valet. "Now look what a mess you've made of things."

"It may have been my idea, but you could have vetoed it," Eli snapped, but in a quiet tone that could not be overheard.

The instant Kyle began bidding on the feisty colt, his friendly rival Amos Shaw raised the price with a bid.

"That ornery cuss," Kyle muttered to Chelsie. "If Amos thinks I'm interested in the colt, he'll jump the bid and it will cost me an arm and a leg."

Chelsie lifted a delicate hand and crooked her finger at Captain Hutton. "Gesture toward me," she murmured quietly to Kyle. "If your friend thinks you were bidding for me, maybe he will back off."

And sure enough, Amos slouched back when Kyle indicated he had been bidding for the lovely lass beside him. It was all Kyle could do to keep from beaming in smug satisfaction when Chelsie purchased the colt without costing him a fortune.

Captain Hutton was disgruntled that he hadn't obtained a higher price for the animal. Sighing disappointedly, he indicated the buyer. When Chelsie tipped her head back to glare directly at Cyrus, he jerked as if he had been stabbed in the back. Bewilderedly, he glanced at Jarred, who sat a good distance away from the servant he had bought a few hours earlier. Spinning about, Cyrus marched over to retrieve the reins to the brood mare that had also been stolen from Chessfield. When Cyrus glanced curiously at Isaac, he pulled his cap low on his forehead and looked away.

"What the devil is going on here?" Cyrus hissed at Isaac.

"The horse that hellion bought came from her estate," Isaac informed his captain.

"What!" Cyrus expelled a string of muffled obscenities and glared murderously at Isaac.

"You told me to fetch a couple more fancy horses," Isaac defended. "You also told me to round up a few extra servants to sell so we would have a full load to carry to the colonies. The chit was wandering round in the pasture when we stole the horses, so I brought her along."

"You fool," Cyrus growled. "She really is a duchess instead of a lowly peasant. Why didn't you tell me?"

"You never want to know where these redemptioners come from, that's why," Isaac growled back. "I don't know why yer in such a snit. Nobody is gonna believe her. One female ain't gonna cause us that much trouble."

"She caused plenty of trouble on the ship," Cyrus countered sharply. "Because of her, we nearly had a riot on our hands.

Putting her in solitary confinement was all that prevented her from attempting mutiny."

"Well, if yer so damned worried, *you* do somethin' about her," Isaac snorted disrespectfully., "*I'm* the one who has to round up unwilling people for you, and you git most of the profit by servin' them quarter-rations."

Cyrus swore under his breath. Isaac may have been content to let well enough alone, but Cyrus wasn't. He was going to do some checking to discover who the man was who purchased Chelsie's redemption papers. He knew Jarred's name, but nothing else, and now he wished he'd never laid eyes on either of them.

Composing himself as best he could, Cyrus grasped the lead rope to the mare and towed her toward the blocks. The look Chelsie bestowed on him caused him to gnash his teeth. Cyrus had come to recognize that defiant stare. He had certainly seen it often enough. That was one witch who not only got mad, but also got even, Cyrus remembered.

In Cyrus's opinion, the best defense was a strong offense. He would have to deal with that feisty chit, but on his terms, not hers. And if she managed to convince Jarred that she was a real duchess, Cyrus would continue to swear up and down that she wasn't. But no matter what, Cyrus would not allow Chelsie to spoil his business of kidnaping unsuspecting citizens from England and selling them as redemptioners. Nor was she going to thwart his theft ring that had brought him a great deal of money. That sassy blond had somehow managed to persuade her master to adorn her with elegant clothes, but she had better not try to have Cyrus arrested! If she did, she might find herself in the same predicament that had landed her in the colonies.

Chapter 5

Jarred caught the silent exchange between Chelsie and Cyrus Hutton. He wasn't certain what visual messages they were conveying, but he knew Cyrus recognized Chelsie. Was Cyrus merely surprised by the peasant's new wardrobe and the position she had quickly attained with the aristocrats? Or was he simply annoyed with her because she had lied about her identity and attempted to brew trouble for him?

His thoughts scattered when Chelsie raised her hand to bid on the mare. Jarred cursed under his breath. Chelsie was trying to purchase another steed, and Kyle made no attempt to stop her. Chrissake, that chit wasn't merely spiteful; she was downright vindictive!

After counting to ten, Jarred managed to corral his stampeding temper. Chelsie may have cost the McAlisters a small fortune, but Jarred swore he would make her regret this ornery prank. Draw his family beneath her spell, would she? Just wait until he got that minx alone!

To Jarred's relief, Chelsie didn't prod Kyle into bidding on the other horses that had been shipped to the colonies. Kyle did, however, bid against Amos Shaw, who had his heart set on a high-stepping stallion. Amos was forced to pay an exorbitant price for the thoroughbred, much to Kyle's delight.

As the McAlister family filed from the auction site to amble through the booths of the country fair, Jarred clamped a viselike grip on Chelsie's arm and drew her aside.

"You'll regret that," he vowed gruffly.

With unflappable hauteur, Chelsie peeled his fingers from her elbow one at a time. "I will let you know when you are allowed to touch me," she sniffed as if she were addressing a peasant. "*Now* you are not."

"Don't play the haughty heiress with me, vixen," Jarred growled. "I know who and what you are. And if those horses you purchased for my father aren't worth their daily rations, I'll extend your indentureship to twenty years to compensate for their cost."

"I thought it would be your wish to be rid of me in a shorter period of time," she mocked as she smoothed the wrinkles from her sleeve—the one Jarred had rumpled with his crushing grasp.

"What I wish is for . . ." Jarred halted in midsentence when Chelsie raised a perfectly arched brow. Damn that wily sprite! She wasn't going to provoke him into wasting another wish. He had blundered away the first without carefully choosing his words. "I'm saving my second wish for something that will cause you considerable distress and satisfy my thirst for revenge," he breathed down her neck. "And *then* I will wish I'd never laid eyes on you."

Chelsie gulped at the faintly dangerous expression on his chiseled features. She didn't have to be a genius to decipher what sort of *distress* he had in mind for her. Unless she misread that devilish look, Jarred intended to make her pay for her indentureship and for the cost of the horses without any money exchanging hands. For certain, she would wind up the loser. From all indications she would become his humiliated whore before she ever got around to meeting Kyle's oldest son, who had not taken time off from his practice of medicine to attend the fall fair. Chelsie had the unshakable feeling she would be in need of a doctor when Jarred got through with her. This overpowering giant would gobble her alive!

Luckily, Chelsie was one of those individuals whose determination increased in direct proportion to the amount of difficulty she confronted. If she survived Isaac's drugging, solitary confinement, and cruel beatings, she could endure most anything, she reassured herself. This pompous colonial wasn't going to get the best of her, no sirree. She was a Channing through and through, and a Channing never admitted defeat. The word was not in their vocabulary!

When Amos Shaw strode forward, Jarred set aside his spiteful musings and opened his mouth to make introductions. Before he could utter even one syllable, Kyle curled his arm around the devastating blond and drew her close, as if she were one of the family. That really got Jarred's goat.

"Amos, meet the Duchess of Chessfield. Chelsie, this is one of our closest neighbors, Amos Shaw."

After a quick round of how-do-you-do's, Kyle announced that Chelsie had purchased the horses for him and that Amos's broken-down stallion would never stand a chance on the tracks against the colt with winged hooves. While Kyle and Amos immersed themselves in a spirited discussion over who'd made the best purchase, Daniel and Grant led Chelsie away to show her the sights. Jarred, who had yet to enjoy the reception he'd anticipated after his long absence, was left to amble aimlessly beside Eli.

"From the look of things, Chelsie has made a place for herself in Kyle's heart. I only hope Neil will be as fond of her as the rest of the family seems to be," Eli mused aloud.

"I hope you aren't including me as the 'rest of the family,'" Jarred grumbled. "Your brainstorm has evolved into a nightmare that I'll probably live to regret."

A sly grin tripped across Eli's lips as he strolled past the pastry booth where Chelsie was wolfing down goodies with both hands. She had been starved for more than a month, and she was taking this opportunity to compensate for all the meals she had missed.

"If you didn't already have a fiancée from a fine upstanding family, you could marry Chelsie yourself and save the McAlisters from this charading duchess," Eli suggested.

"Now why would I want to do that?" Jarred snorted.

"Probably for the same reason you dragged that high-strung minx back to your room and then chased after her once she spirited herself away," Eli surmised, flinging Jarred a goading smile. "Suppose you tell me where you found her and why you took her to the hotel."

"She isn't the first wench who caught my eye," Jarred defended, without directly answering the question. "I don't know why you're making such a to-do about it." Hell, Jarred didn't know why he felt compelled to herd that minx upstairs to his room. He just had, and that was that!

"Nay, she isn't the first chit," Eli agreed. His gaze sobered and he peered intently at Jarred, who had masked his emotions behind a careful, blank stare. "But she is the first one you bought and planned to keep for apparently no other reason except that you wanted her." He thoughtfully stroked his chin, never taking his eyes off Jarred, waiting for that well-disciplined mask to crack. "Seems a mite peculiar behavior for a man who I thought always had his head on straight."

"I'm suffering shell shock after the battle at Great Meadows," Jarred muttered tersely. "I'm entitled to make a few mistakes after what I've been through."

With that, Jarred stamped off in a huff, and he didn't even know why. This charade was Eli's idea, but Jarred felt just as guilty. He was the one who had shepherded that green-eyed witch to his room. Three wishes? Bah! His first, second, and last wish should have been that he'd never allow himself to get mixed up with that wildcat. Damn her! Little Miss Channing was giving Jarred McAlister of Easthaven conniption fits!

Chelsie indulged herself in food and drink and enjoyed Grant and Daniel's attention. Although they didn't want to be looked upon as brotherly types, that was the way Chelsie perceived them. But Grant and Daniel didn't seem to mind. Just escorting the duchess around the fair was pleasant in itself. She had but to look as if she needed something and they both ensured that she had it. Chelsie was appreciative of the trinkets and appetizing snacks they purchased for her. But most of all, she was thankful for the opportunity to enjoy life once again, instead of merely enduring it, as she had on the schooner.

By the time the festivities ended for the night, Chelsie was a bit too tipsy to walk a straight line. Irrepressible giggles persisted in bubbling from her lips. The nightmare was finally over, and she was celebrating her freedom by gulping each drink thrust into her hand.

Grant had made several suggestive overtures during the course of the evening, and Daniel had insisted she needed the affection of a younger man. Chelsie was too inebriated to take either of them seriously. She didn't have a care in the world. She'd managed to retrieve her father's stolen horses and escape captivity. What could be better?

"I think you've had enough fun for one night," Jarred growled as he yanked the cup from Chelsie's numb fingertips.

She blinked her blurry green eyes in surprise. "Where did you come from?" she slurred, nodding sluggishly. "Ah, I remember now." A silly smile crossed her face. "You rose from the bathtub without a . . ."

Jarred snatched her to him so quickly that her words tumbled from her tongue in an inarticulate mumble. "I'm taking the duchess back to her room at the hotel before she makes a fool of herself," Jarred declared as he whisked her away from his young brothers.

"You must be the black sheep of the family," Chelsie tittered carelessly. "The rest of the McAlisters are a pleasant sort." A muddled frown clouded her brow as she glanced back at the fuzzy images of Grant and Daniel. "Aren't they staying at the hotel too?"

"They are residing with friends in Annapolis," Jarred explained.

"I was hoping to room with Daniel and Grant. They are marvelous companions," Chelsie slurred, then grinned impishly into Jarred's thunderous scowl. ". . . Unlike their sourpuss of an older brother."

Jarred didn't pick up the gauntlet, although he was sorely tempted. He merely kept an iron grip on his temper and propelled Chelsie along the path that led from the site of the country fair to the abandoned streets of the city. One glance behind him assured him that Eli did not approve. The valet stomped along several yards behind them, glaring at Jarred's back.

"What did you expect me to do with her?" Jarred snapped in defense of the fourth disdainful glower he received from Eli. "She has one set of clothes, after all. Stashing her where my family is staying would provoke too many questions."

Eli quickened his step to pace beside Jarred and the intoxicated beauty who was being dragged along faster than she could comfortably walk. "If the duchess is staying in our room, where will we be staying?" he demanded to know. "The hotel is filled to capacity." When Jarred didn't respond immediately, Eli growled under his breath. "I am not sleeping in the lobby with the huddled

66

masses who have begged to bed down on the floor!"

When Chelsie stumbled on the hem of her skirt, too sluggish to keep the swift pace Jarred had set, he scooped her up in his arms. "Foolish little imp," he muttered into her moonlit features.

The rum dulled Chelsie's senses and drowned her notorious temper. She was in no mood to protest being carried to the hotel or to pick a fight with this irritating rake. The feel of his arms cradling her was pacifying. Sighing tiredly, Chelsie laid her head against his sturdy shoulder and closed her eyes.

It had been an eternity since she'd been cuddled in her father's loving arms. After all she'd endured of late, she needed to be held and comforted, even if Jarred was doing the holding and comforting. It soothed the wrinkles from her troubled brow, and the inebriating drinks had already taken the edge off her nerves. Chelsie felt content in Jarred's arms.

"Mmmmm . . . you feel good . . ." Chelsie breathed against his neck. Like a kitten snuggling up to a cozy hearth, Chelsie buried her head against the lapel of his black waistcoat. Inhaling the musky scent of his cologne, Chelsie laid her arm around his neck and expelled another weary sigh. "A most comfortable pillow . . ."

Jarred peered down at the petite bundle of ruffles and lace. Despite his irritation with the events of the day, Jarred smiled to himself. Strange, how this sprite brought out such a myriad of emotions in him. She amused him with her antics and her daring. She frustrated him to no end with her spiteful pranks. And she aroused him.

He knew what he wanted from Chelsie—the same thing he wanted from every other woman who wound up in his arms. But it was no longer as simple as appeasing his lust for an intriguing wench. Chelsie had burrowed her way into his family and had portrayed the regal duchess superbly. There were times when she almost had him believing she was an heiress, and he knew better, for God's sake!

When Chelsie came closer, Jarred's body reacted to their close contact. She smelled of pastry and freshly baked bread and the whole outdoors. In one day Jarred had acquired a peculiar feeling of possession for this firebrand. She was his after all, bought and paid for with his own money.

The kiss they had shared that afternoon still lingered on his lips, tormenting him, leaving him wanting for more. He had been jealous of his own brothers when they groveled at Chelsie's feet, when she blessed them with her radiant smiles. Him? Jealous? He had never felt that way with other women, and there was no reason why he should now.

When his three brothers swarmed around Abi Shaw, Jarred was never stung by this blasted possessiveness. In fact, he didn't mind at all. Jarred had proposed to Abi to pay a debt he felt he owed her and because Kyle had been on a rampage to have at least one of his sons married.

Abi was a lovely, reserved widow who would make any aristocrat a fine wife. She wasn't the least bit demanding of his time or attention. She was amiable, shy, soft-spoken—she had all the soothing qualities a gentleman expected in a wife. And even though she was everything a man of his position needed, Jarred couldn't quite make himself settle down to that socially acceptable life of the Maryland gentry. His affection for Abi wasn't strong enough to force him to make sacrifices. He'd been born under a wandering star, and his restlessness and thirst for adventure led him back and forth between the untamed wilds and civilization.

Jarred sighed. Perhaps one day he would be ready to put down roots and give his father the grandchildren he so badly craved. But not now, not when he was distracted by this blond hellion who had passed herself off as a dignified duchess. It would be a fulltime job keeping one step ahead of Cyclone Chelsie to ensure she didn't cause him more trouble than he'd asked for by involving himself in this ridiculous charade.

Aye, this spirited minx would probably be the spark Neil needed in his life. But she was also the obsession Jarred *didn't* need in his! There was no explanation for this ill-fated attraction, but Jarred kept seeing that bewitching face materialize from his bubble bath. He could see forever when he peered into the wide horizon of those emerald eyes. All Jarred's previous relationships with women had proceeded in the normal, expected manner—the flirtation, the seduction, the conquest, and then flight. But with Chelsie, nothing had progressed in the usual fashion. He flirted and she flew. He sought to seduce and this blond-haired spitfire yielded only partially. And the only conquest was self-conquest—

Jarred's. He had spent the better half of the day trying to tell himself he didn't want this minx in his bed as badly as he thought he did.

A reluctant smile pursed his lips as he scaled the steps to his room. He had to admit this vixen challenged him in ways no other woman had dared try. And she'd met his challenge, turning the tables on him so skillfully that he was left to fume, but in resentful admiration of her ability to charm his family out of their silk stockings.

What he needed, Jarred decided, was to break this magical spell Chelsie had cast upon him. He needed her in his bed. Once he had made love to her, she would no longer hold this mystique over him. She would become just another conquest and his fascination would evaporate. That was the way it had always been before. Once he appeased his needs, he'd be content to give her up to his older brother, who needed another preoccupation in life besides tending the sick. The doctor desperately needed to treat himself, and Chelsie was just the medicine. She could breathe life into Neil. His older brother didn't have to know about Jarred's brief affair with Chelsie, nor about her true identity. Things would work out splendidly for everyone if Jarred could satisfy this obsessive craving just once. Then he would never spare this minx another thought, he convinced himself.

When Jarred reached the door to his room, Eli stepped in front of him to open it and then stood in his path, an immovable barrier. "Don't think I don't know what you're thinking," Eli bit off. "I've known you since you were just a scrawny little lad." He brandished a stubby finger in Jarred's face. "If you do what you look like you're planning on doing every time you glance down at that sleeping bundle of fluff, don't expect me to keep silent about it."

"You forget your place, Eli," Jarred growled.

"Look who's talking! Maybe Chelsie isn't really a duchess, but we've made her one. Your father believes it and so do Daniel and Grant. If they *think* she is, then she *is*."

Jarred pivoted sideways to barge into the room, forcing Eli to move or be mowed down. "That is the craziest thing I've ever heard," Jarred scoffed. "And I'm in no mood for a lecture."

Carefully, Jarred laid Chelsie on the bed and watched her coil herself into a tight ball, as she had when she was forced to sleep in a crowded niche beside other passengers crammed together like sardines on the ship. Her lovely features were soft — like a cherub at rest. She was absolutely enchanting, and Jarred stood there a moment quietly admiring her beauty.

When he finally spun about, Eli leveled him a condescending glare. "If you make your bed here and sleep in it with Chelsie, I'm going to hold you responsible for whatever happens," he declared.

He regarded Eli's inflated chest and the stubborn set of his chin. "What do you intend to do? Tattle to my father and force me to make a respectable woman of her?"

"I just might," Eli blustered. "Would you want a woman your own brother had bedded? What if Neil *does* take a fancy to Chelsie?" Unblinking gray eyes riveted on Jarred. "You could complicate matters just because you don't have enough will power to curb your lusts."

Jarred stuffed his hands in his pockets and paced the floor, pausing occasionally to glance at the sleeping beauty.

"If you are in need of a woman, there are several brothels hereabouts, but leave Chelsie alone. In fact, I think 'tis best if you stayed the night with the rest of your family and let me keep a watchful eye on the duchess," he suggested.

Jarred stopped short. "The last time I left Chelsie in your care she was on the street, courting disaster, and in trouble in five minutes," he reminded him.

Eli's chest swelled so, he nearly popped the buttons from his shirt. "I'll be ready for anything this time," he declared with confidence. "Besides, she's well into her cups, thanks to your two eager-to-please brothers. Chelsie won't cause me any trouble."

Jarred rejected the suggestion. "You stay with my family and I'll stand guard over Chelsie," he insisted.

Eli opened his mouth to protest, but the stern expression that was etched on Jarred's face indicated the debate had ended. Jarred was like a stone when he made up his mind. It would take an earthquake to crack him.

"Have it your way. You usually do," Eli grumbled. "But keep in mind what I said. You are asking for trouble by staying here and tempting yourself. I won't be bailing you out if you wind up with a sinking ship."

"Your loyalty after all our years together is touching," Jarred mocked as Eli stamped about, collecting his belongings.

Eli jerked himself up to full stature. "Don't ask me why, but I've taken a liking to that saucy sprite. There's something special about her. And if she really does have a father somewhere who can throw his weight around, you're going to be sorry, just like Chelsie has said time and time again. I can't wait to hear you talk your way out of this one, counselor," he smirked as he stuffed his garments in his satchel and snapped it shut. "You may find yourself in court, representing yourself in the most important case of your life!"

"This was your idea in the first place," Jarred countered.

"I dreamed up the idea to keep you from doing something you might later regret," Eli shot back. "But I was not the one who dragged Chelsie here." A taunting smile tugged at the corner of his mouth as he waddled toward the door, satchel in hand. "You go right ahead and do what you want, but just remember, you'll pay somehow or other. You can put all that fancy education you acquired in those uppity schools in England to good use when the Duke of Chessfield comes looking for his long-lost daughter."

He paused by the door to fling Jarred a curious question. "While you were gadding around London, you didn't happen to run into the Duke of Chessfield, did you?"

"I doubt there is one," Jarred sniffed.

"Well, if there is, and if he *does* have a daughter, and if Chelsie *is* that daughter spending the night with you, you can prosecute yourself or let the Duke do it for you. But either way, you won't have a smidgen of defense. You'll be guilty as hell and I'll testify against you."

With that spiteful remark Eli breezed out the door. He couldn't say for sure if he had gotten through to Jarred, but he had made a valiant effort. Chelsie was not the kind of woman a man could take for granted. She had a mind of her own and a temper hot enough to start a forest fire.

Aye, if Jarred knew what was good for him, he would curb his lust or look elsewhere for satisfaction. If he tampered with that blond wildcat, he was asking for trouble. Hopefully, this was one time Jarred wouldn't go looking for trouble. That was an unnerving habit of his. He seemed to delight in testing his abilities to their limits. But battling the French and Indians in the wilderness was one thing. Seducing a lass who might be the daughter of an influential duke was another matter entirely. And by damned, Jarred had better not mess with Chelsie, Eli growled to himself. For if he did, he would get no sympathy from his valet when it came time to pay the piper!

Chapter 6

When the door eased shut behind Eli, Jarred stared pensively at the far wall, digesting his valet's parting remark. He racked his brain, trying to recall if there was a Duke of Chessfield. But Jarred had been far too interested in the ladies and the sights of London, not to mention his studies, to learn the names of all the dukes and earls who pranced through court. Besides, what were the chances of Chelsie truly being one of the wealthy gentry of England? Slim and none, Jarred wagered.

Jarred knew from his experiences in London that many a maid could mimic the manners of aristocrats. It was a game with them. Envious women imagined themselves as ladies of quality and breeding. Jarred had met his fair share of women who paraded about, attempting to lure their colonial cousins who had been shipped to the mother country to receive proper educations. Those conniving wenches spent half their time searching for foolish pigeons to pluck or latch onto for security. If they could invite a proposal of marriage and sail to the colonies, they could greatly improve their stations in life.

Chelsie could be one of those mercenaries who used her wiles and her beauty to better herself. Anyone could copy the habits and mannerisms of gentry and drop a few names here and there. That didn't make Chelsie a bona fide lady. She might have spent time with aristocrats, perhaps as a servant, but she didn't have the personality of nobility. Most of the upper crust of English society were arrogant to a fault, reserved and refined. But Chelsie had too many rough edges to be an aristocrat. And she wasn't the least bit inhibited.

Eli was fretting for nothing, Jarred assured himself. Chelsie was a misfit who didn't have a place on this planet. The good Lord hadn't known what to do with that feisty minx, so he had stashed her on a ship bound for the colonies and washed his hands of her. And if she really did have a father, which she probably didn't, he wouldn't care less where she was, so long as she was out of his way.

Comforted by those thoughts, Jarred stared down at the soft bundle of beauty who lay on his bed. A wry smile crossed his lips as he ambled over to remove Chelsie's slippers and tug the full petticoats from beneath her gown. She couldn't very well sleep in the only set of clothes she had, now could she?

Jarred leaned onto the edge of the bed to unfasten the stays on the back of her dress. Gently he pulled the garment downward to reveal the lacy chemise beneath it. When he tugged on the hem, the gown slid to her waist. Sliding a hand beneath her hip, Jarred drew the wrinkled garment away and tossed it over the back of a nearby chair.

When he turned back to the barely clad imp, a knot of desire unfurled inside him. Lord, she was lovely. Her shapely legs were exposed by the short chemise and her silky arms lay gracefully upon the sheet. Her glorious blond hair was in disarray, and the creamy mounds of her breasts were dangerously close to spilling from the confines of the sheer bodice.

Jarred went hot all over, even while Eli's fiery sermon echoed in his ears. He was tempting himself to the limits of his resistance, he knew. But demons of curiosity had hounded him all day. He had envisioned how this sassy leprechaun would look after he'd seen her wet gown clinging to her arresting curves and swells. But even his active imagination couldn't do this minx justice. Her skin looked as soft and exquisite as satin, and Jarred surrendered to the temptation of touching what his eyes beheld.

And sure enough, the texture of her flesh was as smooth as it looked. A forbidden hunger gnawed at him, leaving Jarred craving more. He wanted to devour Chelsie with his eyes while he caressed every magnificent inch of her voluptuous flesh. He needed to end his ridiculous fascination for this troublesome nymph.

In all his thirty-two years, Jarred had never been so unscrupulous. He had turned into a Peeping Tom. He was taking unfair advantage of Chelsie, who had drunk herself senseless. She was weary and intoxicated, and she didn't have the faintest idea that her delicious body had become the object of Jarred's attention. He was a scoundrel of the worst sort, and if Chelsie had been in command of her senses, she wouldn't have hesitated in telling him so. But she was fast asleep and Jarred couldn't stop himself from wanting her. He ached to feel her body molded intimately to his, to satisfy the obsession that had tormented him all day.

Cursing his lack of restraint, Jarred drew the flimsy chemise away and watched Chelsie stir when the cool air whispered over her bare skin. Jarred's heart hung in his chest like a rock. He couldn't draw a breath or force his eyes to blink. He simply sat there feasting on the most exquisitely sculptured body he had ever seen. And he had seen plenty of them. But Chelsie put all other females to shame. She was a dainty, perfectly formed portrait of unsurpassed beauty.

Now they were even, Jarred rationalized as he devoured Chelsie with his scrutinizing gaze. She had seen him rise from the tub wearing nothing but bubbles. Now he knew what lay beneath those layers of expensive fabric. Chelsie was a love goddess, one who could arouse and delight a man in the most incredible ways.

Jarred's conscience had taken leave of him, driven away by his overactive male desires. He was through fighting the feelings that ricocheted through him. He wanted Chelsie, and there was no reason why he shouldn't have her, he told himself.

Reaching out, Jarred doused the lantern and hurriedly peeled off his own clothes. As he stretched out beside the naked nymph, every inch of his flesh became sensitized. He could feel the warmth of her luscious body, feel the silky texture of her skin brushing intimately against his.

With a tormented groan, Jarred encircled Chelsie in his arms, bringing her full against him. For a moment he was content to hold her, to inhale the tantalizing scent of her, to absorb her body into his.

When Jarred had tugged away Chelsie's gown, he had unknowingly incited the haunting nightmares that had plagued Chelsie for the past month. The feel of a man's arms folding around her unleashed the tortured memories of the degradation and injustice

75

she'd suffered. Through her rum-induced dreams, Isaac's whisk-ered face appeared like a specter in the night.

Sluggishly, Chelsie had turned away from the goading smile that was plastered on Isaac's homely face. But his captive arms still held her chained to him. His disgusting hands were upon her, mocking her, belittling her. He had come to harass her after she had gone another round with Meredith Holt—the shameless har-lot who had pleasured every sailor who glanced in her direction. But fool that Isaac was, he thought Meredith was his woman, and he punished Chelsie even when it was Meredith who had picked the fights.

Chelsie could almost smell the musty odor of the dark niche Isaac had shoved her into. She had caused trouble and he had come to seek fiendish reprisals by tugging at her clothes and threatening rape. The other passengers knew his intent and started a ruckus to divert him. But this time their yelps hadn't distracted Isaac. He had put his disgusting hands on her, forcing her to endure his rough kisses, threatening to pour his noxious potion down her throat again if she didn't cease her screaming and curs-ing.

His arms were around her, forcing her to accept the feel of his body pressed familiarly to hers. And this time Isaac would ravish her, despite the howls of the other passengers, despite her attempt to break free.

Chelsie could stand no more. She thrashed for release from the chaining arms. A whimpered cry burst from her lips when Isaac's sneering face leaped at her from the darkness. Behind him, her full mouth pursed in a devious smile, stood Meredith Holt, whose conniving lies had so often caused Chelsie to suffer Isaac's abuse. Goading laughter echoed through her dreams. Chelsie could feel the sting of Isaac's doubled fist, hear the taunting chortles of the female voice.

In a burst of fury, Chelsie lunged at her nemesis, then blocked the countering blows. She could hear Isaac cursing and scowling, threatening to strike her again, swearing to take her once and for all, just to humiliate her.

While Chelsie was struggling in the arms of her recurring night-mare, Jarred was growling in frustrated bewilderment. His sleep-ing beauty had come to life like a clawing tigress. Her nails dug into his chest, peeling away flesh. Her uplifted knee rammed into the private parts of his anatomy, causing him to yelp in a voice that was an octave above normal. Chelsie had suddenly come unglued, and Jarred had a fight on his hands simply trying to counter the flying knees and fists!

"Don't touch me, damn you, Isaac!" Chelsie hissed as she kicked the vicious apparition to splinters. She saw the whip clutched in his fist and shrank back before she felt its agonizing sting on her flesh. "Nay . . ."

And then the ruthless bastard was shaking her. His fingers dug into her forearms like spikes, cutting off circulation, bruising her skin. Chelsie heard his menacing growl, but she was too drugged with rum to decipher his harsh words. When he shook her again, Chelsie spluttered in frustration. She would die in the foul-smelling bowels of this ship and be tossed overboard as bait for the sharks. Her father would never know what had become of her. Her last memory would be that of Isaac's birdlike features boring down on her as he covered his body with hers. God help her! She didn't want to die with Isaac's memory tormenting her through all eternity.

"Chelsie," Jarred snapped in exasperation. "Chel, it's me—Jarred."

Still there was no response except her frantic writhing and wailing. She was cursing Isaac with every ragged breath. Tears boiled down her flushed cheeks and she refused to open her eyes to see that it was all only a nightmare.

Jarred could have kicked himself for provoking this maddening dream. Chelsie might not have been a duchess, but she had obviously suffered horrifying abuse at Isaac Latham's hands. Had Jarred known the hell she had been through, he would have dealt severely with that scrawny scalawag.

"Chelsie, for God's sake, wake up!" Jarred muttered, giving her another hard shake.

Finally the deep, commanding voice filtered through her dreams. Over and over she heard her name echo through the long corridor that led to reality. Her tangled lashes fluttered to reveal Jarred's handsome features framed by the moonlight that came through the window.

Something snapped. For weeks she had battled Isaac. She had

77

remained firm and defiant through her dreadful trials. But realizing she was in Jarred's comforting arms left her clinging to him for compassion. Chelsie shouldn't have been in his arms at all, and she didn't have the faintest notion how she had gotten there. But it didn't matter how or why . . . she was safe. For the first time in weeks she had awakened from her nightmare without facing the cruel, tormenting reality of hell on earth.

Like a homing pigeon returning to roost, Chelsie wrapped herself around Jarred's solid frame, still unaware there was nothing but bare flesh between them. Unrestrained tears streamed down her cheeks.

"It's all right, Chel," he murmured comfortingly. His lips grazed her perspiring forehead, his fingers combed through the wild tendrils of her hair. "Isaac will never harm you again, I promise. I won't let him near you. You're safe in my arms."

"He was going to . . ." Chelsie burst into sobs and squeezed back thoughts of the haunting prospect that had come so close to reality that horrifying night a week earlier.

"I know," Jarred whispered as he massaged the tension from her back. "You haven't learned about love, only about lust and abuse. But there is more between a man and a woman than what Isaac did to you. 'Tis tender and warm, and far from frightening. . . ."

"Is it?" Chelsie tipped her head back to gaze into his tender smile. "How could it be?" she questioned, muffling a sniff.

The nightmare still weighed heavily on Chelsie's mind. She had seen Meredith and her lovers tumble about, poking and prodding at each other like wild animals. She had felt Isaac's hands upon her breasts and thighs and fought him with every ounce of strength each time he tried to strip her from her clothes. Those things which went on between a man and a woman had been vulgar and distasteful. It was a direct contrast to the tender kisses Jarred had bestowed on her earlier that day. And perhaps it was that tingling memory that made her wonder if there truly *was* more to sex that the disgusting acts Meredith performed with everything in breeches.

Although Jarred had done nothing to frighten her, Chelsie had endured too many near-brushes with disaster not to be cynical of men. Thus far she had learned a lot about cruelty and lust and nothing about love. Because of her hellish experiences, Chelsie feared intimacy, afraid it would coincide with the nightmares of the past.

Jarred sensed the trauma Chelsie had experienced and he sought to erase her fears with tenderness. Seeing her shaken and vulnerable tugged at his heartstrings. He needed to be here with Chelsie just now, to help her heal those emotional scars before they poisoned her against all men forevermore.

Gently, his hand cupped her quivering chin and he brushed his lips over her tear-stained cheeks. Slowly he withdrew to peer into those haunted eyes that were cloudy with emotion.

"When a man cherishes the woman in his arms, he pleasures her as well as himself," Jarred told her, his hypnotic voice soothing her anxiety.

Again his lips descended upon hers, worshipping her, melting the tension that caused her to tremble like a leaf. "I think you need to be loved as much as I long to love you, Chel. Let me show you the difference between a nightmare and a wild, sweet dream ... ."

His kiss was as intoxicating as colonial rum. In his gentleness Chelsie found immeasurable strength. And in his comforting strength she discovered compelling gentleness. Chelsie surrendered to his soft, velvety voice and a melting kiss. She didn't question why they were abed together. Chelsie needed him at that moment, needed him as she had never needed a man. She was too drowsy and intoxicated to question her reasoning. The feel of Jarred's sheltering arms was enough to quell her fears. His soft kisses and resonant voice were like a soothing balm that healed her wounds.

It didn't matter that he was promised to another woman. It didn't matter that he intended to thrust her into his older brother's arms. Right now there was just the two of them lying together in moon shadows and Chelsie couldn't think past this magical moment.

Warm, bubbly sensations channeled through her when Jarred's light caresses wandered to and fro, sensitizing her innocent body. The tingling sensations became wild, uncontrollable shudders of excitement when his fingertips explored unclaimed territory. His breath was moist against her flesh as he spread a path of kisses along the column of her neck and shoulder. The feel of his hair-roughened body brushing provocatively against hers ignited inter-

79

nal fires that leaped through every fiber of her being.

A soft moan tripped from her lips as his practiced caresses worked their black magic on her skin. Helplessly, Chelsie arched upward to meet his seeking hands, to rekindle the coals of desire that he left to burn each place he touched. She gasped when his tongue flicked at the rose-tipped peaks of her breasts, when his fingertips mapped the supple terrain of her body. Waves of pleasure undulated through her, intensifying her need for him. Suddenly, Chelsie was moving toward him, yearning for his skillful touch.

Her naïve body responded to his masterful touch. She marveled at the vivid difference between Isaac's abusive gropes and Jarred's soul-shattering caresses. This was heaven, and her sojourn on the schooner had been a tormenting hell. Jarred knew where to touch, how to bring her innocent body to life. She didn't shrink away from Jarred; she inched ever closer. A tide of pleasure flooded over her and she savored the wondrous feelings that flowed through her body.

Little by little the horrifying nightmare faded to be replaced by indescribable rapture. Chelsie's breath caught in her throat when Jarred's butterfly kisses whispered over her ribs and belly. His knowing fingers found her womanly softness, teasing and arousing her to the limits of sanity. What had begun as a slow, lazy descent into the sensuous world of passion had become a bonfire of desire. Jarred appeased each burning need. Yet in the process, he created another monstrous craving that demanded fulfillment.

Chelsie clutched Jarred to her, wondering at the breathless urgency that suddenly seized her. Her heart threatened to beat even faster. Chelsie held on for dear life as one indescribable sensation after another came over her like the boiling clouds of a thunderstorm. She was being lifted higher and higher, tossed about by the churning winds of passion.

His hands and lips were everywhere at once, weaving her emotions into a tapestry of delicious pleasure. A need as ancient as time itself engulfed her. Having his kisses and caresses roaming upon her naïve flesh was no longer enough. The gigantic craving demanded appeasement and Chelsie arched upward, unable to get close enough to Jarred, unable to satisfy this strange, unexplainable need that uncoiled inside her. She was struck by a feeling of emptiness, an emptiness Jarred had magically created, an emptiness only Jarred could fulfill. He became the flame that warmed her blood, and she needed him as much as she required air to breathe.

"Jarred . . ." Chelsie's voice was a hoarse whisper, full of question, brimming with need.

He crouched above her, shuddering at the maelstrom of emotion that swirled about him. He peered down into Chelsie's shadowed face, watching the moonlight glisten in her eyes. Taking great care not to hurt or frighten this wild dove, he gently guided her thighs apart with his hips. His body trembled with anticipation and a dozen emotions. He didn't have time to analyze it. Never had he shown such dedicated patience with a woman. But Chelsie demanded his tenderness without asking for it. He had taught her the meaning of desire and he had discovered things he had never known about passion, even when he thought he knew it all. He had given of himself. He ensured that Chelsie had no fear of him when he finally came to her. She wanted him. He could see the hunger in her eyes. And he wanted her—desperately.

"Jarred, make the empty ache go away," Chelsie rasped, amazed at her own abandon, baffled by the ripples of unappeased passion that surged through her.

His sinewy body glided over hers and Chelsie tensed at the unfamiliar feeling of being possessed by masculine strength. His body was forged to hers. And then he was the living, breathing flame that set more fires in her blood. Chelsie felt only a small stab of pain before pleasure drenched her innocent body and swept her out to sea with the tumbling waves of ecstasy. Wild, throbbing tremors went through her and she became aware of nothing but the man who had taken complete command of her mind, flesh, and soul. Before she could gasp at the pleasure of it all, Jarred's mouth slanted across hers, sharing each ragged breath.

Ever so slowly he moved within her, setting the languid cadence of lovemaking. Her arms enfolded him, holding him to her as if she never meant to let him go. She met each thrust, hungering for more, aching to seek an end to these maddening feelings of rapture that demanded more than she knew how to give. The feel of his muscular body gliding upon hers and then receding like a drifting tide left her suspended in ecstasy. Her heart thundered so furiously Chelsie could barely inhale a breath. Frantically she clutched at Jarred, waiting . . . for what? She didn't know.

She feared she would eventually die. What she was experiencing was such wild, dizzying torment that Chelsie couldn't remember where she was or what she had been doing before Jarred had transformed her. Incredible sensations bombarded her from inside and out. Ineffable feelings seemed to roll like a stone tumbling down a hillside, gathering momentum, shattering as it collided with other boulders along the way.

Her nails clenched in the taut muscles of Jarred's back as the ardent crescendo of pleasure swelled out of proportion. Chelsie cried out when her body was caught in the grip of the most wondrous feeling imaginable. It was pure and sweet, and she was left dangling in space while the converging sensations burgeoned inside her until she swore she would burst.

When Jarred shuddered against her, Chelsie clung to him. She was shocked by the lingering sensations that took forever to ebb, amazed that she was still alive when she swore she had breathed her last breath.

For what seemed forever, Jarred wandered through the entangling maze of heady sensations and scattered thoughts. Never had lovemaking been so devastating. Chelsie's wild, uninhibited responses made him feel every inch a man. He knew she had experienced passion's unrivaled pleasures and he had discovered sensations that far exceeded his wildest imagination. With this spirited nymph in his arms he had sailed over rainbows to chase the sun. He was numb to all except the lingering ecstasy that blanketed his spent body. Jarred never wanted to leave her side.

Tender emotion streamed through him as he raised his raven head to peer into Chelsie's elfin face. This incredibly wild-hearted sprite had fulfilled his every wish without realizing it. He felt at peace for the first time in his life.

Placing one last kiss to her petal-soft lips, Jarred forced himself to ease down beside her. Still he couldn't pull away. Chelsie needed to know he wanted to go on holding her long after the loving was over. And he needed to hold her until these warm, possessive feelings faded. Chelsie had been roughly abused in the past, and Jarred vowed to erase every tormenting memory, to assure her that he wouldn't leave her alone to fall into the arms of her recurring nightmares. Torment such as what she must have suffered during her voyage lay buried in a shallow grave, he imagined. She could try to ignore it, but when she let her guard down and attempted to sleep, the phantoms would taunt her. Only time and understanding would permanently bury those ghastly memories.

Odd, how quickly he had learned to read her needs. Jarred seemed to know what she needed far better than she did. He was puzzled by this strange feeling of protectiveness. Her independence and insolence annoyed him at times. But deep beneath that stubborn pride, Chelsie was a vulnerable little girl who needed his tenderness.

"You were right," Chelsie sighed, surrendering to the need to cuddle against Jarred's warm, hard strength. "There is a world of difference. . . ." Lazily, she leaned back in his encircling arms. Her hair sprayed across the pillow as she tucked her head against the crook of his shoulder. "Do you make it a habit of healing the hidden wounds of abused women?"

A deep skirl of laughter reverberated in his massive chest. Gently he reached down to limn her elegant features. "My brother is the doctor in the family," he reminded her huskily.

"He may mend broken bodies, but you heal bleeding souls," Chelsie assured him.

"My only degree is in law," Jarred chortled in answer to her sleepy grin.

"Educated in England," she guessed as her lashes fluttered against her cheeks. Chelsie was too tired to keep her eyes open. When she inhaled, it was thick with the tantalizing aroma of the man who lay beside her, holding her as if she were fragile crystal.

"Aye, at Middle Temple, as a matter of fact," Jarred replied, his voice still heavy.

"And where did you learn to seduce women?" Chelsie asked with candor. "As proficient as you are, you must have acquired a degree in love as well as law."

Jarred tittered softly as he rested his chin on the top of her silver-blond head. "I graduated from Chelsie Channing's school of love," he teased her.

She peeked at his dark face. "Surely you don't expect me to

believe I was your first experiment with passion."

Chelsie held her eyes open for another moment. The drugging effects of the rum and Jarred's intoxicating lovemaking had drained every ounce of her strength. Chelsie had experienced every human emotion during the course of the day, and they had taken their toll. There was no reservoir of energy to draw upon. And so she slid into the hazy darkness to drift through the memories Jarred had weaved so skillfully about her.

Jarred felt her petite body slump against him. She was slipping away from him, but he reluctantly let her go. The three months of battling the French and keeping watch over his own shadow so the Indians wouldn't sneak up to lift his scalp before he was through with it caught up with him. At long last Jarred allowed himself to completely relax. He no longer had to sleep with one eye open and one ear tuned to the sound of approaching danger. He slept like a baby, cradling Chelsie's curvaceous body in his arms, soothing her each time the nightmare threatened to engulf her.

For Chelsie, the night she spent in Jarred's arms was as close as she had come to the security and comfort of her own bed in six hellish weeks. Jarred had chased away the specters and granted her one night's peace. He was the cozy blanket she cuddled into. He made her believe in life again and eased her bitterness toward men. He was the injection of pleasure she needed when she'd been swamped by disillusion and despair. He wasn't offering forever, but Chelsie wasn't asking for more than the night. Her recent experiences had taught her to take one day at a time, hoping tomorrow would be far better than the day before. She had learned to relish each pleasant moment, to stifle the resentment and attempt to cope with the cruelties that had befallen her.

Each time Isaac's scowling face intruded into her sleep, Jarred was there to shake her awake. He replaced the hideous image that tormented her with his gentle smile. And in the dark hours before dawn, Jarred came to her again, whispering promises of dreams, teaching her more about the bliss of lovemaking. And again Chelsie experienced sensations she never believed possible. She wondered if this was the dream that interrupted the nightmare of reality. Rapturous emotions poured out of her like wine streaming from the rim of an overflowing goblet.

She tried not to think, to differentiate between dreams and

reality. There would be time enough to contemplate when dawn came. But for that space in time she reveled in the magical sensations Jarred aroused in her without questioning her incessant need for him. What they had shared, whether real or fantasy, chased away the horrifying memories of the past. And for the first time in a long time, Chelsie enjoyed a few hours of sweet, peaceful sleep.

Chapter 7

Shafts of light sprayed across Chelsie's eyelids. Her head throbbed like a drum. Suddenly she was suffering the illusion that she was still aboard the pitching schooner and her stomach was rolling with the waves. With a doleful groan, she pried open her eyes, then quickly shut them when the blinding sunlight hit her face.

The feel of Jarred's body stirring beside her jostled her awake, sick as she was. Chelsie lay fighting her way through the jungle of tangled thoughts that cluttered her mind. With diligent concentration she tried to recall where she was. The ship? Crammed alongside the other passengers? Nay, she had survived that ordeal . . . she had run aground and escaped. But if she had, why was her stomach topsy-turvy?

With considerable effort, Chelsie sorted through the events of the preceding day. Vaguely she remembered seeing Jarred through a fog, remembered cuddling against him . . . Warm, tingling sensations made Chelsie flinch when bits and pieces of an erotic dream swirled in her mind. And then reality shook her like an earthquake.

What had she done? Her gaze darted to the brawny giant sprawled beside her in bed. Yesterday she had sworn she hated Jarred with a passion. And yet the previous night, under the influence of rum and frightening nightmares, she had . . .

Chelsie swallowed back the nausea that climbed to her throat. Had she not one iota of integrity? She had suffered with the nightmares before (every night, in fact) and she had never turned to the first warm body within reach! Holy Saints! Her life was ruined. She had been seduced by a man who had a fiancée waiting for him. She had become the body Jarred clutched to him to ease his sexual craving. And what was infinitely worse was that she hadn't even resisted his touch! So just exactly what did that make her? A concubine? Damn . . .

Humiliated no end, Chelsie inched away to locate her chemise. She stared at the garment and frowned bemusedly. When had she disrobed? Had Jarred watched her? She didn't recall worming out of her clothes . . . She saw telltale stains on the sheets—at the exact spot Jarred was looking at when he opened his eyes.

Chelsie wasn't sure which one of them looked more shocked. Jarred wasn't permitted to rouse gradually from his sleep. He was jolted awake by the stark implication of what he had done.

A virgin? For God's sake! He knew Chelsie had limited experience with men. He had presumed by Chelsie's unfinished comment the previous night that Isaac had forced himself on her. And he had also presumed that somewhere along the way, Chelsie had tumbled into bed, even if it had been only once or twice before Isaac had his way with her. But obviously, Chelsie's only intimate encounter was with him and he hadn't given it a thought that he might have been deflowering an innocent maid.

The stricken look on Jarred's face, compounded by Chelsie's guilt, set off her notorious temper. "As intelligent as you are, I thought you could have recognized a virgin at first glance," she snapped as she squirmed into her chemise.

"Damn it, you might have told me," he muttered in self-defense.

"You didn't take time to ask before you started teaching me the difference between your brand of passion and Isaac's brutality," she parried. Chelsie couldn't even look at him. Her face was red as a beet.

"I didn't hear you protest," he grumbled as he pushed himself up against the headboard and crossed his arms over his chest.

He could have talked all day without saying that! she silently fumed. Bright red flamed Chelsie's cheeks. Her sudden burst of temper gave her the courage to turn to him. "I was groggy with rum and tormented by nightmares!" she hissed, furious. "You didn't give me time to protest. You just proceeded to seduce me when I turned to you for compassion."

Her green eyes shot sparks as she drew herself up to stare him down. "I hardly think a naïve maid is any match for a worldly rogue like yourself. And I doubt my rejection of your advances would have slowed a man like you down anyway," she sniffed scornfully. "Men love to exert their superior strength over women. Isaac Latham is a shining example of male supremacy in its rawest form, and you are barely a grade above him."

Jarred's blue eyes scorched her. "I'll thank you not to compare me to that disgusting low-life."

"Then don't act like him!" Chelsie spewed.

So much for the truce Jarred had hoped to sign this morning! He and Chelsie were back to swords and daggers already. Their night of splendor was suddenly another of the nightmares Chelsie wanted to forget. Damn it, how was he supposed to know she was completely innocent of men? Nobody had told him, and that information hadn't been embroidered on her sleeve! And, blast it, he had been too caught up in the heat of the moment to realize he was seducing a virgin. It probably wouldn't have stopped him, since he wanted her so badly, he admitted in frustration, but he might have at least hesitated in making love to her.

Muttering under his breath, Jarred unfolded himself to fetch his clothes. Chelsie's startled shriek halted him in his tracks. When he glanced back, Chelsie's expressive green eyes were drinking in every inch of his naked body. If she had missed a scar or birthmark he couldn't imagine how. Her perusal was *that* thorough!

Jarred couldn't help himself. This was no time to provoke this hellion further. But his flippant remark escaped before he could help himself. "If you're finished looking me over, I'll put my breeches on."

Chelsie's face colored before she could wheel around to stare at the wall. "You did that on purpose, damn you," she growled.

She couldn't help herself. She was flustered and she reacted without thinking. Being a slammer and thrower by nature, her hand automatically folded around the lantern and she put it to flight, forcing the naked rake to dodge.

When the lantern made its crash and the coast was clear, Jarred raised his tousled head and peered at Chelsie from over the edge of the bed. A wry smile pursed his lips as he scrutinized the fuming beauty, who stood in a skimpy chemise that did more to entice than conceal her voluptuous figure from his all-consuming gaze.

"After what we shared, I hardly think there is a need for modesty," he remarked as he unfolded his swarthy frame, causing Chelsie to blush again.

In her present mood, everything Jarred said set her off. Chelsie responded to his callous comment by snatching up the marble figurine on the nightstand and hurling it at him. Jarred cursed and ducked, and the second improvised weapon thudded against the wall an instant before a sharp rap resounded at the door.

With a wordless scowl, Jarred snatched up his breeches and stepped into them. Cursing in fluent profanity, Chelsie wiggled into her rumpled gown, sought out the farthest corner, and promptly stamped into it.

When the door swung open, Eli assessed the growling Jarred, whose bare chest was a mass of healing claw marks sustained when Chelsie was fighting her way from the arms of her recurring nightmare. But Eli didn't know that . . . his imagination supplied the answer to his silent question. From the look of things, Jarred had raped Chelsie just to appease his voracious appetite.

Flinging his master a disdainful glower, Eli pushed his way into the room, only to confirm his worst fears. The tangled sheets and stains had Eli mumbling a string of colorful curses. His sympathetic gaze flew to Chelsie, who was as white as flour, except for the splotches of embarrassment that pulsated on her cheeks.

"Obviously what I said to you last night didn't penetrate that wooden head of yours, did it?" Eli sneered at Jarred, who looked as unapproachable as a starved tiger. But Eli didn't care. He was outraged by what he thought had transpired, despite his warnings. "You had no intention of taking my words to heart because you were too busy dreaming up ways to get the duchess into your bed."

"Mind your own business," Jarred bit off as he pulled on his crumpled shirt.

"Somebody better mind yours," Eli snorted sarcastically. "You've got your business in bad shape, and your father and I raised you to behave better!"

"Don't preach!" Jarred roared.

Eli's chest swelled and his wrinkled face puckered in a condescending scowl. "Don't keep doing things that prompt me to deliver sermons," he countered crisply.

Jarred already felt like a heel, and Eli was making matters worse. Because of Eli's intrusion, Jarred and Chelsie weren't allowed to resolve their differences. Jarred needed time to collect his wits. And before he blurted out some hateful remark to that fiery minx or his meddling manservant, Jarred stomped out the door. Chelsie detested him. Eli was disappointed in him and Jarred was . . .

Heaving a frustrated sigh, Jarred aimed himself down the hall. He didn't know what the hell he was at the moment. There were too many emotions struggling to master the others. Jarred didn't know what he felt or what he wanted. And that indecisiveness was an unfamiliar sensation that agitated Jarred even more. But of one thing he was certain: he didn't regret the night of splendor he and Chelsie had shared. It was rare and sweet, even if she hadn't been around enough to know that. Jarred had, and that thought haunted him all the way down the steps and into the street.

When the door banged shut behind Jarred, Chelsie stomped over, opened the portal, and slammed it so hard that dust fell from the woodwork. She had relieved some of her pent-up frustration but not nearly enough to satisfy herself, so she reopened the door and slammed it again.

Eli's shoulders slumped as he watched her vent her anger on the door. "I'm sorry, Chelsie," he murmured apologetically.

Tears welled up in her eyes and she bit her trembling lips. She would have thanked the valet for his compassion, but she feared her voice would shatter. Chelsie was too angry, upset, and humiliated to speak, so she simply nodded mutely.

Resolutely Eli walked up to her. Gently he cupped her quivering chin, forcing her to meet his somber gaze. "Tell me the truth, princess," he said in a soothing tone, "are you truly a duke's daughter? The truth, Chelsie. I want to hear the God's truth. . . ."

Chelsie shook her head affirmatively. "Aye," she managed to say without her voice cracking completely. "I didn't lie to you or to him. And that *is* the God's truth. I was abducted against my will, and my father doesn't know what has become of me."

"I was afraid of that." Eli frowned pensively. "Then 'tis up to me to right this wrong." Swiftly he strode over to fetch an envelope and paper from Jarred's satchel. When he approached Chelsie, he extended the quill and parchment. "Write a letter to the duke and tell him where you are and what happened. I'll see to it that the message is posted and on the first ship to leave port."

A relieved smile crossed her lips. At least Eli believed her and had offered to help. It was a pity Jarred wasn't so sensible as his kindly manservant. But then, what did she expect from a pompous two-legged rat who ravished virgins for sport? Damn him!

Determined of purpose, Chelsie sank down and poured out her frustration on paper. She informed her father of Isaac and Cyrus's treacherous deeds and named Jarred as the horrible, insensitive man who'd bought her indentureship without believing her story. In her present frame of mind, she made Jarred out to be Satan himself. And at the moment, that was how Chelsie viewed the blue-eyed rogue who had stolen her virginity. Had she stopped to consider her father's reaction to such a letter, she might not have condemned Jarred so harshly. But she didn't. She wanted Jarred's head on a platter to appease her humiliation. She vented all her anger onto the parchment that would soon be on its way to the Duke of Chessfield. Evan Channing had a temper that made his daughter's look positively sedate! The duke possessed several endearing qualities, but his temper was legendary. And when Chelsie threatened Jarred on occasion by saying, "Wait until my father gets here," she issued no idle threat. The Duke of Chessfield was a fire-breathing dragon when it came to his precious daughter.

Before Chelsie folded the letter, another thought came to her and she hastily jotted a postscript, asking Evan to bring Moonraker, the prized silver-gray stallion that stood at stud at Chessfield. This she asked because of her affection for Kyle McAlister and his mutual love of horses. She knew her father would consider it an odd request, but Chelsie liked Kyle, even if he had spawned one impossible, horrible, infuriating son. But they couldn't *all* turn out perfect, she supposed.

"Don't worry about a thing," Eli comforted her as he slid her letter into the envelope and tucked it in his vest pocket. "I'll see to it that Jarred accepts his responsibility. He will marry you after what he—"

"I don't want him," Chelsie interrupted bitterly. "I will *not* marry a man who treats me like a harlot. And I'm not sure I want *any* man. They're all more trouble than they're worth . . . present company excluded," she added, peeking up to toss him a sheepish smile.

"You and Jarred are hell-bent on making each other miserable," Eli grumbled. "Forgive me for saying so, Chelsie, but you're as stubborn as he is."

"Thank you for insulting me," Cheslie expelled a caustic sniff. "I would prefer to be compared to a viper—which Jarred is, come to think of it," she added acrimoniously. "And when my father arrives I intend to see Jarred hung by his heels in a snake pit so he can stare at his viper cousins face-to-face."

"Vindictive little thing, aren't you?" Eli chuckled at her poisonous frown. "I would have expected a real duchess to be above such petty revenge." A wry smile crossed his ruddy features. "If I wanted to get even, I'd play along with this scheme and let Jarred think you didn't give a tittle about him, that he isn't worth lowering yourself for."

"I *don't* give a tittle," she declared with great conviction.

Eli smiled again. "Nothing gets to a man like Jarred as much as thinking he doesn't make a difference, that he's made no impression on a lady. It seems to me the best revenge of all would be to have Jarred fall in love with you." He slid Chelsie a discreet glance to gauge her reaction. "That would be justice for our highfalutin' lawyer, don't you think?"

Chelsie returned Eli's mischievous smile. "I think I shouldn't spare Jarred McAlister another thought, but concentrate my efforts on you, Eli," she chortled affectionately. "You have more sense than the illustrious counselor."

Eli fairly beamed. "Are you proposing, duchess?"

"Would you accept?" she queried saucily.

His smile faded. "Aye, if I thought there wasn't more between you and Jarred than either of you will admit."

"There is absolutely nothing between us," Chelsie insisted in a stern voice. "I detest him, for obvious reasons."

"As you say, duchess." Eli bowed gracefully. After doing an about-face, he swept toward the door. "I'll post your letter. Let's hope it sails quickly to the Duke. I'm sure he is eager to know what has become of you."

Chelsie stared pensively after the stocky servant. Perhaps Eli was right. Maybe she was going about this all wrong. The sweetest revenge possible would be needling Jarred until he was ready to admit defeat and by making him fall in love with her. Their rocky relationship was headed nowhere anyway. Jarred had a fiancée awaiting him . . . For some reason that thought cut Chelsie to the quick.

A moan escaped from her lips when the previous night's memories enshrouded her. Tingling reminders of the pleasure they'd shared tapped at her betraying body. Jarred had been so kind and gentle with her, teaching her the difference between sex and love-making. And she had needed his tender touch. There had been something compelling about that blue-eyed devil. Chelsie had felt it the moment she saw him staring at her from across the oversized tub they'd shared. Now they had shared far more than a bath, and she could barely tolerate herself for allowing their relationship to progress to such an intimate state.

Odd, she mused as she paced the room. Intuition whispered that Jarred was the kind of man who could fulfill her dreams, yet instinct warned her not to get more involved than she already was. What chance of happiness could she have if she found herself falling in love with a man who was promised to another woman, a man who intended to match her with his older brother?

Chelsie heaved a frustrated sigh. Why was she sparing Jarred a single thought? This was no time to become sentimental. The intimacy between them had no place in either of their lives. Circumstances beyond her control had led to their night of passion, but it wasn't going to happen again, she promised herself. She needed Jarred McAlister as much as she needed the plague. When her father arrived to fetch her, she was going to return to England without looking back.

She was suffering these sentimental feelings because of her wounded morals, she concluded. It was right and proper that a woman should love the man who took her to his bed. She was trying to compensate for her feelings of guilt by attaching false emotions to their one-night affair.

Well, men weren't hounded by guilt when they hopped from

one bed to another, she reminded herself. Why, then, should she? And if she dared to think for one minute that Jarred felt anything for her, she was deluding herself! He couldn't have much respect for women if he bedded one female while he was engaged to another. Chelsie had no desire to find herself perched on the third side of the eternal triangle. She disliked Jarred and she shouldn't let her conscience hound her. What if she *had* surrendered to Jarred's tantalizing kisses? It wasn't the end of the world. If it didn't mean a thing to Jarred, then it meant less to Chelsie and it would serve him right if he made more of the moment than she did!

Eli was right, she realized with a start. Her special brand of revenge would come in bringing that pompous colonial down a notch. When she was finished with him, he would be sorry he'd toyed with her. She was going to make him wish he'd never met her. He would learn not to play with a woman's affection. If she accomplished nothing else, maybe she could teach him not to take women for granted. Surely Jarred's fiancée would appreciate the lesson that suave debonair rake was about to learn.

Jarred was going to sit up and take note of Chelsie Channing, just see if he didn't! He would realize there was at least one woman who wouldn't fall at his feet and beg for the crumbs of his affection. She was going to challenge him on every front. Jarred might not ever come to love her, but he would certainly remember her. If he *did* accidentally fall in love with her, she was going to brush him off. Once Jarred had been satisfactorily humbled, he might make his fiancée a suitable husband. But Chelsie didn't want that blue-eyed rogue. No siree, she didn't need Jarred McAlister at all!

And before she began her crusade to charm that blue-eyed devil out of his socks, she was going to have her revenge. Chelsie hurriedly arranged her coiffure and exited the room, prepared to put her plan into action. And Jarred McAlister was going to be sorry he'd ever crossed Chelsie Channing from Chessfield!

Cold blue eyes shifted from one weatherbeaten face to another, searching the bustling wharf for Isaac Latham. Jarred had stamped from his room, annoyed with himself, irritated with

Chelsie, and furious with the man who had turned Chelsie's sleep into one of fitful nightmares. Jarred felt the need to punish Isaac for the physical and emotional scars he had placed on Chelsie. He couldn't compensate for the endless days of torture she'd suffered at Isaac's hands, but he could certainly give Isaac what he'd dished out.

So much for following the pledge to uphold the law, Jarred thought to himself. There were times when a man had to become judge, jury, and executioner. If he dragged Isaac to court, he would probably manage to get off without a sentence for beating an insolent indentured servant who sacrificed her civil rights when she signed her redemptioner papers. And if he *did* take Isaac to court, Jarred would have to expose Chelsie as the servant she was, instead of the duchess she pretended to be. Besides, Jarred preferred to knock the living daylights out of Isaac Latham, rather than drag that scalawag to court. Next time that bastard would think twice before he abused a woman!

The moment Jarred spotted Isaac swaggering across the deck of the schooner, he hopped onto the gangplank and made a beeline toward him. When Isaac pivoted to face him, Jarred came uncoiled like a human spring.

Since Jarred was one of four brothers, he had engaged in his share of fistfights. And after the years he had spent in the wilderness and in battle, he was no stranger to the techniques of knocking his foe to his knees. It was a combination of anger, frustration, and outraged fury that doubled Jarred's fist and provoked him to take his irritation out on the wiry sailor who had mistreated Chelsie in only God knew how many ways. Chelsie hadn't gone into detail, but Jarred could guess that Isaac had spared no pity.

One meaty fist connected with Isaac's stubbled jaw. His head snapped back and the force of the blow caused him to slam into the taffrail. But Jarred wasn't finished with Isaac, not by a long shot. He jerked the staggering sailor upright and backhanded him across the cheek.

Holding Isaac by the lapels of his peacoat, Jarred sneered down into his pulsating face. "The next time you decide to abuse a defenseless female, remember the beating you're taking," he snarled. "And in case your memory is short, let me give you

95

something else to remind you of this little chat we're having."

Jarred lifted his knee, catching Isaac in the groin. Simultaneously he cocked his right arm and targeted the jaw he had already knocked black and blue. An agonized groan gushed from Isaac's lips as he wilted like a flower.

Like a panther Jarred pounced down to hoist Isaac onto shaky legs. "Now tell me the truth," Jarred scowled. "Is Chelsie Channing a duchess or a peasant?"

Isaac licked the blood from his lips and glared murderously at Jarred. "You son-of-a-bitch," he hissed.

"Answer me, damn your worthless hide," Jarred growled.

"Nay," Isaac replied, spitefully. "She's a no-account bitch who changed her mind halfway across the Atlantic." He smiled mockingly. "What did you do, mister high-and-mighty? Bed that sassy minx? I s'pose now yer wishin' she was a real lady instead of a peasant, just to ease yer pride."

Isaac's lips curled in a taunting sneer. "Well, she ain't gentry. She came to me in chains at St. Katherine's near the Tower of London, just like all the other convicts who were to be deported from England. She's a lyin' little thief. She ain't got no family or a fancy family crest. And if you slept with her, you stooped as low as any man could get."

Rage billowed inside Jarred and he felt like a bomb about to explode. Isaac's ridiculing words stoked the fires of his temper so completely that he yielded to the blind fury that churned inside him. All the experience and training Jarred had gathered from wrestling with his brothers and from fighting the French and Indians in the wilderness took command of his taut body. He held nothing back when he leveled another blow to Isaac's smirking face. Flesh connected with flesh, and the force of the blow was so fierce and potent that Jarred could have felled a grizzly bear.

Isaac spun like a top and fell back against the rail with such momentum that he cracked his kneecap. A howl burst from his lips when Jarred punched him in the ribs, knocking him against the unyielding rail a second time.

If Jarred hadn't grabbed him by the nape of his jacket and jerked him around to deliver one last blow, Isaac would have collapsed on deck. The beefy fist put Isaac's lights out in a flash and he pitched backward, binding his injured leg in an unnatural position that tore tendons and ligaments loose.

"What the blazes is going on here?" Cyrus Hutton demanded to know as he emerged from the stairwell.

Jarred wheeled about, his blue eyes flashing. "You and your crew will shortly be restricted to land," he announced sharply. "Chelsie Channing's abusive treatment and lack of proper nourishment during her voyage is subject to investigation. When I acquire the list of passengers and question them, we will see if you are operating a legitimate business. Until further notice, you and your crew are drydocked."

"Now wait just a damned minute, McAlister," Cyrus blustered. "I've got merchandise to deliver from the Colonies to England."

"Your clients can look elsewhere to transport their goods," Jarred told him in no uncertain terms. "One look at Chelsie indicates she wasn't given her allotted rations of food. You've been starving your passengers and tucking the extra margin of profit in your pocket. 'Tis a wonder any of the indentured servants arrived alive, considering you probably stacked them together like a flock of sheep and forgot to feed them."

Flinging Cyrus one last murderous glare, Jarred stormed from the deck. When Jarred was out of sight, Cyrus grabbed a bucket and dumped water on his unconscious first mate.

Shaking the daze from his spongy brain, Isaac propped himself up on both elbows and grimaced at the searing pain in his leg. He focused on his captain, who was sporting two fuzzy heads, as best Isaac could tell between the circling stars that swam before his eyes.

"What did you tell him?" Cyrus muttered in question.

"Nothin' that will incriminate us," Isaac croaked as he tried to move his throbbing leg. "I told him Chelsie was a peasant and a thief."

Cyrus breathed a sigh of relief before he assisted Isaac to his feet. "We're setting sail immediately. McAlister plans to impound the schooner, and I don't intend to wait around until he comes back."

Isaac latched onto an improvised cane that would enable him to stand on his injured leg. Scowling curses, he stared after the man who cut his way through the crowd on the wharf. Isaac was a vengeful man who didn't take kindly to being knocked around by some overbearing aristocrat. Chelsie and her ferocious guard dragon hadn't seen the last of Isaac Latham! They would both pay, Isaac vowed vindictively. Still muttering, Isaac dug into his pocket to fish out the gold locket he had yanked off Chelsie's neck the night he had kidnaped her.

"Damned troublesome bitch," Isaac growled, glaring at the expensive necklace. For a moment he contemplated throwing the evidence into the sea, but the pendant was worth a fortune. Meredith Holt was already wearing the elegant ring he had stolen from Chelsie. He also intended to give the pendant to Meredith as a gift, but this was not the time to have the locket floating around Annapolis. What he didn't need right now was for McAlister to catch sight of it. Since the Channing family crest and Chelsie's name were engraved on it, Jarred would know Isaac had lied.

"Where are you going?" Cyrus inquired as Isaac limped across the deck.

"I got somethin' to do before we launch," he mumbled absently. "I'll be back . . ."

Bemused, Cyrus watched his first mate hobble across the gangplank and shuffle along the dock. Swearing fluently, Cyrus stomped over to give orders to his crew. The minute Isaac returned, they were opening sail. Annapolis wasn't the only port in Chesapeake Bay. He would sail up to Baltimore and enlist other clients, he decided. No matter what that growling aristocrat said, Cyrus wasn't staying put. He would fill the hull of his schooner with cargo and set off to England as soon as the storms eased up. And there wasn't a damned thing Jarred could do about it!

Chapter 8

Jarred had stopped to confer with one of his associates who also held a seat on the Maryland Common Council. By the time he filled out the necessary papers for the investigation of Captain Hutton's activities, he was behind schedule. The Maryland Assembly was to convene in midmorning and Jarred had yet to bathe and change after his fisticuffs with Isaac.

As Jarred weaved his way through the streets, the proprietor of the boutique caught sight of him. The plump little man scampered outside, waving a bill and smiling broadly.

A muddled frown creased Jarred's brow as he regarded the rotund proprietor of the shop where he had purchased Chelsie's new gown. Jarred had paid for the garment and the other paraphernalia the previous day. Why was the man flagging him down?

"The duchess left before I had the chance to tally her purchases," the owner explained. "She instructed me to send the bill to your room at the hotel." He laid the exorbitant expenses in Jarred's hand. "The duchess has an eye for style and fabric. I know she will do my creations justice."

Jarred stared goggle-eyed at the list of expenses Chelsie had incurred while he was in the process of beating Isaac to a pulp. For God's sake, what had she done? Bought a new garment for every day of the blessed month? Cursing silently, Jarred extracted his purse. When he finished counting out the payment due, his pouch was empty and would need to be replenished the moment he returned to his room.

Forcing a smile, Jarred bid the proprietor adieu and marched toward the hotel. Thunderation, that minx had cost him a fortune! When he got his hands on Chelsie, he was going to shake the stuffing out of her. Did she think he was made of money? She was beginning to believe she really was a duchess and now she expected to dress like one. Aye, he intended to extend her wardrobe. But he hadn't planned to purchase garments that were stitched with gold and silver thread!

Damn her, wasn't it enough that he had torn Isaac into bite-sized pieces to avenge her mistreatment? Wasn't it enough that she turned him inside out when he allowed himself to dwell on the sweet memories they had created between dusk and dawn? He was feeling bad enough about deflowering a virgin and Chelsie seemed determined to make him pay dearly for what he had done to her. But Jarred had the inescapable feeling that making him pay for her extravagant wardrobe wasn't going to pacify her completely. It would probably be the beginning of a long, tormenting penance for him. . . .

Jarred stopped short when he breezed into his room to see mounds of boxes piled on the bed. Eli was shaking out the frilly new purchases, but that blond hellion was nowhere to be seen. So much for strangling her lovely neck for her mischievous prank, Jarred thought resentfully.

"Where is she?" Jarred questioned, an unpleasant edge to his voice.

Eli bit back an amused grin and turned to face Jarred's black scowl. "The duchess was invited to attend the second day of festivities at the fair," he informed Jarred. "Your father sent Daniel and Grant to fetch her. The agenda for the day includes a puppet show, the military parade, a fiddling contest and cudgeling bouts." Eli set the yellow satin gown aside and picked up the next garment in the stack. "And of course, Kyle invited her to join him at the horserace later this afternoon. He brought the strawberry roan gelding from the plantation to enter in the heat against Amos Shaw's brown mare. You know how excited your father gets about these races. Nothing would please him more than to finally beat Amos at the meeting."

"I'm surprised Papa didn't decide to match the new colt he purchased against Amos's swift brown mare," Jarred snorted. "Chelsie has him believing the colt sprouts wings the moment a race begins."

Eli chuckled at Jarred's bitter tone. "Actually, Kyle did consider racing the copper dun colt. But Chelsie advised him to wait until the next meeting in the spring. She feared the colt hadn't had time to recover from his voyage and that he should be permitted time to get his land legs. She also thought the colt required proper exercise before he was thrust into a grueling race."

"Chelsie advised . . . Chelsie thought," Jarred mimicked. "After a mere two days, I'm already fed up with what that vixen thinks and feels."

Eli turned back to his chores before his sly smile betrayed him. "After what you did to that poor, innocent lass, she deserves to have a few opinions," he declared. "I advise you to be nice to her before she decides to tell your fiancée what happened."

The remark prompted Jarred to sniff contemptuously.

"If I were you (which of course I'm not, thank God), I would try a different tactic besides this half-civilized warfare you've been practicing on Chelsie," Eli stated. "It seems to me a man can catch more flies with honey than with vinegar. Kill her with kindness, and she will become your adoring servant. But attack her with insults, and Chelsie will counter by spiting you at every turn."

"Spare me the philosophical jabber and say what you mean," Jarred ordered as he snatched up fresh clothes and headed toward the door.

"If you want to ensure that Chelsie doesn't cross you, make sure she falls in love with you. A woman in love is *far* easier to control than a firebrand who is spoiling for a fight," Eli suggested. "Give her no reason to hate you and she won't."

Jarred peered at his manservant for a long, ponderous moment. "Now why would I care if that feisty spitfire fell in love with me?" he questioned.

Eli shrugged nonchalantly. "There are some women who make better friends than enemies. I think the duchess is one of them."

"She is *not* a duchess," Jarred muttered sourly. "And because of her, I just beat the hell out of Isaac Latham for abusing her while she was on board the ship. I demanded the truth from him and he swore she was no better than her fellow countrymen who sailed west to secure a better life than they endured in England."

"If you beat the tar out of Isaac, that was incentive enough to provoke him to lie to you about Chelsie," Eli declared with conviction.

"Nay, it was incentive enough for him to confess the truth," Jarred contested.

"And you're a fool if you take the word of a blackhearted scoundrel who beats women," Eli burst out in exasperation.

"Nay, I'm a fool for standing here and listening to the ravings of a lunatic who has become mesmerized by a wily witch," Jarred shouted back. "You're as bad as the rest of my family. Chelsie has you believing she's just a notch below royalty. Well, she isn't! She's just another dispensable female like all the rest."

" 'Tis mighty cynical talk for a man who has a fiancée and a mistress," Eli snorted disrespectfully.

A frown clouded Jarred's brow. "*You* know why I asked Abi to marry me," he muttered.

"Aye," Eli grumbled. "But you've gotten obligation mixed up with sentiment. And what are you going to do about the duchess?"

Jarred opened his mouth to say . . . damn it, he didn't know what he intended to say, so he said nothing at all. Clamping his jaw shut, he flung Eli a withering glance and strode out the door with his clean clothes and towel in hand.

After Jarred left, Eli grumbled under his breath. Jarred was stubborn to the core. Just wait until Chelsie's father showed up! Jarred Bull-headed McAlister was going to be sorry he'd trifled with her! She deserved better than she was getting, but Jarred had taken the word of two scoundrels over Chelsie's because of his lack of faith in women. And Chelsie hadn't helped her situation all that much, Eli thought with a heavy sigh. She could provoke Jarred faster than anyone he knew. When her temper got the better of her, she started slamming doors and throwing things. And all of a sudden she and Jarred were at war—same fight, a different battleground. Lord, trying to get the two of them to sign a peace treaty was exhausting,

Eli decided as he sank down on the edge of the bed.

Chelsie and Jarred were good for each other. They set off a myriad of previously untouched emotions in one another. But both were too cynical and high-strung to see that. And after what had happened between them the previous night. . . .

Eli muttered under his breath. Sweet mercy, Jarred had better hope the Duke of Chessfield was an understanding man. If he wasn't, Jarred was in serious trouble! Even a distinguished aristocrat like Jarred didn't tamper with a duchess without paying his due. And Jarred would one day, Eli prophesied. The letter was on its way to England, and Jarred had better come to his senses and do the right thing by Chelsie, or he was going to be sorry!

Irritable, Jarred marched downstairs to the bathhouse to bathe and shave. The moment he stepped into the spacious bathing room lined with huge, circular vats, the memories rushed back to torment him. As he sank into the steaming bath, he wondered if a lovely leprechaun with green eyes would rise before him again. But this time the only sound to break the silence was the humming drone of a man scrubbing himself on the far side of the room.

Jarred plucked up sponge and soap and lathered his chest. Once and for all, he was going to wash away the tormenting memories of the innocent young beauty who had tempted him past all resistance. The scent of jasmine would no longer cling to his skin. The taste of honeyed kisses would no longer linger on his lips. He wasn't going to recall the splendor they had shared in the moonlit shadows. He was going to cleanse Chelsie Channing from his mind, now and forevermore.

Make Chelsie fall in love with him? Ha! Why should he? Jarred asked himself sourly. Besides, the minx didn't know what love was . . . not that he did either. He had wandered through affairs, never finding a female who made him want to think in terms of forever.

As sweet and charming as Abi Shaw was, Jarred knew he didn't love her. But he *did* need to marry her, to pay his debt to her. He liked her well enough to wed her. She wouldn't compli-

103

cate his life. But one thing was certain, he didn't have any sentimental feelings for Cyclone Chelsie. And he wasn't at all sure there *was* such a thing as love. If there was, did he have the capacity to feel that emotion? Could he draw tender feelings from a spitfire like Chelsie, even if he wanted to?

Jarred slumped back against the edge of the tub and sighed in frustration. Trying not to think about that emerald-eyed sprite was exhausting. Confronting her was exasperating. She was as quick-witted as he was, and he had to stay on his toes to keep one step ahead of her. Making love to her was devastating. But loving her and having her love him would probably be disastrous, considering how their personalities clashed. Chelsie would never soften toward him, even if he did try to woo her. Not that he wanted to, mind you. Why should he? She was a lying little thief who was using him as much as he had used her the previous night.

Eli's theory was madness, Jarred decided. It would accomplish nothing to attempt to win Chelsie's affection. She didn't have any to give away. And if she did, she should concentrate on his older brother. Neil could provide for her and she couldn't hope for more than to become a doctor's wife. Jarred was too restless to remain home for extended periods of time. That was why he consented to manage and oversee his family's four plantations scattered hither and yon. He kept busy checking on the estates, negotiating contracts for the sale and transportation of their tobacco crops. And that was why Jarred had volunteered to journey into the wilderness with the Maryland militia. He liked being on the move. He was an adventurer who had been born to wealth and position. But all the money in the world didn't compensate for the restless longings in his soul.

His need to roam was another reason why he had yet to set a wedding date with Abi Shaw. Jarred kept procrastinating, hoping one day he would be ready to settle down and raise a family. But for now he thrived on being involved with the battle on the frontier, the debates in politics, and the challenges of managing all four plantations. He was satisfied with his life. The only thing he didn't like was this frustrating preoccupation with a saucy peasant who had somehow managed to take up permanent residence in his head. And why did he keep thinking about those three wishes she had promised him? Blast it, they were going to turn out to be curses, he just knew it!

"Wishes . . . curses . . ." Jarred shook his head in dismay. He had wished to have Chelsie in his bed and she had been. Try as he may, he couldn't conjure up another female who had pleased and satisfied him with such lively passion. Chelsie had prophesied that he would soon wish he had never laid eyes on her. Well, he was already wishing that, but he wasn't going to voice the whim, or he would waste another wish, the same way he'd expended the first—requesting she behave like a duchess for his family's benefit. But if he had just one meaningful wish it would be . . .

"Bah!" Jarred growled, flinging aside the sponge. Chelsie wasn't a leprechaun *or* a duchess, and she couldn't make dreams come true or grant wishes. She was a witch who cast evil spells on unsuspecting men and then drove them mad with tormented memories of nights that shouldn't have existed. . . .

A devilish smile quirked Jarred's lips when Eli's words flitted through his mind. Maybe his servant *did* have a point. Whether Chelsie was witch, leprechaun, or woman, he could control her if she felt even a smidgen of affection for him. If he could cool her fiery spirit, she would be far easier to handle. And if she did happen to fall in love with him, she would be putty in his hands.

Well, it was worth a try, Jarred supposed as he stepped from his bath. What did he have to lose? Nothing could be worse than battling that fiery nymph whose temper had already become legendary. Why, he and Chelsie might even become friends. Of course, Jarred wasn't quite sure what he would do with her, even if they did come to terms. Having that blond-haired temptation at Easthaven would be asking for more trouble than he already had. She had the other McAlisters wrapped around her dainty finger as it was.

Maybe it would be best to sell her redemption papers to one of his many associates who would treat her with kindness. Servants were always in demand in the colonies. Chelsie could remain in Annapolis, working as a house maid, and Jarred could check on her when he was in town.

Aye, that was the best solution. After he gave his report

about the goings-on in the Ohio Valley to the Maryland Assembly, he would make arrangements for Chelsie. But right now he didn't have a moment to spare.

Jarred expelled a deep sigh as he mounted the steps to his suite. He couldn't recall being so undecided about a woman before. But Chelsie had come into his life like a whirlwind. One moment he wanted to keep her with him, the next he was thinking of leaving her in Annapolis. One instant he wanted to forget what they had shared, the next he was aching to take her in his arms again. For God's sake, what was a man supposed to do about a frustrating female like Chelsie Channing? Jarred wished he knew the answer to that baffling question. He was sure it would make him a much happier man.

Decked out in the latest fashion, Chelsie stood beneath her parasol, bookended by Kyle and Grant McAlister. Daniel, who had fluttered around her like her personal lackey, had rushed off to fetch Chelsie a mug of sillabub—a concoction of wine and cream that teased her taste buds.

Chelsie had been treated to every aspect of the colonial country fair since Grant and Daniel had come to fetch her that morning. She had watched farmers sell and trade livestock, viewed a wrestling match between two muscular giants, and giggled in amusement when several young men attempted to chase down greased pigs in the muddy arena.

Determined to put aside her troubled thoughts, Chelsie had enjoyed the second day of festivities and the charming company of the McAlister clan. She felt carefree and full of spirit. Kyle treated her like the daughter he'd never had. Things were going splendidly until Kyle ushered Chelsie toward their rented carriage that would carry them in style to the racetrack on the far side of the fairgrounds.

Just as Chelsie stepped into the coach, a dagger whizzed past her, ripping a hole in her plumed bonnet and knocking it from her head. The stiletto stuck in the opened door of the carriage with the hat dangling from it.

Kyle wheeled around at once to seek out the scoundrel who dared attack the duchess. Grant darted off in every direction at once to apprehend the blackguard, but the assailant had lost himself in the milling crowd.

Chelsie was lifted up into the coach for protection while Kyle fussed over her like an overprotective father. "I'm fine, truly," she insisted as she inspected the gash in her bonnet. "I . . ."

But before she could continue, Grant and Daniel clambered into the coach to offer her a drink and some consolation. When the carriage sped off, Chelsie eased back in the cushioned seat, shrugging away the questions. Although she had a pretty good idea who might have tried to dispose of her, she couldn't point an accusing finger at Isaac Latham without revealing how she knew the ruffian. Feigning innocence, Chelsie responded to the concerned inquiries with several "I don't knows."

From that moment on, Kyle, Grant, and Daniel became her fulltime bodyguards. When they arrived at the track, Kyle's sons were assigned the task of keeping watch over Chelsie's blind side while the patriarch scuttled off to ensure his strawberry roan gelding was being properly tended by the trainers.

With great enthusiasm, Chelsie viewed the first few heats of the races. Scores of bets were placed before each race and money exchanged hands the moment the winners crossed the finish line. Kyle returned to take his place beside Chelsie, but his attention was glued to his gelding and Amos Shaw's long-legged brown mare.

"I see I'm not too late to witness this grudge match between the McAllisters and the Shaws," Jarred chuckled.

Chelsie involuntarily flinched at the sound of Jarred's rich, baritone voice. She didn't dare glance back. By now Jarred must have known she had billed him for the numerous gowns she'd purchased at the boutique. Fortunately he wouldn't attack her with his own family as witnesses. Chelsie spitefully hoped Jarred had cursed her when he'd discovered what she'd done. It served that rascal right for stealing her virginity, and he'd only *begun* to pay. Just wait until he received the bill for the jewelry she had bought to adorn her royal blue brocade gown and the other garments sewn from the finest fabric in the colonies.

While Chelsie was ignoring him, Jarred studied her rigid back and the arrogant tilt of her chin. At least his money had been well spent, he mused as his eyes took in Chelsie's expensive clothes and curvaceous figure. The gown Chelsie had selected was cut from the finest silk. Layers of ruffles and lace rimmed the full skirt and sleeves. The garment accented her trim waist, and Jarred was anxious to see what she looked like. Unfortunately, Chelsie refused to face him. All he got was the cold shoulder.

When Chelsie had composed herself, she granted Jarred his wish. With feminine grace she pirouetted to grace him with a sunny smile that was a mite too pretentious to be sincere.

"Hello, Jarred," she murmured in her sweetest voice.

His eyes were immediately drawn to the plunging neckline of her blue gown. The bodice was tight, stiffened with stays of whale bone. There was so much of her neck and chest revealed by the daring décolletage that Jarred had difficulty lifting his gaze. Each time Chelsie inhaled, her full breasts threatened to spill forth. And like waiting vultures, Jarred's brothers were ogling the luscious display with masculine appreciation.

Jarred swore under his breath, then bit back another colorful curse when he noticed the expensive necklace that encircled Chelsie's swanlike throat. His annoyed gaze fell to the matching ring and bracelet on the arm she offered him. Striking a pose, Jarred grasped her fingertips to brush a kiss to her wrist, even though he would have preferred to take a bite out of her delicate hand.

"When am I to receive the bill for your new jewels, duchess?" he growled as he stepped closer.

Chelsie blessed him with another dazzling smile that rivaled the brilliance of her new jewels. "I requested the proprietor to deliver the bill tomorrow," she replied. "Your colonial craftsmen are masters. I'm very impressed. They charge high prices for their jewelry, but the workmanship is second to none."

Jarred leaned close to her ear with the pretense of offering a compliment. "Nay, dear duchess," he contradicted in a threatening tone that would have sent a lesser woman diving for cover. "Your *audacity* is second to none."

"Why, thank you, Jarred," she purred as she reached up a jeweled hand to pat his tense jaw. "You flatter me. But a lady does *so* enjoy being noticed and complimented by a gentleman.

You must know how dear you are to me. And I adore your family so."

Chelsie strategically curled her hand around Kyle's elbow, giving it an affectionate squeeze—one that earned her a pleased wink from the patriarch. "Your father has made me feel at home here. When the duke arrives, I know he will be most grateful to all of you for the hospitality and generosity you have shown me."

What father? Jarred thought. This minx didn't have one. Holding his tongue, he focused his attention on the race about to begin. When the pistol exploded, five horses lunged from the starting line and thundered neck-and-neck down the stretch. For a few seconds the roan gelding held his slim lead and Kyle yelled and cheered his horse on to victory. Chelsie, who was immediately caught up in the excitement, chimed in to encourage the gelding.

Jarred stood back, his gaze fixed on the stunning blonde in blue silk. Although he was irritated as hell with Chelsie for her latest prank, he couldn't contain the smile that spread across his lips when she wasn't looking. She was a bundle of barely restrained spirit, rooting for the McAlister horse as if it were her own. Reluctantly Jarred admired her spirit. She was a source of boundless energy. She bounced up and down, calling to the gelding to quicken his pace and take to the inside of the track. Her jeweled hand was clenched around Kyle's elbow while they both dispensed with gentlemanly and ladylike conduct to loudly encourage the roan.

For the life of him, Jarred couldn't figure out why he had grown so attached to a woman who frustrated him no end. While he had been delivering his state-of-war report to the assembly her wide green eyes and heart-shaped lips kept materializing before him. In the brightly lighted assembly room, he kept seeing a dimly lit corner where two lovers clung together in passion's embrace. The memories followed like his own shadow, preoccupying him, distracting him. Jarred kept wondering where Chelsie was, what she was doing. He kept picturing his younger brothers fawning over her as they had the previous evening. This wild-hearted beauty had filled his thoughts to overflowing, and Jarred wondered how he was ever going to route this gorgeous minx from his mind.

Kyle's annoyed scowl interrupted Jarred's contemplations. He glanced up to see Amos Shaw's brown mare stretching out to ease ahead of the strawberry roan. Kyle took racing very seriously, and he was crushed by the defeat, galled that Amos had enjoyed another victory.

"That is my fifth consecutive loss at the meeting," Kyle muttered disappointedly. "I'll beat that ornery old coot if it's the last thing I do!"

"Just you wait until the spring," Chelsie consoled the disgruntled patriarch. "The copper dun colt will run circles around Shaw's mare."

The nag probably couldn't run without tripping over his own hooves, Jarred mused. Chelsie was filling his father with false hopes.

"The first thing I have to do is calm the colt down," Kyle muttered. "We had one hell of a time leading the colt to the livery stable for the night. He protested my trainer's handling. I feared he would kick his way out of his stall when I stopped by last night to feed and water him."

"I'm sure he'll settle down when he is adjusted to his new surroundings," Chelsie consoled Kyle. "Even horses are nervous when they find themselves thrust into unfamiliar situations. The colt is high-strung, and I'm sure the voyage was a harrowing experience for him. He was only responding to instinct, fighting back to counter his fright."

Her gaze darted briefly to Jarred, who had no trouble deciphering the comments. Chelsie may have been discussing the colt, but the remark carried an underlying meaning. In other words, Jarred hadn't been compassionate and understanding of the trials Chelsie had faced during *her* voyage. But Jarred was bemused by her last comment. Was she suggesting that she was partly to blame for this battle that was going on between them? Did she imply that she was fighting back at her unpleasant situation and that Jarred had been her scapegoat?

Jarred barely had time to mull over those questions when Chelsie peeked up at him from the rim of long, curly lashes. He was miffed by the faint smile that hovered on her soft lips. For an instant Jarred swore she had forgiven him for stealing her innocence. But even if Chelsie had forgiven him, Jarred hadn't forgiven himself. If he had known she was pure and naïve, he would never have . . .

Hell, yes he would have, the sensible side of his brain scoffed. He had wanted that delicious elf in his bed since the moment he laid eyes on her. Jarred had seen to it that Eli trotted off to spend the night elsewhere. And Jarred had known what he wanted, what he intended. He had planned it all. But he hadn't counted on deflowering a virgin, for God's sake!

Jarred forced himself not to rehash the events that had led to a night of unequaled passion and a morning after that had put him and Chelsie at odds once again. He wasn't going to touch her ever again, he promised himself.

After conferring with a fellow assemblyman, Jarred had made arrangements for his newly purchased bondswoman to work for his associate. By the end of the week, Chelsie would be garbed in an apron and cap, tending to the household duties of one of Annapolis's most respected politicians and lawyers.

While Jarred was lost in thought, Amos Shaw approached his rival. Beaming like a lantern, Amos drew himself in front of Kyle. "Well, my friend, it seems you have another debt to pay."

Muttering sourly, Kyle fished into his pocket. "Just wait until next time," he snorted. "You will be paying me when I enter my new colt in the race."

"That skinny-legged nag with the oversized head?" Amos snickered. "The colt doesn't stand a chance against my brown mare, or the new stallion I purchased." Teasingly, Amos waved the coins under Kyle's nose—one that was out of joint. "It was a pleasure betting against you, Kyle. I never mind taking your money." Amos strutted off.

Kyle scowled in annoyance. "If I live long enough to outrun that rascal, I'll flaunt my victory in his face the same way he flaunts his in mine. Damned ornery buzzard!"

Chelsie comfortingly patted Kyle's inflated chest. "Your time is coming," she prophesied. "You will have your revenge. I'm convinced that we all have our day of reckoning." Her clear green eyes shifted to Jarred. "Justice is always served to those who plan ahead and wait."

A wary frown knit Jarred's brow. What was waiting at his

day of reckoning? he wondered. Chelsie was a master at speaking to one member of his family and aiming invisible barbs at Jarred. Her wit and intelligence were dagger-sharp. Jarred had the uncomfortable feeling he had made a crucial mistake when he'd pitted himself against this wily witch.

When Jarred glanced away from Chelsie's impish smile, his eyes landed on Eli's wry grin. "What do you find so amusing?" he demanded.

Eli crossed his arms over his thick chest and shrugged lackadaisically. He was the only one who knew about the conflict between Jarred and Chelsie. His respect for her abilities had increased rapidly in the past few minutes. In Eli's estimation, the illustrious assemblyman, lawyer, and soldier had met his match in Chelsie Channing from Chessfield. Jarred was finally getting what he deserved—a feisty female who matched his dynamic, strong-willed personality. Jarred was vividly aware of her and this secretive relationship between them was beginning to stain his every thought and color all conversation.

If the hostility between these two sparring challengers carried an electrical charge there would have been lightning bolts leaping back and forth between them. But the amusing thing about it was that the rest of the McAlisters didn't have the foggiest notion they were standing on the battlefield while these two enemies waged their war of wills. Ah, this was ripe, Eli mused, stifling a snicker. He relished watching the quick-witted lawyer match wits with Chelsie's keen mind.

"With your background in raising and breeding thoroughbreds, maybe you can offer me some advice about the colt," Kyle was saying to Chelsie. "I'm determined to make that copper dun gelding a winner."

What background? Jarred thought cynically. Chelsie had obviously boasted her expertise to Kyle. Lord, that ornery chit was setting his poor unsuspecting father up for the fall of his life!

"Chelsie won't be around to guide you in training the colt," Jarred inserted. "I have made arrangements for her to stay with one of the assemblymen from the upper council until her father arrives."

"She can't stay in Annapolis," Grant declared. "Not after

112

what happened this afternoon."

A puzzled frown clouded Jarred's brow. "What are you babbling about?"

"The attempt on Chelsie's life," Daniel hurriedly supplied. "We were preparing to climb into the coach to drive to the starting line when a dagger notched a slice in the duchess's bonnet." Daniel indicated the slit near the crown of her plumed hat. "Two inches lower and Chelsie would have had her hair and her skull parted."

Jarred's shocked gaze flew to the curvaceous blond who had taken yet another adversity in stride. Most women would have been lying in a dead faint after such a brush with catastrophe. But Chelsie merely smiled, shrugged, and made light of the incident.

"The only discomfort I suffered was a rip in my bonnet," she insisted. "There is no need to make a fuss. It was probably just an accident. Perhaps a young lad carelessly hurled the dagger and he was simply too embarrassed to step forward to own up to his mistake."

"Accident or no, I insist that you sojourn at Easthaven until the duke arrives," Kyle demanded in the firm tone he employed when he wanted control of a conversation. "There is no need for you to spend more time in Annapolis than necessary after the incident. I, for one, do not take the matter lightly."

Jarred didn't take the matter lightly either! Unless he missed his guess, Isaac was punishing Chelsie for causing him trouble. Jarred felt personally responsible for the attempt on Chelsie's life. He had provoked Isaac and the miserable scoundrel had struck back in his own cowardly way.

"Aren't you staying for the other races?" Kyle queried when Jarred spun around and strode away.

"I have unfinished business to transact," Jarred threw over his shoulder. His eyes were magnetically drawn to the shapely blonde and Jarred had to force himself to focus on his father and his valet. "Eli can accompany Chelsie back to her hotel room after the festivities are over."

When Jarred disappeared in the crowd, Grant ambled up beside Chelsie and smiled curiously. "Your hotel room?" he asked quietly. "I meant to ask you why my brother's satchels were in your room when we arrived to fetch you to the fair this morning."

The probing question caught Chelsie off stride. With considerable effort she fought down the blush that threatened to stain her cheeks. "Eli asked if he could remove Jarred's belongings while the maid cleaned his room. And in turn, Eli moved my belongings into your brother's room while the maid tidied my suite."

Relief spread over Grant's handsome blond features. He didn't want to find himself in competition with his brother while he was wooing this fascinating beauty. It was true that Jarred had a fiancée on the string, but he was never lacking for womanly attention. Women flocked to Jarred like birds instinctively migrating south for the winter. Grant was having enough trouble keeping young Daniel at a respectable distance from the enchanting duchess without having to worry about Jarred's intentions toward her.

"You're getting a mite nosy," Eli snorted as he wedged his way between Grant and Chelsie like a protective shield. "Just like the lady said, I moved the luggage around and you best mind your own business before you offend the duchess with your rude questions."

"I wanted to take the lady to dinner," Grant replied. "But I did not wish to overstep my older brother." His eyes searched Chelsie's flawless features, gauging her reaction to his remarks. "Just because Jarred has a fiancée doesn't mean he rolled over and died. We all know Jarred has an eye for the ladies. Chelsie is a rare beauty. I hardly expect my older brother not to notice. If that is all he has been doing. . . ."

"Grant McAlister, mind your tongue before I bob it off," Eli growled as he brandished a fist in the young man's face. " 'Tis bad enough that you voiced that lurid remark, but 'tis worse that you allowed the duchess to overhear it!"

Grant bowed apologetically. "Forgive me, Chelsie. In truth, all I wanted was your charming company at my dinner table tonight. I wish to make my intentions known without offending you or my brother. I would be honored if you would accept my heartfelt invitation."

Although Eli was shaking his head no, Chelsie nodded affirmatively. "I would delight in dining with you, Grant," she assured him.

And why shouldn't she? Jarred had no control over her, no control at all, Chelsie reminded herself rebelliously. And she had been starved for six weeks. If a man wanted to take her out to dinner, she wasn't about to turn him down. Now if only she could restrain herself from eating with both hands to curb this voracious appetite she had developed after being deprived of nourishment!

"The duchess will be in *her* hotel room," Eli announced indignantly. Grabbing Chelsie's arm, he steered her through the crowd. "We will expect you at seven, and not a moment before."

Kyle chuckled as he watched Eli lead the shapely lass away. "I don't know what you said, but you managed to stir up Eli's fatherly instincts," he observed.

"It would seem so," Grant murmured. "All of a sudden the whole brood of McAlisters and their servants have taken a fancy to the lovely duchess. I wonder if Neil will also fall beneath her spell."

"That would suit me just fine," Kyle enthused. "Chelsie would make him a fine wife."

"She would make *me* a fine wife," Grant sniffed in offended dignity. "Neil will have to take his place in line, because I found her first."

"Chelsie would do herself a favor if she married a younger man," Daniel interrupted as he tapped himself on the chest for emphasis. "Me . . ."

Grant snickered at his lovesick brother. "You have only just graduated from King William's School for Boys. And you have yet to begin your studies in England. I hardly think you are ready to take a wife."

"At least I'm old enough to know better than to insult a properly bred young lady by suggesting she is sharing a room with my older brother," Daniel blurted out.

"You have a big mouth, Danny," Grant scowled, shooting his father a hasty glance. And just as he feared, Kyle looked as if he had swallowed a pumpkin. "I would dearly love to stuff my fist in it."

115

"You're the one who said it," Daniel taunted. "I only repeated it."

Before Daniel and Grant could come to blows, Kyle stepped between them. "No wonder none of my sons are married," he grumbled. "They are so busy squabbling among themselves, they haven't the time or inclination to take a wife to fight with. And if you ask me, you both have big mouths that need gags stuffed in them!" A frustrated sigh escaped the patriarch's lips. "At this rate I'll never have a daughter-in-law — or grandchildren."

And that was what Kyle wanted most of all, besides defeating Amos Shaw on the racetrack, that is. He feared there would not be another generation of McAlisters to carry on the family tradition. For years he had harped at Neil and Jarred to provide him with daughters-in-law and grandchildren, but to no avail. The eldest son knew all there was about having babies and delivering them, but still he had none of his own. And Jarred had involved himself in the longest engagement in history and refused to set a wedding date. At this rate, Kyle swore he would go to his grave without knowing if the McAlisters were to become an extinct species!

Standing rigidly between his two sons, Kyle refocused on the horses that were lining up for another race. Damn, he muttered. He was already out of sorts after losing the race to Amos Shaw. Having Daniel and Grant fussing over the duchess and making insinuations about Jarred's involvement with her wasn't helping his disposition a tittle.

Yet after two days of sharing Chelsie's delightful company, Kyle decided there were two things he wanted from life — seeing Chelsie married to one of his sons (he didn't care which one), and savoring a victory over that ornery old coot Amos Shaw!

Chapter 9

An annoyed scowl shaded Jarred's brow when he met the young lawyer he'd sent to deliver the legal documents to have Captain Hutton's schooner impounded. One look at the dock and Jarred knew Hutton had set sail without permission.

"The ship was already out to sea when I arrived with the necessary papers," the young man explained.

Swearing a blue streak, Jarred reversed direction to stamp along beside his associate. Jarred was annoyed that he wasn't able to have Hutton and his crew punished for exploiting indentured servants. But what bothered him most was wondering if Isaac was running around loose or if he had sailed with his captain.

If Isaac wasn't the one who had made the attempt on Chelsie's life, who then? Could it truly have been a careless youngster too ashamed to own up to his foolishness? Or had Isaac managed to vent his vengeance, then return to the ship before it sailed?

By the time Jarred returned to the hotel, he was no closer to an explanation. Determined to pursue the investigation, Jarred asked Chelsie to list the names of as many passengers as possible so his associate could follow up on the inquisition. It wasn't until the studious-looking young man scuttled out the door that Jarred noticed his luggage was nowhere to be found.

Jarred posed the obvious question to Eli, who immediately puffed up like a toad.

"Grant already noticed your belongings in Chelsie's room," he grumbled. "She already had to dream up an explanation on

117

the spur of the moment."

"That shouldn't have been too difficult for her," Jarred smirked, casting Chelsie a taunting glance. "The duchess is already becoming an accomplished liar."

Before Chelsie could fling a suitably crushing rejoinder, Eli blurted out, "Your younger brother is coming to take the duchess to dinner. I don't want Grant asking any more embarrassing questions than he already has."

Jarred wheeled about to hurl Chelsie a frosty glare. "I don't recall your asking permission to accept my brother's invitation."

Too late Jarred realized he should have been more tactful with the feisty spitfire. He and Chelsie were still at odds, and she took immediate offense to the remark.

She elevated her chin so she could look down her nose at the imposing figure of the man who towered over her with such infuriating effectiveness.

An amused smile pursed Eli's lips. The two most stubborn creatures on earth were staring each other down. Eli took his leave. He had seen Chelsie in action on several occasions and he knew she was competent in handling herself against Jarred.

"I do not feel obligated to answer to you," Chelsie declared tartly. "I will go where I please, with whom I please. Grant is far more entertaining than his older brother, and I relish every opportunity of avoiding you."

Steel-blue eyes riveted on Chelsie's obstinate frown. What was there about this she-cat that constantly got his dander up? Everything she said had rubbed him the wrong way since this morning. "You should feel obligated," Jarred muttered. "If not for me, you could have been sold to some lecher who used you for his sexual pleasure. He could have made your life hell."

"He already has," Chelsie countered in a tone that cut Jarred to the quick. "He has virtually enslaved me. He used me for his pleasure while he had a fiancée waiting in the wings. I cannot imagine how my situation could be much worse!"

Jarred's breath came out in a rush. "What is it you want? My proposal of marriage to compensate for your loss of innocence?"

"What I want is your head on a platter and your heart fried," she sputtered.

118

How dare he even think she would want to be tied to him? Being his servant was humiliating enough. Marriage proposal, indeed! That was the very *last* thing she wanted from Jarred McAlister.

"Do not flatter yourself," Chelsie sniffed. "If you were the last man on earth I wouldn't wed you and bed you."

A smile quirked Jarred's lips as his eyes made a sweep of her alluring figure. "As I reminded you once before, you voiced no protest last night while you were lying in my arms."

Chelsie didn't hit him, but she looked as if she wanted to. Her emerald eyes flashed as she glared at his mocking grin. "It wouldn't have mattered if I *had* protested," she parried. "You made your intention clear enough when you joined me in bed without awaiting an invitation."

"Where did you expect me to sleep?" Jarred retorted. "You seem to forget, this is my room and you are garbed in clothes I purchased for you. All you have is mine, *Duchess*." He made the title sound like a curse, and that is exactly how he meant it.

Chelsie wanted to slap him silly. *Damn him*. He made her so furious she swore she would go blind with rage. She could have bought him out ten times over, and he was flaunting *his* domination and wealth in *her* face!

"If you were a gentleman, you'd have made other arrangements and you most certainly wouldn't hold the fact that you purchased a few garments over me."

"A few?" Jarred hooted sarcastically. "I doubt the queen herself has such an extensive wardrobe!"

Chelsie shrugged as if he had scored no points with his remarks. Besides, there were more important matters on her mind at the moment. "I demand to know what sort of explanation you intend to give your brother Neil if you *do* manage to make a match between me and a man I have never met." One delicately arched brow fell. "He is a doctor, after all. I'm sure he would realize he wasn't the first man to wind up in my bed. Shall I confess all to him, and tell him his own brother seduced me to ensure I would be a satisfactory lover for his eldest brother?"

Jarred's lips curled in a menacing growl. Now he was the one who looked as if he would like to hit something to ease his irritation—preferably her. But it did her heart good to level a verbal blow that ignited Jarred's temper. Usually he was the picture of poise and self-control in these never-ending battles of theirs. But for once he was furious, and it took visible restraint not to snatch her up and shake the stuffing out of her.

The truth was that Chelsie delighted in annoying Jarred. He may as well be angry, she reckoned. She wanted to share the company misery loves so well. Chelsie felt used and humiliated, and she wanted this raven-haired devil to suffer right along with her.

"That was not the way it happened," Jarred ground out, once he had put a stranglehold on his temper. It was not an easy task, mind you. Chelsie could get under his skin faster than any woman he had ever known. She had an uncanny knack of saying *just* the right thing to agitate him. How did she do it?

"Then how did it happen?" Chelsie purred caustically. "I certainly was in no condition to undress myself *or* you. And I couldn't care less about you or your doctor brother."

Jarred managed to catch himself before he rapped out a suitably nasty rejoinder. He had learned it was futile to fight fire with fire where Chelsie was concerned. She was far too intelligent to be outclassed in verbal debates, and she wasn't bad in physical combat, either. And as Eli had said, there were times when a man had to kill some women with kindness. This, it seemed, was one of those times, and this was definitely one of those women!

"It happened like this. . . ."

His arm stole around her waist, bringing her supple body into familiar contact with his, sending goosebumps across her skin. Holding her wide-eyed gaze, Jarred lowered his head. His eyes were fixed on her lips, and he was vividly aware of how quickly he could lose himself in the dewy taste of her. The scent of jasmine warped his senses, and Jarred forgot what they were arguing about. Suddenly he was back to wanting this sassy minx in the same wild ways he had the previous night.

Chelsie promised herself she would remain as rigid as a flag-pole, refusing to submit to his persuasive tactics. She would bring this arrogant colonial down a notch. She wasn't going to feel a thing except repulsion for the man who had stolen her virginity. He would never arouse her desires again.

Famous last words. . . .

The moment his sensuous lips slanted across hers, Chelsie's brain malfunctioned. Jarred overpowered her with a tenderness she couldn't fight, didn't want to fight. She couldn't recall her name or the reason she was annoyed with this sapphire-eyed rogue. The forbidden memories from the previous night fogged her mind, arousing and exciting her. Jarred had pleasured her then and he was pleasuring her now. But Chelsie would have preferred to die than admit it to this rakish devil.

Jarred had only meant to prove that Chelsie was as much at fault for what happened as he was. But their kiss didn't feel like he was proving a point, at least not the one he had in mind. It felt more like the eruption of a steamy geyser. All the turmoil of sensations he had experienced in the darkness came flooding back, drowning him in bubbly emotions. All of a sudden he wanted only what they had shared—the mindless rapture of possessing and being possessed by this wild, sweet witch.

Strange, Jarred had never felt so out of control with any other woman. It was as if his body had a will of its own, one not regulated by rational thought. He felt himself gathering Chelsie closer, as if he couldn't get enough of her. His hands glided up from her tiny waist to rediscover her shapely contours. His fingertips brushed over the soft mounds of her breasts, longing to feel her satiny flesh beneath his inquiring caresses without garments to hinder him. He wanted all of her, and one kiss wasn't going to be enough to pacify him, not when he knew how it felt when they made wild, sweet love.

Chelsie gasped at his intimate touch. She wanted to fling herself away from him, truly she did. But her body instinctively arched toward his tender caress. She was entranced by the delicious memory that rivaled nothing in her twenty years of limited experiences with men. The sensations welled up inside her, aching for release.

Jarred McAlister was a magical wizard, she decided. He could make her body respond to him against her wishes. One minute she was so angry with him she was seeing red, and the next second she was yielding to his skillful kisses and caresses.

121

Had she been a harlot in another lifetime? Chelsie asked herself. Why did she sway toward Jarred, grasping at these sensations of splendor as if she meant to hold onto them forever? She had never been permissive with other men who courted her. Why should this infuriating colonial be the one to arouse her in the most incredible ways?

As Chelsie's resistance went down, her arms slid up his broad chest and curled around his neck. She had to hold him close. *Had* to, mind you! Suddenly she was starved for him, impatient for him. It was utter madness, a crazy obsession! But Chelsie couldn't help what she felt.

The clean, fresh aroma of the man who held her so expertly in his arms surrounded her like a fuzzy white cloud. Each breath she inhaled was so thick with the arousing scent of the man that her senses took flight and abandoned her when she needed them most. Her sense of taste and touch betrayed her as well. She was left craving more, like a blind man yearning for sight.

Suddenly all reserve fled and Chelsie was kissing him back. Damn her shameless soul, she was relishing every moment in his embrace. How could she fight this handsome rogue when she was her own worst enemy? And how could he transform her *no* into *yes* when she swore she would never kiss or touch him again?

Through the cloudy haze that engulfed her brain, Chelsie heard Eli's quiet words whispering to her. If she were smart, she would employ this encounter to her advantage. If she planned to make this rake fall in love with her, she could enjoy the ultimate victory over him and also explain the reason she surrendered to his touch. It would be easy enough to say her response was just an act, just like the one he thought she was portraying as a duchess. She could savor these exquisite feelings and Jarred would never have to know that he stirred her as no other man ever had.

She would inflame his dreams and leave him burning on a hot flame. She would make him want her and he would carry her memory around with him like a curse. And when she went her merry way, Jarred could take her memory with him to his marriage bed. He would get what he deserved for toying with women all his life.

And when the time came to leave, she would declare that her affection for him was just a charade. Jarred would never know she found unparalleled pleasure in his sinewy arms. She would never confess the truth. Let him think what he would . . . let him fall beneath her spell for a change. Although she wasn't an accomplished lover, she could make a man desire her . . . couldn't she? How difficult could it be to make a man surrender to his animal lusts?

If Chelsie was fretting over her ability to bewitch Jarred, she was worrying for naught. Jarred was hopelessly lost to the taste and feel of this luscious beauty. He didn't give a thought to Abigail Shaw or to his oldest brother. He wanted Chelsie with a passion. She filled some strange, previously untouched need inside him. It was as if she had tapped a deep well and was drawing out emotions he didn't realize he had in him. Chelsie was feisty, infuriatingly stubborn, contrary and staunchly independent. But when he dared to touch her, he wanted her. It was as simple as that. . . .

And suddenly Jarred was a prisoner of his own primal needs. With a muffled groan he scooped Chelsie in his arms and took her toward the bed. Only making wild, passionate love to this saucy nymph would satisfy him. He had grown addicted to her. Chelsie kindled fires in him that only she could extinguish. He needed her to appease these monstrous cravings, to fulfill the hunger that rose from nowhere to leave him starved for her and her alone.

Jarred gently laid her on the bed. Her eyes met his, knowing she was seeing the reflection of her own uncontrollable passion. It was all wrong, she knew. But when Jarred kissed and caressed her, he made it all seem so right and natural.

As he sank down beside her, Chelsie surrendered to her insatiable need to have his moist lips upon hers. Her body melted against his, feeling the rapid beat of his heart thudding against her breasts. The steady burn of desire had unfurled inside her, and she swore she would become a flaming torch before Jarred appeased the incredible need he instilled in her. . . .

A sharp rap at the door froze them in mid-kiss. With a muffled curse, Jarred unfolded himself and drew Chelsie up beside him. "Who is it?" she chirped, her voice quavering with unfulfilled passion.

"Grant. Are you ready, duchess?" came the warm masculine voice from the hall.

"Crawl under the bed," Chelsie whispered urgently to Jarred.

"What?"

When he simply stood there gaping at her, Chelsie gave him an impatient shove. "I already had to explain what your luggage was doing in my room. I have no desire to fumble through an excuse as to why you are here. At the moment I can barely think straight."

A roguish grin spread across his rugged features. "Are you admitting I arouse you?"

Another rap at the door had Chelsie swearing under her breath. Still Jarred hadn't stirred a step, and he didn't intend to until she had admitted that he set fire to her blood.

"All right, for crying out loud," Chelsie muttered. "'Tis true. Now will you please do your gloating under yonder bed?"

After pressing a triumphant kiss to her lips, Jarred scrunched down to slither under the bed where Eli had stashed his satchels. Jarred was far from comfortable, but he was relieved that Chelsie had finally admitted there was something between them, whether either of them wanted something going on between them or not! Maybe it was male pride that prompted him to taunt her . . . Jarred wasn't sure. But he didn't want to be the only one affected by this ill-fated attraction.

Once Jarred disappeared beneath the overhanging bedspread, Chelsie swept toward the door. Pasting on a cheerful smile, she greeted the handsome blond who awaited her.

Grant's critical gaze flooded over Chelsie's titillating figure. A provocative smile crossed his lips as he offered her his arm. "At last I have you all to myself. I have been looking forward to this . . ."

Meanwhile, under the bed, Jarred was muttering uncomplimentary epithets. Grant had a way with women, rake that he was. He was attracted to that bedazzling minx, and Jarred damned well knew it. He understood why this spirited beauty appealed to Grant . . . but what Jarred *didn't* understand was his fierce possessiveness. He'd taught Chelsie the meaning of passion. And if Grant laid a hand on Jarred's property, he would . . .

Eli chuckled heartily when Jarred's ruffled head protruded from beneath the bedspread like a turtle emerging from his shell. "Looking for your luggage, counselor?" he taunted unmercifully.

Scowling, Jarred bounded to his feet. "I sorely resent sneaking around as if I were afraid to confront my own brother."

"With Chelsie's stunning good looks and sharp wit, she should have the chance to pick and choose her suitors without having to field questions concerning her relationship with you," Eli contended as he walked around to the opposite side of the bed to drag out the luggage. "And just exactly what *is* your relationship with the duchess?"

Jarred glared at his incorrigible manservant. "We don't have one," he lied to save face.

"After last night I'd say you do," Eli scoffed in contradiction. "Just wait until the duke gets here. You're going to have a hell of a lot of explaining to do."

"There is no duke, for God's sake!" Jarred screamed, his patience depleted. "Isaac swore up and down that Chelsie was an orphan who wound up in prison for thievery. She's a convict. Can't you get that through your thick skull? She even stole my purse of coins after she clubbed you over the head. Why have you been taken in by that sassy minx?"

"Why have *you?*" Eli questioned. "You think she's a thieving peasant, yet you can't keep your hands off her. And you don't want to treat Chelsie like a duchess because you don't want to believe she really *is* one. But she is, and you have a responsibility to her after last night."

Muttering grouchily, Jarred extracted his watch from his pocket. "Is this lecture going to be long-winded? I'm rather pressed for time, and I'd prefer not to have this conversation at all."

"You always say that when *I'm* winning the argument, counselor," Eli said smugly. When Jarred stamped toward the door, Eli frowned curiously. "Where are you going? I hope you aren't entertaining thoughts of interrupting Grant's intimate dinner with the duchess. They make a charming couple."

"For your information, I'm due at the Tuesday Club in ten minutes," Jarred snapped.

Eli nodded agreeably. "Good. You and the local dignitaries can gather round the table at the tavern and engage in your political discussions while Chelsie and Grant eat and drink and do whatever it is young couples do to get better acquainted. . . ."

Ah, the power of suggestion, Eli mused wickedly. It played havoc with this frustrated man. And that was exactly what Jarred was. He didn't know what he wanted these days. He was bound by his sense of obligation to Abi Shaw and his commitment to the welfare of the colonies. But beneath that well-disciplined shell was a man whose brain was at war with his masculine desires. He couldn't quite let go of Chelsie . . . that was obvious. He had been growling and snorting like an angry bull ever since Chelsie had taken her place in the McAlister family. She no longer depended on Jarred for much of anything. That rankled him. He wanted that independent hellion to need him, and he didn't even know why!

For a long moment Jarred peered at his valet, trying to decipher the thoughts that chased each other across his weatherbeaten face. "I thought you wanted to see Chelsie married to Neil," he reminded Eli.

"She could marry *any* of the McAlisters and it would suit me, even if *you* should be the one to wed her . . . considering what happened last night."

"Will you forget about last night?" Jarred grumbled as he stalked toward the door. "It didn't happen the way you think."

"Why should I forget about it?" Eli smirked. "You haven't. I saw Chelsie when she traipsed off with Grant. It looked to me like she'd been soundly kissed, and I don't have to be a genius to figure out who did the kissing." A thought furrowed his brow. "I wonder if that will give Grant any amorous ideas. You know your brother. He adores women—short ones, tall ones, blondes, brunettes. Grant never met one he didn't love at first sight. In fact, he is almost as notorious with women as you are. . . ."

Bang! The door slammed shut so hard the picture fell off the wall. *Damn* Eli. He didn't need to remind Jarred of his younger brother's reputation with the female of the species. After all, Jarred had taught that scamp all he knew, and Grant had better not be practicing his techniques on that green-eyed leprechaun. And she had better not be granting Grant three wishes, either!

When Jarred stormed off, Eli chuckled devilishly. It was good to see Jarred roasting over the fire that was blazing beneath him. It had been ages since Jarred had felt anything except the normal reaction to women. His affairs had been shallow and monotonous. They had soured him toward love and marriage. And Abigail, bless her heart, could not set spark to a man like Jarred. She was shy, retiring, sweet, and kind. Unfortunately, that wasn't what a rambling tumbleweed like Jarred needed to make him put down roots. What he needed was a feisty wildcat like Chelsie, who upset his life and made him consider his priorities. She set fire to Jarred's passions, and he hadn't been the same since she'd turned him wrong-side-out.

Yes siree, Eli mused smugly. Jarred Love 'em-and-leave-'em McAlister had met his match this time. Given half a chance, Chelsie could make him believe in love and commitment. But it would take a strong case to convince a cynical rake like Jarred. He thought all he needed from a woman could be satisfied in a bedroom. But that billy goat of a man was in for an eye-opening experience if Eli could make this match before Jarred handed Chelsie over to Neil. The stubborn lawyer needed Chelsie in his life as much as Neil needed a woman in his. But in truth, Chelsie was too much woman for a man like the soft-spoken doctor. It would never work having Chelsie as Jarred's sister-in-law. She had to be his wife or she would have to walk out of his life forever.

Heaving a sigh, Eli paced the room. Now, how the devil was he going to make Chelsie and Jarred realize they were good for each other? Stubborn as they both were, it would take a while, and Eli didn't have much time. The family would be leaving for Easthaven in two days, and Jarred would be coming and going as he usually did. It wouldn't be so easy to get them together.

Damn, if only Eli had a couple of weeks, he might make some headway with those two bull-headed individuals. But he didn't know that even as he was formulating his plans, destiny was molding the future. Within an hour he would have fretful

127

thoughts on his mind, thoughts that overshadowed his desire to see Chelsie and Jarred as man and wife.

Chapter 10

The report of a pistol shattered the night and Jarred's blood ran cold. In the lantern light that cast its golden glow on the streets, Jarred watched in dread as a vast throng scattered in panic. Wild shrieks erupted from women, and men grumbled curses as they stampeded from where the shot was heard. Jarred felt like a fish fighting its way up the rapids as he elbowed through the crowd headed in the opposite direction. Grimly he aimed himself toward Grant's favorite haunt, harboring an uneasy feeling that he knew what he would find when he got there. Sure enough, his worst fears materialized.

The color drained from Jarred's bronzed features when he spied Grant scooping Chelsie up in his arms to brush a kiss over her forehead. Blood stained her shoulder, and her soft whimper cut through Jarred's soul like a knife. Without preamble, he dashed toward Grant to steal Chelsie from his brother's protective arms.

"I'm perfectly capable of taking care of the duchess," Grant muttered in a resentful tone when Jarred cradled the wounded beauty against him.

"Is this what you call taking care of her?" Jarred snorted sardonically. "She got herself shot and you were probably too busy drooling over her to pay the slightest attention."

"What did you expect me to do? Throw myself in front of an unseen bullet?" Grant cried, indignant. "In case you haven't noticed, big brother, it's damned dark out here!"

"Not dark enough for an assailant to miss his target," Jarred retorted.

"Jarred . . ." Chelsie's pained cry brought him back to his senses. Instinctively she snuggled in his arms just as she'd done when her nightmares tormented her. "My shoulder . . . it hurts so bad it's making me . . . nauseated. . . ."

Jarred cursed under his breath. "Don't just stand there, Grant. Fetch a doctor." Lord, how Jarred wished Neil had come with the rest of the family to Annapolis. Chelsie needed him desperately.

Grant stared in all directions at once, and Jarred growled at his paralyzed brother. "For God's sake, are your feet nailed to the ground? Fetch Doc Hester!"

Pivoting, Jarred sought out the closest carriage and ordered its occupants out of it. With Chelsie bundled in his lap, Jarred instructed the driver to rush them back to the hotel.

As Chelsie was jostled in the speeding coach, her stomach pitched. When another searing pain shot down her arm, she snuggled closer to Jarred's solid chest, burying her head against his shoulder.

Jarred was suffering all the tortures of the damned. Watching Chelsie shudder in pain tore his heart in two. Oddly enough, when she was wounded, he bled. Seeing her in a weak, vulnerable condition scared the hell out of him. Him—a man who possessed nerves of steel on the battlefields where the French and Indians were terrorizing the colonial borders. Him—a man who rarely buckled in the face of disaster. But at the moment he felt as stable as a house of sticks . . . the slightest breath of wind would have blown him down.

Hadn't Chelsie suffered enough? First there had been Isaac's tormenting abuse, then the haunting nightmares, and now this. Who the devil was trying to dispose of her, and why? Had Isaac remained in town to finish the task he'd begun that afternoon? Those questions tormented Jarred all the way to the hotel, but he couldn't conjure up a satisfactory answer.

The moment Jarred burst through the door, Eli's jaw sagged. Barking a command to fetch hot water and bandages, Jarred eased Chelsie into bed. When Eli darted off to gather supplies,

Jarred loosened Chelsie's stained gown, despite her feeble protests. Only a faint blush of embarrassment colored her otherwise ashen cheeks, and Jarred made short work of removing her clothes.

"I never knew a woman who attracted trouble the way you do," Jarred declared as he inspected the gash on her shoulder.

Chelsie shrank from his touch—one that burned like fire against her tender flesh. "You needn't add insult to injury," she choked out.

A rueful smile grazed his lips as he combed the tangled mane of silver-gold away from her perspiring face. "If it makes you feel any better, I'm sorry."

"It doesn't," Chelsie muttered and then winced when she tried to squirm to a more comfortable position. Her shoulder throbbed in rhythm with her thundering heart. "The only thing that would make me feel better is having you flat on your back with a hole in your shoulder."

"Bitter, aren't we?" Jarred teased softly.

"Extremely," Chelsie muttered, her voice thick with resentment.

"I would have taken the shot myself to spare your agony," Jarred assured her with a tender smile.

"How gallant," Chelsie sniffed. For the life of her she didn't know why she was taking her frustration out on Jarred. This wasn't his fault, after all. But she had become accustomed to verbally attacking him. It was second nature to her.

Chelsie's caustic comments played havoc with Jarred's temper. He was deeply concerned about this feisty hellion, and she was throwing snide remarks at him. His compassion may not have made her feel better, but her insensitivity wasn't helping matters.

"I'm trying to be nice," Jarred said as he tucked the quilts around her naked body.

"Stick to something more familiar," Chelsie suggested flippantly. "And I'll have you know I could have undressed myself, thank you very much!"

Before Jarred could counter her indignant remark, Eli burst through the door, slopping hot water everywhere. His worried gaze flew to Chelsie's wounded shoulder. Swiftly he handed the supplies to Jarred. Dipping a cloth in the water, Jarred cleansed the oozing wound. He had seen Neil in action often enough to learn the proper procedure.

Chelsie gasped in pain when the water trickled over her injured shoulder. Her hand instinctively clutched Jarred's, as if squeezing him would somehow lessen her pain, but it didn't. Her shoulder still burned like hell.

"Drink this," Eli murmured compassionately.

Chelsie obeyed, but the ale didn't soothe the sting . . . it only set fire to her throat. When she sputtered and coughed, the jarring motion aggravated her tender shoulder and she cried out in pain.

"Don't make things worse than they already are," Jarred snapped.

"I only wanted to help," Eli defended. "I was trying to numb her pain."

When Eli stepped back, Jarred squeezed the cloth over the wound and Chelsie yelped again. "You're enjoying this, aren't you?" she accused.

"Nay, I am not," Jarred told her matter-of-factly. "My wish is that you were as good as new."

" 'Tis one wish I cannot grant," Chelsie croaked, overwrought with pain and fighting like the devil to maintain her composure. Unshed tears misted her eyes, but she refused to give in to them.

"Ah, would that you could, little leprechaun," Jarred murmured.

There was something in the way Jarred smiled down at her that calmed her nerves. She gazed up at him, her bitterness evaporating. For a moment they simply stared into each other's eyes, sharing some silent secret Eli couldn't decode.

If there wasn't something going on between these two, Eli swore he would eat his boot, sole and all. This catastrophe brought them a step closer together, even if they were trying to pull in opposite directions. They cared for each other in their own special way. Those hidden feelings were simmering just beneath their shells of stubborn defense.

The spell was broken when Grant barged into the room with Doctor Hester following in his wake. Jarred unfolded himself, and the physician immediately took the vacated spot at Chelsie's side.

"I had no idea dining out was such dangerous business," the physician teased as he investigated Chelsie's wound. "You will have to take supper in bed for a few days, young lady."

Chelsie nodded as the doctor fished into his bag for a scalpel and some antiseptic. The shiny instrument severed Chelsie's delicate composure.

"Jarred . . ." Her good arm instinctively went out to him, silently beseeching him to clutch her hand.

Jarred was beside her in less than a heartbeat, holding her quaking hand in his, forcing her to look at him instead of at the sharp scalpel that was about to cut its way into her flesh. "Grant, why don't you and Eli go fetch us all a drink while the doctor tends the duchess," he suggested without ever taking his eyes off Chelsie. "I don't think she needs an audience just now."

Reluctantly, Grant and Eli backed toward the door. Chelsie didn't see them leave. Her frantic gaze was glued to Jarred's tanned face, concentrating on the intriguing lines and crow's feet that were carved in his handsome features.

"This will help you sleep," Doctor Hester said gently as he spooned laudanum into her mouth. "You will need time to recuperate after I remove the buckshot. Don't use your arm any more than necessary."

The instant the scalpel sought out the pellets that were embedded in her shoulder, Chelsie bit back an anguished screech. Her nails clenched Jarred's arm, but he felt nothing save Chelsie's pain. His eyes locked with hers, offering her a reassuring smile, attempting to provide the comfort and compassion she so desperately needed.

It seemed to take forever for the laudanum to take affect. Chelsie would have preferred the doctor wait until she was asleep before he began probing and poking. But the physician refused to run the risk of allowing infection to take hold. He wanted the pellets removed and the wound stitched as quickly as possible.

When the worst was over, Chelsie sagged on the bed, her body trembling with pain. She wanted to cry, but she refused to reduce herself to tears.

Once the wound had been bandaged, the doctor motioned for Jarred to follow him to the door. "Keep her sedated with laudanum through the night," he instructed, handing Jarred the bottle of medication. "The incisions were deep, and there is a risk of infection. Keep a close watch on her and call me if her temperature rises dramatically. I expect she will run a bit of a fever, but I don't want her to reach the point of convulsions."

Jarred nodded bleakly, but when he turned back to Chelsie, his anxious expression was masked behind a casual smile. "Close your eyes, duchess," he requested. "I'll be watching over you while you sleep."

"I really don't hate you," Chelsie slurred out, the laudanum working like a truth serum. "I should, you know, but I don't. . . ." Her eyelids drooped and her body sank into the mattress.

"I truly don't dislike you either," Jarred whispered softy. With the greatest of care he eased down beside the wounded nymph to press a fleeting kiss to her brow. "Sleep now. . . ."

Chelsie melted like a trusting child when Jarred grasped her hand. His presence calmed her fears as nothing else could, and she drifted into foggy dreams.

By the time Grant and Eli returned, Jarred was totally exhausted—mentally, physically, emotionally. His thoughts and feelings were a tangled jungle that Jarred couldn't fight his way through. Seeing Chelsie lying so still had Jarred muttering spitefully at whoever had taken a shot at her. Chelsie was such a vibrant, spirited young woman. It seemed unnatural for her to be lying abed like a . . . a corpse.

Jarred expelled a frustrated sigh. He and Chelsie might be at odds, but Jarred hadn't wanted anything to happen to her. She'd been through enough terrifying ordeals already. He *did* care about her, he realized. If he *hadn't,* he wouldn't have purchased her indentureship against his better judgment. He wouldn't have allowed his family to think she was more than a thieving peasant. Jarred still didn't know what he was going to do with this saucy sprite, but he couldn't leave her in Annapolis with a would-be assassin running around loose. And he wasn't at all sure he could give this blond-haired beauty up to

134

any of his brothers, no matter how badly Neil needed a woman in his life or Grant wanted one in his.

Grant, who held himself personally responsible for Chelsie's catastrophe, was downing ale like a thirsty camel and cursing himself for not paying closer attention to his surroundings. He was well aware that an attempt had been made on her life earlier that afternoon, and he had been too mesmerized by the green-eyed duchess to protect her. Eli, visibly shaken by the incident, was matching Grant glass-for-glass, wishing Chelsie had remained in her room in the first place. And Jarred was drinking steadily, although he proceeded at a more reasonable pace than his brother and his valet.

Each time Chelsie moaned in discomfort, all three men vaulted to their feet to hover over her. After two hours of keeping constant vigil, Jarred ordered his brother and valet out of the room.

"I'm staying here," Grant insisted. "*I'm* the reason she was wounded."

"*I'm* staying. *You're* going," Jarred contradicted firmly, but he found himself in the middle of an argument nonetheless.

"I'm not leaving." Blue eyes clashed with blue, neither man intending to give an inch.

Eli clutched Grant's arm, shepherding him toward the door. "Don't argue with your brother. You'll wake Chelsie."

Hesitantly, Grant allowed himself to be propelled into the hall. But his eyes lingered on the sleeping beauty whose bare shoulders protruded from the coverlet. Reflexively, Jarred walked over to draw the quilt beneath Chelsie's chin and then asked himself why he was being so overprotective, even with his own brother. It wasn't as if Grant hadn't caught a glimpse of feminine flesh before!

A tender smile rippled across Jarred's lips as he folded himself onto the edge of the bed to ensure that Chelsie's temperature hadn't risen. He had only sat down when inaudible phrases tripped from Chelsie's ashen lips. As if pursued by demon spirits, she began thrashing. Her head rolled from side to side and she grimaced at the pain she was inflicting on herself.

While Chelsie fought her recurring nightmare, Jarred swore

fluently. If she didn't lie still, she would rip a stitch and the doctor would have to be recalled to repair his seam. Jarred was frustrated as hell. He had consoled Chelsie the previous night and they had wound up sharing passion's wild embrace. But lying there comforting her seemed to be all that soothed her while she was a prisoner of her tortured dreams. She had consumed a large dose of laudanum and shaking her awake was practically impossible without inflicting more pain on her. She was trapped in dreams and Jarred could do very little except curse her plight.

Carefully he stretched out beside the tormented beauty, murmuring softly to her, wondering if she could even hear him. Instinctively Chelsie inched closer to the hard masculine form beside her, just as she'd done the previous night. Jarred had become the pillow she rested upon, the rock she leaned on when trouble overwhelmed her.

Jarred pondered the strange attachment that had developed between them. It was an unconscious bond that strengthened with each passing hour. Aye, he hungered for this proud pixie the way a man craves a lovely woman. But their relationship entailed more than a fleeting encounter with passion. What he felt for this sassy lass was unlike what he'd felt in his previous affairs. Circumstances had widened the dimensions of his feelings for Chelsie. It wasn't love, of course, he assured himself sensibly. But there was a strong attachment of some sort. Perhaps he saw something of himself in her when he peered into those fathomless emerald eyes. Perhaps . . .

Chelsie's muffled shriek jerked Jarred back to the present. When she began to thrash once again, he held her close, whispering soft utterances of compassion. After a quarter of an hour, she sank back into a deep sleep and Jarred half-collapsed in exhaustion. Fretting over this wild sweet witch was wearing him out. God, he would give most anything to have Chelsie back on her feet. Their fiery arguments were far better than stewing over her while she was wounded and vulnerable.

Finally Jarred's weariness overcame him, and he followed Chelsie into dreams. As the night wore on, they settled deeper and deeper into each other's arms. Only when he was holding her curvaceous body to his could Jarred find peace. Like two restless souls searching for a port in the storm, Jarred and Chelsie clung to each other, wrapped in forbidden dreams of a night that should not have existed, wishing they were not so magnetically drawn to each other when they had no future together.

Chapter 11

A startled gasp gushed from Grant's lips when he breezed into Chelsie's room unannounced. His eyes popped when he spied his older brother abed with Chelsie, cradling her against his bare chest. Although Jarred had the decency to wear his breeches, Grant puffed with so much indignation he nearly split his shirt seams.

"What in the sweet loving hell do you think you're doing?" he snorted.

"What does it look like?" Jarred snorted back before prying open both eyes to meet Grant's condescending glower.

"It looks as if you'd planned to do more than give aid and comfort to the wounded, that's what!" Grant muttered as he slammed the breakfast tray onto the nightstand.

"She was having nightmares," Jarred mumbled in defense. He eased away from Chelsie's side.

"So naturally you laid down beside her while she was stark naked," Grant smirked. " 'Tis possible, big brother, to offer consolation while standing on both feet." His flashing blue eyes skipped to the creamy flesh that lay exposed by the drooping quilt and he growled again. "And don't tell me who undressed the duchess before Doctor Hester examined her. I don't think I want to know." Huffily he paced the room, sparing Jarred mutinous glares at irregular intervals. "I was the one who was interested in courting the duchess, and you wound up abed with her. Thanks a hell of a lot, big brother. The next time I want you to stand in my stead, I'll let you know!"

Eli, who had trailed along behind Grant, stood propped

against the wall, listening to the conversation with wicked glee. Jarred was getting himself in deeper and deeper. Now he had Grant fuming. Jarred couldn't keep his distance from the dazzling sprite. He was drawn to her like a moth to a flame, and he was getting his wings singed.

"Nothing happened, for God's sake," Jarred grumbled while he paced parallel to his furious brother. "I didn't think she needed to be left alone after what happened yesterday."

"If I had known what you intended to do while she was drugged with laudanum, I wouldn't have let you near her. And I hope Abi Shaw doesn't get wind of this." His derisive glare sliced Jarred in half. "It would demolish her to know her unfaithful fiancée has made another indiscreet play for another woman."

"That's enough!" Jarred bellowed. "You will have plenty of time to cater to the duchess if you are feeling slighted. I have decided to transport her to the plantation so Neil can oversee her convalescence."

"You are going to move her in her condition?" Grant croaked in disbelief. "And what about your conferences with the assembly committees? How do you plan to be in two places at once?"

Jarred waved his hand for silence. "The conferences on defense will have to wait. Chelsie's welfare is my foremost concern at the moment. 'Tis your duty to inform Papa and Daniel that we are leaving as soon as we can transport Chelsie to the wharf and board our schooner."

"But the horses will have to be loaded, and the—" Grant began, only to be cut off by Jarred's impatient scowl.

"Surely you can handle those minor matters. After all, it isn't the first time we've shipped horses back and forth from Annapolis."

"But 'tis such short notice. We planned to stay a few more days . . ."

"See it done, Grant," Jarred demanded. "The sooner Chelsie is in Neil's care the better. He is the best physician in the colony and Chelsie deserves the best."

Grant relinquished his argument. Once Jarred made up his mind to something, he wanted it done immediately. "Very well,

I'll see that everything is ready and waiting when you bring Chelsie on board. But I still don't think it wise to move her so soon after she was shot."

"She won't even know she left her bed," Jarred assured him. "Now go." His arm shot toward the door and Grant threw up his hands in defeat and left.

After spouting orders to Eli, Jarred crammed his garments in a satchel and neatly folded Chelsie's new purchases into the one he had emptied. Hurriedly he went downstairs to purchase the quilt and sheets upon which she lay. Jarred was just on his way back upstairs to await Eli, who had gone to fetch a stretcher, when the silversmith approached him. But Jarred didn't even bat an eye as he surveyed the charges for Chelsie's jewelry. He simply paid the man and continued on his way.

When Eli came upstairs with the string of servants who had accompanied the McAlister family to Annapolis, Chelsie was carefully transferred onto the stretcher and transported downstairs while Jarred fired orders like bullets to ensure her comfort and protection. Chelsie was still drugged with laudanum, and as Jarred predicted, she didn't know she had been moved.

A crowd of curious bystanders parted like the Red Sea when the entourage proceeded onto the street. Jarred had covered Chelsie's head like a corpse, and murmurs rippled like waves through the crowd. It was Jarred's hope that her assailant would assume she had not survived her wound. And the sniper did assume just that. A wry smile bordered her assailant's lips as the not-so-dead duchess was toted to the waiting wagon. Mission accomplished, the assailant wedged through the crowd of onlookers and disappeared from sight without being recognized.

Kyle McAlister was beside himself as he marched back and forth across the deck of the schooner. Concern etched his wrinkled features when the stretcher was lifted from the wagon and carried onto the deck. Chelsie seemed so full of undaunted spirit, so carefree and alive. And now . . . Kyle squeezed his eyes shut and cursed the disaster that had left Chelsie wounded. He had begun to consider the green-eyed nymph as one of his own, and it crushed him that she had been struck down in the company of his son. Kyle vowed then and there to see that Chelsie wanted for nothing during her rehabilitation. He fully intended to compensate for this tragedy, to ensure that Chelsie was protected and comfortable until her father arrived.

When Chelsie was settled on the bed of the most spacious cabin on board, the McAlisters set sail up the bay to the secluded estuary near their plantation. Traveling by the numerous waterways was the rule rather than the exception in Tidewater country. Jarred would never have considered moving Chelsie if the journey had to be made by land. The roads that joined the cities and towns of the colonies were washboarded and plagued with ruts. Even the King's Highway that led from Annapolis to the populated centers to the north and west left a great deal to be desired, especially for a wounded traveler.

While Chelsie swayed back and forth between wakefulness and sleep, the McAlister clan carefully monitored her condition. She had only to look uncomfortable and her passel of mother hens were fluttering around her.

In less than three hours the schooner eased into the tree-choked estuary and private dock. After sending one of the servants on ahead to alert the household and make preparations, Chelsie was uplifted on her stretcher and carried to another waiting wagon. She was too drowsy to take note of the magnificent estate that set on the rise of ground above the private dock on Chesapeake Bay. All she saw was the inside of her eyelids and drifted back and forth between nightmares and reality.

Within an hour, Jarred had settled Chelsie into the guest room adjacent to his suite, despite Grant's protests. Grant would have preferred to have the ailing duchess in the room beside his, but very few men—even family—argued with Jarred and won. He was a very determined man—the most determined and stubborn one in the McAlister clan, as a matter of fact. And what really infuriated Grant the most was that there was a private door leading from Jarred's boudoir into Chelsie's room. After what Grant had seen in Annapolis, he wasn't sure Jarred needed his own special entry into Chelsie's suite. Good God, Jarred had already wound up in her bed!

The moment Chelsie was settled, Neil appeared in the hall, ready to tend his patient. His gentle brown eyes swept over Chelsie's exquisite features before they drifted to Jarred. "I hope you have a believable explanation to offer Abi," he murmured as he eased down to remove Chelsie's bloodstained bandages. From what Grant tells me, you have been hovering a mite too close to the duchess to be just an innocent party caught up in the lady's string of disasters."

Jarred gnashed his teeth. First it had been Grant who scolded him for his attentions to Chelsie and now Neil. Well, by damned, he didn't have to answer to any of his brothers if he didn't want to!

"Are you going to tend our patient or lecture me?" Jarred muttered crankily.

"I'm very versatile," Neil declared as he inspected the wound. "I can do both."

"Blast it, Chelsie was without a proper escort in the colonies and then she was wounded while she was in our care. What would you have me do? Waltz off and leave her to fend for herself?" Jarred was suddenly defending himself, even when he hadn't planned to.

Soft laughter rattled in Neil's chest. Slowly he turned to study his brother's inflated chest and black scowl. "I have discovered a cure for oversensitivity, Jarred," he teased. "Shall I have Eli fetch you some of my miracle pills?"

"I'm not oversensitive," Jarred snorted derisively.

"If you say so," Neil patronized him.

"I do say so."

Jarred's vehement denial brought Chelsie awake. Her lashes fluttered up to meet a pair of chocolate brown eyes embedded in a handsome face which bore a striking family resemblance to Jarred and his brothers. Neil was not so muscular as Jarred, but he was every bit as good-looking, in his own refined way. There was something about his reassuring smile that made Chelsie immediately let down her guard. Reflexively she offered Neil a feeble grin and expelled a weary sigh.

Her blurry gaze drifted to Jarred, who looked a mite tired and haggard himself. Dark circles ringed his eyes, and there was a strained expression on his unshaven face. His clothes looked as if they had been slept in, and bloodstains splotched the front of his wrinkled shirt.

A muddled frown puckered her brow when she surveyed her elaborate surroundings. "Where am I?"

"The McAlister estate," Neil responded as he examined her seeping wound. "And I am Jarred's older brother."

"Doctor Neil McAlister," Chelsie murmured in recognition. " 'Tis nice to make your acquaintance, although I would have preferred it to be under more pleasant circumstances. Jarred has nothing but praise for you and your medical abilities. According to him, you are the pick of the litter."

Jarred bit back a growl. My, but Chelsie was laying it on thick. She knew the role Jarred had asked her to portray for Neil, but for God's sake, she didn't have to play the part of a smitten maid quite so well! She had flashed Neil one little smile and already he was melting!

"I'm flattered, Miss Chelsie Channing from Chessfield," Neil chortled. "The competition in my family is stiff, and glowing accolades from one of my brothers is rare. But your compliment far exceeds any praise offered by Jarred."

Jarred rolled his bloodshot eyes and swore under his breath. He didn't need Neil's wonder drug for oversensitivity. But what he could use was a cure for nausea. This sticky sweet scene was making him sick. Jarred wanted Chelsie and Neil to be on friendly terms, it was true. But they didn't have to get along quite so well. Damn this little witch. Even while she was lying here weak and wounded, she could still charm the wings off an angel, and she had made very quick work of Neil!

"Jarred, you may take your leave," Chelsie requested hoarsely. "I find myself in very competent hands."

The dismissal, courteous though it was, got Jarred's goat. He had stood like a posted lookout over Chelsie. He had purchased her indentureship, her wardrobe, and her jewels. He had soothed her troubled dreams and nursed her through a long, harrowing night. And she was showing him the door! Thunderation, a little gratitude would have been nice!

When the door banged shut behind him, Chelsie focused absolute attention on Neil's kind face and on the thick, chestnut-brown hair that capped his head. He was bending over her, concentrating on packing a fresh poultice on her wound.

"Before things get completely out of hand, I thought you and I should have a private chat," she began, her voice gravely from lack of use.

One dark brow elevated acutely, then Neil smiled down into her enchanting features. "Oh? This sounds serious."

"It is," Chelsie confirmed and then grimaced when the poultice oozed into the wound. "Jarred and Eli's ultimate purpose for bringing me here was to supply you with a wife, whether you wanted one or not. They seem to have your best interests at heart, but I do not condone their methods. Before they manage to push me into your lap, I want you to know I protested their matchmaking. 'Tis my belief that a man and woman should decide for themselves if they wish to be married. 'Tis not a decision to be made by well-meaning friends."

Neil choked on his breath. Chelsie's candor caught him off guard. Jarred and Eli's intentions vaguely annoyed him. But Neil was an easygoing fellow who'd learned to take the disappointments of life in stride. He rarely got excited and he kept to himself most of the time, satisfied with the way of things . . . except for one aspect of his life. And aside from one depressing thought that kept tormenting him, Neil was well-adjusted. He was too dignified to allow his temper to get the better of him and . . . he liked this straightforward beauty quite a lot. . . .

"I see," he said, composing himself and restricting his eyes to the wound on her shoulder. "I appreciate your honesty, Chelsie."

"I am giving you fair warning, because I want you to understand that I did *not* come here husband hunting and I do *not* wish to be a party to this scheme. And in my own defense, I should like to think I could find my *own* mate, if I desired one. You do not need to feel obligated when Jarred or Eli push me in your direction."

Neil was silent for a moment while he studied the pale beauty whose tangled tresses sprayed across the pillow like streams of sunshine. With deliberate concentration he focused on his task of rebandaging her wound. "I suggest that we play along with my brother's scheme. It will prevent the entire family from interfering." A cryptic smile pursed his lips as he

144

tossed Chelsie a quick glance. "You have already managed to brighten my day. Your presence here might be just what we all need. I think you and I are going to get along just fine."

Chelsie didn't understand his exact meaning, but she was relieved Neil had taken the news so well. Intuition told her Neil had plans of his own. Silently she watched him, battling the demons of curiosity that leaped up at her each time Neil broke into a wry smile. Finally weariness and the lingering effects of the laudanum overcame her and she drifted off to sleep before Neil completed his examination.

A slow, mischievous smile curved the corner of Neil's mouth upward as he climbed to his feet. Chelsie's appearance in the house was a blessing in disguise. Her honesty gave Neil the opportunity to keep one step ahead of his younger brother. Things were just getting interesting, he mused as he ambled toward the door. And after what Grant had told him about Jarred overstepping his bounds of propriety the previous night, it left Neil to wonder. . . .

The moment Neil opened the portal, Jarred was there, waiting like an expectant father. "Will she be all right?" he wanted to know that very second.

Neil feigned a look of surprise, then glanced back at the dozing sprite. "I suppose so," he replied. "To be honest, I was so distracted by that bewitching young lady, I almost forgot about doctoring her. She is breathtaking, isn't she, Jarred?" A rakish grin spread slowly across his full lips, making his eyes shine like ebony. "Mmmm . . . this is the part I like best about being a physician. I never mind examining lovely patients. I have a license to peek. . . . "

Jarred could feel the fury rising from the pit of his belly, flowing upward toward his cheeks, leaving him hot under the collar. For a half-second he toyed with the spiteful retaliation of breaking the doctor's fingers, wondering what they had touched during the examination. Damn it, this was Eli's stupid idea. Jarred had dragged Chelsie home to lift Neil out of his doldrums, and he had taken an instant liking to Chelsie. Maybe that was what Jarred wanted in the beginning, but it damned sure wasn't what he wanted now! And Neil had better not be taking privileges by gaping at Chelsie's curvaceous body under the pretense of giving her a medical examination! Blast it, his straightlaced brother had just come untied!

With a wordless growl, Jarred followed Neil downstairs, annoyed with himself for feeling something besides pleasure when he learned his older brother was smitten with Chelsie. It was the first time in two years Neil had shown an interest in women. He had wallowed in self-suffering bachelordom until Chelsie came along. And poof . . . one look at that gorgeous witch, and Neil had been captured in her spell.

Frustrated no end, Jarred threw himself into the duties he had neglected while he had been away for the past three months. Grant had assumed the tasks of managing all four plantations, but there was much to be done before the tobacco crops were harvested. There were shipping arrangements to be made and buyers to be contacted in England, not to mention the stack of legal papers and business ledgers that awaited him. Grant drew the line at filling out the tiresome ledgers. When Jarred returned after a long absence, he always found stacks of bills and notes to be entered into the accounts and ledgers.

And while Jarred was burying himself in his paperwork, a pair of sparkling green eyes and heart-shaped lips superimposed themselves on the parchment. Chelsie's stunning image kept crowding its way into his mind's eye to distract him.

Witch, Jarred grumbled resentfully. She had taken his entire family by storm, and now she was trying to work her black magic on him. She was a deported thief who pretended to be a duchess, and Jarred, fool that he was, had brought her here. Now Neil and Grant were fussing over her, and Daniel clung to her like a leech. Kyle was popping into her room once an hour, asking if she needed anything to make her more comfortable.

And then of course there was Eli, who had long been subject to Chelsie's devastating charm. Jarred seemed to be the only one with any sense left when it came to Chelsie, and he didn't have enough sense to brag about. For God's sake, he would have been checking on her too if he could have wedged his way into her room during the daylight hours.

Jarred heaved a tired sigh and slammed the ledger shut. He had accomplished his mission by delivering Chelsie into Neil's competent hands. Jarred was trying to keep his distance so Neil could have his chance to court Chelsie, but it was damned difficult. When he wasn't with her, he was thinking about her constantly, and he hadn't been with her for more than ten minutes since her arrival. Consequently he was thinking about her all the damned time! For God's sake, how long was this preoccupation going to last? It was driving Jarred up the wall!

Part Two

If a man could have half his wishes
he would double his Trouble.
Ben Franklin

Chapter 12

For five days Chelsie was catered to, coddled, and fussed over like a newborn infant. It wasn't that she didn't appreciate the constant attention, but she was suffering from a severe case of cabin fever. The walls of her elegantly decorated room were shrinking, and she felt smothered by the incessant string of humanity that trailed in and out of her boudoir.

Neil came to check on her at regular intervals. Eli and Kyle entered to cheer her up by keeping her posted on how the colt and mare were adjusting to their new surroundings. Rebecca McAlister Brooks, Kyle's widowed sister, who had lived at Easthaven for more than a decade, came to provide Chelsie with companionship. Grant visited her, apologizing for being unable to save her from disaster. But Daniel was by far the worst. He was the epitome of manly devotion, and his infatuation for Chelsie was obvious to the point of being ridiculous. He insisted on cutting her food into bite-sized bits and feeding it to her as if she were paralyzed from the neck down. He was there constantly, fluttering over her, making eyes at her, fawning over her without a smidgen of gentlemanly reserve.

But what bothered Chelsie most was Jarred's absence. Not once had he come to check on her, at least not to her knowledge. She knew he was wandering around somewhere because she occasionally heard his peal of laughter ringing through the halls and his footsteps echoing in the room that adjoined hers. But the door between the two chambers had never opened. Yet in her troubled dreams she remembered hearing the deep resonance of his voice and feeling his comforting arms. She knew it must have been the laudanum that confused memories with reality. What other explanation was there?

Chelsie found herself waiting to catch a glimpse of Jarred's handsome visage each time the door opened. But she was always disappointed. Odd, she had so quickly grown accustomed to his presence, and how quickly he had made himself scarce. Obviously Jarred was relieved not to have sole responsibility of her and was content to let the rest of his family wait on her hand and foot.

That thought hurt Chelsie more than it should have. How could she miss the companionship of a man who had apparently discarded her from his thoughts and now wanted her out of his life? She hadn't given a fig whether a man lost interest in her before. Why should she harbor these ill-found feelings of loneliness for Jarred? He was an engaged man!

Tormented by forbidden fantasies, Chelsie threw her legs over the edge of the bed. She intended to sneak out of the house to prowl the darkness. Chelsie thrived on fresh air and the whole outdoors. She had been cooped up as long as she could stand, and extended periods of confinement made her edgy. She had been polite and attentive to her flood of well-meaning visitors, but she sorely needed space.

Although her arm and shoulder were tender, the rest of her body needed exercise. That was her diagnosis, not Neil's. He had insisted she stay in bed for two more days. Chelsie feared she would go stark raving mad if she followed the doctor's instructions to the letter.

Weaving unsteadily, Chelsie peeked around the door that joined Jarred's vacated room. She tiptoed into the chamber to borrow breeches and a shirt. Trying to fasten herself into her ladylike garments would put too much strain on her arm and would be impractical for what she had in mind.

After rummaging through the dresser drawers, Chelsie located a buckskin shirt and breeches. Fumbling with her sore arm, she tied the baggy garments about her as best she could. When she had resituated her injured arm in the sling Neil had made for her, she breathed a long sigh. Free at last!

Upon investigation, Chelsie discovered that the terrace doors that led from Jarred's room opened onto a balcony that wrapped around the back of the sprawling brick mansion. Smiling in eager anticipation, Chelsie crept outside. Clamping her good hand on the railing, she eased onto the vine-choked trellis and cautiously descended into the garden below. Her eyes were immediately drawn to the stables. Oh, what she wouldn't give to sit astride Trumpeter and feel the wind caressing her face!

Giving way to impulse, Chelsie aimed herself toward the stable. No one would know about her midnight ride. She could chase the wind on Trumpeter's back, then brush him down before returning to her room. She would feel ten times better because of her nocturnal prowling.

Trumpeter's whinny brought a contented smile to Chelsie's lips. The copper dun colt had always been one of her favorites in her father's stable. Evan Channing, like Kyle McAlister, had a penchant for fine horses and for hunting and racing. The duke always had at least one entry for the English Derby and had come close to winning the Triple Crown in England. Chelsie knew her father would be distressed over her disappearance and the loss of this high-bred colt. Evan envisioned greatness for Trumpeter. He was sired by a prized Arabian and the thoroughbred mare that had also been stolen by Hutton and his crew of pirates.

Trumpeter was a high-spirited colt that still had a great deal of training to undergo, but his potential was limitless. Chelsie didn't know how they would work out the details when her father arrived to inform Kyle he had purchased stolen horses. Well, she would worry about that later, she decided. For now, she just wanted to canter Trumpeter across the meadow to rejuvenate her spirits.

After leading the colt outside, Chelsie drew him to the fence so she could climb on his back without a saddle. When she was finally astride the prancing colt, a contented sigh escaped her lips. For the first time in almost eight weeks she had found a substitute for being at Chessfield. On occasion, when she was restless, she had sneaked Trumpeter from the stables at Chessfield to gallop across the countryside like a lost spirit.

Pressing her knees to Trumpeter's flanks, she trotted down

the path. The colt pranced in anticipation of the run, knowing Chelsie would eventually give him his head. A faint smile pursed her lips as she remembered the difficulty this colt had given his trainers at Chessfield. Trumpeter wasn't particularly fond of men, but he had always been putty in Chelsie's hands. Since he'd first come into the world as a wobbly, long-legged foal, Chelsie had been at his side, encouraging him with a gentle voice. When the trainers had difficulty with him, Chelsie insisted she be allowed to work with the contrary colt, and her father had permitted it.

Now this high-stepping colt and the mare were Chelsie's only contact with her past, and she relished the opportunity of reminiscing about better days that entailed a carefree existence on the other side of the ocean. For this space in time she could pretend she was sailing over the plush meadows of Chessfield, that she was only a few steps away from the grand stone mansion that was perched on a hillside of emerald green.

As Trumpeter stretched out to cover the moonlit path where Kyle exercised his horses, Chelsie allowed her thoughts to flow unhindered. She contemplated her secret affair with Jarred, one that brought unwanted pleasure which mingled with an unfamiliar kind of pain. Chelsie didn't want to find herself drawn to Jarred. She was uncomfortable with what she was feeling for him. She honestly missed his crooked smiles, his challenging glances, and even their fiery arguments. There was an empty space in her life, one that hadn't been there until that raven-haired rake had come and gone.

Forcefully Chelsie pushed aside her foolish whim and forbidden memories. She refused to let Jarred upset her. Men were dispensable, a necessary evil. She didn't need him. When her father arrived, she would go home where she belonged and leave Jarred to his fiancée. Abigail Shaw was welcome to him, Chelsie assured herself.

The crisp breeze beat against Chelsie's face and she felt her spirits soar when she pressed against Trumpeter's muscular neck, clinging to his mane. Trumpeter was familiar with the shadowed path. He had been put through the paces daily, but he had protested his male riders, giving them fits. With Chelsie on his back, his hooves sprouted wings. Without command he slowed his pace and circled to retrace the lane that led back to the stables.

Before Trumpeter thundered back in the direction they had come, rousing the servants, Chelsie commanded him to slow his pace. She slid from his back a good distance from the stable to prevent being discovered. As she rounded the corner, the moonlight caught on the muscular frame of the man who had propped himself casually against the wall to watch her.

A startled shriek erupted from Chelsie's lips, but Jarred pounced like a tiger, covering her mouth before her cry of alarm shattered the silence. Wide eyes lifted to Jarred's grinning face. When she recognized who had caught her sneaking about in the darkness, she relaxed in his steely arms. Chelsie wasn't pleased to have Jarred looming over her, interrupting her nocturnal prowling. But better him than someone else, she reckoned. She could deal with Jarred when he scolded her. They had become proficient at arguments, and Chelsie prepared herself for her expected lecture on staying in bed, where Neil had put her.

Jarred's scornful gaze swept down Chelsie's outlandish attire. "Nice clothes," he smirked at the oversized garments that looked suspiciously like his own.

"Thank you. The man I stole them from has impeccable taste," Chelsie replied, peeking up at him through long, curly lashes. "Why haven't you come to see me?"

Jarred dropped his hands from her waist the instant before they began to roam of their own accord. "I didn't think you would miss me, since you and the good doctor were getting along so well . . . which reminds me." His brows furrowed as he stared at the sling. "I thought Neil said you were to remain bedfast for two more days. I doubt that a midnight ride on that contrary colt was on his list of prescribed therapies."

" 'Tis a mental therapy," Chelsie defended. Her chin tilted to that defiant angle Jarred had come to know so well. "I needed fresh air."

"So naturally you sneaked into my room to steal my clothes and then crept to the stable to select the wildest steed you could find and took flight in the darkness with a half-mended arm," he snorted sarcastically. "That prank suggests you *need* mental

155

therapy, minx."

"Have you been visiting your fiancée tonight?" Chelsie wasn't sure she wanted to know, but she had to ask. It was none of her business, but she felt the need to switch topics of conversation before Jarred scolded her more than he already had. She always became defensive, and then they wound up in a shouting match. Their arguments were as regular as clockwork, and she was in no mood for one tonight.

An amused smile quirked Jarred's lips as he stared down into her elfin face. Jarred wasn't surprised that she changed the subject of conversation, but he was baffled by her interest in what he had been doing. Lately his family had been hovering over this lively sprite, and Neil had spent more time with her than all his other patients put together. Quite honestly, Jarred was startled that Chelsie had noticed he hadn't been around and that she was curious about where he had been and with whom.

"Nay, I haven't seen Abi since I returned from the wilderness," he answered. Jarred knew he shouldn't be taking a bold step toward Chelsie, but he needed her back in his arms. He was suffering an obsessive need to hold her. Impulsively he laid his hands on her hips and drew her supple body against his. "I have been in Annapolis, discussing important matters of state." Jarred wasn't sure, but he thought he detected relief in her shadowed features. "I just returned home to find Easthaven haunted by an apparition on horseback. . . ."

When Chelsie realized her good arm had slid up to toy with the coal-black hair that lay recklessly across his forehead, that she was studying him as if he were a masterpiece of art, she froze. Why did it seem so natural to touch this rake as if he were hers? It was absurd. She shouldn't be taking privileges with him, nor he with her. Awkwardly Chelsie glanced away, then retreated a respectable distance.

"I suppose I should brush the colt down and put him back in his stall," she said lamely.

"I suppose you should," Jarred quietly agreed, watching her every move, studying each enchanting expression that teased him in the shadows and the moonlight.

Inhaling a steadying breath, Chelsie grabbed Trumpeter's

156

mane and led him back to the stable. After fumbling in the dark, she located the curry brush and set to work on him. Chelsie murmured constantly to him while she worked, as if she were chatting with a dear friend. With her chore completed, she ambled outside, but Jarred had disappeared into thin air. She was disappointed and shocked to realize she had anticipated seeing him. The man kept her emotions in perpetual turmoil, but blast it, life was dull when he wasn't around.

It was inconceivable that she could have missed him in the first place and that she longed for his companionship. Her—a woman who had never needed a man in her life, a woman who never had difficulty squeezing every iota of pleasure from each dawning day! Chelsie shook her head in wonder. She didn't need Jarred. And he certainly didn't need her. Why was she depressed when he wasn't around? Why did their brief encounter in the darkness leave her yearning for more?

Giving herself an inward shake and a stern lecture on the foolishness of harboring a tittle of affection for a man who had one woman on a string and only God knew how many others drooling over him, Chelsie marched around to the back of the mansion. Her thoughts of Jarred dispersed when she began her difficult climb up the terrace. Coming down the trellis one-handed hadn't been easy, but she had managed. But going up was another matter entirely. Each time she lifted her slippered foot, it caught on the dangling hem of her oversized breeches. And with only one arm to maintain her balance, Chelsie had one hell of a time maneuvering up the ivy-covered lattice.

When one foot slid from its resting place, Chelsie muffled a squawk. She knew she was about to fall, and the thought of winding up with both arms in slings flashed through her mind. Damn it all, how was she going to explain when she was found sprawled in the shrubs below?

To her surprise, a hand slid around her waist, balancing her the split second before she lost her footing and plummeted to the garden below. My, but Jarred darted through the darkness like a disembodied spirit, disappearing and reappearing at the most unexpected moments.

"Idiotic nymph," Jarred growled as he flattened himself

157

against her back. "Why didn't you employ the conventional method of entering a house by coming through the front door the way everyone else does?"

"If one is sneaking off into the night, one doesn't parade in and out the front door," she snapped.

"I suppose you have reverted to your bad habits — ones left over from your previous life of crime," Jarred speculated.

She didn't argue. Jarred was her judge, jury, and gaoler. He had made up his mind that she was a liar and thief, and nothing would convince him otherwise. In this ever-changing world, Jarred's stubborn mind was ever-constant. Confound it, if only she had her locket and her emerald ring, she could prove she was who she said she was.

When Jarred pressed closer to prevent losing his footing, he accidentally mashed against Chelsie's injured arm. Instinctively she jerked away. But considering she and Jarred were hanging on the trellis like acrobatic monkeys, that was not a wise thing to do. Her abrupt movement caused Jarred's hand to slip from its anchored position on the lattice.

"Argh . . . !" Jarred's voice erupted in a howl when Chelsie tried to reposition herself on the trellis. Her heel caught him in the groin. Reflexively he doubled over. One hand had already been jarred loose, and now the other was groping to latch onto the trellis. Unfortunately, Chelsie had reached for the same spot to steady herself, and they wound up holding each other's hand, clinging to nothing but air.

"Oh, for God's sake," Jarred growled as he clawed the vines that snapped in his hands.

"Shh . . . shh . . . ! Chelsie sputtered, struggling desperately to keep her balance.

It was a valiant attempt to regain their footing . . . valiant, but futile. The thin strips of lattice weren't sturdy enough to support the two oversize birds who were fluttering in the vines. When Chelsie and Jarred sagged backward, the excess strain on the lathe caused the trellis to snap loose. Although Jarred and Chelsie managed to plaster themselves to the lattice, the entire thing tore loose from its nails and tilted backward.

Like a giant redwood felled by a lumberjack's ax, the two-some and their broken lattice crashed into the shrubs below. A growl that sounded almost inhuman erupted from the tangled bodies and broken lattice and mass of prickly shrubs. The animal howl was loud enough to wake the dead and did indeed rouse the entire McAlister clan.

Candles blazed in the windows on the second story. Through several terrace doors the McAlisters appeared, clutching their robes around them. Loud whispers wafted from the balcony as the family tried to locate the source of all the noise.

"Who's there?" Kyle's voice boomed.

"It's me, for God's sake," Jarred bellowed back. "Send Neil down here. I think I broke my blessed arm!"

A stampede thundered into Kyle's room, through the hall and down the steps that led to the door. Kyle, Rebecca, Daniel, Neil, Grant, and Eli trotted around the shrubbery to remove the broken lattice and choking vines from the victims.

The congregation wasn't surprised to see Jarred sprawled in the bushes with his left arm tangled in a most awkward position. But what shocked them out of their nightclothes was finding Chelsie lying face-up on top of Jarred, cradling the wounded arm, which she had reinjured during her fall.

"What in the sweet loving hell is going on here?" Grant growled at his brother. It wasn't the first time he had posed that gruff question. Jarred seemed to have an uncanny knack of winding up with Chelsie, whether it was lying in a bed or in the bushes.

"Save the interrogation until later," Jarred bit off. Grimacing, he tried to move the arm Chelsie had fallen on. The task caused him to suck in his breath and hiss in pain. "Get me the hell out of here!" he roared in frustration.

Eli and the McAlister clan scrambled around the thick shrubs to pull Chelsie to her feet and then dragged Jarred from the bushes that held him fast.

"For heaven sake, Chelsie," Neil muttered as he pulled back her buckskin shirt to examine the bloodstained bandage. "I thought I told you to stay in bed. Lattice climbing is not recommended for mending patients . . . and what the blazes are you doing in Jarred's clothes?" he added when he got a good look at her.

"Stop asking questions and examine my arm," Jarred growled

as he held the throbbing appendage against his ribs. "A little first aid would be nice, Doctor McAlister."

Neil stamped over to his brother and glared at him furiously. "If this arm isn't broken, I might just break it," he muttered spitefully. "I thought you'd outgrown such childish pranks years ago."

"What are you doing back from Annapolis in the middle of the night?" Kyle wanted to know. "And why were you sneaking Chelsie out of the house?" His brown eyes narrowed accusingly on Jarred. "You have a lot of explaining to do, son."

The two injured patients were herded back to the house. Jarred was thankful for the time to formulate his thoughts. He wasn't sure if he could satisfactorily explain the incident without incriminating Chelsie. Why he shouldn't place the blame where it belonged, he didn't know. But protecting her had become second nature, and he didn't want his family to think this shenanigan was her fault. For several minutes Jarred conjured up and rejected several flimsy lies. But they all sounded a mite far-fetched to him. How was he going to talk himself out of this one?

"Just look at this," Neil scolded as he indicated the ripped stitch on Chelsie's shoulder. "Now see what you've done, Jarred?"

Chelsie's face flushed and she tugged the gaping shirt back in place before all the McAlisters saw more of her than she intended. "It wasn't Jarred's fault," she declared, wincing at the burning pain in her shoulder. "It was mine."

"I don't need a woman taking the blame for my foolishness," Jarred muttered crankily.

He had yet to formulate his excuse and Chelsie was already shouldering the responsibility for their crash into the shrubs. But Jarred refused to let her explain. It would only provoke more questions about what a dignified duchess was doing sneaking around at midnight, riding Kyle's prize colt.

"I returned from Annapolis and thought I would check on the duchess," he declared. "Chelsie uttered the desire of inhaling fresh air and seeing the plantation house from the outside instead of from her four walls. I gave her my clothes because I thought it would be easier for her to worm in and out of them

160

without straining her arm." So far, so good, Jarred complimented himself. His lie sounded reasonable.

"You could have used the back door instead of the trellis," Grant snapped derisively. "The whole story sounds fishy to me."

"Would you care to try again?" Eli snickered at the ruffled-haired rake whose face was a mass of scratches and whose clothes were snagged with leaves and stems of ivy.

"It was my fault," Chelsie insisted. "I borrowed Jarred's clothes and sneaked down the trellis for some fresh air. I knew Neil would protest, so I chose to be discreet. I have a terrible aversion to being cooped up." Her pleading gaze lingered on each concerned face. "Jarred was just returning when he heard me thrashing on the lattice. And he attempted to rescue me. Everything happened at once. When he tried to help me down, the lattice gave way and we fell. Now please examine his arm. I feel personally responsible for his injury."

It was that placating look in those emerald eyes that did it. Although his family had flung Jarred dubious glances while he offered his rendition of the incident, no one questioned Chelsie. They merely accepted her explanation and then turned their attention to Jarred's mangled arm. Once again he had been upstaged by this lively minx and she was crowding him from the limelight that was rightfully his. And what rankled Jarred most was the realization that Chelsie Channing pulled as much weight than Kyle McAlister's second son! All Chelsie had to do was murmur her sad little story about suffering cabin fever and then bat her big green eyes and the whole clan melted. Damn, that spellcasting witch beat anything Jarred had ever seen. She could probably declare that the sun rose in the west and his family would accept her word for it.

Jarred was bent completely out of shape after his family accused him of lying and turned right around and accepted Chelsie's story. She hadn't bothered to mention her wild ride on that contrary colt, of course. Neil would have been hopping up and down in indignation, and Kyle wouldn't have believed she could even stay on that spirited steed without a saddle or rein and one arm in a sling. Blast it, Jarred should have left Chelsie hanging by two fingers on the lattice instead of shinnying up the tree and tramping across the trellis to save her. He should have left her there until she mildewed. Damned troublesome wench. She not only got herself in trouble, but she dragged Jarred down with her!

And confound it, if he had truly broken his arm because of her, he was going to hold it over her for the rest of her natural life. She would *never* be free of her indentureship. By damned, he would demand a lifetime of service to compensate for all the trouble she'd caused him!

Chapter 13

After a thorough examination of Jarred's arm and the gashes from the shrubbery that marred his face and back, Neil diagnosed that his brother had sustained a severe sprain. Nothing was broken, but according to Neil, something should have been. When he finished wrapping the injured arm, Neil placed it in a sling.

"A matched pair," Neil declared with a faint smile. "Both of you are confined to your rooms. Neither of you will be scaling the lattice until I sign a clean bill of health."

"Aye, doctor," Chelsie murmured obediently.

Jarred gaped at the spirited misfit. Never had he heard her employ such a subservient tone. He swore her voice would crack.

While Rebecca escorted Chelsie to her room, Eli accompanied Jarred to his. The moment the door eased shut, Eli burst into snickers.

"Things haven't been so lively around here since you and your brothers were playing childhood pranks."

"You were right. That woman is a walking disaster," Jarred grumbled. "Now she has *me* jinxed."

Eli grinned. "I'm beginning to understand what really happened," he mocked at the scowling patient. "Chelsie, overpowering as she is, forcefully attacked you and shoved you up the lattice alongside her. When she saw her chance to get even with you, she knocked you into the shrubs and purposely landed on your arm. Although she intended to break it in at least three places, you wound up with only a few tendons and ligaments pulled. 'Tis a pity that big bully of a woman didn't pick on someone her own size. You poor defenseless man, you."

"I can do without your sarcasm," Jarred growled.

"Then don't blame Chelsie for your woes," Eli countered. "Just because you aren't man enough to handle that uninhibited pixie is no reason for you to. . . ."

"I can handle her," Jarred snapped.

"Nay," Eli argued, delighting in getting Jarred's dander up. "Maybe it would be best if Chelsie *did* match up with Neil. As active as she is, she needs a doctor on twenty-four-hour call. You should stick with Abi. She is much more docile and she never causes you a smidgen of trouble. When you finally get around to marrying her, your life will be calm, sedate and predictable," he added in a ho-hum tone.

"When I want your opinion of what I need and want, I'll let you know," Jarred snorted. After peeling off his snagged shirt, he plunked down on the bed.

"I think you should marry Abi—the sooner the better," Eli insisted. "That will give you more than enough reason to keep your distance from Chelsie before she manages to break her neck—and yours as well."

Jarred rolled his eyes in disgust. He was quickly growing tired of Eli's satirical prattle. "I thought you had decided it was truly Chelsie I should marry and forget my obligation to Abi."

"I changed my mind after tonight," Eli announced. "You don't really want a wife. All you need is a hostess who knows her place and stays in it. Chelsie would be far more than that, and I don't think you could devote the time it would take to tame her. She's just like that copper dun colt Kyle purchased—strong-willed, spirited, tenacious, and difficult to handle."

"Not when *Chelsie* rides him, he isn't," Jarred murmured, momentarily distracted by the vision of Chelsie's wild mane of hair trailing behind her as she flew across the meadow on the steed's back. Jarred had watched her in mute amazement when he realized she had climbed onto that barely manageable colt without a saddle or bridle. She had the most incredible knack of handling a steed that gave its trainers fits. The colt had responded without protest to her commands.

The color drained from Eli's ruddy complexion. "That's what

she was doing when she sneaked out of the house?" he croaked in stupefied astonishment. "Wounded arm and all?"

"Wounded arm, and without a saddle or bridle," he confirmed. "The colt can fly with that witch on his back. He became her magical broom."

Eli sat down before he fell down and mumbled to himself for a full minute. Was there nothing Chelsie wasn't afraid to try? The daring little imp! Nothing slowed her down, not even a lame arm or a fall in the shrubs. Why, by the following evening, she would probably be back to her nocturnal prowling. And Jarred would be one step behind her, Eli predicted.

Aye, Jarred put up a fuss, but he was watching out for that green-eyed pixie just like the rest of his family. Jarred simply couldn't leave her alone, even after he had spent the better part of the week avoiding her like the plague. How long would it be before this billy goat of a man realized he was engaged to the wrong woman?

Lost in thought, Eli murmured a quiet goodnight and ambled downstairs to his room. When the door closed behind him, the portal that adjoined Chelsie and Jarred's room creaked open. Two wide emerald eyes in an enchanting face framed by a wild spray of silver-blond hair appeared around the edge of the door. Tentatively Chelsie stepped into the room to peer somberly at Jarred.

"I came to apologize," she said quietly.

Jarred didn't hear her. The moment she stepped into the lantern light, he was distracted by her revealing gown, which displayed her delectable curves and swells. The diagonal neckline of the sheer garment exposed her bandaged shoulder. Trouble though this leprechaun was, she could steal a man's breath away with her dazzling beauty.

There were few women who had been blessed with an over abundance of good looks. They were stunning whether they were at their best or worst. Chelsie was one of those rare beauties who drew a man's admiring gaze and held it fast. Peering at this emerald-eyed imp had become an obsessive hobby of Jarred's.

Each night he had crept into Chelsie's room to check on her while she slept. He had been there to soothe her when troubled dreams converged upon her. He had stood back and studied her elegant features, fighting the illogical attraction, wanting her in the worst possible way. No one knew of his late night visits, but he was always there — wanting her, willfully restraining himself from satisfying his hungry desires, and then chastising himself for wanting her so badly. It had become a vicious cycle that constantly tormented Jarred. But torment or no, he found his footsteps taking him to her room and leaving him standing there, aching to reach out and touch her as intimately as he once had.

"Jarred?" Two delicately carved brows knitted over her concerned eyes. "Are you all right?"

Jarred gave himself a mental slap and scolded himself severely for trolling through a sea of whimsical thoughts. "Aside from having my arm very nearly twisted out of its socket and having you and the lattice fall on me, I'm getting along splendidly," he replied sardonically.

"No need to worry." Chelsie squared her shoulders and raised a proud chin in response to his resentful remark. "Next time I sneak from the house, I won't include you in my follies."

"There won't *be* a next time," Jarred said in no uncertain terms.

"Is that a decree or a threat, counselor?" she questioned.

"Both. I wish for once you would. . . . " Jarred caught himself before he wasted another wish.

"You wish for what?" she prodded, grinning impishly. "That we had never met? That I had not put this tormenting curse on you?"

Jarred rolled from the bed. In two swift strides he was towering over Chelsie. It amazed him that when he came within two feet of this saucy chit he was entrapped in that mystical aura that hovered around her. Her alluring scent teased his senses. The revealing gown inspired cravings that had lain dormant for almost a week. Her parted lips seemed to beg for his kiss, and Jarred felt hard-pressed not to take her sweet mouth under his.

Jarred wanted her madly, but he didn't want to want her. He knew what she was — a phony duchess who possessed far too much rambunctious spirit to have descended from royalty. She was trouble with a capital T, and if he didn't take her in his arms this very instant he was going to burn himself into a pile of frustrated ashes!

When he was standing this close to temptation, his mind and body could never agree. He wanted to be logical and sensible, but his flesh was weak, refusing to accept his brain's good advice.

Why should he keep fighting the compelling attraction? Jarred asked himself as he stared down into those enormous eyes that danced with living fire. All his noble self-restraint had earned him nothing but maddening exasperation and an ache in his loins. He had kept his distance for one agonizing week, and still the yearnings hadn't ebbed. And it didn't appear they would fade soon. Jarred was stuck with an insane craving and Chelsie was the cause and cure of the curse that tormented his waking hours and played havoc with his good humor. He had always prided himself in possessing an even disposition. But lately he was as sour as clabber, thanks to his obsessive hunger for this sassy virago.

Jarred tugged Chelsie close and lowered his head to capture her petal-soft lips, savoring and devouring them. She offered no protest and Jarred almost wished she would. It might bring him back to his senses. Might? Jarred laughed at himself. It was only wishful thinking on his part. He never could leave this enticing beauty alone, good intentions or no.

Chelsie gave no thought to rejecting his one-armed embrace. It was crazy and insane, but she yearned for this blue-eyed rake. She had become addicted to his masterful kisses and the feel of his gentle hands. He could make her pulse patter like hailstones. He knew how to make her innocent body respond to the sweet, potent magic of passion. She needed him to ease the longings that she had suppressed for more days than she cared to count. She wanted to absorb his hard, masculine flesh, to become a part of his invincible strength.

Her right arm slid upward as she arched shamelessly toward him. Her quaking body delighted in making familiar contact with his. Chelsie felt as if she were coming home from a long, aimless voyage on an empty sea. A tiny sigh escaped her lips as Jarred kissed her. She would sacrifice her last breath to enjoy another dozen kisses like this one. It was hot and explosive, and she felt warm, giddy, and incredibly alive!

A throb of desire pulsated through Jarred's veins when Chelsie's luscious body brushed suggestively against his. What an irresistible temptress she had become! She made him glad he was a man. She made him ache to satisfy the monstrous craving that had been held in check for what seemed eternity.

Jarred had considered easing his need for a woman while he was in Annapolis, but a pair of sparkling green eyes kept tormenting him. He hadn't wanted just any feminine body to pacify his lust. He had wanted this blond-haired minx in his arms, and any other female would have been a meager substitute for the rapture he had discovered with this witch-angel.

"What spell have you cast upon me?" Jarred's voice was a harshly disturbed whisper. His hand glided down the silky fabric that clung to her curvaceous figure, aching to mold her bare flesh to his. "I know what you are, but when I touch you I can think of nothing but holding you . . . loving you. . . . "

A mischievous smile dangled on the corner of her lips as she leaned back to meet his all-consuming gaze. "I am what I have become," she taunted him as she traced the cleft in his chin. "And you will become what I make of you. . . . "

It was the vibrant flash of fire in those expressive green eyes that had first sparked Jarred's fascination and lured him back against his will. When he stared at this beguiling nymph, he lost the good sense he had been born with. She made life an adventurous game, a constant challenge. Jarred couldn't seem to get enough of her.

"What is your intention, witch?" he chortled, his voice raspy with unfulfilled desire. "To turn me into a pillar of stone, a pile of sand?"

Chelsie gave her head a negative shake, sending the silver-blond tendrils rippling down her back. "Nay," she contradicted huskily. Her fingertips investigated his chest, feeling his whipcord muscles flex and relax beneath her inquiring touch. It was the first time Chelsie had permitted herself to explore his powerful physique. He reminded her of a sleek panther—a mass of potential strength who moved with lithe grace and lightning speed. "I was leaning more toward turning you into a human torch." Wantonly her body glided against his and her adventurous hand trekked along the band of his breeches, causing Jarred's heart to skip a beat.

"Feed the flame," he groaned in tormented pleasure. Instinctively he clutched her against him, letting her feel the extent of his desire for her. "God help me, but I want you the way I've never wanted another woman. . . . "

Chelsie had intended to be satisfied with a few dozen kisses. But his raspy words and the feel of his bold manhood pressing against her thigh was her undoing. Suddenly she needed to recapture that mystical night when she'd awakened to find herself in Jarred's brawny arms. The forbidden memories of rapture had followed in her shadow, teasing her, leaving her to burn. She feared she would never earn the respect and devotion of this restless man, but she needed him to love her just now, even if he could offer no more than physical pleasure.

Chelsie detested herself for stooping to this, for allowing herself to be content with a few sparse crumbs of his affection. But all her firm resolutions evaporated when she was molded to his hard, masculine contours. Jarred had become her anchor in an unfamiliar sea. He had been there to see her through each storm, to protect her when she feared she couldn't remain afloat in turbulent waters. Wanting and needing him had become as natural and reflexive as breathing.

Chelsie wasn't sure how and when they wound up on Jarred's four-poster bed. But they were there—kissing, touching, removing the hindering garments that separated them. Chelsie satisfied her craving to learn his muscular body by sight and touch, to return the pleasure she had discovered when Jarred introduced her to the dark sensuous world of passion. Chelsie was amazed at the power she seemed to hold over him. It was gratifying to know she could shatter his composure as thoroughly as he had shattered hers.

Her hand was never still for a moment. She investigated his masculine terrain, memorizing the exact location of each taut muscle and tendon, measuring the wide expanse of his shoulders and chest. Chelsie marveled at this lion of a man. There was something unique about Jarred McAlister. Although he had the education and manners of a gentleman, he was as strong as an ox and as agile as a jungle cat. He hadn't spent all his life studying law, that was for sure. There was a wild nobility about him, a dynamic sensuality that seeped through that veneer of sophistication when his guard was down. Whatever Jarred was, he was not a dandy or a weakling. He was all man, every swarthy, virile inch of him. . . .

All thought scattered. Chelsie's senses took flight in wild abandon when Jarred's light caresses worshipped her. His fingertips ran the length of her spine, then lifted over her shoulder to circle lazily around the rose-tipped crests of her breasts. His warm breath whispered his need for her as his sensuous kisses mapped every sensitized inch of her flesh.

Jarred had one-handedly set her body aflame. If he was discomforted by his injured arm, he certainly didn't show it. And Chelsie forgot she had ripped a stitch during her fall to the shrubs. Her body was numb to all except the exquisite sensations Jarred's kisses and caresses evoked in her. He made her impatient with wanting, a slave to the forbidden memories they had created so many nights ago in the hotel in Annapolis.

He couldn't seem to get close enough to the fire that scorched him inside and out. His hot, greedy kisses drifted over her silky skin, relishing the soft texture of her curvaceous body. His hand weaved over her belly and then retraced its erotic path to the dusky peaks of her breasts. His moist lips tracked along the pulsating column of her neck, leaving bonfires burning in the wake of his kisses and caresses.

This is what he had craved each night he'd crept into Chelsie's room. But he had confined himself to simply worshipping her exquisite body from afar. He had vowed he would allow his brother the chance to charm this nymph. It killed him to stand aside and pretend he had never touched this wild, sweet dove, that he didn't want her in his bed.

But those days of restraint had taken their toll. Jarred was through pretending he didn't crave the wild splendor he had discovered in Chelsie's arms. He was like a desperate man who was impatient to claim this lovely treasure as his own. Although his conscience still tormented him, it was no match for his male desires. Chelsie brought his primal instincts to life and he responded because it was impossible not to. There was simply something about this green-eyed enchantress that silently called out to his restless soul and lured him to her.

A groan of unholy torment bubbled in Jarred's chest when Chelsie touched him, urging him closer, confessing her need for him. His body uncurled upon hers as he came to her. His heart slammed against his ribs and stuck there when she arched upward and murmured his name like a mystical incantation. Jarred was hopelessly and completely lost to the feel of her supple body beneath his, to the melodic sound of her voice, to the shuddering sensations that bombarded him.

Jarred felt himself losing complete control when her body moved in sensuous rhythm with his. The cadence of their lovemaking was frantic and urgent, stirring a savage splendor. Jarred had become the flame within her, and he burned with the heat of a thousand suns as the holocaust of passion engulfed him. He felt her nails digging into the rigid tendons of his back like a cat flexing her claws. He felt her soft, luscious body joined intimately to his. They were flesh-to-flesh, soul-to-soul and heart-to-heart. Jarred trembled in the sublime ecstasy of becoming a living, breathing part of this inexhaustible bundle of energy and spirit.

The pleasure that streamed through every fiber of his being was so intense that Jarred ached in places he had forgotten he had. Lovemaking had never been such a complex experience that entailed the mind, body, and spirit. Chelsie touched every part of him, spinning his emotions into a tapestry of unrivaled rapture. She was teaching him things he never expected to learn about lovemaking, as if *she* were the instructor and *he* were the novice!

Although Jarred swore he knew all there was to know about passion, Chelsie left him wondering what he had been doing for the past decade when he took a woman in his arms. Whatever it was, it didn't hold a candle to the blaze of desire this firebrand ignited within him. She had him burning alive, and nothing could extinguish the flame until it had run its course.

She stirred the most remarkable sensations. It was as if he were soaring in motionless flight, drugged by some intoxicating potion that left him lightheaded. He had transcended the realm of physical satisfaction somewhere along the way. His soul had cast off the encumbering garments of flesh to sail across spar-

171

kling sunbeams and glide over the arc of rainbows. . . .

Suddenly the wild sensations that channeled into the core of his being erupted like a cloudburst. Streams of ineffable pleasure rained upon him. His body shuddered as the emotions poured forth, numbing his body and mind to all except the feel of this mystical enchantress who had showed him new dimensions of passion.

Sweet mercy, if he was so devastated by this nymph's lovemaking when she used only one hand to sensitize his flesh, he wondered how he would survive when she had recovered from her injury. The first time Jarred had made love to her she had responded to him, satisfying his every whim. But she had not dared to touch him intimately in return. This time she had made love to him with magical inventiveness and naïve ingenuity. Her bold caresses had melted him into puddles of liquid desire. He marveled at the power she held over him.

Jarred expelled a ragged breath and sought to collect his wits. He didn't have enough strength left to contemplate how Chelsie had worked her black magic on him. She just had, and that was that.

The hurried trips back and forth from Annapolis, compounded by a long, hectic week, piled on top of three hair-raising months of battle in the wilderness, left Jarred exhausted. All he wanted was to drift toward that hazy horizon that lay far from the obligations and pressures of reality. With a contented sigh he closed his eyes and faded into the sweet hypnotic dreams Chelsie had spun around him.

Carefully Chelsie eased away when she heard Jarred's methodic breathing. The sight of him sleeping peacefully in the moonlight tugged at her heartstrings, and she cursed her vulnerability for a man who would never see her as his equal, but rather his pawn of pleasure.

Blast it, each time Jarred came within ten feet of her, she couldn't see past those sparkling blue eyes. She fell into those mysterious pools and could not swim out until her feminine desires had been fulfilled. Where was her firm resolve when she needed it most? How could he make her melt like snow on a campfire each time his mouth took possession of her lips and his hands enslaved her with tender caresses?

172

Had she no willpower, no pride? Jarred had chosen his mate in life, and Chelsie, fool that she was, had overlooked his commitment to Abi and reveled in the indescribable rapture she had discovered in his arms. What was she trying to prove? That she had misplaced the good sense she had been developing these past twenty years? And why did she presume that she, a virtually inexperienced woman, could ever make a man like Jarred fall in love with her, just for spite or for any other reason? Eli had put that ridiculous notion in her head, and she should have rejected the idea before it took root.

Well, from now on she was going to treat Jarred McAlister the way she had treated all other men. She would ignore his wily charms and keep him at arm's length. This ill-fated affection she felt for him was over and done. She was not going to fall in love with a man who could offer her only stolen nights of ecstasy while he upheld his obligation to his fiancée.

Jarred had started out by using her and he was still using her to satisfy his lusts. If she were smart, she would never let herself forget that. Chelsie told herself she was only experimenting with passion because it was new and mysterious. Jarred had unlocked her hidden desires and brought them to life. But all the desire in the world couldn't compensate for the strong emotional bond involved in loving a man with all her heart and soul. She knew Jarred wanted her body. But there was a vast difference between wanting and loving. Chelsie may have shared his passion, but Abi had his respect and his commitment. Chelsie cursed herself for accepting one without the other.

She was just a passing fancy to Jarred and he was only the time she was killing until her father arrived to take her home. That was all it was, she convinced herself as she wormed into her nightgown and crept toward the door. She was playing at love like a naïve little girl playing house. But there was no enduring affection between her and Jarred. Desperation had thrown them together and Eli and Jarred's scheming had kept them there. Jarred wanted her because he wanted all women, not just Chelsie. She was a conquest, a convenience—and she must never let herself be deluded into thinking she was special to Jarred. Neither of them could seem to break their bad habits—a curiosity that refused to fade, a passion that fed upon itself like a sickness.

A rueful smile pursed her lips when the memories of their secret splendor threatened to buckle her resolve. If things had been different in the beginning, she might have loved this complicated man of many moods. Had they met at a different time and place, perhaps this cursed attraction could have evolved into lasting affection. But when a man and woman made their first acquaintance in a bathtub, nothing proceeded in a normal fashion. Jarred had an obligation to Abi Shaw, one he didn't seem inclined to ignore. And to him, Chelsie was just a peasant charading as a duchess, a toy he played with in between his obligations.

Her affair with Jarred had been an eye-opening experience. At least now she knew that it was her wealth that had lured other men to her the last few years. Their soft words of affection were a ploy, and they hadn't meant a single word they said. Ah, wealth was a curse, Chelsie mused. Now that she was a pauper in Jarred's eyes, she could see herself as she really was. She had been a sought-after prize for fortune hunters. But none of them desired the woman beneath the expensive gowns and jewels. What they offered was superficial affection, bought and sold with her fortune. They wanted the wealth she could provide, not the personality attached to her fortune.

All this soul-searching made Chelsie's spirits drop. Suddenly she wasn't sure who she really was or what she wanted. She had once been a spoiled, sophisticated heiress with the world at her feet. Now she was just a woman trying to protect her wild heart from the one man who had come as close to taming it as any man ever would.

Her obsession for that blue-eyed devil wasn't helping matters. The war her conscience was waging against her feminine desires had Chelsie so confused and frustrated that she wanted to scream. But of one thing Chelsie was certain: she was going to be heartbroken if she allowed herself to become too attached to Jarred. He was the one man who could break her spirit, because she was vulnerable where he was concerned. Damn him for confirming her suspicion that men had never been interested in her as a person, only in her body and her tempting fortune.

Damn him for making her care for him, when she knew better than to risk her heart on a lost cause!

Chapter 14

Chelsie froze in her tracks when she stepped into her room to find a shadowed figure lounging in a dark corner. After her near brushes with catastrophe, her first instinct had become flight. Wheeling about, Chelsie aimed herself toward Jarred's protective arms, even though she had just resolved to observe the limitations of their relationship.

" 'Tis only me, duchess." Neil's quiet voice halted her in midstep.

Swallowing with a gulp, Chelsie pivoted to seek out Neil's refined features in the crisscrossed shadows.

Slowly he unfolded himself from his chair, stuffed his hands in his pockets, and ambled toward her. After he had peered at her for a long, thoughtful moment, a wry smile rippled across his lips. "Are you in the habit of doing this much nocturnal prowling, my dear?"

Chelsie couldn't meet his inquisitive gaze. Guilt puckered her bewitching features. Dropping her head, Chelsie studied her bare feet as if something there had suddenly demanded her attention. "I suppose you want an explanation," she murmured awkwardly.

"Nay, I have heard enough explanations for one night." He grasped her forearm and gently propelled her toward her bed. "I came by to ensure that you and Jarred didn't need medication for the pain. Obviously neither of you required a doctor's attention. It seems you have devised you own sedative. . . ."

It was fortunate the darkness concealed the explosion of color that enflamed Chelsie's cheeks.

Once Neil had tucked his patient in bed, he sank down beside her. Another grin tugged at his lips. "I hope you realize you have the dignified lawyer of our family behaving like the prankster he was in his youth. And considering you are both invalids, you have been a mite too active this evening. . . ."

"It won't happen again," Chelsie tried to assure him, but Neil pressed his forefinger to her lips to silence her.

"It doesn't matter, duchess. Nothing has changed." A low chuckle rumbled in his chest as he gave way to the impulse of combing his fingers through those glorious strands of silver and gold. "Well, actually, things *have* changed," he allowed. "But for appearance's sake, everything will remain the same. Since you rebelled against lying in bed for two more days, I will permit you to join us downstairs for meals and enjoy a little physical activity . . . within reason . . . if you understand my meaning . . . ."

Chelsie blushed again.

"Papa has invited the Shaws to dine with us day after tomorrow. There is one member of their family I think you should meet." Although Chelsie refused to lift her eyes, Neil reached beneath her chin, tilting her flushed face to his unblinking gaze. "You and I will continue our courtship as if nothing has happened, and I will not disclose the fact that you and Jarred have. . . . " He let the sentence hang in midair, but the technique was just as effective as if he had bluntly described what she and Jarred had been doing.

"Neil, I promise I will never. . . . "

Again his index finger brushed over her lips to shush her. "You needn't make promises to me, duchess. All I ask is that you be my escort for the dinner party. In exchange for your charming company, I will keep silent. We will let tomorrow determine the direction of the future."

Chelsie almost wished she *had* fallen in love with Neil. He was such a kind, understanding man, and he refused to pass judgment. He could have embarrassed her no end if that had been his want, and he could have blabbed her shameful mistake to his father. But Neil was offering to become her confidant. He was helping her shoulder the burden of her shame by becoming her escort while Jarred courted his fiancée. . . .

The thought stung her. Chelsie wanted to kick herself for surrendering to her wanton desires. Jarred had no affection for her whatsoever. Damn her foolish heart! She was never going to let Jarred that close again!

"I want you to dress in your most fetching gown for the party," Neil requested. "I should like to have the company of the most remarkable young woman I have ever met."

"You are a saint," Chelsie murmured. "And I would be honored to be your escort for the evening."

"Nay, I'm no saint," Neil contradicted. "But at long last there seems to be a flicker of light at the end of the dark tunnel." Neil paused at the door, half-turning to meet Chelsie's frown. "You are that light, Chelsie. And if things unfold the way I hope they will, we might both enjoy our hearts' desire."

When Neil exited, Chelsie contemplated the situation. What the devil was Neil babbling about? Flickering lights in tunnels? Heart's desire? Her heart's desire was to go home where she belonged and forget the nightmare which brought her here. And more important, she wanted to forget the man who had come to mean more to her than he should have.

"Flickering lights indeed!" Chelsie sniffed bitterly. The only flickering lights she wanted to see were the flames set under Jarred McAlister. If he hadn't taken advantage of her in Annapolis, none of this would have happened. Chelsie would have been the same as she always was—energetic, carefree and . . . and innocent of men! Damn him for making her want him so. She had been much happier when she was naïve of men and ignorant of the powers of passion. She was a ruined woman because of Jarred. But did he care what would become of her? And what if she carried his child . . . ?

The unsettling thought caused Chelsie to worm beneath her quilts. She wasn't sure she could endure seeing that roguish McAlister smile on the face of her own child, not when she could never win the affection of her child's father. And what would her own father say if he knew what she had done?

Chelsie shuddered to think how Evan Channing would react to the news that he was to become a grandfather without first becoming a father-in-law. Kyle McAlister was so eager for grandchildren he would probably accept the child, even if he had to send the mother away with some believable excuse to save the family's reputation. And Chelsie would never allow Kyle to force Jarred into a marriage he didn't want. How would Jarred's fiancée react if she were caught in the middle of a scandal? Chelsie groaned miserably. When she was in Jarred's arms, everything seemed so right and natural. But when reality came rushing back like a tidal wave, the passion they shared seemed so wrong, so complicated.

All the trouble that could come about because of her careless affair with a philanderer who already had a fiancée was more than enough reason for Chelsie to renew her vow to avoid Jarred. Just think of all the complications that could evolve! Neil already knew what had transpired between them, and Grant had made plenty of speculation. If she and Jarred had created a child, they would make a hopeless situation impossible.

Chelsie wanted children, a passel of them, to satisfy her own craving for the brothers and sisters she'd never had. But she'd never imagined herself with a child and without a husband. That was putting the cart before the horse. Sweet mercy, she had to forget Jarred McAlister existed. She had already flirted with disaster!

That troubled thought followed Chelsie into fitful dreams — ones that became entangled with recurring nightmares. But again, just as it happened so often of late, she imagined she heard Jarred's soothing voice comforting her. And finally, the tormenting memories faded and Chelsie was granted a few hours of undisturbed sleep.

The rap at Chelsie's door sent her scrambling behind the dressing screen. Before she could accept while she was half-dressed, Jarred sailed into the room as if he owned the place.

"You could have announced yourself," she scolded harshly. "My room is not the local grog shop, where you can come and go as you please."

A muddled frown knitted Jarred's brow. What had put this minx in a snit now? He hadn't seen her since that night two days ago, when they had been as close as two people could get.

179

"I came to check on you," Jarred declared as he pushed the door shut. At Neil's insistence, his left arm remained in a sling that was damned inconvenient. Jarred had cursed his lame appendage a dozen times the past two days while he caught up on his chores that had been neglected while he was battling the French and Indians at Fort Necessity.

"As you can plainly see, I am alive and well, thank you very much," Chelsie announced in a tone that invited another bemused glance from Jarred.

Grumbling under her breath, Chelsie wrestled into her expensive gown that had been purchased with Jarred's money. That was the only consoling thought to ease her simmering temper.

"What in Hades is the matter with you?" Jarred demanded.

"Nothing. I'm happy as a lark," Chelsie snapped.

Without being requested to assist her, Jarred strode across the room to single-handedly tackle the stays on Chelsie's gold satin gown. But his hand was immediately slapped away and he was awarded a disdainful glare for his efforts.

"If I want your help, I will ask for it," Chelsie bit off as she pivoted to give him the full effect of her frigid glower. "Now what is it you want?"

"I want to discuss what happened the other night," he began, gauging her reaction to the topic of conversation.

The statement was not well received. Chelsie bristled. "Nothing happened," she declared with conviction. If he had come to instruct her about how she was to behave with his fiancée underfoot, he needn't have bothered.

An amused grin pursed Jarred's lips and his blue eyes twinkled. "If you think nothing happened, one of us is a fool," he murmured in that low, seductive tone that was meant to buckle her defenses. It didn't work.

"If the shoe fits . . ." Chelsie sniffed sarcastically, steeling herself against his dark, magnetic charm. Drawing herself up, she swept across the room to arrange the freshly washed mass of silver-blond hair that trailed down her back.

Jarred gnashed his teeth. For some reason this firebrand was spoiling for a fight, and there wasn't time to do their typical arguments justice. Their guests would be arriving any minute.

"Abigail Shaw is a very delicate, reserved young widow,"

Jarred explained. "I don't wish to—"

Chelsie promised herself she would hold a tight rein on her temper, but Jarred's apparent consideration for his fragile fiancée rubbed Chelsie the wrong way. Damn him! What about Chelsie's feelings? Did they count for nothing? Was this the way a gentleman always behaved when he confronted the disaster of having his intended bride meet his mistress? Never in her worst nightmare had she expected *she* would be the mistress her lover cautioned before meeting his would-be wife!

"The poor, dear woman," she cooed, her tone nowhere near sympathetic. "By all means, we must take every precaution to spare her feelings, even if we have to tread all over mine. We wouldn't dare upset sweet, delicate Abi, would we?"

"Oh for God's sake, that's not what I meant," Jarred growled in irritation. Just *once* he would like to verbalize a thought without Chelsie leaping to the wrong conclusion. She was always interrupting him in midthought. With this sharp-witted, defensive shrew, he was never allowed to finish a statement before he found himself in the middle of an argument.

"Isn't it?" Chelsie spun around, her green eyes flashing. "You don't want me to suggest or imply there is something going on between us while dear Abi is underfoot." Her breasts heaved with every agitated breath. "Do you think I would boast of our reckless encounters? If you do, you are a conceited ogre. I detest myself for falling into your bed a second time. But it will not happen again, because I have endured quite enough humiliation these past two months, thanks to you and Isaac Latham."

Jarred had always prided himself on remaining cool and controlled while those around him floundered about. But Chelsie had the incredible knack of setting him off. Her volatile temper seemed to ignite his. And all of a sudden he was fuming, even when he swore up and down he wouldn't let this spitfire get under his skin . . . again.

"Are you positively *certain* it won't happen again?" Jarred scoffed into her stubborn features. "If you think what is between us is over, then you are the fool, Chel." To prove his point, his arm stole around her waist, pulling her resisting body to his. "You are beginning to believe you are who I have allowed you to become. Now you think you are so close to

181

royalty that I am beneath your lofty station."

His full lips were a hair's breadth away from hers and Chelsie cursed when her heart lurched in her chest. The powerful cross-currents of emotions caused her brain to malfunction. And when this devil touched her, her betraying body reached out to his. She detested her weakness, despised the forbidden sensations that rose from their shallow graves to haunt her.

His mouth came down on hers, stealing her breath and her protest. Chelsie didn't want to remember, to reexperience this wave of ardent sensations. But rejecting the feelings was like trying to erect a wall to restrain a cyclone. Nothing could stop the swirling sensations that engulfed her when she was in Jarred's arms. The simple truth was that he aroused her, and all the determination in the world wasn't going to change the way her body instinctively responded to the feel of his solid strength pressing intimately against hers.

Jarred fed her growing hunger with his arousing caresses. His hands were everywhere at once, crumbling every barrier of defense he encountered. As always, when he dared to touch this enticing package of temptation, he lost control. . . .

Saved by the knock at the door, thank the Lord! Chelsie breathed a shuddering sigh and fought for composure.

The crisp sound echoed across the room, forcing Jarred to retreat. Why did he always end up pulling this firebrand to him? It was becoming as natural as their arguments. They couldn't seem to have one without the other!

"Who's there?" Chelsie croaked.

"Neil," he announced cheerfully. "Are you dressed, duchess?"

"Give me a moment," she pleaded. Her gaze flew back to Jarred's suddenly indiscernible expression.

For an instant their eyes locked and Chelsie cringed when Jarred broke into a roguish grin—one that she would have delighted in smearing all over his craggy features if there had been time. Sweeping into a bow, Jarred silently mocked her surrender.

"As you say, duchess, nothing happened then or now." Leaving her to fling him a go-to-hell glare, Jarred rose to full stature and silently tracked toward the door that joined his room to hers.

Inhaling a frustrated breath, Chelsie marched over to open the portal for Neil. "Would you help me with the stays?" she requested, her voice not so steady as she would have liked. "They are giving me fits with one arm in a sling."

Neil's perceptive gaze settled on her kiss-swollen lips and then lanced off the adjoining door. "Are you sure it isn't my brother instead of the gown that is giving you trouble, my dear Chelsie?"

Her shoulders slumped and she nodded begrudgingly. She couldn't lie to Neil. He was a dear, kind man who offered compassion and understanding. "Aye, it was," she reluctantly confessed. "You don't by chance have an antidote for Jarred in that medical bag of yours, do you?"

Neil chortled softly as he fastened the last stay. "Nay, but don't fret, duchess. Tonight you can repay my younger brother for the torment he is causing you by giving him an ample dose of his own medicine."

Her nose wrinkled at the unsatisfactory suggestion. "What I would prefer is for you to give Jarred a personality transplant," Chelsie grumbled spitefully.

Another chuckle, one that came so easily when he was with this lively lady, burst from his lips. "As soon as I figure out how to perform such difficult surgery, I'll make Jarred my first patient," he promised.

"I would greatly appreciate it," Chelsie murmured with a long sigh.

The amusement evaporated from Neil's refined features as he clutched Chelsie's hand in his own. "I would be greatly pleased if you pretended to have eyes only for me. Sometimes a man needs to feel needed in a way that only a beautiful woman can provide. I request your constant attention. . . ." Gently he lifted her hand to press a light kiss to her wrist. "Will you indulge my vain whims, Chelsie?"

How could she refuse that warm, endearing smile and that soft-spoken voice that had the ability to smooth the wrinkles from her soul? She couldn't. Chelsie returned his smile, even though she didn't have the foggiest notion what Neil hoped to accomplish with this charade. Ah, another charade, Chelsie mused with a disconcerted sigh. If she kept this up much longer, she wouldn't know who or what she was.

"You will be the object of my devout attention," Chelsie assured him with a graceful curtsy.

"Thank you, duchess. I am counting on that," he murmured as he escorted Chelsie into the hall. The faintest hint of a smile hovered on his lips. If Neil played his cards right, Jarred was the one who would suffer most this night. And it served him right, Neil thought to himself. No man should trifle with a duchess without paying his dues. And tonight would determine whether Jarred's engagement to Abi could endure the test. . . .

Chapter 15

The spacious dining room boasted a hand-carved mahogany table and plush chairs upholstered with silk damask. Shiny silverware and sparkling crystal goblets set upon the lacy tablecloth. Decanters of mint-sling, pumpkin flib, and sangaree were positioned at each corner of the table. The expensive china topped off the place settings that had been fussed over for the past hour by Rebecca McAlister Brooks, who delighted in entertaining guests. She loved to organize formal dinners and plan activities. It was her true calling in life.

Sighing in satisfaction, Rebecca carefully scrutinized the room. She had seen to every facet of this evening's affair, down to the last minute detail. Everything had been done according to her precise specifications and she intended to play the gracious hostess. Ah, if only there were more opportunity to plan her social functions. She lived for these formal gatherings of family and friends!

Chelsie stifled a grin as she watched Rebecca flit about, indicating where the family and guests were to sit. The merry widow had followed the same procedure the past two days when Chelsie descended from her room to take her meals with the McAlister clan. Rebecca was a likable, vivacious character, but she had as big a fetish for giving parties as Kyle did for hunting, fishing, and horse racing. Since the death of her husband, Rebecca had adopted her brother's family as if they were her own, and she had eagerly accepted Kyle's invitation to take up residence at the plantation. Now she ruled the roost at Easthaven and dreamed up excuses to entertain family and guests.

"You and Neil will sit there," Rebecca announced, gesturing to the far end of the table. "We will let young Daniel occupy the other chair beside Chelsie, since he has been hovering around her like a devoted puppy. And Grant can take that seat . . ."

Although Rebecca was still rattling on about who was to sit where, Chelsie didn't hear another word. Her heart slammed against her ribs when Jarred appeared in the arched doorway with a voluptuous brunette on his arm.

Chelsie had expected Jarred's fiancée to be attractive. But Abi Shaw was nothing short of a raving beauty. A mass of shiny brown curls dangled around her oval face. Her almond-shaped brown eyes were enchanting. Her full, pink lips were pursed in a smile that was neither too sweet nor the least bit pretentious. Her olive complexion was utterly flawless, and she was a perfect match for the striking raven-haired rake who stood beside her garbed in fashionable royal blue velvet breeches and matching waistcoat.

Chelsie's eyes turned a dark shade of envious green even while she assured herself she didn't care if Jarred had a stunning fiancée. Abi's appearance caused Chelsie to sidle closer to Neil, as if the kindly doctor could cure her ill-founded jealousy. It wasn't that Chelsie was jealous of Abi's statuesque poise and classical beauty, mind you. It was the courtly, respectful way Jarred treated the young widow that cut Chelsie to the quick. He viewed Abi as a visiting queen and Chelsie as a thieving peasant. Damn him. Nay, double damn him, she corrected.

"How nice to see you again, duchess," Amos Shaw greeted, dragging Chelsie from her tormented musings. "I was most distressed to hear about your difficulties in Annapolis. But I see you are mending nicely under Neil's watchful eye."

"All the compliments about Neil's skills as a physician are well founded," Chelsie murmured, turning her adoring attention to her escort. "But I have also discovered the good doctor to be charming company. I haven't minded being injured. Indeed, 'tis the perfect excuse to spend so much time with Neil." For effect, Chelsie batted her enormous green eyes and blessed the eldest brother with a melting smile.

Jarred rolled his eyes in annoyance. Why did it always get his goat when Chelsie played the part of a regal duchess so damned well? And that disarming smile she bestowed on Neil had Jarred grinding his teeth. Why, for God's sake, was he so jealous?

When Amos introduced his lovely daughter to Chelsie, she expected to experience immediate dislike. But there wasn't a haughty bone in Abi's body. She was graceful, poised, generous and sincere with her affection, and positively charming.

Well, so much for hating her competition on sight, Chelsie thought as Neil drew out her chair for her. Wasn't the "other" woman supposed to be spiteful, greedy, and conniving? Abigail Shaw was anything but! In fact, Abi was one of the nicest, warmest individuals Chelsie ever had the pleasure of meeting. *And Abi is not your competition,* her feminine pride assured her.

Whatever was between Chelsie and Jarred was over. Chelsie didn't have the heart to hurt a woman as amiable as Abi Shaw. She was every bit the lady—modest, personable, and most delightful company. The longer Chelsie visited with Abi, the more she realized she could never strike a note of discord between the comely brunette and her miserable, infidel fiancé. The truth was, that rascal deserved to be raked over the coals for dallying with another woman. And what turned Chelsie wrong-side-out was that *she* was that other woman!

It would have boosted Chelsie's pride considerably if Abi could have had one noticeable fault instead of all those charming virtues to her credit. When Chelsie counted all her failing graces and compared herself to Abi, she realized she would never be the lady Abi was.

Chelsie was too spirited and vivacious to be contained within the narrow confines of womanhood. Her father had never deprived her of social outlets for her rambunctiousness. And because Evan Channing rarely denied Chelsie her whims, she had grown up doing exactly what she pleased and saying what she felt. She had become more the misfit than the lady. That was painfully obvious when she compared herself to Abi Shaw, who was very nearly perfect, in Chelsie's estimation.

After the conversation veered from politics to raising tobacco, Abi turned questioning eyes to the elegant blond who held Neil's undivided attention.

"Tell us the news from London, Duchess," she requested with sincere interest. "I have not had the pleasure of touring abroad since our fund-graising mission to improve the schools and education in the colonies."

Chelsie darted Jarred a discreet glance, watching him wince as if he feared she would fumble when placed on the firing line. Well, Jarred the cynic McAlister was going to be surprised. London was her stomping ground, and she had to pretend nothing.

"London is as London always is," Chelsie began as she touched her napkin to her lips. "Concerts are constantly being held at Covent Gardens to entertain the gentry who congregate there for the season."

One thick brow rose as Chelsie cited the favorite haunts of the rich and famous. Big deal, Jarred mused as he sank back in his chair to view this phony duchess in action. So what if Chelsie knew where the wealthy aristocrats passed the time? Obviously she had heard of these places—who hadn't? At least she was playing her part superbly. No one would have guessed that in actuality she was a peasant with a princess's tastes.

"Many visitors from the colonies still flock to the New England Coffee House to exchange news from home and compare their experiences in London," Chelsie went on to say. "The tavern of Mile End still serves the finest currant wine to be had in all England, and the Goose Green Fair has attracted hundreds of eager visitors."

"My favorite site was always the Garden of Medical Plants at Chelsea," Neil inserted with a nostalgic smile. "I could spend days there and at Gresham College, viewing the scientific collections."

Chelsie smiled impishly at Neil. "I much prefer the theater to the botanical gardens. David Garrick has transformed British theater into a fascinating art with his incredible acting abilities."

Of course this wily actress preferred the theater, Jarred silently smirked. Just look at the performance she was giving! She should receive an award for her portrayal of a regal duchess.

Her attention refocused on Abi, who listened eagerly to references of places she had once visited while staying with relatives in London. "If you are active in the committee for bettering education in the colonies, you should contact Dr. John Fothergill and Thomas Hollis. They have been instrumental in assisting colonists who come to London to study medicine, law, and the fine arts. They are both eager to supply the most up-to-date literature. I'm sure they would be most cooperative and very useful in your undertakings."

Wearing a mocking grin, Jarred raised his glass in silent toast. "Is there anyone you don't know in London, duchess?" The question sounded innocent enough to the others who were seated at the table, but Chelsie knew that Jarred was subtly taunting her.

"Personally?" Chelsie displayed a tolerant smile. "There are many aristocrats to whom I have been formally introduced in court," she qualified. "But I cannot say that I know each of them well. Because of my father's interests in racing and politics, I have had many opportunities to meet not only statesmen and other distinguished gentry, but also foreign dignitaries."

"Jarred met quite a few potentates while he was studying in England," Kyle interjected. "He made contact with John Hanbury, who has been supplying a market for our colonial products. John treated Jarred like a son while he was abroad. And in turn, Jarred has offered him legal advice in land speculation here in the colonies. When Grant traveled to London, he was received into John's home with open arms."

"I'm sure the duchess has met John," Jarred remarked, casting Chelsie another taunting grin that made her yearn to rearrange his ruggedly handsome features. "She seems to know everybody who is anybody."

Chelsie pasted on an artificial smile and put a stranglehold on her stemmed goblet, wishing it was Jarred's neck. "Aye, my father has done business with John Hanbury on occasion," she informed him in a honeyed tone. For a long, deliberate moment, Chelsie allowed her gaze to glide over Jarred's broad chest and the sling that cradled his wrenched arm. Too bad she hadn't broken that appendage when she fell on him, she mused spitefully. "I'm sure we have a great many friends in common, since Jarred traveled extensively with the aristocrats of London."

Mischief flickered in her eyes. "After getting to know you these past few weeks, Jarred, I'm certain we have another mutual acquaintance. Surely you have tripped the light fantastic with Sir Francis Dashwood, the fast-living leader of gentry who is a member of Parliament. He loves to entertain guests at what he refers to as the Hell-Fire Club — his privately owned establishment on the grounds of his sprawling country estate."

Jarred was in middrink when Chelsie suggested he had consorted with Dashwood. To those less familiar with London, the remark meant no more than Jarred's association with a member of Parliament. But to Jarred it was a well-aimed stab in the back. He had sucked in his breath so quickly, shocked by Chelsie's subtle insinuation, that he nearly strangled. The sangaree lodged in his throat and he wheezed and sputtered to catch his breath.

Kyle reached over to whack his son between the shoulder blades before he choked to death on his drink. Chelsie peered at Jarred with those enormous green eyes that seemed full of sympathy and concern, though they were, Jarred knew, anything but!

Jarred was absolutely certain that nothing would have pleased her more than to see him reduce himself to severe coughing spasms. And he was right. Chelsie delighted in giving Jarred exactly what he deserved. Judging by Jarred's startled reaction to her remark, the rascal knew all about Sir Francis Dashwood and his perverted orgies and black masses which were held at the Hell-Fire Club.

When Jarred finally regained his breath, Chelsie smiled questioningly. "You have seen Dashwood's fascinating garden, haven't you?" she taunted him, loving every minute of it.

"As a matter of fact, I have," Jarred croaked like a sick bullfrog. "Have you, duchess?"

The gardens to which Chelsie had referred lay far from the tower of Dashwood's elaborate manor, surrounded by a thicket of trees that protected them from the rest of the estate. One particular garden had been carefully laid out to form the offensive picture of a naked woman, made entirely of shrubbery. Fountains placed at strategic points had visiting ladies blushing profusely.

If that wasn't lurid enough, an abbey had been built on the grounds near the ruins of a medieval monastery. Dashwood and his evil order of the Friars of St. Francis played the sacrilegious roles of the apostles in a parody that ridiculed holy ritual. Pornographic paintings had been sketched on the ceiling, and the most incredible collection of graphic books in all of England lined the shelves of Dashwood's secluded library. The perverted lecher had even stooped to importing prostitutes from London and dressing them as nuns when he held his demented orgies.

Chelsie smiled like the Cheshire cat in response to Jarred's question about whether or not she had frequented the grounds. She wasn't about to say yea or nay, even though she and one of her more adventurous friends had sneaked into the garden to ascertain if all the sordid rumors they had heard were true. They were!

"Ah, what scrumptious dessert," Chelsie enthused as the servant set the creamy pudding before her.

"If Dashwood's estate is a must, I shall have to make a note to visit it when I begin my studies at Middle Temple," Daniel announced, having grown tired of being excluded from the conversation in which the light of his life was the focal point. It was bad enough that Daniel had to watch his oldest brother fawn over Chelsie. But being left completely out was the last straw for the lovesick pup.

Jarred glanced quickly at Grant, who had accompanied him to Dashwood's club. Grant was doing a magnificent job of hiding his amusement behind the glass poised at his lips. Chelsie had buried the hatchet in Jarred's back with her references, and Grant almost burst out laughing when his brother strangled on his drink.

"By the time you arrive in England, Dashwood's club may no longer be in existence," Chelsie predicted. "I have heard gossip of public scandal. Some of Sir Francis' activities have been questioned by other members of Parliament, my father included. If, by chance, he is driven from public office and into seclusion, perhaps Jarred can provide you with a visual picture of the intriguing garden. Jarred strikes me as a man very much interested in *hort*iculture. . . ."

This time both Grant and Jarred choked on their drinks. While they sputtered and coughed, Chelsie bit back an ornery grin. It did her heart good to catch Jarred off balance. It served that rascal right after all the humiliation and frustration he'd put her through.

Score one for the duchess, Jarred thought as he wheezed to inhale a breath. Sooner or later *someone* was bound to ask him to describe those sordid gardens at Dashwood's estate, he just knew it! And he would be forced to lie through his teeth. There was no way in hell he was going to inform the guests that a naked woman had been etched in shrubbery. Damn Chelsie's hide! She had purposely put him on the spot.

When the meal finally ended, Jarred couldn't wait to take a stroll around the grounds with harmless Abi Shaw on his arm. She didn't require that Jarred be mentally alert every second. Unfortunately, Neil invited himself to join the engaged couple and Jarred was forced to sharpen his mental weapons once again, since Chelsie would be accompanying them. Of all the rotten luck!

And Chelsie held true to form. She didn't let up for a minute. She mentioned every shady tavern within a hundred miles of London, asking if Jarred was familiar with the establishments and their notorious dens of prostitution. Although there were some sixteen thousand gin mills and infamous taverns in London, Chelsie insulted Jarred by suggesting he had frequented one and all. And she inferred that he had sipped ale at the other seven thousand taverns and adjoining brothels in the London suburbs. Within an hour Jarred had been poked by so many sharp jibes that he felt like a human pincushion. Enough was enough!

"Neil, why don't you show Abi the new colt and mare Papa purchased in Annapolis while the duchess and I pause to rest," Jarred suggested, fighting to disguise his irritation. "My arm is beginning to pain me a bit, and I'm sure Chelsie's is too."

"My pleasure," Neil murmured, taking Abi's arm to lead her away.

"My arm isn't . . ." Chelsie started to protest.

Jarred clamped his hand over Chelsie's mouth only to have his fingers chewed. "Ouch! Damn!" he growled, then promptly removed his hand.

"I prefer to join Abi and Neil," she insisted as she aimed herself in the retreating couple's direction.

Jarred caught her arm as she breezed by and dragged her back beside him. "You are going nowhere until we have a private conversation, *witch*," he hissed, his voice ominous and threatening.

A lesser woman would have shrunk from the lion's muted growl. Chelsie, however, did not. She deflected Jarred's murderous glare without batting an eye.

"We have nothing to say to each other," she declared, elevating a stubborn chin.

"We have plenty to discuss, and I have just begun talking," he snapped brusquely.

"What a pity," Chelsie sniffed in a flippant tone. "I am already through listening."

When Chelsie wormed for freedom, Jarred yanked her back to breathe down her neck. "One word from me and you will be exposed for the charlatan you are," he muttered menacingly. "I do not intend to spend the remainder of the evening wondering if Duchess Porcupine intends to stab me with her poisonous quills."

"You wouldn't be offended if you hadn't slept your way across England, entertaining all the whores who flock around Lady Guise's bagnio, where explicit works of art are painted on the ceilings for the amusement of each concubine's male guest," she sniped. "When your father informed me you had studied law and taken the bar examination, he presumed you earned a respectable degree in London. Little does Kyle know the *bars* you *examined* were the ones that were situated beside the bordellos of not only famous but also obscure courtesans."

"I am not a connoisseur of ceilings in bagnios, and I will have you know I have not spent more time on my back than on my feet," Jarred flashed furiously.

"Nay?" One dainty brow lifted as she raked the fuming rogue with scornful mockery. "You certainly couldn't prove it by me."

"Nay, I have not," Jarred confirmed in a booming voice.

"How refreshing to learn you earned your law degree the proper, respectable way." Her marveling tone was filled with sarcasm. Chelsie implied she didn't believe him for a minute.

"And quit trying to change the subject," Jarred scowled. "We are discussing your mischievous prank, not my escapades in England."

"I have not once offended your fiancée," Chelsie reminded him sharply. "That was what you demanded of me, and I have honored your request. In fact, I like Abi. 'Tis a pity you aren't good enough for a lady such as she."

"You will be pleased to know I. . . ." Jarred's voice trailed off when his family and their guest paraded out of the front door to inspect Kyle's prize colt and brood mare.

"I will be pleased about what?" Chelsie prompted in a quieter voice. "That you agree you aren't good enough for Abi and that you plan to kill yourself to spare her a life with you as her husband? How noble and gallant of you."

Jarred studied the sassy vixen, wondering how she would look wearing a choker formed by his fingers. As for himself, Jarred loved the idea.

"If I carried the situation to such extravagant extremes, I should marry you so you could make my life hell . . . as if you haven't already," he muttered acrimoniously. "Those three wishes you granted me are indeed curses."

"I have already told you I wouldn't marry you if you were the last man on earth," Chelsie sneered, but not loudly enough to be overheard by the approaching family and guests.

"And I wouldn't ask you if you were the last woman," Jarred assured her hatefully. "I'd kill myself first."

"I'll fetch the pistol," she offered spitefully.

And there they stood like two tigers scrutinizing their opponents, wanting to pounce but unable to satisfy their vengeance without making a scene in front of the congregation that was sweeping down the brick path to interrupt them.

If only Chelsie could have gotten her hands on this infuriating varmint, she would have shaken him until his pearly white teeth fell out. Oh, how she would love to give him another taste of his own medicine—delivered to his mouth via her fist!

Chapter 16

Kyle McAlister wedged himself between the duchess and his son, unaware that he had strolled onto a battlefield with two warring foes. "Come along, Chelsie," he insisted. "Amos wants another look at the colt that is going to beat his stallion in the next race."

"That will be the day!" Amos expelled a volcanic snort. "Your spindly colt will trip over his uncoordinated legs and fall on his face long before he outruns the quality thoroughbred *I* purchased. Besides, your trainer informed me the colt doesn't take kindly to instruction. You have to learn to control him before you can put him on the track," he goaded Kyle.

It was with great relief that Chelsie ambled alongside Kyle, leaving Jarred to trail behind with his younger brothers. And it was fortunate that Kyle had interrupted them when he had, Chelsie mused as she tossed Kyle a cheery smile. She had seriously considered knocking the tar out of his second son.

"Perhaps you should enlist the duchess to train your contrary colt," Jarred suggested, smiling sardonically. "She is an authority on contrariness."

Although Chelsie winced at the barb that referred to her midnight ride on Trumpeter, Kyle took the suggestion at face value. " 'Tis an excellent idea," he enthused. "Chelsie informed me that she is familiar with the English technique of training horses. Perhaps she can convey the latest skills to my trainers."

"I'm sure she can," Jarred smirked. "Indeed, I doubt there is anything Chelsie cannot do and do exceptionally well."

"Why, thank you for the kind compliment," Chelsie replied

with a sugar-coated smile. "I would be more than happy to tend the colt."

Jarred growled under his breath when Chelsie opened the colt's stall. Although the trainer issued a warning that the steed delighted in kicking his attendants every chance he got, Chelsie reached out a gentle hand and spoke softly to Trumpeter. The fidgety colt ceased his stamping and snorting and stood stock-still while Chelsie eased around to face him.

"Well, I'll be damned," Kyle breathed in disbelief. Each time he went near the high-spirited animal, Trumpeter came unglued. But when Chelsie stroked his velvet muzzle, the copper dun colt was putty in her hands.

"High-bred champions require a tender touch and soothing words," Chelsie murmured to Kyle. "This steed has a generous heart, I think. In time he will come to accept you. Once you have gained his trust, he will run himself into the ground to please you."

"It looks to me as if the colt is partial to women and mistrusting of my male trainers," Kyle said, softly stupefied by the abrupt change in the steed's temperament.

"From the look of things I would say you have hit upon the problem," Jarred murmured as he watched Chelsie charm the feisty colt into behaving like an obedient puppy.

"The colt doesn't seem to be the least bit intimidated by you," Kyle said in a bewildered tone. "You possess a rare gift of gentleness, duchess."

There she was in the limelight again, Jarred thought disgustedly. Chelsie this . . . Chelsie that. She was always upstaging him and doing something to impress Kyle. The old man would be in for the shock of his life if he discovered this little sorceress was nothing but a thieving pauper who had a unique rapport with animals. Most witches did have a way with creatures, Jarred reminded himself sourly.

Trumpeter lowered his head, nudging Chelsie when she paused from stroking him. Tittering, Chelsie playfully scratched his forelock. "With your permission, squire, I would like to work with the colt."

" 'Tis a waste of time," Amos declared matter-of-factly. "That leggy animal will never outrun my stallion or my brown mare on the track."

"He might if Chelsie trains and rides him," Kyle muttered in offended dignity.

"Papa!" Jarred pushed his way past his brothers to confront his father face-to-face. "That is absurd. You cannot ask the duchess to become your lady jockey!"

"Of course he can," Chelsie contradicted, unoffended. "I would be delighted to accept Amos's challenge on the track."

"This is ridiculous!" Jarred snorted derisively. "I forbid it!"

Jarred knew he had lost the debate the moment he stared into his father's unrelenting gaze. He wanted a victory over Amos Shaw so badly he could taste it. Kyle would put the King himself on that long-legged colt if he thought he had a chance of winning this grudge match.

A broad smile spread across Kyle's face and he nodded affirmatively. " 'Tis settled, then. Chelsie will ride the colt at the meeting in Annapolis next spring. And if the duke arrives before that time, he will remain as our houseguest until after the race."

"Do you honestly think a dignified duke is going to permit his daughter to ride in this match between two proud old fools?" Jarred sniffed disrespectfully. "For God's sake, the duke wouldn't believe you had the nerve to ask her in the first place!"

"My father won't complain," Chelsie assured Jarred whose cynical glare was cutting her to shreds. "The duke is of the opinion that a woman has a right to do whatever she is capable of doing. And I have ridden in more than one English race."

"Of course you have," Jarred countered, his mocking tone negating his words. "I'm sure you have also flown to the moon."

"Jarred McAlister, mind that runaway tongue of yours!" Rebecca scolded her nephew. "That is no way to speak to a properly bred young lady. You were raised better than to talk like that!"

Jarred rolled his eyes skyward, summoning divine patience. Now his aunt was taking up for that sassy little charlatan. This lie he had concocted had mushroomed to incredible proportions. It was all his fault for allowing his family to believe

Chelsie was of royal heritage. Damn it, he should have had his head examined for bringing this minx to Easthaven. She was double her weight in trouble!

"As soon as Neil deems your arm is properly healed, you can begin training the colt," Kyle announced with a bright smile.

"Why wait?" Jarred questioned, his voice heavy with sarcasm. "The duchess is so extraordinary, I wouldn't be surprised if she could ride that feisty colt bareback . . . with one hand . . . in the dark. . . ."

"*Now* who is being ridiculous?" Kyle growled.

Ah, if only Kyle knew the truth—Chelsie had already accomplished that very feat. And Jarred wouldn't have been toting around his arm in a sling if he hadn't tried to cart Chelsie back to her room by way of the trellis without the rest of his family knowing what she had been doing at the stroke of midnight.

"It seems to me Neil should have quarantined Chelsie in her room. Those who have spent too much time around her appear to have developed a case of incurable idiocy," Jarred exploded in frustration.

"I will *not* have you making such disrespectful remarks about the duchess," Daniel blustered, glaring at his older brother.

"Oh, shut up, Danny," Jarred snapped. "You aren't the damsel's knight in shining armor!"

When Daniel puffed up with irritation and looked as if he was contemplating knocking Jarred flat, Grant grabbed his taut arm, holding the youngest McAlister at bay.

"Calm down, Danny," Grant soothed. "Our older brother is in another of these black moods that have been plaguing him of late. As much as you would like to try, I don't think you will be able to beat him out of his bad temperament." A ridiculing smile pursed Grant's lips as he focused his attention on Jarred, who looked as if he were chewing on a lemon rind. "As you said, big brother, those who get too close to the duchess have developed a severe case of stupidity. And you have been closer to her than the rest of us. . . ."

Although the remark was spoken so confidently that no one overheard, Jarred felt his body go rigid with anger. He wanted to throw something—starting and ending with that sassy little firebrand who had turned him wrong-side-out and put him at odds with his family.

It was obvious that Daniel was hopelessly infatuated with Chelsie and Grant had been fascinated with her since the day he'd met her. The rest of the family was no better, Jarred mused resentfully. They all came to her defense and ostracized him for pointing out the idiocy of their behavior. All three of his brothers were so bedazzled by Chelsie's vibrant personality and blinding beauty they didn't even know they had been *had!* It was up to Jarred to ensure things didn't get completely out of hand, and in his estimation, the situation had just reached a critical point! Damn that vixen, she was making fools of all the McAlisters.

"Speaking of Neil. What became of him?" Amos questioned, changing the topic of conversation before the McAlister brothers came to blows. "And where has Abi wandered off to?"

At the sound of his name, Neil appeared from the back of the stable. Thrusting his hands into his pockets, Neil ambled toward the congregation who surrounded Trumpeter's stall. His twinkling brown eyes settled on Chelsie and then shifted to Amos.

A muddled frown gathered on Jarred's brow. "I thought Abi was with you."

"She was," Neil affirmed as his attention circled back to Chelsie. He broke into another cryptic grin that worried her more than a mite. "But Abi decided to return to the house. You just missed her."

Chelsie surveyed Neil's mysterious smile and felt a lump of apprehension constrict her throat. Surely he hadn't informed Abi of what he had inadvertently discovered about Jarred and Chelsie. He was her friend and confidant . . . wasn't he? Abi had better not be in tears, dashing off to dry her eyes before she was forced to face her father, the McAlisters, and her philandering fiancé!

"Perhaps I should check on her," Jarred mumbled as he pivoted on his heels. "I'll leave the winged colt and his mystical mistress to their disciples of black magic."

"My, but Jarred has been in a fit of temper tonight," Kyle sighed as his second son stomped off in a huff. "I think he needs Abi's soothing disposition to calm him down." His sparkling gaze darted to Amos. "I would like to see those two set their wedding date. A two-year engagement is plenty long enough, and I am anxious for grandchildren."

"I suggested a spring wedding to Abi, but she tactfully indicated that I should mind my own business," Amos chuckled. "Neither of them seem as eager as we are."

Chelsie fell silent, absently brushing her hand over Trumpeter's broad head. Why did it strike a sensitive nerve to hear Kyle talk of marrying Jarred off to Abi? She didn't give a tinker's damn what that devil did as long as he wasn't doing it with her, Chelsie tried to convince herself.

When the others ambled back to the house for a game of piquet, Chelsie strolled around the sprawling estate. It was the first chance she had to view the magnificent plantation in daylight. The three-story brick dwelling towered in the sunset like a monument to sophistication and propriety. A wide veranda encircled the back and north side of the mansion and a breezeway connected the two wings that jutted off to the east and west. A tall colonnaded porch loomed over the front door, forming a grand entrance to the stately manor. A stone's throw from the gigantic structure were the detached kitchen and servants' quarters, all of which were whitewashed and well manicured.

Inhaling a sigh of appreciation, Chelsie drank in the awe-inspiring sight of the McAlister plantation. The last rays of sun splashed across the carpet of thick grass, bathing the still of the evening in shades of bronze, copper, and gold. Easthaven held an unmatched elegance with its colorful gardens and numerous outbuildings, stable, and private wharf.

Her assessing gaze swung back to the mansion to peer at the many chimneys that reached up into the cloudless sky. Thin curls of smoke drifted upward to put a faint blemish on an otherwise flawless landscape. In some ways this plantation reminded Chelsie of Chessfield. The self-contained community was immaculate, displaying its owner's appreciation for esthetics. Even the stable where Kyle kept his prize horses was tended with great care and pride. The horses themselves were treated as if they were members of the family.

Aye, Easthaven was the picture of elegance and it soothed

her troubled soul just to gaze upon it. Oh, how she would have delighted in swinging onto Trumpeter's back to thunder across the meadow, as she had done so often at Chessfield. Reluctantly her eyes drifted back to the manor. Since the McAlisters were entertaining guests, it would be rude of her not to join them, though she would much prefer to be elsewhere, especially while Jarred was underfoot. She would only punish herself by going inside and staring at Jarred from a distance—wanting him when she shouldn't and couldn't have him. And undoubtedly, she would be forced to resist the urge to harass Jarred out of mere childish vindictiveness.

Mechanically, Chelsie strode toward the great house, telling herself she didn't really want Jarred, that he was just a bad habit she had difficulty unlearning. But when Jarred's rich baritone voice wafted its way from the parlor, her heart wrenched in her chest. This evening should have confirmed the fact that Jarred belonged to another woman. But Chelsie, despite her firm resolve, couldn't quite let go of this ill-fated attraction for a man who was definitely off limits to her. Blast it, she did feel something for that impossible man, even when she hadn't wanted to. Chelsie hated to admit it, but she did care. It hurt to know she was nothing more than an answer to Jarred's physical needs in stolen moments of passion.

Composing herself as best she could, Chelsie breezed into the room if she didn't have a care in the world. Jarred was in the process of analyzing the difficulties on the western frontier. When he paused from his soliloquy to glance at her, Chelsie turned to Neil and flashed him a smile. Pretending not to notice that Abi was sitting cozily by Jarred's side, Chelsie gracefully sank down beside Neil. She was, however, greatly relieved that Abi didn't look as if she had been crying a bucket of tears. Apparently Neil hadn't divulged her sordid secret to Abi.

"I'm afraid the American west has become the battleground for England and France, who invent war just because they are natural-born enemies," Jarred said bleakly. "But this time the situation has reversed its usual pattern. Ordinarily the battle begins in Europe and spreads to America, as it has done in the past two French-and-Indian wars. This time the shots we fired at Great Meadows set off the chain reaction that will inevitably spread through Europe.

"France has cast her greedy eyes on the rich valleys of the Ohio River, claiming it as part of her empire. Our colonists on the outposts of civilization fear the intrusion of the French troops will inevitably lead to their domination in the heart of the continent. The French insist that LaSalle claimed all lands bordering the Mississippi and Ohio Rivers. The British base their right of settlement on Cabot's discovery and exploration of the interior of the continent."

Jarred paused to sip his pumpkin flib and then eased back on the sofa, stretching his long legs before him. "The French have made allies of several Indian tribes who are driving out colonial settlers right and left, pushing them back toward our coasts. The militias we sent to build forts along the frontier have met with fierce resistance. For three months I fought alongside Christopher Gist and Lieutenant Colonel Washington, struggling against overwhelming odds. We entrenched ourself at the hastily constructed palisade we called Fort Necessity. But we were outnumbered and forced to surrender to the strong forces of the French and Indians. Without regular army recruits from England, we cannot hope to match the white-coated, well-drilled French army officers and their cunning allies who hide in the forest and ambush their enemies with alarming success."

"What suggestions did you offer to the governor and the Assembly?" Kyle questioned somberly.

"I cannot see any hope of fending off the French without British support," Jarred replied in a grim tone. "The French are trying to take advantage of our colonists and the Crown has been dragging its feet about issuing ultimatums to France. Maryland and Virginia are ready for all out war, but King George the Second maintains that, at present, he is officially at peace with France. However, the Crown has finally agreed to send reinforcements with General Braddock as the commander of the expedition."

"I doubt General Braddock will be of much use to the colonies," Chelsie interjected without thinking.

She was bound to incite an argument with Jarred when she spoke her mind. She usually did. He always took offense when

202

she voiced her opinion. Sure enough, Jarred countered with a ridiculing smile.

"I should have known the general is a personal friend of yours, duchess. Do tell us why the general won't suit our purposes," Jarred invited, even though he looked as if he didn't give a whit what she thought. He didn't.

"Edward Braddock was not cut out to fight on the outposts of civilization," she prophesied. "He may be a brilliant military strategist on designated battlefields where he is accustomed to fighting a gentleman's war, but he knows nothing of tactics on the frontier. I don't think Braddock will adjust to battling the French and Indians in the manner you have just described to us. Bushwhacking is not Braddock's style. He would consider himself too dignified to stoop to such sneaky tactics. In Europe, battles are called off because of darkness and inclement weather. The general and his staff retire to their lavish headquarters to feast, plan their strategy, and lounge in the arms of their mistresses. Braddock will be reluctant to leave his paramour, since he is so fond of her."

Shocked gasps rippled through the room. Jarred was the only one who wasn't caught off guard by Chelsie's frank appraisal of General Braddock and his philosophy of war. Even if they rarely agreed on any issue, Jarred had come to expect Chelsie's candor.

"I'm sure the general will be open to suggestions from seasoned frontiersmen who have spent the past two years in conflict against the French and Indians. And surely the general can tear himself away from his beloved lady long enough to answer our call for assistance."

Chelsie gave her silver-blond head a negative shake. "The lady in question means the world to Edward." Her pointed gaze pinned Jarred down. "There are some men who hold love in the same high regard as patriotism and honor. The general's curse comes from the fact that he is unable to marry the woman he loves and his downfall will be his refusal to sway from his customary methods of battle. I rather suspect he will insist upon fighting European-style, with his men standing in columns, marching elbow-to-elbow, and firing only upon his command. I fear the regular army will fall like sitting ducks in

203

their bright red uniforms that can be spotted a half mile away in a fog and two miles away on a good day when visibility is clear."

Her bleak prediction had Jarred muttering under his breath. "I hope that isn't the case, but if the campaign should happen to go awry, the Assemblymen from each colony are preparing to send delegates to Albany to discuss the need for our own plan of defense against invasion. The French have proved their desire to make themselves the lords of the North American continent. If we do not unite and establish our own funds to support our own strong military defense against intruders, we may find ourselves pledging allegiance to the King of France.

"When are you and the other delegates leaving for Albany?" Abi inquired solemnly.

Jarred was leaving? Chelsie should have been overjoyed by the news that this infuriating man would be out of her hair for an extended period of time. Unfortunately, that was not the case. The news had the reverse effect on her.

"I am to meet with George Washington in Richmond at the first of next week. Then I will travel to New York for the convention," Jarred informed his fiancée. "I will have to impose on Neil to accompany you to the ball the Newtons are giving week after next. I doubt I will be back in less than a month." His gaze swung to Chelsie, flinging her a smug smile before he focused his attention on his older brother. "Will you stand in my stead, Neil?"

"As you wish, Jarred," Neil quietly affirmed.

Chelsie fumed. She would have had to be an idiot not to realize Jarred had purposely requested that Neil accompany Abi. That would leave Chelsie the odd man out, so to speak. That role was becoming familiar to Chelsie. Jarred was always shoving her aside as if she counted for nothing. And that was exactly what she was worth, in his opinion. Damn his soul! Just wait until her father got here to confirm that she was who she said she was. Jarred McAlister would realize he had made a complete ass of himself. He would probably change his tune when he learned she was a wealthy duchess. Most people did. But Chelsie would know that deep down inside, Jarred didn't like her all that much, no matter what he said to compensate for treating her so abominably. As far as Chelsie was concerned, Jarred had dug his own grave.

"I also hope I can impose on Grant to oversee the workings of the plantations while I'm away again," Jarred added as he glanced hopefully at his blond brother. "The paperwork is all in order and the arrangements for shipping and selling the crop have already been made."

"I doubt I can properly fill your shoes, big brother," Grant teased playfully. "But I shall fumble along as best I can."

"Well, enough of this serious talk," Rebecca announced as she vaulted to her feet. "I have been waiting all night to display my talents at the spinet while the rest of you dance."

As soon as his sister struck up a lively tune, Kyle took Chelsie's hand and led her in the minuet. Before the song ended Daniel cut in, holding Chelsie a mite closer than necessary. Chelsie danced with every man in the crowd except Jarred, who didn't bother to request the opportunity to spin her around the floor. He stuck to Abi like glue.

Although Chelsie would have relished the chance to tread on Jarred's feet, he was wise enough to take a wide berth around her. Chelsie was responsible for his sprained arm, and Jarred was sure that ornery minx had designs on his feet as well.

Finally Chelsie could tolerate no more. Seeing Jarred and Abi together had an unsettling effect on her emotions. Employing the excuse of a throbbing arm, Chelsie retired to her room to pummel her pillow. She was in a quandary: things were not working out as she had anticipated. The idea was for her to make Jarred fall in love with her so she could jilt him for treating her so horribly. But she wasn't enjoying one smidgen of spiteful satisfaction. In fact, she felt. . . .

Chelsie didn't know exactly how she felt. She was confused by some odd emotion that she couldn't comprehend, and she was irritated by this ridiculous jealousy she had no right to experience when she saw Abi and Jarred together. If only she could go home where she belonged! Perhaps she could return before her father had time to pack his belongings and come to fetch her. If she could borrow money from Kyle and book passage to London, she could forget about that blue-eyed rake.

Surely Kyle wouldn't hesitate in giving her a loan . . . surely he would, she realized with a dejected sigh. Kyle was depending on her to train Trumpeter and satisfy his thirst for victory over Amos Shaw. As much as Chelsie wanted to go home, she couldn't overlook Kyle's generous hospitality. She had made an obligation to Kyle, and her father had taught her to respect a promise made. And perhaps her emotions wouldn't be in such turmoil, since Jarred wouldn't be around to frustrate her. It would be good practice for her to grow accustomed to life without that raven-haired rogue. When she finally returned to England she would never see Jarred again, and she would slam the door on the past.

Clinging to that encouraging thought, Chelsie peeled off the sling that cradled her left arm and slid between the sheets. From this day forward, she wasn't going to spare Jarred Mc-Alister another thought. He was going to become a closed chapter in her life. And when he returned from the convention in Albany, she would be immune to his dark, sensual charm. Why, in a couple of days, she probably wouldn't even remember how her body trembled when it made familiar contact with his. She would forget the sound of his baritone voice, the compelling fragrance of his cologne. She wouldn't be entranced by those hypnotic blue eyes that danced with devilry. She would never again crave his skillful kisses and those soul-shattering caresses. . . .

This wasn't helping matters one whit, Chelsie realized when betraying tingles trickled down her spine. Remembering what she planned to forget about Jarred McAlister provoked the forbidden memories to emerge from the shadowed corners of her heart. And if she wasn't careful, she was going to fall in love with that stubborn, inconsiderate, impossible man! *That* she didn't need, especially when she was trying so hard to put their reckless affair in proper perspective.

After an hour of tossing and turning, Chelsie swung out of bed and stamped her foot. She felt like slamming a few doors and throwing things. But since she had been living under the McAlister's roof, she was forced to limit her tantrums. Among other things, she had learned several lessons in self-control. She had resorted to giving herself silent pep talks, but they hadn't helped to reduce her frustration one tittle. Jarred's tormenting memory still preyed heavily on her mind. Feeling incredibly restless, Chelsie slipped her tender arm into the sling and tiptoed into Jarred's room. Rifling through the dresser drawers, she located the clothes she had borrowed for her midnight ride a few days earlier.

Chelsie wiggled from her gown and shrugged on the ill-fitting clothes. With swift, precise strides, she crossed the room and sailed onto the terrace.

A startled gasp erupted from her lips when she ran right smack into the last person she wanted to see — Jarred.

"Going somewhere, duchess?"

His voice was husky with unfulfilled desire — a condition aggravated by standing and watching Chelsie peel off her clothes while she was unaware she had a captive audience of one. Jarred had returned to his room, but he too was too restless to sleep. Aimlessly he had ambled around the terrace to wrestle with his troubled thoughts. Hearing the quiet creak of the door, he pivoted in the shadows to watch the apparition float across his dark room. His all-consuming gaze hadn't missed one alluring detail when Chelsie stood in the moonlight to shuck her nightgown. It had been difficult to stand outside on the balcony when he ached to scoop her up in his arms and caress what his eyes had beheld.

Why did this minx have to arouse and torment him so? He had an obligation to Abi. Yet his gaze constantly strayed to this blond-haired hellion. This battle of mind over body was wearing him out. Try as he may, Jarred couldn't get her off his mind. And for the past ten minutes he had been circumnavigating the terrace, telling himself he was not going to sneak into Chelsie's room to check on her the way he usually did when no one was around to know he constantly watched over her while she slept.

Chelsie mustered all her will-power, determined not to crumble beneath the velvety resonance of Jarred's voice. She hated it when that male sensuality came pouring out and caused goose bumps to cruise across her flesh. When he used that seductive tone of voice, it reminded her of the times they had lain in

207

each other's arms and he had whispered his need for her . . .
Chelsie caught herself the instant before the tantalizing memory
buckled another barrier of her defense.

"I'm going riding," she announced in a tone that brooked no
argument.

"Not on McAlister stock, you're not." Jarred towered over
her, fighting like the devil to keep from pulling her luscious
body to his.

Chelsie retreated a step before she was completely suffocated
by his nearness. Why did she have to be so vividly aware of
him? And why did he have to resort to that other tone of voice
that got her hackles up? First he bombarded her with that
provocative whisper that aroused secret memories, then he
switched to that annoying tone teeming with arrogance and
male supremacy.

"The copper dun colt is my horse," she snapped. "Why do
you think Trumpeter responds so readily to me?"

Jarred hooted in disbelief. This witch honestly expected him
to believe she was a sophisticated duchess and that the horses
were from her father's stock! Where did she get such audacity?
And who did she think she was talking to, anyway? The village
idiot?

"I'll tell you exactly why that colt buckles beneath your will.
'Tis the same reason I have been bedeviled by you. You are a
witch, and you have cast your spell on all of us!"

Chelsie curled her fingers, itching to encircle Jarred's thick
neck. "You are going to feel very foolish when my father shows
up, just see if you don't."

Another intimidating chuckle tumbled from his lips. "What
do you plan to do? Weave another of your incantations to
make this imaginary duke materialize from thin air?"

He was really asking for it, and Chelsie had to restrain
herself. Before she yielded to a spiteful retaliation that entailed
hitting Jarred's aquiline nose, Chelsie wheeled away.

Jarred's lean fingers fastened on her elbow, spinning her
around to face his intimidating smile. "Come down off your
high horse for once. You have no need to play your charade
with me. After all, I'm the one who landed you this role and
provided you with the necessary costume to make you look the

part."

"I hate you," Chelsie sputtered, unable to contain her frustration a moment longer.

"The feeling is mutual," Jarred growled.

The words were no more out of his mouth than he yielded to the irrepressible urge to capture those full, pouting lips. For a man who had just sworn his animosity, Jarred had the most peculiar way of showing how he felt. He hadn't meant to kiss her. He had spent the better part of the evening telling himself he was never going to get this close to temptation again. And he wouldn't have if Chelsie hadn't disrobed in front of him, leaving him to burn like a human bonfire.

When his sensuous lips rolled over hers, Chelsie feared her knees would fold. The searing imprint of his body upon hers melted her defenses. And he called *her* a witch? Ha! *He* was the one who wove magic spells and had her doing things she promised herself she would never do again. She was kissing him back. God, not again . . . this wizard pressed those warm, possessive lips to hers and she didn't have a defense left. It happened every blessed time!

When Chelsie came up for air, she was slapped in the face by cold, harsh reality: kissing this rake would solve absolutely nothing. That was what had gotten her in trouble in the first place. For once she was going to take firm control of her desires, refusing to let them dominate her common sense. She had to start denying herself the pleasure of his kisses and caresses sometime. If not now, she feared she never would!

Chelsie was prepared to crash through walls, if necessary, to remove herself from Jarred's close proximity. She was far too aware of him, too confused by the crosscurrents of emotions that hounded her. She wanted to be anywhere but here . . . with him . . . Especially with him!

Before Jarred could grab hold of her, Chelsie flung herself away from him and shot across the balcony like a discharging bullet. Quick and agile as he was, he was way too slow. Desperation put wings on Chelsie's feet, and she had already swung a leg over the railing before Jarred could shove his stalled mind into gear and pounce on her.

With a wordless scowl, Jarred bounded toward the railing

and leaned over to clench his fist in the nape of Chelsie's shirt. With his feet planted on the balcony, Jarred doubled his big body over the rail to keep a firm grip on the witch who was about to spirit off into the night.

Chelsie never did care much for being manhandled. Her temper exploded when Jarred refused to loosen his grip. Hissing obscenities, Chelsie clamped her hand on the trellis and dug her feet into the niches between the lathe when Jarred tried to hoist her back up to the terrace. Mustering every bit of strength, Chelsie pulled her feet from their precarious resting place on the trellis and let herself drop a quick two feet — using only her good arm as her lifeline.

Jarred was left holding her entire weight in one hand — the hand that was clenched in the collar of her shirt. A muted growl gushed from his lips when Chelsie's wily tactic abruptly yanked him off balance. Since his left arm was in a sling, he couldn't brace himself against the railing. And with his tall frame folded over the railing, he was top-heavy — especially since he was supporting his own weight as well as Chelsie's. Needless to say, gravity got the better of him.

A string of curses spewed from his lips as he passed Chelsie on his way down. The human fly had latched herself onto the trellis and secured her feet beneath her. But Jarred was in the process of making a swan dive without a pond of water beneath him. Frantically Jarred tried to contort his body in midair so he could grasp at the lattice. Unfortunately, he had only managed a ninety-degree turn before he crashed into the shrubs below — shrubs that still retained his imprint after his fall from days past.

When Jarred toppled from his perch, Chelsie instinctively closed her eyes and prayed that he wouldn't break his neck. She had winced when she heard Jarred land with a cursing thud in the bushes. Hesitantly she pried open one eye to see Jarred's limbs entangled with the branches of the shrubs. Swallowing with a gulp, she shinnied down the trellis to determine if there were any bones in his body that hadn't been broken at least once.

"Jarred? Are you all right?" Chelsie whispered to the tangled form in the bushes.

"Hell no!" Jarred grimaced, trying to move the ankle of his left foot—the foot that was practically wrapped around his neck! The attempt caused excruciating pain, and Jarred didn't try again.

"Don't move," Chelsie advised.

"I don't think I can," Jarred groaned miserably. He hurt all over. He knew the feeling well . . . thanks to this walking disaster with mischievous green eyes and silver-blond hair, he had found himself in the same predicament twice in one week.

Frantic, Chelsie darted around the corner of the house and breezed through the front door. Like a flying carpet she sailed up the steps to reach Neil's bedroom. Without knocking, she barged in to find Neil bare-chested and in the process of removing his breeches.

"Come quick," she insisted breathlessly. "Jarred fell in the bushes. This time I think he broke his ankle."

This was no laughing matter, but Neil couldn't help himself. Jarred had looked ridiculous with shrubs jutting out from under his arms and legs the last time Neil had come to his rescue. That same undignified picture popped to mind again, and Neil couldn't even mask his amusement behind an artificial cough.

"It isn't funny," Chelsie chastised him on the way down the steps. "I think Jarred is hurt."

Neil came to a screeching halt when he rounded the corner to find his brother's brawny body tied in knots. Another grin found his lips before he could smother it. Jarred swore vehemently.

"Don't you say anything, damn it," he snarled at Neil. "Not *one cursed word*. Just get me the hell out of here . . . again!"

Cautiously Neil leaned into the shrub to straighten the leg that suddenly seemed to have more joints than usual. Even though Jarred growled and hissed like a rabid dog, Neil dragged him from the shrubs.

"Don't put any weight on that leg," Neil instructed as he looped Jarred's arm over his shoulder for additional support.

"I'm not *that* stupid," Jarred muttered resentfully. His brother was treating him as if he didn't have enough common sense to fill a thimble.

"Nay?" Neil smirked unsympathetically. "Then how is it that you managed to fall into the same shrub twice? Are you training for a career as an acrobat?"

Neil's sarcasm was not well received. Jarred was already furious with himself for falling pell-mell into the bushes, and he was angry with Chelsie for involving him in another of her madcap escapades. Mostly with Chelsie, he decided, flashing her a murderous glare. If not for her clever tactic, he would have been standing on the terrace, pulling her back beside him instead of landing in the shrubs, bruising his pride and twisting his ankle. Lord, that was all he needed. He was already carrying one arm in a sling. Now he would require a crutch for walking. How was he going to explain this latest disaster to the rest of the family?

As Neil assisted his injured brother around the side of the house, Chelsie trailed a few steps behind them. Her shoulders slumped dejectedly. She hadn't meant to cause Jarred to take a spill. She had only tried to discourage him from stopping her from descending the trellis. If he hadn't truly hated her before, he most certainly did now, she reckoned. Maybe he was right. Maybe she was jinxed and her curse had begun to rub off on him.

When they reached the front of the house, Chelsie darted to Jarred's side to help him up the steps. But as luck would have it, she reached for his arm — the one that had been reinjured in his second fall.

Jarred sucked in his breath when Chelsie's attempt to assist him inflicted more pain on his already throbbing shoulder. "For God's sake, woman, don't touch me!" he yelped. "You've done enough damage for one night." With a quick glance to his brother, Jarred made a bitter request. "When this walking disaster finally does succeed in killing me, make sure her name is listed on my death certificate under cause of . . ."

Chelsie let go of his arm as if she were touching live coals. "I'm sorry, I didn't mean—"

"You're not sorry," Jarred growled as he hobbled up the steps. "And you are *just plain mean*. I saw you laughing at me on my way down."

"I was not!" Chelsie protested hotly.

"You were too!" Jarred harshly accused.

"If you two don't keep your voices down, the whole house is going to know what is going on," Neil muttered.

Both Jarred and Chelsie quickly clamped their mouths shut. Without daring to glance at Jarred, Chelsie opened the front door and stood back to let the two men enter. When they reached the landing, Neil smiled gently at Chelsie, who was chewing on her bottom lip, wondering if Jarred would ever forgive her for making him fall, cracking his ankle and wrenching his arm . . . twice. . . .

"I suggest you go to bed, duchess. I'll take care of Jarred," Neil volunteered.

Nodding in compliance, Chelsie went toward her own room. But it was well into the night before she managed to sleep. She kept hearing all sorts of growls and hisses in Jarred's room. He was furious, all right, she realized bleakly. He would never forgive her. Chelsie imagined this last escapade would keep Jarred from ever coming near her again. It proved to be an effective but rather drastic method of putting a halt to this star-crossed love affair. And it was certain that Chelsie would need to keep a low profile for the next few days. If she dared to venture too close to Jarred, even if only to express her sympathy and apology, he would most likely strangle her.

Blast it, she hadn't meant to hurt him, not really. But he would never believe that. Jarred Bull-headed McAlister had never believed anything she said! Why would he start now?

Chapter 17

After searching every nook and cranny in the mansion, Jarred hobbled outside to locate Chelsie. Since the dinner party four days earlier, Chelsie had avoided him completely, not that he would have been receptive to her visits.

For the first two days after his fall, Neil had kept Jarred bedridden and his left leg elevated. And for those two days Jarred lay there staring at his foot—one that was draped with cold packs to reduce the swelling. He had begun to understand why Chelsie had sneaked off into the night after she had been wounded. Staring at the same four walls day in and day out was monotonous.

Although Jarred hadn't forgiven that human hurricane for causing him to fall, twist his ankle, and reinjure his shoulder, his temper had ebbed. And before he left on his trip, he intended to give that misfit a few instructions . . . not that it would do any good, Jarred mused as he ambled outside in search of Chelsie. That independent minx had the infuriating habit of doing as she pleased. Jarred wasn't thrilled about leaving her to her own devices for an extended period of time. Since Eli was accompanying him to Albany, there would be no one at the plantation who knew the truth about Chelsie. That worried Jarred.

When Jarred limped into the stable on his cane, Kyle was conversing with his trainers and the copper dun colt was not in his stall. A rumble of thunder shook the rafters and Jarred frowned in concern. It was late afternoon and he hadn't seen hide nor hair of Chelsie or the feisty colt she had taken it upon herself to train. Blast it, that chit didn't have sense enough to come in out of the rain, and she was carrying this game of avoiding Jarred to ridiculous extremes.

Another peal of thunder reverberated through the stables, spurring Jarred to action. With determined strides, even though he still had a noticeable limp, Jarred marched over to retrieve his stallion from the stall.

"Where are you off to in such a rush?" Kyle wanted to know. "Did Neil give you permission to put excessive strain on that ankle after you stepped in a hole and twisted it?"

"I intend to find Chelsie," Jarred threw over his shoulder as he tossed the saddle onto his steed. "And nay, Neil didn't give me permission, but my ankle is feeling considerably better."

Jarred had concocted the convenient lie about stepping in a hole and about his ankle's condition improving. All this to protect that high-strung chit who always managed to get herself into trouble and take Jarred with her. Lord, why did he bother with that jinx of a woman?

"I think the duchess is taking this training business a mite too seriously," Jarred muttered as he shoved the bit into the roan stallion's mouth. "There is a storm approaching, and Chelsie isn't familiar with the type of storms that plague the coast. England is not accustomed to raging winds and lightning. The British expect only fog and drizzling rain." Grimacing, Jarred placed his left foot in the stirrup and swung into the saddle. "And the marsh can be treacherous if one doesn't know what to expect during a storm. There is no telling what Chelsie might do, since she isn't aware of the dangers of threatening weather conditions in these parts."

Gouging his steed, Jarred trotted from the stables, looking in all directions at once. Damn it all, where was that minx? She hadn't employed the practice track to exercise the colt. Wherever she was training that long-legged nag was anybody's guess.

When the clouds piled higher in the sky, Jarred felt a stream of panic trickle down his spine. He had been searching for over an hour and hadn't found a trace of that misplaced nymph. Veering east, Jarred aimed himself toward the coast. A sudden stillness settled around him — the eerie stillness which suggested the world was holding its breath, waiting for the thunderstorm to break loose.

The sound of carefree laughter wafted its way toward Jarred and he growled several explicit curses. Chelsie was amusing herself while he made a frantic search, worrying himself sick. Propelling himself in the direction of her laughter, Jarred galloped the stallion through the skirting of trees that surrounded the estuary where their private wharf was situated. To his irritation and utter amazement, he saw Chelsie perched in a skiff, holding the rope that was attached to the colt's halter. Was she taking the animal for a swim? What sort of crazy training program was that?

When Jarred skidded to a halt on the rocky slope, Chelsie glanced up. The contented smile that hovered on her lips evaporated when she spied the muscular form of the man who sat rigidly in his saddle, glaring at her. Jarred looked indignant. His appearance spoiled what had been a productive day of training Trumpeter. Chelsie was pleased with herself for thinking of Jarred only a mere dozen times during the course of the day. At this rate he would be off her mind completely within a few years. The amount of time she spent battling memories of Jarred's had diminished with each day she'd avoided him.

She regretted causing him to sprain his ankle, and he'd cursed her for constantly dragging him into trouble. To pacify him, she had conveniently avoided taking meals with the family when she knew Jarred would be at the table. And now here he was, come to rake her over the coals again for only God knew what.

"Get out of the water," Jarred bellowed at her. His good arm shot toward the churning clouds that rumbled above them.

Chelsie peered up and frowned bemusedly. In England, one could expect to be drenched by looming clouds, but she had no aversion to getting wet. She couldn't imagine why Jarred looked so put out with her for borrowing the skiff and rowing out into the bay. . . .

All of a sudden Chelsie didn't have time to consider Jarred at all. The calm before the storm gave way to a fierce downdraft of wind that whipped down the hillside and put whitecaps on the waves that scudded across the bay. Before Chelsie blew out of the boat, she grabbed the oar to paddle ashore. Unfortunately, the gusty gale was billowing against her, and her one-armed attempt to row to the wharf had her going in futile circles.

Trumpeter's shrill whinny and wild-eyed stare brought Chelsie's head around. Without considering her own safety, Chelsie tossed the rope into the water, allowing Trumpeter to thrash toward shore before he panicked and injured himself by becoming entangled in his rope.

Jarred swore in colorful expletives when he saw what Chelsie had done. She was without an anchor, and she had loosed the colt that might have been able to tow her ashore. For God's sake! How did she think she was going to save herself on the choppy sea? By walking on water? Well, she had best start walking, and she had damned well better be quick about it . . . !

Chelsie's piercing scream froze Jarred's thoughts. A lightning bolt struck the cresting waves so dangerously close to the skiff that Jarred's heart seemed to stop. The accompanying crash of thunder echoed in his ears, clanging a peal of doom.

Chelsie had been so startled by the lightning bolt she instinctively vaulted to her feet, capsizing the skiff. A snake of dread slithered down Jarred's spine when the howling wind and angry sea drowned Chelsie's bloodcurdling shriek. Blinded by terror—something he had never experienced in all his life—Jarred gouged his stallion, forcing him down the steep slope and onto the planked wharf. The steed protested with every step. But Jarred's harsh growl and forceful tug on the reins discouraged the animal from defying his master.

As the sky opened to pour buckets of rain that were driven hard by the roaring wind, Jarred snatched the rope from Trumpeter's halter. As the frightened colt floundered to shore

217

and trotted away, Jarred dallied the rope around the pommel of his saddle. When Chelsie's head bobbed to the surface, he bellowed at her to catch hold of the rope. Although Jarred's aim was accurate, the angry waves shoved Chelsie backward, snatching the rope from her reach.

Even though Chelsie had swallowed a good deal of water, she managed to screech Jarred's name when she burst back to the surface. Her one-armed attempt to fight the oncoming swells of water had exhausted her. She knew she was going to die. Jarred's handsome visage flashed before her eyes time and time again. Wasn't that the way it happened the instant before one went to meet one's maker? This was the beginning of the end, Chelsie realized grimly. She would go to her watery grave with Jarred's name on her lips and his memory tormenting her soul through all eternity.

Jarred would be glad to be rid of her, of course. She had caused him nothing but trouble. But just wait until the duke arrived, Chelsie mused as she sputtered to catch another breath. Jarred would be sorry. Evan Channing would chew Jarred up one side and down the other for not promptly returning his one and only daughter. . . .

"Damn it, Chel, grab the rope!" Jarred blared over the howling wind and pelting rain.

Blinking back the water that clouded her vision, Chelsie groped for the end of the rope that lay upon the surface like a long, winding snake. Her fingers numbly folded around the lifeline, but it took every last ounce of strength to hold on when Jarred urged his stallion along the wharf, towing her ashore.

When another clap of thunder rumbled above her, Chelsie instinctively shrank away. The rope was yanked from her hands.

Cursing fluently, Jarred untied the rope from the saddle and secured it onto the jutting poles at the end of the wharf. After fastening the other end of the rope to his waist, he inhaled a deep breath and dived into the water. By the time he reached the spot where Chelsie had been the moment before, there was nothing but a few drifting strands of silver-blond hair floating on the surface. Jarred twisted the tendrils around his hand and yanked her head from the water.

Chelsie would have shrieked in pain if she hadn't swallowed another gallon of water. All she could do was sputter and cough to catch her breath (or rather, what little there was left of it). Holding the rope in his injured arm and clamping Chelsie in the other, Jarred wrestled the sling from his shoulder and used it to secure Chelsie to him. Grimacing in pain, Jarred maneuvered around to grasp the rope with his good hand and pulled himself toward shore.

For what seemed forever, Jarred inched toward the wharf, feeling Chelsie's dead weight beside him. When he finally reached the dock, he yanked Chelsie up and shoved her onto the planks. Ramming the heel of his hand against her shoulder blades, he forced the water from her lungs and waited an anxious moment for her to breathe on her own. The explosion of lightning and thunder muffled Chelsie's agonized sob, but it was the sweetest sound Jarred had ever heard.

When Chelsie struggled to her knees, Jarred stared into her dazed green eyes and felt his overworked heart flip-flop in his chest. He had seen that haunted look on her face when she was tortured by nightmares. It always cut his composure to shreds. He could face danger unafraid. He could confront disaster without fear for his own safety. But seeing that tormented, helpless expression on Chelsie's bewitching features always got to him. It was the only time in their stormy relationship that Jarred felt this staunchly independent minx needed him.

Flinging aside his sentimental thoughts, Jarred hoisted Chelsie to her feet. Leaning on the limping Jarred for support, Chelsie wobbled along the wharf on weak knees, fighting the blustering winds that sought to knock her down. Jarred steered her toward the small storage shack that was built into the hill, but Chelsie set her feet, refusing to stir another step.

"Where is the colt?" she choked out.

"He headed for the cover of the trees," Jarred growled into her peaked face. "Forget about him. You're the one who needs looking after. For God's sake, you nearly got yourself killed!"

219

"I'm surprised you didn't stand aside and watch me meet my demise," Chelsie mumbled deflatedly. "Then I wouldn't be causing you to have so many unfortunate accidents and I would be out of your life forever."

"If that's what I truly wanted, I would have let you sink like a rock," Jarred snapped back at her. "But I don't, damn it."

Rain-soaked lashes swept up to meet the scowl that was plastered on Jarred's bronzed features. "You mean you truly don't hate me for causing you so much trouble?" she queried hoarsely.

Jarred expelled his breath in a rush and smiled in spite of himself. Tenderly he reached up to push a renegade strand of wet hair from her face. "Nay, I don't hate you, Chel," he murmured as he focused on the tantalizing curve of her lips. "But don't ask me to define what I feel, because I'm not sure I can explain it, even to myself. . . ."

The moment Jarred kicked the door shut behind him, Chelsie knew he meant to kiss her, and she knew she should object. But rejecting him would mean denying herself the warm, intense pleasure that awaited her. She longed to absorb his strength after she had come so close to breathing her last breath.

Jarred groaned in defeat when he felt his body sway instinctively toward hers. He needed to hold her, to assure himself that she really had survived the ordeal. He needed to feel her petal-soft lips beneath his, to forget how close he had come to losing her to the storm-tossed sea.

When his lips rolled over hers, Chelsie abandoned all thought. Her lashes fluttered down to block out the terrifying feeling of helplessness that had plagued her a few minutes earlier. When his questing tongue probed deeper, Chelsie felt herself being dried from inside out by a fire that threatened to burn out of control. The chill of death was quickly replaced by passion's billowing flame, and Chelsie followed the heat to its source. Her quaking body meshed against Jarred's lean, hard contours. She ached to become part of him, to cherish the wild, compelling sensations that splintered into every fiber of

220

her being.

An uncontrollable shudder rocked Jarred's soul when he felt Chelsie's supple curves melt against him. He was as desperate to possess her tempting body as he had been to save her from drowning. It was that same frantic urgency to spare her life that seized him now. Roughly he clutched her to him, guiding her hips to his, savoring and devouring her all in the same instant. He couldn't seem to get close enough, couldn't appease this impatient need to feel her silky flesh lying intimately beneath his.

"Chelsie . . . love me," Jarred growled in tormented desire. "I want you, just the way I always have . . . madly . . . obsessively. . . ."

And love him she did. Each caress provided exquisite pleasure. Each kiss left him moaning in sweet, maddening torment. Her hands and lips wandered everywhere, tunneling beneath the damp garments that separated flesh from flesh. Jarred had never allowed the woman in his arms to take the initiative in lovemaking. But he granted Chelsie that privilege plus a dozen more. When she pressed him to his back on the planked floor of the storehouse, Jarred went down without complaint. He was like a puppet moving upon command, responding to the black magic this inventive witch wove over him.

That same strange sense of power overcame Chelsie as it had once before. It was as if she were suddenly in command of this swarthy giant. She reveled in giving him pleasure, in touching him boldly. Her kisses and caresses grew more intimate each time Jarred groaned in sweet agony. Her hands skied down his shoulder to follow the dark hair that descended over his muscular belly. Her adventurous caresses stroked the hard columns of his thighs and traced the lean muscles of his hips, seeking out each ultrasensitive point and driving him mad with wanting.

Bracing herself on one arm, Chelsie glided upon him and then withdrew like the tide teasing the seashore. The sheer impact of her luscious body gliding upon his made him go hot all over. Each time her silky flesh whispered over his, Jarred's heart very nearly beat him to death. She was practicing exqui-

site torture on him, making him want her so badly he swore he would die long before she got around to satisfying the ache that throbbed in rhythm with his pounding heart.

His black lashes swept up to see her enchanting face in the shadows. Suddenly he was lounging on the wind swept grass of the emerald isles. Lips as quenching as summer rain drifted over his mouth. Again, her curvaceous body half-covered his in the most incredible kind of caress. And then she settled exactly upon him.

The torment ebbed to be replaced by the wild crescendo of a melody that strummed in his soul. He was moving in hypnotic rhythm, experiencing one indescribable sensation after another. Mindlessly he clutched Chelsie to him and held on for dear life. He could feel himself letting go, even while he eagerly pressed her hips into his. It was a strange parody that Jarred couldn't quite comprehend. The tighter he clutched her luscious body to his, the closer he came to losing his grasp on her—and on reality.

Having come so close to dying in the angry sea had made every moment precious to Chelsie. She savored each ineffable sensation that ricocheted through her body. She was on fire. Sparks danced down her spine, and nothing but passion's sweet release could tame the leaping flames. The blaze fed upon itself, burning hotter with each breathless moment of pleasure. Chelsie wasn't sure she could endure the erotic explosion that burst inside her. She kept reaching upward to grasp that elusive feeling of contentment, aching to seek an end to desire's wild devastating torment.

And then it came—that phenomenal sensation that satisfied the unbearable hunger and left her suspended in time and space. It was as if she had scattered in all directions at once—a mass of diverging feelings flung through the dark universe, revolving in timeless flight. The curtain of darkness that enshrouded her parted to reveal a sun-speckled rainbow. Chelsie could feel the warmth of colors brushing over her skin, hear the pacifying thud of Jarred's heart beating in rhythm with hers. Ever so slowly she came back into herself . . . she was

222

suddenly reminded of the fairy-tale about the king's men who tried to put Humpty Dumpty back together again and she wondered if she, too, would ever be the same.

That peculiar analogy caused Chelsie to giggle giddily. Jarred's brand of lovemaking was like being torn apart by tormented pleasure and then being glued back together again. She was enjoying the most satisfying feelings of contentment, even if loving Jarred was completely exhausting. It drained her thoughts, her emotions, her energy. Chelsie couldn't move, didn't want to move. Jarred's warm strength cushioned her, and she felt oddly pacified for the first time in days.

"Would you mind telling me what you're cackling about, witch?" Jarred murmured as he absently brushed his hands along the shapely curve of her hip.

"I doubt you would understand," she sighed tiredly. "You were not there."

Jarred grinned rakishly as he rolled to his side, taking Chelsie with him. "I thought I was, little green-eyed leprechaun," he chortled. "Surely you don't think you got where you were all by yourself . . . where were you?"

Chelsie blushed. That was an intimate question she chose not to answer.

"Tell me," Jarred prodded, peering into those animated pools of green, entranced.

"You wouldn't believe where I was," she assured him, trying to turn away.

His hand traced the delicate line of her jaw, uplifting her face, forcing her to meet his penetrating gaze. "Tell me."

"Very well then, if you promise not to laugh," she stipulated.

"Cross my heart," Jarred vowed, straight-faced.

A curious frown knitted her brow when a fleeting thought skipped across her mind. "Do you make it a habit of cross-examining all your lovers, counselor?"

"Nay, actually I never cared to know before," he admitted and then wondered why he had offered that confession. He wasn't sure he wanted Chelsie to know she wasn't just another smile and a moment of pleasure to him. That's all she should have been. But she had burrowed into his heart, when he would have preferred her not to have been there at all.

"I found myself in one of Mother Goose's nursery rhymes," she admitted sheepishly. "I know it sounds peculiar, but . . ."

"Which one?" Jarred questioned, stifling a chuckle.

"Humpty Dumpty and his fall from the wall—" Chelsie had no sooner alluded to the eggshell of a man than Jarred burst out laughing. Chelsie whacked him on the chest. "You promised not to laugh, and I will *never share* my private thoughts with you, *ever again*," she pouted.

"I have heard lovemaking described as life's little death, but never as the shattering of eggshells," Jarred snickered in amusement.

"Then you haven't loved until desire shatters you to pieces and passion's release molds you back together," Chelsie burst out without thinking. She blushed a half-dozen shades of red.

The mocking smile faded from his lips. Gently, Jarred limned her exquisite features. His eyes met and locked with hers, pensive and probing. "Is that how it is for you when we make love, Chel?" he inquired huskily.

"Aye," she reluctantly confessed. "You please me very much."

"And you please me," Jarred admitted as he sought her sweet lips. "Too much, I fear. . . ."

It took only one kiss to rekindle the flame that never seemed to completely burn itself out. It flickered anew each time Jarred caressed this mystical nymph. Chelsie had walked into his life, turned it upside down, and touched all his emotions. This blond-haired sprite's name was attached to every sensation imaginable—anger, fear, frustration, amusement, and mindless desire. Jarred had never experienced fear until he found himself afraid of losing Chelsie. She could bring a smile to his lips or stamp a disgusted frown on his face. She could leave him cursing a blue streak faster than anyone he knew. And when she made wild, passionate love to him . . . ah, there were no words to describe those wondrous sensations. . . . At least, there weren't until Chelsie compared passion to a splintering fall into oblivion. Suddenly he was falling, his emotions exploding inside him, flinging him in all directions at once. . . .

In the aftermath of love, Jarred wasn't sure anything could put him back together. He felt completely scattered to the four winds.

"Jarred?" Chelsie peered curiously at the odd expression that captured his handsome face. "Are you all right?"

He gave his ruffled raven head a negative shake. A faint smile hovered on his lips as he stared up at the enchanting vision that hovered over him. "I'm not sure anyone can put me back together again. . . ."

His teasing remark brought an impish smile to her lips. He hadn't made any commitment, but he had implied that he was as thoroughly shattered by their lovemaking as she was. Her hand glided over the broad expanse of his chest, teasing and arousing him. Making love to him twice should have been enough, but it wasn't. Tomorrow Jarred would be on his way to Richmond and then to Albany, and she wouldn't see him for only God knew how long. She prayed that when he returned, she would no longer be carrying a torch for a man she could never have. But for now, she was going to engorge herself on his passion. The storm that raged outside the storehouse would be nothing compared to passion's tempest. . . .

"God, not again . . ." Jarred groaned as her wandering caresses surveyed his masculine terrain, making his pulse leap. Suddenly he was back to wanting her in the worst possible way. "I swear I can't get enough of you . . ."

Twisting, Jarred rolled Chelsie to her back, amazed at her ability to arouse him so thoroughly and so quickly. One touch and he was on fire. One kiss fanned the flame and he was lost to that holocaust of passion that burned reason from his mind and left him craving this wild, sweet witch whose uninhibited brand of lovemaking beat anything he had ever seen.

Jarred wondered dazedly if he would ever overcome this maddening obsession. With each passing day his need and desire for Chelsie seemed to get worse instead of better.

Mmmm . . . there was nothing better than holding Chelsie in his arms and setting sail on another intimate journey. . . . How

225

could he ever deny himself these wondrous pleasures? Why should he try? He needed her. She had become as necessary to his life as breathing.

Jarred growled in anticipation as she arched shamelessly toward him, sending waves of ecstasy rippling into the core of his being. Chelsie made him thankful he was a man—the man who was allowed to share this quintessence of ecstasy. This was as good as it got, and Jarred was experienced enough to know. Chelsie made things happen. She was a spark that ignited all kinds of fires and Jarred wondered how he was going to forget the secret splendor they had shared if Neil decided to marry this high-spirited nymph.

That troubled thought evaporated in the fog that clogged Jarred's brain. He didn't want to think about losing this emerald-eyed nymph. He wanted only to concentrate on loving her, on committing each of these wondrous sensations to memory before he rode away to New York instead of lingering in the never-ending circle of this magical leprechaun's arms. . . .

Chapter 18

"Thank God," Kyle breathed when Chelsie and Jarred trudged into the mansion three hours later. "We were about to send out a search party."

Although the rest of the family swarmed around them, Jarred shouldered his way through the crowd and pulled Chelsie toward the spiral staircase. "We'll be down later," he said as he whisked Chelsie up the steps. "Have the cook fetch something hot for us to eat. We're chilled to the bone."

"Speak for yourself," Chelsie teased softly, flashing Jarred an elfish grin.

Jarred couldn't contain the rakish smile that surfaced on his full lips. He wasn't the least bit cold . . . on the inside. But for appearance's sake, it was the proper thing to say after one had dived into the bay during a thunderstorm.

Once Chelsie had changed into dry clothes, she ventured downstairs to take her evening meal and field the barrage of questions fired at her. She had explained that she had taken the colt swimming to strengthen his legs against the resistance of the water without putting unnecessary strain on his ankles. Kyle shook his head in wonderment.

"Those Englishmen have made a science of training horses," he sighed. "Ah, that I should be so knowledgeable in conditioning all *my* racehorses."

"The technique has proven very effective for injured animals," Chelsie explained. "And it also lessens the chances of injury in the first critical weeks of a colt's training. My father always uses swimming to condition his steeds after an injury. It

227

allows the animal to strengthen its endurance while the injury heals. But I had no idea I was about to become a victim of a hurricane when I took to the water! Rainstorms at home are not so fierce and deadly."

"I'm thankful Jarred found you in time," Rebecca breathed in relief. "If he hadn't, the afternoon could have proved disastrous for you, and you haven't even healed from your shoulder wound."

"Aye," Kyle chimed in, his eyes twinkling with wry amusement. "We don't want anything to happen to you. I had hoped to keep you with us indefinitely." His gaze swung past Jarred to settle on Neil. "In fact, I had hoped Neil would work up the nerve to propose so we can keep you in the family permanently."

"Papa!" Neil scolded his outspoken father.

Kyle carelessly shrugged off the rebuke and focused on Chelsie. "I have noticed that you and my oldest son have been getting along splendidly. I openly admit I would be delighted to have you as my daughter-in-law, the mother of my grandchildren. I've waited a decade to enjoy children underfoot. Since all my sons have been dragging their feet to the altar. . . ." His pointed gaze landed on Jarred, who found himself frankly annoyed with the conversation. "It seems I must take it upon myself to make the match." His mischievous gaze circled back to Chelsie, whose cheeks were splotched with a becoming blush. "Will you consider marrying us, duchess? We would be pleased and honored to have you in the family."

"Marry all of you?" Chelsie tittered nervously, attempting to make light of an uncomfortable situation. "Is it socially acceptable for a woman to have several husbands in the colonies?"

"Take your pick," Kyle offered generously.

"I will be only too happy to marry her," Daniel volunteered with great enthusiasm.

Jarred shoved his little brother back down before he could fully gain his feet. "You aren't marrying anyone until you have completed your studies in England," he grumbled sourly.

Damn, Kyle had grown impatient. He was so eager to ensure

228

he would have grandchildren that he was offering Chelsie a blanket proposal. The thought of Chelsie married to any of his brothers turned Jarred wrong-side-out.

"If you don't mind, I would like to handle the matter myself," Neil interjected, shooting his father a silencing glare. But he wasted his time—Kyle was not to be put off.

"You have been handling your romantic endeavors all by yourself for years and you never seem to have time for courting while you are attending to your ailing patients," Kyle sniffed. "If you don't have the nerve to speak for yourself, I will do it for you."

"Marriage is a serious commitment, and I—" Neil began.

"Don't I know it!" Kyle snorted. "How do you think you and your brothers got here? Your mother and I took wedlock and children very seriously."

"Kyle!" Rebecca scolded, glancing hastily at Chelsie. "Don't embarrass the dear girl. We all know you have become attached to her, but you are being a mite too pushy."

"I am greatly honored that you would accept me as a daughter-in-law," Chelsie said gently. "But . . ."

"Then it's settled," Kyle interrupted before Chelsie could add any stipulations. "Rebecca can plan the wedding and you can decide if Neil or Grant would suit you best."

Daniel slumped dejectedly in his seat. Grant perked up and grinned cheerfully. Neil smiled wryly and Jarred sat there and sulked.

Gracefully, Chelsie rose to her feet. "It has been a long, harrowing day. If you will excuse me, I would like to contemplate my options in my room . . . after I have digested all the water I swallowed while I floundered in Chesapeake Bay."

As she swept out of the room, Jarred glared at his father. "You put the duchess on the spot," he muttered grumpily. "I think it best if you let Fate take its own course, instead of tampering with it. Chelsie is very much her own woman, and I think she should do what she wants to do . . . without your pressure."

"And I think *you* should restrict yourself to matters that

concern you, Jarred," Kyle replied, casting his second son the evil eye. "You have your own wedding to plan, and you have been neglecting your commitment. If Chelsie's engagement is going to last as long as yours has, 'tis time to set the wheels in motion." Kyle's fist hit the end table, rattling the cups and saucers. "Blast it, I want grandchildren, and I swear all my sons have avoided marriage just to spite me!"

"It would have been nice to part on a friendly note," Jarred growled as he got up from the sofa. "I will be gone for only God knows how long, and my farewell on the eve of my departure entails a repetitive lecture on marriage and babies. And to make matters worse, I have just returned from a three-month absence upon which I was rudely shuffled aside to make welcome the Duchess of Chessfield." Blue eyes sparked fire. "It seems to me you should adopt Chelsie and disinherit your disappointing sons who cannot seem to provide you with the daughters-in-law and grandchildren you want so desperately."

When Jarred stamped off in a snit, leaving the room in silence, Rebecca scurried over to the spinet. Her fingers flew over the keys in a lively tune, giving the McAlisters the chance to smooth their ruffled feathers. It didn't improve Kyle's mood, but it kept him from harping on the monotonous subject of matrimony—a topic he had already run into the ground on this and numerous other occasions.

Chelsie was contemplating the ceiling when Jarred eased open the door that joined their rooms. Against her will, her heart unfolded invisible tentacles, reaching across the room to touch him. He wore nothing but a velvet robe, and the shadows concealed his craggy features. But it didn't matter . . . Chelsie had memorized each line on his face, and his image had long been branded on her mind. She could close her eyes and conjure up that handsome face at will.

Silently Jarred approached the bed to stare down at Chelsie's moonlit face. "Don't allow my father to force you into doing something you do not wish to do while I'm gone," he quietly advised her.

Chelsie took immediate offense. Why? She wasn't certain why that remark rubbed her the wrong way, but it did. Maybe it was because she was already feeling the emptiness of knowing Jarred wouldn't be around, even when she swore up and down she didn't want this handsome devil underfoot to tempt her. Or perhaps she was simply agitated at herself for missing him when he wasn't even gone! And one couldn't overlook the fact that having Jarred tell her what to do always set her off. It was probably the combination of many things that stoked the fires of her flammable temper, she reckoned.

"I should defy your father, but 'tis perfectly all right for me to submit to your whims in all matters . . . is that it?" she bit off.

Jarred plunked down beside her, muttering under his breath. Here he was in the middle of an argument, and that was the last thing he wanted when he sneaked into Chelsie's room. "Damn it, I didn't come here to fight with you. I came to apologize for dragging you here and for involving you in this scheme to marry Neil. I should never have let Eli talk me into this."

"Why? Because I'm not good enough for your older brother?" Chelsie sniffed, wondering why she was spoiling for battle, purposely baiting Jarred.

His sinewy arm sank into the mattress beside her shoulder as he loomed over her. "Don't try to put words in my mouth, woman. I'm the lawyer around here. I can speak for myself, even if my father doesn't think any of his sons were born with tongues that could rattle off marriage proposals."

When Chelsie tried to present her back, Jarred pushed her onto the sheet and peered intently at her. "I just want to hold you tonight, Chelsie," he said in a soft, persuasive tone that melted her completely. "I feel as if I'm about to lose something very precious to me."

Of all the things she expected Jarred to say, that wasn't even on the list! And fool that she was, she fell for his softly uttered words.

231

"I want yours to be the last face I see before I rise early in the morning to travel to Richmond. Please, Chel, I need to hold you, to lie beside you all through the night. . . ."

A mist of tears clouded her eyes. Chelsie knew she should have sent him away. But damned if she could muster the willpower to order him back to his own room. The very fact that Jarred had asked instead of commanded threw her off guard. He was different, somehow. He was no longer the willful, domineering man he portrayed to the rest of the world. He was once again the gentle, considerate lover who tugged at her heartstrings and dissolved her common sense.

As Jarred stretched out beside her, Chelsie instinctively snuggled against his solid strength, savoring the musky scent of him, reveling in the contentment of having him beside her, holding her as if she meant something special to him.

A quiet sigh escaped Jarred's lips as he gathered Chelsie close. "Making love to you isn't even enough at times," he confessed, baffled by this overflow of sentiment.

He had never murmured such admissions to any other woman, but it was different with Chelsie. It had always been different with this feisty sprite. He needed her as he'd never needed another woman. She touched something deep inside him, and it was something more than a mere physical craving. She was so strong, determined, independent. Yet for some reason Jarred wanted her to need him. As strong, determined, and independent as he was, he needed her . . . if that made any sense. Despite his attempt to fight what he felt, even when he didn't quite understand what emotion was tugging at his heart, he had the inescapable feeling he was about to lose this spirited nymph to one of his brothers. It was going to kill him to return home and learn that Neil or Grant was engaged to this curvaceous blonde who monopolized his thoughts.

"Sometimes I just need to be with you when the loving is over, before I have to go away. I won't be able to hold you close each time your memory torments my thoughts," Jarred whispered as he spread a row of butterfly kisses along the swanlike column of her neck. "Let me stay the night, Chel. I long to

232

compensate for all the long, lonely nights ahead of me, when I will want to hold you and cannot. . . ."

That really did it. How was she supposed to tell Jarred to take a hike after the softly uttered confessions he had murmured against her neck, sending a skein of goose bumps sailing over her flesh? She couldn't. She was hopelessly lost to the husky sound of his voice, to the feel of his hair-roughened flesh molded familiarly to hers.

Although she refused to break down and cry, the teardrops trickled down her cheek. This would be the very last time she could lie in Jarred's protective arms. When he returned from his journey, she would have to keep him at arm's length, for her heart's sake, for Abi's sake. This was good-bye, Chelsie reminded herself ruefully. Jarred knew it, too. He must have. That was why he had come to her room. They both knew he had an obligation to Abi and that this ill-fated affair of theirs must come to an end before they ended up hurting others. Jarred didn't love her, Chelsie told herself sensibly. And she had tried very hard not to love this restless rake. Oddly enough, the qualities about him that often infuriated her were the very ones she could not help but admire—his willfulness, his sense of duty and responsibility, his persistence, to name a few. She and Jarred had touched each other in some special way, a way that entailed more than primal passion.

Even when she argued with him, it was her attempt to build barriers between them, a protective device that hadn't worked as well as Chelsie had hoped. Thus far, nothing had saved her from this growing attachment for Jarred. Aye, she could list his failings until she was blue in the face. She could even conjure up a few faults that he didn't really possess, just to battle this illogical attraction to him. But there was a vast difference between thinking and feeling when it came to keeping her perspective about him. Her head was having a hard time ruling her reckless heart.

While Chelsie cuddled closer, she reminded herself that she must break this strange, unexplainable bond between them now and forevermore. Abi Shaw was too kind and generous a woman to be hurt. Chelsie had but to close her eyes and she could envision Abi's lovely face. It made Chelsie feel guilty and ashamed of herself. She was tormented by her feelings for Jarred. They obviously had no future. She was haunted by the fact that she was betraying a woman who deserved better than this.

But just once more before she let go of him forever, Chelsie needed to sleep in Jarred's brawny arms. Then she would let him go, not just tomorrow, but for all the tomorrows to come. It was best for everyone concerned, even if Chelsie died a little inside when Jarred rose at dawn and walked out the door to assume his obligations to the colonies—and to the woman he would one day marry.

"Jarred . . ." The most peculiar sense of loss overwhelmed Chelsie. Her stomach felt like a bottomless pit. The emotions she had fought so hard to suppress had risen to her throat. "Even if we . . ." she stammered, struggling to formulate her thoughts, which had picked a miserable moment to force themselves to her tongue. "I fear I have . . . I hadn't meant to . . . but I think I've . . ." A frustrated sigh gushed from her quivering lips.

Jarred shook with silent laughter. Never did Chelsie have difficulty speaking her mind! It was amusing to listen to her fumble around like a tongue-tied idiot. "That was splendidly put, little leprechaun," he teased playfully.

The taunt was the provocation that caused the words she was trying so hard not to say to tumble from her lips. "Oh, for crying out loud, Jarred. I think I'm in love with you. I hadn't meant for it to happen. And in a sense you were right about me. I was a pauper who sought a treasure I am only beginning to understand. But rest assured, I will be over loving you by the time you return. I won't go on like this . . . I can't . . . it's tearing me apart. . . ."

Her frantic confession both pleased and tormented Jarred. He looked down into her puckered features and his heart twisted in his chest. Against his better judgment, he wanted this fiery hellion, even when he had made a permanent commit-

234

ment to Abi. Jarred was a man who was ruled by his sense of obligation, and he was not accustomed to letting his heart get in the way of logic. But Chelsie's admission was ripping him to pieces, bit by bit. He wanted something he couldn't have, and his absence would give his father the opportunity to press for a marriage between Neil and Chelsie or between Chelsie and Grant. But one way or another, Jarred feared he would return home to find himself giving the bride away.

Damn it. If he hadn't needed a bath that day in Annapolis, none of this would ever have happened! He would never have been captivated by this silver-blond genie who rose from his tub to complicate his life. Lord, how he wished. . . .

The emotional turmoil caused Jarred to clutch Chelsie desperately to him. "And sometimes just holding you isn't enough, either," Jarred growled in exasperation. "I feel like loving you again . . . I need you, Chel. . . ."

As his warm, demanding lips descended upon hers and his practiced hands flooded over her quaking body, Chelsie surrendered to the emotions that swirled inside her. She hadn't expected Jarred to admit he loved her, for she knew he didn't, but he could at least have said he liked her, just a little. . . .

Chelsie's thoughts vanished in the haze of pleasure that enshrouded her when Jarred worked his passionate magic on her. It no longer mattered that she might simply be a diversion, the feminine body he turned to when he wanted to appease his masculine desires. God help her, she did love him, even if she could never have him as her own, even if he couldn't return her affection. Chelsie couldn't say for certain how Jarred really felt about her. He wanted her body, she knew. But if he felt anything stronger than physical attraction, this elusive lawyer was keeping his own counsel.

Forgoing her pride, Chelsie followed the whispering of her heart, expressing her love for him in all the ways Jarred had taught her, weaving her affection for him in each worshipping kiss, each admiring caress. She would have a month to get over loving him, but tonight she was going to express the emotions that had burgeoned inside her since that afternoon when she found herself staring into the most fascinating pair of blue eyes she'd ever seen.

Loving Jarred was to be both her reward and her punishment, she realized dismally. Chelsie hadn't thought there was a man on earth who could please and satisfy her. After discarding a score of marriage proposals from the best prospects in Europe, Chelsie had stumbled onto the one man who wouldn't and couldn't wed her. And although she wouldn't be able to stay forever with Jarred, she intended to spend eternity in his arms — the eternity of loving him between dusk and dawn . . . and this she did, completely.

Jarred got no sleep whatsoever. Not that he complained, mind you. But the hardest thing he had ever done was to leave Chelsie's silky arms just as the first rays of sunlight sprinkled across the room to bathe her curvaceous body in a golden glow and encircle her lovely hair with a mystical aureole. He was tormented by her confession of love, wondering if she truly meant what she had said, baffled by the strange constriction in his chest.

Was it love that tormented him so? And if it was, what in the name of heaven was he going to do about Abi? And worse, what if Chelsie did something drastic, like marry one of his brothers to ensure they never shared another splendorous night of passion? She promised not to love him when he returned, vowed to smother her affection until it withered and died. And come to think of it, what sort of love was it that fit into a designated hour? Could this saucy minx turn her affection off and on, like a machine? What sort of fickle nonsense was that? One either loved or one didn't, and the feelings didn't go away when one snapped one's fingers — unless one was a leprechaun with supernatural powers.

Frustrated, Jarred peered down at the sleeping beauty and fought his way through the tangle of thoughts that cluttered his mind. He was tired and cranky and confused about his own feelings and . . . blast it, why had Chelsie even admitted she loved him at all, if she was only going to grant him one night of affection? By tomorrow she would probably wade out of the shallow infatuation she felt for him and turn her charms on his brothers. . . .

That haunting speculation caused Jarred to snatch up a paper and quill to hurriedly jot Chelsie a note. Quietly he tiptoed over to place the letter on the pillow where he had slept . . . well, not exactly slept, Jarred amended as he moved silently back to his own room. This seductive sorceress had kept him awake, teaching him a few dozen more things about passion that even *he* hadn't believed possible. It was killing him to leave her behind, knowing she would be out of his reach when he got back.

Trying not to think at all, Jarred swung into the saddle, barely acknowledging Eli's presence beside him. But he was burning with a fever that only this green-eyed leprechaun could cure. Jarred couldn't shut out the titillating visions that danced in his head. His mind was reeling with wild, fantastic memories — ones he swore would haunt him for the next month. And sure enough, he was right!

Part Three

If she some other swain commend,
Though I was once his fondest friend,
His instant enemy I prove;
Tell me, my heart, if this be love.

When she is absent, I no more
Delight in all that pleased before,
The clearest spring, the shadiest grove;
Tell me, my heart, if this be love.
George Lyttleton

Chapter 19

Mustering a cheerful smile, Chelsie descended the steps, garbed in an elegant green gown. It had been a week since Jarred had ridden out of her life and she had closed the door on the past. Chelsie had cursed herself time and time again for admitting she loved Jarred. But what hurt the worst was that he hadn't returned her confession. He had said he wanted her, but wanting and loving were poles apart. Yet Chelsie reluctantly admitted nothing was going to change the way of things, even if she had earned Jarred's love. He was still obligated to Abi, and neither of them could have betrayed her for the world. But what baffled Chelsie most about the last night she had spent in Jarred's arms was the note he had left on his pillow.

Chelsie had awakened to find an empty space beside her, and she had stared bemusedly at Jarred's parting message.

I had to leave a note for fear you wouldn't even notice I had gone.
Jarred

Not notice? Blast it, the man had left a void the size of Chesapeake Bay in her heart when he departed. Who wouldn't notice? And why on earth had Jarred left such a note in the first place? That didn't sound at all like the self-confident rake she had come to know. Just when she thought she had him figured out, he did something unpredictable. The note was a shining example of the inconsistency that plagued men in general, and Jarred in particular. What was the purpose of that message? To keep her on a string while he flitted about Albany?

Well, Jarred wasn't keeping her on a short leash! He wasn't going to play on her sentimentality with his ridiculous notes. Chelsie had resolved never to spare him a thought, to forget the ecstasy they had shared, to smother the blossom of love that had unfolded its fragile petals in her soul. . . .

But the road to hell was paved with good intentions, Chelsie mused with a deflated sigh. Forgetting Jarred was the most difficult task she'd ever undertaken.

The moment Kyle appeared at the foot of the steps, Chelsie pasted on a greeting smile and shoved the thought of Jarred out of her mind. Kyle had invited her to ride with him to the country church for Sunday services. The rest of the family was scheduled to follow in a larger carriage. Why Chelsie was allowed the privilege of riding with Kyle, she didn't know. She had the uneasy feeling she had been singled out so Kyle could quiz her about her choice of a husband. Since Jarred had left, she had been alternately courted by both Neil and Grant, and constantly doted on by Daniel, who was out of the running, but who refused to admit defeat to his brothers. Not an hour had passed that one of the McAlisters hadn't invited her to go riding or for a stroll, fishing, hunting—any activity that granted her privacy with one of them.

"Well, have you made up your mind about my sons yet?" Kyle abandoned all tact and went straight to the heart of the matter.

Awkwardly, Chelsie fiddled with the folds in her gown and glanced in every direction except Kyle's. "How am I to pick one worthy mate when each of your sons is brimming with charm and personality?" she hedged.

Kyle popped the reins, sending the carriage lurching forward. "You needn't be tactful with me, duchess. Are you or are you not interested in one of my sons?"

"I like them all," Chelsie admitted honestly. "But if . . ."

Kyle's body tensed beside her and Chelsie's words died beneath the clatter of the carriage that approached from the west. She had the feeling Kyle's interest in marrying his sons off wasn't his only reason for inviting her to ride to church with him this bright, crisp Sunday morning. She caught the glitter of anticipation in Kyle's dark eyes as the Shaw's carriage approached. If she hadn't been preoccupied with other thoughts, she might have been able to predict why Kyle refused to wait for the rest of the family: he had harnessed his prize trotter to this smaller carriage for one purpose. Kyle had every intention of racing Amos to church, just as he did every Sunday morning, only Chelsie didn't know it was a ritual. But she was about to find out!

In the distance Chelsie could hear the clip-clop of hooves and Amos's deep voice urging his steed to quicken his pace. Chelsie clutched the edge of the buggy when Kyle snapped the reins over his trotter, accelerating their speed over roads that weren't fit for the pace set by a turtle.

Despite Kyle's attempt to maintain the lead, Amos's horse eased up beside them. Chelsie glanced over to see Amos grinning like a baked possum and Abi's pretty mouth clamped shut in blatant irritation. Although Chelsie was annoyed that Kyle hadn't informed her of his intentions, she was faintly amused by these two fierce competitors and their obsession with horse racing.

Amos cracked his whip over his steed and Kyle countered by cheering his horse on in a loud, boisterous voice that rang through the countryside like a church bell. Wheels creaked and mud splattered as the carriages whizzed down the straight stretch of road that led to the quaint stone church. Little did Chelsie know this was merely a warm-up exercise for the races which were held every Sunday after prayer meeting. There were at least a dozen racing enthusiasts who congregated after church to match their prize trotters against the Shaws and the McAlisters.

"Damn it all," Kyle scowled when Amos's carriage inched into the lead. "Forgive my language, duchess. . . ."

Sheepishly he glanced at Chelsie, whose bonnet no longer sat primly upon her head. Had she known the speed with which she was to be spirited to church, she would have nailed her bonnet in place! Hanging on for dear life, Chelsie watched Kyle resort to the whip and bellow at his steed to quicken his gait. Both of the horses had lowered their heads and plunged toward the church, as they did each Sunday. The laboring animals remained neck-and-neck until they were but a hundred yards from the church. Both drivers were yelling at their horses and snapping their whips in the air as if they were about to win England's coveted Triple Crown.

A muttered curse tripped off Kyle's tongue when Amos's steed beat him by a nose. As Kyle stamped on the brake, Chelsie clenched her fists on the edge of the seat to prevent catapulting head over heels to the ground. The coach skidded sideways in the mud left by a recent storm, slamming Chelsie against Kyle's shoulder. A muffled groan escaped her lips when her tender arm collided with his elbow.

"I'm sorry," Kyle apologized all over himself. "I was so preoccupied with the race, I forgot all about your mending arm."

"I'm fine," Chelsie chirped, her voice indicating she was nothing of the kind. Inhaling a steadying breath, she resituated her cockeyed hat on top of her head and flicked the splatters of mud from her gown.

"Another Sunday, another victory," Amos taunted as he strutted past the carriage with Abi wobbling unsteadily beside him. "Better luck next time, Kyle. . . ."

Kyle gnashed his teeth as he assisted Chelsie from the coach. "Confound that Amos," he seethed. "He even gloats on Sunday . . ."

"While some of us resort to cursing," Chelsie reminded her pouting companion. "Neither of those are saintly qualities, squire. I only hope the Lord appreciates the speed with which his flock arrives for prayer meeting, rather than the language and manners they employ along the way. More's the pity that we sinners have one or two more transgressions for which we must repent in the 'getting here' ". . . .

Kyle snickered at the witty beauty. "If the good Lord could see his way clear to letting me win just one blessed race, I could eliminate my need to repent for swearing on the Sabbath," he defended.

"Then it would be you doing the strutting and Amos doing the cursing," Chelsie predicted, tossing the gray-haired squire a teasing smile.

"Ah, Chelsie, I do so enjoy your wit," Kyle sighed as he gave her an affectionate squeeze. "You have to marry one of my sons or I will be forced to marry you myself. You always manage to brighten my days."

Nodding a humble thank-you, Chelsie tucked her hand in the crook of his elbow and ascended the steps to await the arrival of the rest of the family, who were journeying to church at a more prudent speed.

When the services were over, the McAlisters and the other members of the congregation strolled down the road to witness the weekly races that were held after church, weather permitting. Before Chelsie could join the McAlisters, Abi approached her.

Chelsie tensed in response to the grim expression on Abi's comely features. Her heart thudded in anticipation of an unpleasant scene. If Neil had dared to tattle to Abi about what was going on between Chelsie and Jarred, she would never forgive him. This could prove to be the most awkward conversation of her life. With bated breath Chelsie stood first on one foot, then the other, waiting for Abi to formulate her thoughts.

Abi knotted and unclenched her tapered fingers in the folds of her pink satin gown. Gathering her nerve, she finally met Chelsie's expectant smile. "I know 'tis not my place to ask, and you probably don't think 'tis any of my business, but . . . ah . . . I . . ." She stammered nervously, glancing one direction, then another.

Chelsie was most sympathetic toward Abi's uneasiness, but there was no way to smooth over this conversation. She felt as awkward as Abi did. And when this ordeal was over, Chelsie swore she was going to strangle Neil for tattling. Damn him!

She thought he was her confidant and friend.

Inhaling a courageous breath, Abi plunged ahead before she lost her nerve. "I must know if your intentions toward Neil are sincere," she blurted out in a rush. "Kyle informed me that he is hoping to announce your engagement to his oldest son at the Newtons party next week."

Neil? Chelsie frowned. That was not the direction she expected this conversation to take. What in the blazes did Abi care who Neil married? Had she appointed herself his guardian angel?

Noting the astounded expression on Chelsie's enchanting features, Abi rushed on. She had not heard one word of the sermon after Kyle leaned over to boast once again that he expected Neil to propose to Chelsie. She had heard that remark the previous week, and she was compelled to discuss the matter with Chelsie.

"If you are truly in love with Neil then I shall not interfere. But I must know you will cherish him as much as . . ." Abi dragged in another breath of air over her galloping heart. ". . . As much as I do." There, she'd said it. It nearly killed her to force out the secret confession, but it had been hidden in her heart for more than a year, and the words refused to be restrained a moment longer.

Chelsie's jaw sagged and she stared at Abi. "But what about Jarred? I thought. . . ."

Abi clutched Chelsie's arm and led her to the wooden bench beneath the stately shade tree. "Three years ago when my husband accompanied Jarred into the wilderness to oversee the construction of forts to ward off Indian raids, the militia was attacked and Jeffrey was killed along with three other men. I know Jarred held himself personally responsible for my loss. And being a man of honor and obligation, he proposed marriage to me after the proper period of mourning. Overwrought, I accepted his gracious offer, certain I was fortunate to have a man as wonderful as Jarred."

Heaving a sigh, Abi continued while Chelsie hung on her every word. "But Jarred is a very busy man who has the duties of the Assembly and the McAlister plantations to occupy his time. He is also a commander in the militia, and he never hesitates to answer the call for assistance on the frontier.

"When Jarred was unable to accompany me to social functions, he deputized Neil to escort me so I would not be left to sit at home alone." Abi's gaze dropped to her lap, where her hands were still clenched in the folds of her gown. "It was Neil I fell in love with," she admitted in a tremulous voice. "He is kind and generous and loving. But I had already made a commitment to Jarred, you see, and Neil is too much the gentleman to betray his brother. I don't even know for certain how he feels about me. He would never commit himself or become his own brother's rival and I'm miserable. . . ."

Muffling a sniff, Abi lifted her cloudy eyes to Chelsie's unblinking stare. "I think perhaps Neil knows I have grown much too fond of him, but he is far too superb a man to embarrass me with his speculations. I even thought Neil cared for me in his own quiet way . . . or at least until you came into his life."

"Abi, there is . . ." Chelsie interrupted, but Abi grasped her hand, beseeching the lively duchess to allow her to finish.

"I am only telling you this because I care so deeply for Neil, so deeply that his happiness is my foremost concern," she murmured. "And I could *never* hurt Jarred, who has been so considerate and obliging since the death of my first husband. I know which man I want, but I would never cause dissension in the McAlister family." Her tortured gaze lifted to Chelsie. "And if you honestly love Neil, I will do nothing to stand in your way. I will accept your marriage and make no attempt to cause discord. I want him to be happy, even at my expense, because I love him enough to let him go, if that is for the best."

Chelsie slumped back and frowned pensively. Her thoughts reverted to her first conversation with Neil. It had sounded odd at the time, but now Chelsie began to understand what Neil meant when he said the situation would work to both their advantages. That rascal! He had purposely tried to make Abi jealous and force her hand. He was not the kind of man who would interfere in his brother's engagement, it was true. Apparently he felt it would be far more acceptable for Abi to break her long-term engagement with Jarred. And Abi, torn by guilt and her secret love, had tried to accept her fate gracefully, just as she had nobly accepted the loss of her first husband. She was too much the lady to pit brother against brother. And Neil was too much the gentleman to vocalize his desire for his brother's fiancée.

No doubt they had loved each other from afar. When Jarred had trotted off to attend to his obligations, they had cherished each moment they were thrown together. They had probably scorned themselves for wishing Jarred would be called away, and yet they longed for the chance to enjoy their precious moments together and live their secret dreams.

After several minutes of silent reverie, Chelsie nodded determinedly. "If you are in love with Neil, then 'tis high time you declared your feelings for him," she insisted.

"Oh, but I couldn't do that!" Abi croaked, aghast. "It has taken me a week to muster the nerve to approach you with my shameful confession. 'Tis far too brazen and improper to ask Neil to marry me! And how would I ever face Jarred . . . ?"

"I think Neil shares your carefully guarded affection," Chelsie announced, cutting Abi short. "I also think Neil has been courting me just to make you jealous. I am fond of Neil, but we share a friendship that might be likened to that of brothers and sisters. As for Kyle, he won't be the least bit insulted if one engagement is broken, so long as it is quickly replaced. Indeed, I think he will be elated." A mischievous grin pursed Chelsie's lips. "And I have a suggestion as to how to draw out Neil's confession, but I will need your help."

Abi cast Chelsie a dubious glance when she spied that impish smile that made the duchess's eyes sparkle like polished emeralds. "I'm not so sure I could be a part of any scheming. . . ."

Chelsie stared Abi squarely in the eye. "Do you love him enough to marry him or don't you?" she demanded.

"Is Neil going to hate me for whatever devious scheme you are planning, duchess?" she queried.

"*I* am going to hate you if you allow Kyle to force Neil and me into a marriage neither of us wants," Chelsie retorted.

Abi fiddled with the folds of her skirt. An indecisive frown puckered her brow. She cared deeply for Neil, but her constitution did not easily lend itself to barging up to a man and blurting out her affection, especially while she was engaged to that man's brother. Finally she nodded affirmatively.

"Aye, I do love Neil," she sighed. "And more than anything, I want to be his wife . . . if he will have me."

A satisfied smile crossed Chelsie's lips. "Then I will grant you your wish." Her twinkling green eyes locked with Abi's apprehensive ones. "Now, here is what you are going to do. . . ."

While Amos and Kyle and the other contenders were thundering down the home stretch, staring covetously at the finish line, Chelsie unfolded her scheme to Abi. It was a mite devious, Chelsie did admit. But handling a McAlister was as difficult as fishing a whale from the sea with a cane pole. One needed a large net if one expected to meet with success. And if Jarred felt more than obligation for Abi, that was too bad. In fact, it would serve him right for throwing his fiancée in his brother's lap one too many times. Chelsie shouldn't be the only one around here who was nursing bruised pride, she decided. And besides, it wouldn't hurt Jarred to have a dose of the kind of medicine he had been doling out the past month. He would have to learn to live with his broken engagement, just as Chelsie was learning to live with her broken heart. Now *that* was justice!

Stifling an impish grin, Chelsie marched toward the office that sat just beyond the whitewashed fence encircling the McAlister plantation. Neil's office was beneath a canopy of trees and had been a hub of activity that morning. Patients had come and gone in a flurry, but there had been a lull during the noon hour. Another elfish grin hovered on her lips when she spied Abi's carriage approaching. Right on time, Chelsie thought as she breezed into the office to find Neil restocking his medical bag.

Neil's brows jackknifed when Chelsie sashayed toward him, wearing a most provocative smile. She was garbed in a full skirt and peasant-style blouse that swooped low to reveal the luscious curve of her breasts. A stream of silver-blond hair cascaded over one shoulder, and a delightfully wicked twinkle glistened in her eyes.

The very sight of this saucy nymph alerted Neil as to why Jarred couldn't keep his distance: Chelsie fairly sparkled with untamed spirit. She was the liveliest, most dynamic woman he had met in a long time . . . ever, he quickly amended. My, but Jarred had all the luck with women. He was engaged to the most fetching beauty in Maryland, and he had seduced the most intriguing duchess England had to offer. . . .

Neil's contemplations scattered when Chelsie sauntered over and plunked down right in his lap! "What are you doing?" he grunted in disbelief.

The stunned expression on the doctor's handsome face caused Chelsie to bubble with laughter. "I came for an examination," she declared in a provocative tone. Her fingers speared into Neil's chestnut brown hair, ruffling his well-groomed mane. "And afterward, we can practice being engaged. . . ."

Neil promptly removed her straying hand and held it in his own. "Why are you acting so peculiar? Have you been stealing drugs from my medicine bag?"

"Nay," Chelsie assured him as she kissed his puckered brow. "Why don't you tell my why you think I'm behaving peculiar. After all, you are the doctor. . . ."

Neil was shocked by Chelsie's amorous assault. They had been friends since the moment they met and suddenly she was trying to seduce him. Why? Was she missing that ornery brother of his and turning her affection elsewhere for solace? Undoubtedly!

"Don't you want to inspect my injured shoulder, doctor?" she queried evocatively. Chelsie slid the loose neckline down to reveal one bare shoulder.

"I checked your wound yesterday and it was fine," Neil

250

chirped. He would have vaulted to his feet and found a corner to stand in if Chelsie hadn't pinned him in his chair with his long legs wedged under the desk. "And even if I did, I wouldn't do it here . . . like this. . . ."

"This is your office," Chelsie taunted as she blew in his ear. "What better place for a doctor to get his hands on his patient . . . ?"

"Chelsie! What in the blazes has gotten into you?" Neil let out a startled squeak when Chelsie unbuttoned the top two buttons of his shirt, leaving him to wonder who was examining whom! "You know 'tis Jarred you really want. You are going to regret behaving like this when you come to your senses."

"I *have* come to my senses," she murmured, snuggling closer. "Your father wants me to select a suitable match from his stable of studs, and I choose you."

Neil's eyes were as round as dinner plates. "You don't want to marry me!"

"Ah, but I do," she contested.

"Nay, you don't," Neil argued. "You are pining for Jarred, and since he's gone, you're turning to me for consolation, even though it isn't me you truly want."

"Your diagnosis is all wrong, doctor," Chelsie purred as she toyed with the lapels of his jacket. "Jarred is a page from my past, an unpleasant memory I wish to forget. And you are the man who can make me forget what I don't want to remember. . . ."

"I can't . . ." Neil chirped.

"Why not?" she wanted to know. Her taunting caresses glided over his shoulder to trace the edge of his gaping shirt.

"Because I'm. . . ." Neil grabbed her wandering hand and stared at her frog-eyed. "Because I'm . . ."

It was at that precise moment that Abi entered the office. Neil's wild-eyed gaze flew to the shapely brunette who wore just the right amount of shock and dismay to fit the role Chelsie had demanded of her.

"What on earth?" Abi gasped.

"Abi, what are you doing here?" Neil growled disgustedly.

251

Abi lifted her delicate chin to stare down her nose at the ruffled doctor. "*Why* I came isn't important now. If this is the way of things, what I came to say cannot be said."

Chelsie bit back a giggle. Abi was playing the part of the jilted lover so superbly that Neil was beside himself with frustration. Abi looked as if Neil had just stabbed her through the heart, and she couldn't believe he could have been so cruel. And it was amusing to watch this calm, usually well-controlled doctor unravel at the seams. He was *that* upset about being caught with Chelsie in his lap!

"This isn't what you think it is," Neil blustered as he wormed for freedom. But he couldn't remove Chelsie from his lap without shoving her to the floor and risking another injury to her mending shoulder — one that shouldn't have been protruding from the sagging neckline of her provocative blouse!

One perfect brow elevated to an aloof angle. "Isn't it, Neil?" Abi sniffed disconcertingly. "Do you usually make it a habit of examining your female patients while they are on your lap?"

"Nay," Chelsie responded for the flustered physician. "Only his soon-to-be fiancée."

Theatrically, Abi half-collapsed against the wall and worked up a few crocodile tears to suit the occasion.

"Confound it, Chelsie, get off me!" Neil muttered, his eyes fixed on Abi, who looked as if she were about to faint. "Can't you see Abi needs my consolation."

Stifling a grin, Chelsie finally removed herself from Neil's lap. Like a homing pigeon, Neil flew straight to Abi, who was still bleeding tears.

"I am not marrying Chelsie and she knows it," Neil proclaimed, tugging Abi into his arms before she wilted onto the floor. "I can't."

His lips grazed her forehead. Ah, how long he had waited to hold her to him, to display even a smidgen of the pent-up affection he felt for her. And once he allowed himself to touch her the way he had yearned to do, the emotions came pouring out like floodwaters rushing over a crumbling dam.

"I can't marry Chelsie when I love you," Neil murmured

252

tenderly. "God forgive me for putting you in such a predicament, Abi, but I've wanted you all the while Jarred has been courting you."

Now Abi was crying real tears that streamed down her flushed cheeks. Her face was pressed against Neil's unbuttoned shirt, and she held onto him as if she never meant to let go. For over a year she had wanted to feel his arms around her, but guilt, her own sense of honor and obligation restricted her. All the inhibitions came tumbling down when she finally found herself in Neil's loving arms.

"And I can't marry Jarred when I love you," she whispered, her voice rattling with emotion.

"Well, that settles that," Chelsie declared. The pleased smile on her face was like a rising dawn. My, but matchmaking was a rewarding occupation. Perhaps she should consider a profession in it, even if she couldn't find a match of her own. Although Jarred was free from his obligation, it didn't change things between him and Chelsie. She had expressed her love for him before he left for Albany and he offered no confession of affection in return. And just because he was free to marry didn't mean he wanted to.

The man had been engaged for two years! From the look of things, he was not particularly eager to consider the institution of marriage. And why should he, when he could have any woman he wanted without speaking vows? He had certainly taken what he wanted from Chelsie, so he didn't need to marry *her*. Before that humiliating thought spoiled her mood, Chelsie tossed it aside and concentrated on the loving couple who had yet to let go of each other.

Neil pried his eyes off Abi to survey the impish smile that lit Chelsie's bewitching features. A suspicious frown knitted his brow when he started putting two and two together. "You planned this little scene, didn't you?" he accused.

"I certainly did," Chelsie replied unrepentantly. "And Abi agreed to help me. It seems she has been as miserable as you have. I thought it rather ridiculous for the two of you to be so honorable about protecting your feelings from your tumbleweed of a brother. . . ."

The door swung open once again and Kyle froze in his tracks when he spied Abi in Neil's encircling arms. The abrupt intrusion flung the chummy couple apart so quickly that Chelsie burst out laughing.

Kyle stared bug-eyed at his son. "What the blazes is going on here?" he demanded to know that very second.

Neil drew himself up to proud stature. "Papa, Abi cannot marry Jarred because. . . ." For a half-second his courage failed him. For more than a year he had contained his confession when he wanted to shout it to the world. For over one tormenting year he had hated himself for wanting his brother's fiancée and it had torn him apart. And even now, facing his father with his admission was difficult. Neil inhaled a deep breath and blurted out his feelings. "Because I love her and I would marry her in a minute instead of remaining engaged to her for two whole years!"

Kyle's stupefied gaze swung to Abi who blushed up the roots of her hair. "Do you return my oldest son's affection, Abigail?" he questioned point-blank.

Still blushing beet-red, Abi nodded. The instant Neil held out his hand to her, she dashed back into his protective arms. "Aye," she admitted, her eyes fixed on Neil's refined features. "But I didn't want to shame Jarred or hurt him. He has been kind to me. . . ."

"Pish-posh," Kyle sniffed. "Jarred had his chance and he has been pussyfooting around for two years. If it is Neil you truly want and he obviously wants you, then we shall have a long-awaited marriage." Kyle beamed proudly. "I am so anxious for the two of you to . . ." His voice trailed off when he remembered Chelsie was standing beside the desk. "Oh, dear . . ."

Wearing a wry smile, Neil ambled over to the vivacious beauty who had rattled him enough to force him to admit what he wanted most in life. "Thanks to this lovely lady, Abi and I can enjoy the future we feared we could never have. You have the duchess to thank for forcing us to bring our feelings for each other out in the open."

Kyle sagged with relief. Chelsie didn't appear to be the least bit chagrined by the match. For that he was thankful. Kyle wouldn't have hurt this delightful nymph for the world. "Then the wedding will be held as soon as Rebecca can make the arrangements," he announced enthusiastically.

"What about Jarred?" Abi questioned apprehensively.

"Surely he will be back at the end of the month. And once we have explained the situation, Jarred will accept it because he has no choice. This is obviously the best match," Kyle added with a sly smile to the loving couple. "A month will give us plenty of time to make the preparations." His brown eyes settled on his oldest son and his soon-to-be daughter-in-law. "In fact, I'll see to making the announcement to the others while the two of you discuss your future. And don't fret about Jarred . . . he is man enough to know when to back away graciously."

When Kyle scurried off to inform the family of the exciting news, Chelsie strode toward the door. The last thing Neil and Abi needed now was company.

"Chelsie . . ." Abi's bubbling voice halted her at the portal. "Thank you for making a pass at my future husband," she said with a teasing smile. "But from now on, I'll see to the matter myself."

Chelsie returned the impish grin. "I'll lock the door on my way out, if you intend to see to that matter immediately."

Abi's sparkling eyes lifted to meet Neil's refined features. "Aye, I do. I have waited a long time for this. . . ."

Tittering delightedly, Chelsie eased the door shut and hung up the sign informing Doctor McAlister's patients that he was unavailable. Judging by the look on Neil's face, he had already forgotten his name and his profession.

Chelsie's prediction was entirely accurate. . . .

Chapter 20

Smoldering green eyes blazed across the ransacked study in the massive stone mansion known as Chessfield. Evan Channing had been in a towering rage ever since his daughter's disappearance. For almost three months Evan had turned the countryside upside down trying to locate Chelsie and the two thoroughbreds that had been stolen while they grazed in the meadow.

The door slammed behind Evan and the manor shook as if it had been hit by an earthquake. Evan had always been a door slammer—it was a quirk his daughter had picked up from him when she was in a fit of temper. But no one could slam a door as forcefully as Evan Channing. He was a master. When he was angry or frustrated, the entire mansion echoed and rattled with aftershocks. Doors sagged on their bent hinges, streams of dust trickled from the woodwork, portraits fell from walls. There had been quite a bit of racket at Chessfield of late. The duke had been in a permanent snit, and nothing eased his black mood.

Evan was a large, powerful man and when he was furious, it was suicide to cross him. He was six feet, three inches tall and two hundred fifty pounds of hard muscle—muscle that had remained taut for the past three months since his beloved daughter's disappearance. His flaming red hair remained disheveled. His snapping green eyes constantly shot hot flames, and his full lips were continuously curled in a sneer that sent the average man scurrying for cover.

The servants of Chessfield trod lightly when the duke was

storming around the manor. Luckily for them, he had spent most of his time tearing England upside down trying to locate his precious daughter. For the most part Evan was a fair man who controlled the Irish temper he had inherited from his mother's side of the family. Chelsie's presence in his life had been the buffer that padded that notorious temper of his. She could calm her father when no one else would dare go near him. Chelsie could burst into one of her radiant smiles and Evan's disposition would become sunny once again. But without Chelsie to brighten his days, a cloud of gloom hung over him, turning his disposition black as pitch.

"Damned, confounded, cussed pirates!" Evan roared at the walls. From his extensive investigation, he had learned that a ship had anchored near Chessfield—a ship bearing no marking that could be recognized or tracked down. No one in the area seemed to know whence it had come or where it had gone. But Evan was prepared to bet his fortune that Chelsie had been spirited away against her will. She loved Chessfield and she had been content where she was. It wasn't like her to prance off without telling her father her destination.

Chelsie . . . Evan swore a blue streak when his daughter's visage rose to torment him. Snatching up a priceless figurine, Evan hurled it against the wall. He had amassed great wealth during his lifetime, but it meant nothing without that little green-eyed beauty who was the image of her mother. Chelsie had given his life new meaning after Evan's wife had died. Although his family had arranged his marriage, Evan had grown to love Chelsie's mother. She had come to mean everything to him. Now he lived for the smiles that captured every exquisite feature on Chelsie's bewitching face. But she had vanished into thin air, and Evan didn't have a clue where to look for her. That helpless frustration nagged at him constantly, and he was impossible to live with, especially when dreadful premonitions left him fearing Chelsie had perished.

The faint rap at the door provoked Evan to wheel about. "Who dares disturb me?" he bellowed.

The windowpanes shook.

There was only one courageous soul at Chessfield who would confront this growling Goliath. Doris Wycoff had been Chelsie's maid, confidante and adopted mother, and she was the only one who had the slightest effect on Evan since his daughter's mysterious disappearance.

Bolstering her bravura, Doris pushed open the portal to face Evan's murderous sneer. His imposing stature could send a lion cowering in its den. At forty-five years of age, Evan was still a fine figure of a man. His features were moderately handsome and far from refined. A crop of curly red hair capped his broad head, and thick brows arched over his piercing green eyes. He had the shoulders of a bull, and lately, the temperament of a wounded rhinoceros. Doris wasn't much taller than Chelsie and she looked like a dwarf in comparison to this brooding giant. But she had spunk — something that had definitely rubbed off on the duke's vivacious daughter.

"I've heard just about enough of your ranting and raving for one day. The carpenters from the village have only just repaired the last two doors you ripped off the hinges yesterday. I will *not* be calling them back today to remodel what is left of your study," Doris declared, matching the fuming giant glare for glare. " 'Tis time you sat down and tried to relax."

"I don't want to sit down!" Evan blared as he stamped around the room. "Hell and be damned! My daughter is missing and I cannot rest until I know what has happened to her!"

Doris poured a cup of tea laced with brandy and shoved it toward the fuming duke, who did an about-face to pace back in the opposite direction.

"Drink it," she insisted in a tone that brooked no argument.

Although he hurled his persnickety servant a poisonous glower, Evan did plunk down in his chair and swallow the scalding tea. "Done, madam." His brawny arm shot toward the door and his bushy brows formed a single line over his menacing green eyes. "Now get the hell out of here before I lose what is left of my good disposition! I intend to spend the entire day sulking, and you are interrupting!"

The bold servant didn't budge. Reaching into her apron pocket she extracted the crumpled letter that had arrived an hour earlier. She had taken it upon herself to steam open the curious letter before presenting it to the duke. After reading its contents, she resealed the message before approaching this brooding giant. To Doris's relief the news was encouraging, but she would have had no inclination to present the message to Evan if it had been bad news—not today, not in his horrendous mood!

"This has just arrived," Doris announced as she tossed the letter into his lap.

A dark frown puckered his brows and he stubbornly refused to read the letter while he was seeing the world through a furious red haze.

"I have an idea it might contain news about Chelsie," Doris tempted him. "It came from the Maryland colony, and it looks a lot like your daughter's handwriting on the envelope. . . ."

Doris had barely gotten the last word out before Evan tore into the letter like a starved tiger devouring a feast. His eyes flew over the message, and growls and snorts erupted from his curled lips at irregular intervals.

It was a pity Chelsie had been in such a snit when she penned that letter. But she had been thoroughly annoyed with Jarred at the time and she hadn't said one nice thing about the man who had refused to believe she was who she said she was. She had explained that she had been kidnaped, purchased as a servant, and forced to do her wicked master's bidding.

"Bought my daughter like a lowly slave, did he?" Evan erupted in another earth-shaking bellow that could have raised the dead. Still swearing fluently, he read on, hating Jarred McAlister sight unseen. When Evan got to the part about the ship and crew starving and abusing Chelsie, he was on his feet, storming around the room, muttering curses that would have burned the ears off a priest. Doris, however, was accustomed to these tirades, and she didn't bat an eye at the string of obscenities that tumbled from the duke's lips.

"I'll wring that worthless colonial's neck! I'll tear those vicious pirates limb from limb and hang their remains on the mast of their bloody ship! I'll watch them all die one by one and I'll consign them to the fiery dungeons of hell, so help me, I will!" Evan brandished his fist at the walls.

His green eyes burning, Evan pivoted toward Doris. "Pack our belongings," he hollered at her as if she were stone-deaf. "We are leaving for Maryland within the hour."

" 'Tis already done," she informed him calmly.

"You read my mail—and my mind!" Evan accused harshly.

Doris didn't cower. She raised her pointed chin. "Aye, for your own good," she declared with conviction. "You were in no mood to receive discouraging news today. If Chelsie had not been alive, I wouldn't have given the letter to you until after you had simmered down."

"I do not need you to screen my mail, woman," Evan snapped as he stalked to the door. "I am a grown man!"

"A man with a vengeance," Doris amended as she followed in his wake. "You have been hell to live with, and I shall not tolerate any more of your snarling."

"You will have to listen to it until I vent my fury on those bastards who dared to kidnap and humiliate my daughter," Evan growled.

"And if you don't get a grip on yourself, you will have a seizure before you reach the colonies," Doris told him matter-of-factly. "It will take at least a month, maybe more, to make the voyage, and I will not endure your ravings for two fortnights!"

"Then don't go," Evan bit off.

Doris puffed up like a toad. "Not go?" She expelled a derisive snort. "That girl is as precious to me as she is to you. I promised her mother I would keep watch over her until my dying day, and I intend to do it!"

Evan inhaled a huge breath and his massive chest swelled to phenomenal proportions. Slowly he expelled the air and dropped his head to study the tiled floor beneath his feet. "I will try to contain myself in your presence, woman. But do not expect me to restrain my temper when I get a hold of this

Jarred McAlister and those scurrilous pirates. They will know hell hath no fury like that of a father who has lost his most prized possession!"

"You can give them all the hell you wish," Doris generously offered. "But spare me another tantrum. I have heard quite enough of them the past three months." A curious frown knitted her brow as she studied the postscript on the note Chelsie had sent. "What do you suppose Chel wants with Moonraker?"

"How the devil do I know?" Evan grunted. "If she had wanted the whole blessed stable, I would have ripped it down and set it afloat. I don't care what I have to do to get my daughter back!"

In a flurry, Evan and Doris collected their belongings and clambered into the coach that would take them to London. Behind the carriage, the shiny silver-gray stallion tossed his proud head, protesting being led anywhere. But he went nonetheless, because the Duke of Chessfield was hell-bent on setting sail for Maryland with Moonraker in tow. And God help any man or beast who stood in his way!

Now, Jarred McAlister was not a man who ran from trouble, and he didn't allow it to run from him either. But he was going to wish trouble had taken a detour around him when it came in the form of the ominous Duke of Chessfield. Evan was mad enough to tear Jarred into bite-sized pieces, and man enough to do it. When Chelsie said, "Just you wait until my father gets here," she wasn't kidding!

Chapter 21

While plans were being made for the upcoming wedding, Chelsie battled thoughts of the handsome rake who was attending the convention in Albany by concentrating her time and energy on Trumpeter's training. The technique did not prove to be one-hundred-percent effective, however. Jarred's image kept cropping up at the most unexpected moments. Chelsie hadn't wanted to spare that philanderer another thought, but his memory came uninvited to her dreams. Time and time again, Chelsie assured herself she was through loving that handsome rascal, that she had gotten him out of her system. But each time she saw Abi and Neil together, she whimsically wished Jarred could have been as loving and devoted to her as Neil was to Abi.

The only reason she missed Jarred was because he wasn't there to comfort her when she awakened from a nightmare, Chelsie convinced herself. What she had felt for Jarred was just a childish fascination. She only missed him because she had grown accustomed to having him around, and he was simply a habit that would take time to break. She only yearned for his erotic brand of lovemaking because he had unlocked her feminine desires and permitted them to run rampant. Wanting him had been perfectly natural, and it didn't mean a thing, Chelsie tried to reassure herself. She had been physically attracted to Jarred, and she had mistaken that attraction for love. Jarred felt nothing special for her. In his opinion, she was good enough to bed, but not good enough to wed. She was just a warm body for him to cuddle up to.

When her father arrived, she would return to Chessfield to take up life where she had left off. She would simply pretend these past few months hadn't existed. She would be content with the life she had once known . . . she hoped. . . .

Chelsie heaved a heavy-hearted sigh. After listing those consoling platitudes, she didn't feel one bit better. Thunderation, how could she long for a man who didn't love her and never would? What a fool she was, what a glutton for punishment! The wound on her arm had healed satisfactorily—why was it taking so long for the gash in her heart to mend?

Determined to outrun the tormenting thoughts of a man who didn't want her for what she was and who had never trusted her, Chelsie nudged Trumpeter into his swiftest gait. As if he understood his mistress's need to fly, the steed took off like a shot.

Ah, well, Chelsie consoled herself as she leaned against Trumpeter's neck, feeling the wind rush past her face like fleeting memories. At least now she knew she wasn't woman enough to please any man. The swains who had courted her in England had obviously been after her money. They were impressed by her title, her prestige, and her fortune. They were bedazzled by what she represented. But the truth was that no man found her personality endearing or intriguing. Jarred didn't think she had a shilling to her name, and he wasn't the *least* bit impressed with her. My, but titles held incredible influence, she mused dispiritedly. When she was strolling through England, people looked up to her because she was a Channing. She had enough wealth and influence to make her own rules as she went along. But now that she was under Jarred's thumb, he looked down upon her as if she were a lowly peasant.

In a way, Jarred was right about her. On the inside, she was a pauper who played at being a princess. In England, she had flitted from one man to another, rejecting proposals right and left. But it had never been the real Chelsie Channing those fawning suitors wanted, only her money. If she could have earned Jarred's love without him knowing she was truly an heiress, she would have been assured that men wanted her for herself, not for the wealth and influence she could grant them. But her inability to win Jarred's affection was the true test of her worth. Chelsie was thoroughly convinced that her title and fortune was all men really wanted from her.

That thought was hard on her self-confidence. True, her name had earned her entrance to any door in England and would gain her boundless privileges in the colonies. But on the inside, where it truly counted, she began to wonder if she possessed any unforgettable qualities that could lure a man the way Neil was lured to Abi.

Well, it didn't matter, Chelsie convinced herself. She was going to become a dedicated spinster. She was never going to let another man close enough to hurt her the way Jarred had. Her family was wealthy enough that she would never want for anything. She had no need to marry for money, and she wouldn't marry for love because the one man she could have. . . . Well, just because, Chelsie mused stubbornly, refusing to complete the thought.

Her pride was already smarting. To admit she couldn't marry for love because no one else could take Jarred's place was to accept defeat. What Abi and Neil shared was rare, and Chelsie was an idealistic fool to believe their love was the rule instead of the exception. The truth of the matter was that most aristocrats married for position, and most men and women were fortunate indeed if they ever fell in love with the spouse they were pressured into marrying. Was it any wonder so many men kept mistresses and women entertained lovers . . . ?

Stop this philosophical prattle, Chelsie scolded herself. She had no right to be feeling lonely. The McAlisters had treated her like a queen. She was never at a loss for companionship when she wanted it. Grant had accompanied her to the Newton's party, and she had never lacked for dance partners. Daniel hovered around her like a devoted puppy while she wandered around Easthaven. She had attended the grand reception Rebecca had organized to announce Neil and Abi's engagement, and she had met many of the plantation owners and their families.

Kyle had practically adopted her as the daughter he had never had. He insisted that she ride with him to prayer meeting each Sunday, and he came to her for advice about outrunning Amos's prized trotter. And Kyle had been walking on air when, at Chelsie's insistence, the bay mare from Chessfield was harnessed to his carriage. The mare had defeated Amos's steed by a nose, and Kyle had strutted into church like a peacock. It was Amos who had been forced to beg forgiveness for using colorful curses on the Sabbath.

So why should a woman who lacked for nothing be wandering around like an abandoned child? And why on earth did she search for Jarred on every steed that trotted down the path near Easthaven? Even when Jarred returned, nothing would change. Chelsie had vowed to treat him just like the rest of the family — with friendliness and respect, nothing more, nothing less. What had been between them was over. To live on false hopes would only break her heart, and Chelsie swore up and down she would not return to Chessfield, longing for a man who probably hadn't given her another thought since he rode away from Easthaven. There was no telling how many women had lain in Jarred's arms these past few weeks. Chelsie refused to even hazard a guess, knowing it would only depress her.

The crash of furniture and the furious roar of voices that ricocheted around the walls of the dimly lit tavern in Albany's less respectable district of town had Eli grumbling under his breath. Jarred had been in a black mood for almost a month. Tonight he had gone looking for trouble and found it. Eli, caring friend that he was, had followed Jarred, certain he was bent on self-destruction. After tracking Jarred to a similar tavern of ill-repute a few blocks away, Eli had spied on Kyle's second son while he gulped down one mug of ale after another. When Jarred was approached by a buxom brunette who had planted herself in his lap and practically slobbered all over him, Eli had watched Jarred leave the tavern with the wench to adjourn to her quarters.

Eli had cursed Jarred's indiscretion, but to his bewilderment, the drunken rake had come storming from the doxie's room mumbling a string of curses. Eli didn't have the faintest idea what had transpired, but Jarred hadn't been there ten minutes before he stamped out and headed toward the next tavern. In less than fifteen minutes, judging by the ruckus going on inside, Jarred had picked a fight with anyone who would accommodate him.

Heaving a disgusted sigh, Eli shoved his shoulder against the heavy door and barged into the tavern. Sure enough, Jarred had taken on three of the surliest looking varmints ever to congregate in one place! When a chair flew across the room, Eli ducked and took cover behind an upturned table. Rolling his eyes in disdain, he watched Jarred's doubled fist collide with one stubbled cheek before he wheeled about to attack the brute who came at him from behind. Before the third bully could grab ahold of him, Jarred snatched up another chair and slammed it against the man's broad head. After another five minutes of fists matching powerful fists and bodies flying across the room, Jarred was finally wrestled down and held in place while two of the scalawags took turns punching him.

Drawing his flintlock, Eli approached the three men who were beating the tar out of Jarred. "That's enough," Eli growled. When one of the oversized brutes pivoted to give him a taste of his beefy fist, the valet cocked the trigger and sneered menacingly. "Back off, Goliath. I'd just as soon shoot you as look at you."

The three men finally retreated, leaving Jarred sprawled on the floor. Propping himself up on an elbow, Jarred glared at his meddling valet through bloodshot eyes.

"I don't recall inviting you to rescue me. If I had wanted your assistance, I'd've asked for it," Jarred muttered.

Eli, still holding the drop on the three surly scoundrels, extended a hand to hoist Jarred to his feet. "You can thank me later," he snorted.

"What the hell are you doing here, anyway?" Jarred scowled as he scraped himself off the floor.

"Following a fool," Eli smirked as he slowly backed toward the tavern door. "We're going to the hotel before you get yourself in more trouble than you already have. You always swore Chelsie was a walking disaster, but if you ask me. . . ."

"I'm not asking, and don't you *dare* mention that minx's name around me again," Jarred exploded. Before he reached the exit, he grasped an abandoned mug of ale on the only table that was still standing upright and downed it in one swallow.

Once they were outside, Eli tucked his pistol beneath his coat and grabbed ahold of Jarred's arm. He was weaving about like a besotted ape, and Eli had not enough patience left to fill a thimble. He wanted to hustle Jarred to his room and put him to bed.

Jarred obediently walked the first block in silence, for which Eli was thankful. If the rapscallion became belligerent or unruly, Eli doubted he would be able to handle him. He had met with difficulty the last time Jarred had gone on one of these binges, and they were beginning to occur with alarming regularity. He and Jarred had been in Albany for four weeks, and like clockwork, Jarred had gone out to drink himself insane every third night. Eli didn't have to be a genius to know what was tormenting Jarred, but the damned fool wouldn't admit that his green-eyed leprechaun had taken a permanent hold on him. He just kept fighting the feeling tooth and nail. . . .

A shocked gasp erupted from Eli's lips when out of the blue Jarred reached over to give him an affectionate squeeze. For a moment Eli swore Jarred even meant to scoop him up in his arms. Good God, Jarred was so far into his cups, he didn't know what in blazes he was doing! Sputtering indignantly, Eli whacked Jarred's cheek, then listened to him grumble at Chelsie, and she wasn't even around to hear him!

"That's just what I thought," Eli grunted as he shoved Jarred's arms away a second time. "You see Chelsie's features in every face you confront and you have been trying to drink yourself blind so you won't have to see her. But all the liquor in Albany can't dissolve her haunting image, can it?" His voice rose to a dull roar. "If you'd married that girl, like you should

267

have in the first place, you wouldn't be in such an irascible mood. Now you've started picking fights with an army of brutish giants you can't possibly hope to whip without reinforcements. . . ."

Eli flinched when Jarred tripped over his feet and practically fell on his face. Clutching Jarred's arm, Eli jerked him upright and aimed him toward the hotel. "Damned stubborn, arrogant fool," he muttered irritably. "The sooner you admit you're in love with that pretty little witch, the happier you'll be."

"I hate her," Jarred contradicted over his thick tongue.

"Of course you do," Eli snorted sarcastically. "That's why you made such an ass of yourself tonight. Well, I hope Neil or Grant winds up marrying the duchess. It would serve you right for the way you have treated her. And if I hadn't promised your father I would keep a watch over you, I would have let those three gorillas make mincemeat of you. Maybe they could have beaten some sense into you!"

Still spouting about Jarred's temporary lapse of sanity and his asinine behavior, Eli propelled his master to his hotel suite. In frustration he shoved Jarred onto the bed, where he collapsed into incessant mumblings and thrashed around until he passed out from too much liquor.

Heaving an exasperated sigh, Eli stared down at what was left of Jarred's elegant garments. It was a good thing he and Jarred were to depart for Easthaven the following day, because Jarred was down to his last set of decent clothes, and he couldn't take much more of these beatings. Jarred was punishing himself, Eli supposed. But then, he really couldn't say for certain what Jarred was trying to prove. The man had been moody and as quiet as a clam since they'd left Easthaven.

Unless Eli missed his guess, Chelsie was the haunting thought that refused to go away and grant Jarred a moment's peace. The man was hopelessly hooked on that blond-haired sprite, and he was fighting his feelings for her because he wasn't accustomed to caring so much about a woman. It was a first for Jarred, and he didn't know how to handle it. The more Jarred cared about Chelsie, the harder he fought those unfamiliar feelings that bound him like unrelenting chains.

After tugging off Jarred's boots, Eli gently eased the tattered waistcoat from his shoulders. If Jarred and Chelsie didn't get things straightened out between them before long, Jarred wouldn't have an unbroken bone left in his body. Lord, how many fights could a man pick before his swarthy challengers beat him to a bloody pulp?

Well, this was going to stop, Eli decided. When Jarred woke the following morning, Eli was going to read him the riot act. If Jarred didn't accept what he was feeling, Eli was going to wash his hands of this stubborn rake and let that pack of goons make a meal of him. Damn him, enough was enough!

As the days progressed at a snail's pace, Chelsie began to doubt Jarred would return in time to attend the wedding, which was to be held in Baltimore. The Shaws had several relatives in the northern community, and the wedding party was scheduled to depart the following afternoon. Although Neil graciously offered to postpone the ceremony until Jarred returned, Kyle wouldn't hear of it. Now that he had one of his sons this close to the altar, he wasn't about to reschedule the wedding!

The family gathered their belongings and carted them aboard the schooner bound for Baltimore. As the vessel opened sail, Chelsie peered out across Chesapeake Bay, watching the pungeys and skiffs that followed the lazy, winding creeks that led inland to the plush, green countryside. Waterfowl took flight to escape the intrusion of the schooner that cut effortlessly through the blue-gray waters of the bay and seagulls cried out as they swooped and dived high above the deck.

The previous month, when a thunderstorm had unleashed its fury, Chelsie swore she would lay buried at the bottom of this bay. But Jarred had . . . Chelsie squelched the thought, along with the bittersweet memories of the hours they had spent nestled in each other's arms, waiting out the howling storm. And later that night he had come to her room, whispering his need to be with her before he walked out of her life.

Blast it, Jarred could have at least written to her, couldn't he? If he cared at all, he would have. But he didn't. Those softly uttered words were only a ploy to seduce her one last time before he left her soul to bleed.

"Get out of my mind and my heart," Chelsie hissed at the hauntingly handsome image that rose like an apparition from the murky depths to torment her.

"You miss him, don't you?" Neil's quiet voice sliced through her pensive musings and Chelsie practically leaped out of her skin.

Struggling for composure, she pivoted away from the rail to peer into Neil's refined features. "Who? My father? Aye, I do," she replied with mock innocence.

A wry grin grazed Neil's lips. "I wasn't referring to the duke, Chelsie."

"Nay?" She raised a perfectly arched brow and blessed him with a dazzling smile. "My father is the only man in my life."

Neil chuckled in amusement as he braced his forearms on the rail. "You are as stubborn and proud as my brother. I should tell Papa what has been going on between you and Jarred so he can schedule a second wedding. Nothing would please Kyle more."

Her hand folded around Neil's arm and she gazed beseechingly at him. "If you wish to repay me for seeing that you and Abi were finally allowed to enjoy your hearts' desire, you will keep my secret and spare me the humiliation. 'Tis not the same as it is for you and Abi," she insisted earnestly. "There is so much you do not know. There are things between Jarred and me that have not been resolved—and may never be."

Neil heaved a defeated sigh. It was difficult to deny this sultry beauty her whim when she stared up at him with those enormous green eyes. "Very well, Chelsie, I will honor your request. But whether you admit it or not, you are suffering from a serious heart condition. And I recognize all the symptoms," he murmured, casting her a sympathetic smile. "I carried a torch for Abi for more than eighteen months. How long do you intend to carry yours?"

When Neil ambled across the deck, Chelsie pulled a face at his departing back. Heart condition, indeed! She had tried to explain that her situation was different from the mutual affection he and Abi felt. Jarred wouldn't know love if it walked up and sat down on top of him. He didn't want her in all the ways true love entailed. Love was needing to be with someone in order to give meaning to each day. It wasn't just the joining of bodies, but also of minds and hearts and souls. It was a craving to be a part of someone's life, a fierce longing to share each other's hopes and dreams. . . .

Chelsie blinked. All those feelings were the same yearnings she still felt for that impossible raven-haired devil. After all the silent pep talks she had delivered to herself the past few weeks, one would have thought she would have gotten over Jarred. Damnation, why was falling out of love so difficult? She should have hated Jarred by now. She had categorized all his faults, but that hadn't stopped her from searching for him in every shadow, from wanting him obsessively. She had recognized him as a lost cause from the beginning, and she knew he would never return this one-sided love she felt for him. Jarred didn't want to be tied down, or he would have married Abi long ago. And Chelsie had given him the perfect opportunity to express what he felt for her the night before he left. All he had said was that he wanted her (wanted her body, to be specific).

When Chelsie glanced over her shoulder, Neil was negligently propped against the railing, smiling slyly at her. He probably thought he had given her food for thought and that she was going to throw herself at Jarred's feet, begging for whatever scraps of affection he would toss her way. Well, it was time Neil understood how things were and how they were going to be, Chelsie decided. Neil was standing there so smugly, thinking he knew it all. The fact was, he didn't know beans about her relationship with Jarred—how it had begun and where it was going—and it was time she told the meddling doctor a thing or two.

Drawing herself up, Chelsie stamped over to Neil, who was grinning like a Cheshire cat. "Before you start scheming and

271

thinking it wouldn't hurt to go behind my back to inform your brother that I'm in love with him, there are a few things you should know."

"Did I say I was considering such deviousness?" Neil asked, amused by the spark of fire he saw flickering in Chelsie's emerald eyes. Only just now had he observed the feisty side of Chelsie's nature, and he understood why Jarred had been intrigued by her. Chelsie was extremely high-spirited. It was evident in the way she held herself, the way she approached her challenger. She had tried to contain herself within the limitations of womanhood, but there was no holding back all that vivacious spunk. Chelsie lived for thrills. That was why she eagerly offered to train the copper dun colt, why she insisted on scaling the trellis instead of employing doors and stairs. Her zest for living, her fiery emotions and ungovernable passions were difficult to restrain.

"In the first place, I have already made the foolish mistake of admitting how I felt about Jarred. Not that it made a whit of difference to him, mind you. He said nothing about love when he had the chance, when I dared to bare my heart to him. And since he left Easthaven, I have heard not one word from him," Chelsie blustered. "He doesn't want me the way you want Abi. 'Tis as simple as that."

"Do you love him enough to attempt to win his love? Can you be patient enough to wait until he sorts out his emotions?" Neil asked gently. "My brother is cynical of affection because women have always come to him with little more invitation than an interested glance. He has tried to keep his distance from you, but he was always there when you needed him, and he always comes back when he finds himself *needing* you." Unblinking brown eyes bore down on Chelsie. "You mean something to Jarred. 'Tis evident in the way he looks at you when he thinks no one is watching, in the way he hovers about, keeping sentinel over you."

"Jarred is satisfied with his life, but I cannot continue the same way we have been going. And I know for a fact that I don't mean anything special to him. You are trying to read more into his casual glances than is really there," Chelsie snapped irritably.

Although she was unaware she was taking her frustration for Jarred out on his older brother, Neil understood, and it was difficult for him to suppress his amused grin. He delighted in observing this dynamic side of Chelsie's personality. He could well imagine how Jarred felt when she put him on the firing line. This blond-haired hellion and that ornery brother of his would make the perfect match, once they realized the strength of the bond between them, that is.

"Jarred has never trusted me. He refuses to believe in me and feels no love for me," Chelsie went on, even though her pride was smarting. "What he wants from me is the same thing he desires from any other woman. All we have accomplished is to have complicated each other's lives. As soon as my father arrives, I am going to do Jarred and me a favor by returning home and ending this. . . ." Her eyes dropped to study her slippered feet, as if something there suddenly demanded her attention. "This affair," she finished in a softer voice.

"Putting an ocean between the two of you isn't going to help." Neil cupped her chin, forcing her to meet his solemn gaze.

"Aye, it will," Chelsie insisted.

Neil gave his head a negative shake. "I tried to bury myself in my work to forget the woman I never thought I could have. But nothing could smother her memory, and an ocean won't drown it."

As Chelsie wheeled around to stomp away, Neil scoffed at her stubbornness. "You can't outrun love, duchess. There is no horse swift enough, no schooner fleet enough to escape those intangible feelings. They will reach across the endless miles to touch and torment you," he prophesied. "And even though Jarred refused to offer a confession of affection back to you, you might be surprised to learn that Jarred is suffering from the same heart condition that plagues you."

"He certainly looked healthy enough to me the last time I saw him," Chelsie muttered without a backward glance.

Neil may have been an experienced physician, but he wasn't an authority on his brother. All Jarred had ever wanted from Chelsie was a womanly body to appease his needs. She knew that as well as she knew her own name. He didn't give a fig about the feelings and emotions attached to the body that pleasured him. Jarred didn't want to make room for a woman in his life. He would never settle down. He had his chance to say what he felt the night before he left, and he had said nothing about loving her back, because he didn't. At least he was honest, Chelsie begrudgingly admitted. In his silence he had spoken volumes. Chelsie knew better than to expect more than Jarred knew how to give.

Chelsie was through living on whimsical dreams. She had humiliated herself too many times by succumbing to her wanton desires. She had fallen in love with a man who enjoyed his freedom and who would never give it up. Never again would she confess her feelings for Jarred. If she did, he would probably laugh in her face. She might never get over loving him completely, but she wasn't going to allow him another chance to tread all over her heart. Clinging to that resolution, Chelsie gathered her luggage and waited impatiently for the ship to ease beside the wharf.

A melancholy smile hovered on her lips as she peered at the thriving community of Baltimore. Chelsie felt incredibly ancient all of a sudden. It was as if she had aged at a phenomenal rate these past few months. Not so long ago she had been a spoiled heiress, the apple of her father's eye, the belle of London. But oh, what a metamorphosis she had undergone after she had been bound, gagged, and herded aboard the schooner to be transplanted in Maryland! She had learned what it meant to be starved, beaten, and ridiculed. She had discovered the true meaning of humiliation and despair—as well as the bitter disappointment of unrequited love.

If it was true that one's character was what one had left when one had lost all there was to lose, Chelsie felt she had nothing at all.

She laughed humorlessly at herself. When Jarred had referred to her as a pauper and a thief, she had vehemently protested. But the depressing fact was that Jarred had seen right through her, finding nothing exceptional about her. When she was stripped of her title and her fortune, there was nothing worthy about her to like. All the McAlisters except Jarred liked her because of what she represented. They catered to her because of her prestige. Their attitude toward her lent credence to the testimony that her friendships were based on who she was, not on what she was.

Ah, well, Chelsie mused as she accepted Grant and Daniel's assistance across the gangplank. At long last she had come to know herself. If she had learned nothing else from her ordeal and her one-sided love, it was that her failing graces far outnumbered her redeeming qualities. And knowing herself as she did, it was little wonder that Jarred saw no depth of character in them. She wasn't sure why he had felt the need to shield her from her enemies. Chelsie sighed heavily at the thought. It was probably because of Jarred's innate need to rescue abandoned souls and battle lost causes. She was no more than an obligation, and Jarred was strongly motivated by his overactive sense of responsibility. He thought he was giving her a chance to better herself by buying her indentureship. He had become entangled in his misdirected feelings of protectiveness, and his physical attraction to her had complicated matters.

Now that she understood Jarred's motivations and her own feelings, she could accept things, Chelsie convinced herself. It didn't make the hurt go away, but she had gained valuable insight about herself and Jarred. And when she finally returned home, she would be a better person because of the painful lessons she had learned. She had matured. In the years to come, she would look back on these months and label them her bridge between childhood and adulthood. What a rude awakening it had been! Once she had seen herself through Jarred's eyes, she recognized her shortcomings.

Feeling less confident than ever, Chelsie sank into her seat in the coach. At least Neil and Abi were happy, she nobly reminded herself. It was comforting to know that someone was.

Chapter 22

Narrowed blue eyes squinted into the sun, relishing the view of Easthaven from the rise of ground to the north. The spacious plantation was splattered with a spectrum of brilliant colors that graced the countryside at sunset. Odd, Jarred couldn't remember being quite so anxious to return home. There was always a mountain of work awaiting him and ledgers to be labored over after long absences such as this. But this time Jarred had been eager to return to Easthaven after only one week. Chelsie's memory had followed him like his own shadow, tormenting his days and nights. Her image had colored every conversation and stained every fleeting thought. Lord, she had become a habit Jarred couldn't unlearn, and he had tried. Each night he stewed over who would be there beside her to soothe her haunting nightmares. He speculated on which of his brothers was presently turning his charms on the saucy vixen, and his predictions were tying his nerves in knots.

Jarred had not only ached for her up to his eyebrows, but he longed for her companionship. He wanted to be the recipient of her radiant smiles, to test himself against her quick wit. For the first time in his life, wandering had become an empty substitute for a craving that nothing cured. Even the long, tiring sessions at the Albany Congress hadn't distracted him all that much. He had missed her. And if wishing would have made it so, he would have closed his eyes and wished Chelsie into his arms. Him! The man who had walked away from a dozen affairs without the slightest remorse, without feeling a compelling need to go back and take up where he had left off.

Nothing had eased his obsession for her. It was getting worse instead of better. Her absence in his life left an emptiness nothing could fill.

For the past six weeks Jarred had turned his feelings over in his mind a million times. He had carefully spread his emotions before him, analyzing them one by one. But it was that last maddening night before he'd left Albany that had finally done it. Chelsie's vivid memory had gotten the better of him, and Jarred had marched off to seek solace in a bottle of rum.

Jarred had thought liquor was the answer, that after a few hours of fast and furious drinking, he wouldn't even remember the question. When the curvaceous brunette had planted herself in his lap and offered him sexual favors, Jarred had accepted, since drinking hadn't cured his obsession. He was sure he could love Chelsie's memory away when liquor failed to curb his frustration. Jarred had been determined to forget the hold Chelsie had over him. Without delay he had escorted the brunette wench to her quarters, unaware that Eli had been his constant shadow that night.

The moment Jarred closed the door to grant himself privacy with the attractive doxie, a pair of dazzling green eyes appeared from nowhere. Jarred was convinced it was the rum that was playing tricks with his eyes, but the more he blinked, the more the chit began to take on Chelsie's enchanting features. When the wench curled her arms around him and pressed suggestively against him, Jarred had backed away. *Backed away,* mind you! The feel of the woman in his arms was all wrong. He couldn't bring himself to touch another woman while Chelsie was there to taunt him, practicing her bedeviling powers, even while they were miles apart.

Although Jarred's passions had lain dormant for five agonizing weeks, he had wheeled around to snatch up his discarded coat. Mumbling a flimsy excuse, Jarred had stalked out into the night to make a beeline for another tavern on the rough-and-tumble side of town. Since loving Chelsie's memory hadn't worked worth a damn, Jarred resorted to liquor once more. His hunting expedition for a cure to terminate his preoccupation with that vivacious beauty left him circling back to the bottle. In the smoke-filled tavern, Jarred had again drunk himself half-blind, but still it didn't help. And so naturally he had picked a fight, uncaring if he won or lost, just as long as he had something else to distract him. He had wanted to forget that green-eyed leprechaun who possessed the body and face of an angel and the magical lure of a witch.

The rest of the night was a blur to Jarred. He did recall throwing fists and receiving a few well-aimed blows to his jaw and midsection. And then, of course, he remembered seeing Eli's face puckered in a condescending frown. After that, Jarred drew a blank, but Eli was inconsiderate enough to give a detailed rendition of his behavior the following morning while Jarred was nursing one hellish hangover.

According to Eli, Jarred had referred to his valet as Miss Chelsie Channing from Chessfield. Then, in his besotted condition, he had proceeded to hug the stuffing out of his manservant. Eli didn't take kindly to dragging his master home by the nape of his tattered jacket and tucking him in bed. Nor did Eli appreciate amorous embraces from one of his own kind. For that, Eli had raked Jarred over the coals but good.

Through fuzzy eyes Jarred had watched Eli wag a stubby finger in his face and curse him for behaving like an ass. When Eli glared at him as if he was contemplating knocking the tar out of his master, Jarred assured him it was a waste of time, since he was going to die from his hangover anyway. Eli, who hadn't been the least bit sympathetic, had proclaimed dying was too good for a man who behaved as abominally as Jarred had.

After Jarred had soaked in the bathhouse for the better part of the morning, he had come to his senses. And while he sat there and soaked, he finally realized why he had been acting the way he had.

For weeks Jarred had battled this mental tug-of-war, aching for Chelsie, haunted by his obligation to Abi. No matter how many lectures he had delivered himself, he couldn't let go of the memories he and Chelsie had made. Not the good times

. . . not even the bad times. He thought of Abi and he hated himself for betraying a woman who deserved far better than he could do. He contemplated the distasteful way he'd treated Chelsie, and he cursed a blue streak. Jarred was tired of fighting his attraction for that blond-haired hellion. Abi may have been what a man of his position needed, but Chelsie was the woman Jarred wanted. And it was pure hell when he was in Albany and Chelsie was in Easthaven doing only God knew what with one of his three brothers!

Since Jarred had never been struck by cupid's arrow in all his thirty-two years, he had come to the reasonable conclusion that he was immune. But it seemed the later in life a man came down with the plague of love, the more difficult it was to cure his case.

So he had fallen in love with a sassy peasant who pretended to be a duchess. So what if she had been a beggar and thief in her other life, in England? There were still qualities about her that intrigued him. Chelsie's past and her questionable background no longer mattered. He adored the woman she had become—no matter how she had gotten to be that way. She was keen-witted, feisty, spirited, intelligent, and gorgeous. And maybe she had once been an aristocrat's daughter before disaster befell her family. But somewhere along the way Chelsie had received an ample education. Jarred might never learn the truth about her past, because Chelsie insisted on clinging to that tall tale about being a duke's daughter. And there had been a time or two when Jarred wanted to believe it, despite what Cyrus Hutton and Isaac Latham had told him. But the fact was, Chelsie didn't fit into the mold of the dignified, refined duchess. None of the ones Jarred had met in England behaved anything like this green-eyed wildcat. Duchess, indeed!

But in Chelsie's defense, Jarred *did* admit that he might have concocted such a story if he'd been forced to endure the atrocities she'd suffered at Isaac's hands. And none of that mattered now . . . Chelsie's past didn't interest him. All he cared about was the present—and the future. Things were going to be different from now on, he promised himself. He hadn't decided how to break off his engagement without hurting Abi or insulting the Shaws, but he would work it out . . . somehow. He loved Chelsie, and fighting the attraction had only made him miserable and impossible to live with (as Eli had so bluntly informed him).

The odd stillness that settled over Easthaven had Jarred worried. There wasn't the usual bustle of activity. Chelsie wasn't out exercising that copper dun colt; Kyle wasn't taking his trotter through the paces in anticipation of another Sunday morning race with Amos. Where the hell was everybody?

"This place looks as if it is deserted," Eli observed, squirming uncomfortably in his saddle. Lord, he couldn't wait to part company with his steed. Jarred had been in such a rush to return home, he'd taken no time out to rest. Jarred may not have felt the wear and tear on his bones and muscles, but Eli was getting too old to spend night and day on the back of a horse.

"Something is wrong," Jarred muttered, nudging his mahogany bay stallion toward the stable. "I hope to God Chelsie hasn't gotten herself in some kind of trouble that has affected the entire household."

Before Jarred could dismount at the barn, one of the grooms strode outside. A broad smile split the trainer's tanned face. "We were beginning to wonder if you would make it back in time."

Uneasiness settled over Jarred like a black cloud. "In time for what?" he questioned impatiently.

"Everybody has been talking about it for weeks, and we all thought you would be back from New York long before now," the groom rattled on, refusing to meet Jarred's probing stare. "The squire decided to go ahead without you. You know how anxious he has been to see one of his sons married. And since all the arrangements had been made . . ."

"Married!" Jarred croaked, his eyes popping.

The trainer nodded. "Neil is getting married tomorrow in Baltimore. The family packed up, and . . ."

A disgusted growl erupted from Jarred's lips. Kyle had apparently persuaded Neil to marry Chelsie, and they hadn't even bothered to wait for the second son to return from his duties as a representative to the Albany Congress! Scowling in fluent profanity, Jarred wheeled his steed around and took off like a cannonball.

Eli muttered a few salty curses of his own as he followed in Jarred's wake. Neither of them took the time to let the groom finish what he intended to say. A pity, that . . . if Jarred had known Neil was about to marry Abi, he might not have thundered off so. But all he could envision was Chelsie speaking the vows with Neil, and he *had* to stop that wedding! Once he had finally decided he couldn't live without Chelsie, he couldn't tolerate the thought of losing her to anyone, not even one of his own brothers. He had spent six agonizing weeks trying to forget her, and it hadn't worked a whit. She was in his blood, for God's sake! She couldn't marry Neil when she'd confessed she loved Jarred . . . could she?

Ah, the bitter irony, Jarred thought with an empty laugh. After all these years, he'd finally found a woman who made him forget every other female he had ever known. Now his brother was about to make Chelsie his wife. How could he live in the same house with her, knowing she had once admitted to loving him and had then turned to Neil? Chelsie would be sleeping in his older brother's arms and Jarred would be. . . . The thought twisted in his belly like a knife.

"What are you going to do if you arrive too late to stop that wedding?" Eli asked when Jarred finally slowed the stallion to a walk.

"The first thing we have to do is get there," Jarred grumbled. "Damn it, how could she consent to marry Neil when she said . . ."

"Well, what would *you* have done if you were her?" Eli snorted derisively. "You flaunted Abi under Chelsie's nose and kept her as your mistress. If the duchess sends you away after the way you've treated her, I wouldn't be surprised. In fact, I'd say you had it coming."

Jarred slid his outspoken servant a disdainful glance. "Thank you for your support and encouragement," he mocked caustically. "I don't know how I'm supposed to behave, since I've never been in love before."

"Well, at least you've finally admitted it. That is one step in the right direction," Eli chuckled.

"But there is still Abi to consider," Jarred muttered in frustration. "I don't want to hurt her. Damn it, sometimes I wish I'd never met that green-eyed witch. I was perfectly happy with my life until she came along."

Eli stared at Jarred and scoffed explosively. "For a man who knows his way around the Maryland Assembly and the backwoods of the Ohio Valley, you are a full-fledged buffoon when it comes to affairs of the heart. If you wind up miserable, it would damn well serve you right. For two long months I tried to tell you that you were engaged to the wrong woman."

"What I don't need right now is your criticism," Jarred spat.

"If you'd listened to me, you and Chelsie would've wed last month, and she wouldn't be preparing to marry your big brother," Eli muttered. "But did you listen?" He didn't wait for Jarred to respond; he simply raved on. "Nay, you did not! You just blundered ahead. Now Chelsie is marrying Neil, and you're going to be the one in a deep depression. . . ."

"Oh, for God's sake!" Jarred howled as he urged his steed into a trot, refusing to listen to the rest of Eli's long-winded sermon.

"Damned fool," Eli grumbled as Jarred darted away. If Chelsie married Neil, things would be worse than they already were. Jarred had rebelled against his feelings for that saucy hellion, trying to break the magical spell she'd cast on him, but it hadn't kept him from wanting her. He wasn't accustomed to having a mere wisp of a woman tie his emotions in knots. He had been unusually discontent since the morning they'd left Easthaven more than six weeks ago. *Nothing* had suited Jarred during their sojourn in Albany. And what was going to be infinitely worse was for Chelsie to become Neil's wife before Jarred could tell her how he felt about her. Sweet mercy! Life at Easthaven would be nothing short of hell if Chelsie married the wrong man. Even if it had been Eli's idea to match that sassy nymph with Neil, it would never work now, not after Jarred and Chelsie had become hopelessly involved.

The harder Jarred pushed his steed to reach Baltimore in the nick of time, the more he tried to convince himself he didn't care if Chelsie married Neil. At least it would be over once and for all. If things turned out for the worst, Jarred would take up residence at one of the other three McAlister plantations. Since he couldn't bare to see Chelsie without touching her, he would simply avoid seeing her, except on rare occasions.

And Eli was right, damn him. Jarred had treated Chelsie disgracefully. If by some remote chance he *did* arrive in time to stop the ceremony, he was going to compensate for wronging her. Things were going to be different . . . he would court Chelsie properly, and with the respect she deserved. She had become such an addiction to him that he hadn't cared what happened as long as he had her in his arms, sharing a passion the likes of which he had never known. He had been overprotective of her, irrationally possessive. Yet he'd withheld his love from her because of his long-standing obligation to Abi.

Jarred was the first to admit he hadn't handled the situation well. But, confound it, that was because he couldn't handle that high-spirited nymph who had turned his well-organized life upside down! How was a man supposed to handle a human hurricane?

Through it all Jarred had discovered a special kind of magic in Chelsie's silky arms. Blast it, Chelsie knew what they shared was unique, didn't she? She had even said she loved him. Whether she truly meant it or not was anybody's guess. What in sweet loving hell was she trying to prove by marrying Neil? That she was entitled to her revenge, that she could fall out of love as easily as she fell into it? Or had it simply been the heat of passion that had provoked her confession? Maybe she hadn't meant what she said. Jarred had heard that phrase uttered many times before by the women in his arms. He had no guarantee that Chelsie was sincere. Passion was often mistaken for love.

And what if she *had* fallen for his mild-mannered, soft-spoken brother? That was certainly within the realm of possibility. Six weeks was a long time to leave a desirable woman like Chelsie with another man when that man's father was pushing for a wedding! He should have taken Chelsie with him, even if he had had to dream up some crazed excuse. Well, it was too late for that, Jarred reminded himself bitterly. He had to reach Baltimore in record time, or he could kiss any chance of happiness with Chelsie good-bye.

The journey to Baltimore was the worst trip of Jarred's life. He swayed back and forth between wanting to fight for the woman he loved and accepting his punishment for refusing to stake his claim on her when he had the chance. Jarred was suffering all the tortures of the damned, and Eli offered not one iota of compassion. He gave Jarred hell all through the night. And although Jarred swore he had been punished enough, he was soon to discover he had endured only the first of nine kinds of hell.

None of the McAlisters knew what sort of trouble was lying in wait. And if Jarred had known what he would face in Baltimore, he'd have wished for wings on his feet. Ah, what a difference two hours would have made! Jarred didn't have the foggiest notion that stopping his brother's wedding would soon be the least of his concerns . . .

Chapter 23

Dressed in the elegant gold gown Kyle had purchased for her to wear to the wedding, Chelsie peered at her reflection in the mirror. The young woman who stared back at her made a valiant effort to look cheerful. But on the inside, her spirits were scraping rock bottom. Try as she may, Chelsie couldn't get Jarred out of her mind. She supposed she was still paying penance for casting aside the score of men who had zealously courted her since her season in London. When she finally met a man who made her want more from life than a solitary existence, she was not allowed to enjoy her heart's desire.

Chelsie heaved a heavy sigh as she rearranged the renegade strands of silver-blond hair that slipped from the mass of curls atop her head. Falling out of love with Jarred McAlister was more difficult than she ever imagined. His name and his vision had attached themselves to so many memories that trying to locate one thought which didn't center around that dashingly handsome rascal was next to impossible.

The abrupt rap at the door dragged Chelsie from her pensive deliberations. That would be Kyle coming to escort her to the church. Neil and his other two brothers had left a half hour earlier to see to the last minute arrangements.

Chelsie had barely opened the door when Isaac Latham leaped around the corner to thrust a knife at her throat. Before Chelsie could scream bloody murder, Isaac shoved a gag in her mouth and tied her hands behind her. Wide-eyed, Chelsie peered at the grisly sailor whose stubbled face was twisted in a sinister sneer.

Still glaring at Chelsie, Isaac fished into his pocket for the hastily scribbled note and the locket he had stolen from her during their voyage to Maryland. Now the locket would serve an important purpose: the time had come to permit Jarred McAlister to know the truth about this feisty bitch. After placing the note and the locket in clear sight on the nightstand, Isaac craned his neck around the door. Hurriedly he tossed a hooded cape over his captive and propelled her toward the back staircase.

Twice Chelsie tried to make a dash for freedom, but the cane Isaac kept clamped in his hand proved to be a painful reminder of who held the upper hand. Chelsie blinked back the tears that threatened to spill from her eyes when Isaac whacked her shoulder and ribs, discouraging her from attempting another escape.

After being scuttled down a path that led to a row of hastily constructed shanties near the wharf, Chelsie was bound to the crude table. Without a word, Isaac hobbled out on his cane, leaving Chelsie to speculate on what evil designs this vicious fiend had in mind for her this time. For the life of her, she couldn't imagine what Isaac was doing in Baltimore and how he had found her.

Chelsie's shoulders slumped dejectedly as she surveyed the dingy shack, searching for a means of escape and finding none. Jarred would probably be delighted to know Isaac had materialized from thin air to dispose of her . . . permanently.

Well, this was one sure-fire way of falling out of love with Jarred, she reckoned. It was a rather drastic method of forgetting the only man she had ever loved. If Isaac had his way, Chelsie was not long for this world. She would go to her grave loving a man who would be glad to have her out of his life once and for all.

While Chelsie was wallowing in the depths of despair and futilely struggling to loose the ropes, Isaac was snickering triumphantly. He had been lounging on board the schooner the previous day when the McAlisters had cruised into Baltimore. Cyrus Hutton and his crew had spent the past month contacting would-be clients and loading cargo to be shipped to England. Isaac hadn't anticipated seeing the sassy wench who had caused him so much trouble, but her unexpected appearance had kindled the fires of his vengeance, ones that had festered for more days than he cared to count.

When Chelsie had stepped ashore with the McAlisters, decked out in finery, a mutinous fury had glazed Isaac's eyes. His hand had clenched the gnarled cane that had become not only his constant companion, but also a perpetual reminder of his anguishing confrontation with Jarred McAlister. Thanks to that sassy bitch, Isaac had suffered a brutal beating at Jarred's hands. And because of that beating, Isaac had wound up with a mangled knee that hadn't ever properly healed. Every step he took reminded him of Chelsie Channing and her vicious guard dragon.

Isaac had always been a vindictive man who held a grudge. He also loathed his lowly station in life and detested the gentry because they had been born to titles he could never hope to attain. His hatred for the feisty duchess and the domineering aristocrat had multiplied with each passing day. When Isaac caught a glimpse of Chelsie, he swore to make her and her arrogant lover pay dearly for what they had done to him.

Hell-bent on his purpose, Isaac had gone ashore to follow the entourage and learn what Chelsie and this family of highfalutin' aristocrats were doing in Baltimore. After he'd tracked Chelsie to the hotel, he watched the McAlister men amble down the street to the tavern. Tucking himself in an out-of-the-way corner, Isaac had listened to Grant and Daniel tease Neil about his upcoming wedding. Once Isaac had discovered what he wanted to know, he'd returned to the ship to make his plans. Now he'd put the first phase of his scheme into motion. He had taken Chelsie as bait to lure out Jarred, and he could almost taste his sweet revenge. When he was through with Chelsie and those haughty aristocrats, they would all be roasting in hell!

After knocking on Chelsie's door for the third time, Kyle frowned. Where the devil was the duchess? They had agreed to ride to the church together. Kyle shrugged. Perhaps Chelsie had decided to travel with his sons, too anxious to wait for Kyle, who had fussed with his clothes and appearance to ensure he looked his best for this monumental occasion.

Scurrying down the hall, Kyle rapped on his sister's door. Within a few minutes, Kyle and Rebecca were on their way to the church. They were unaware that Chelsie had not reached her destination but was, instead, tied in knots in a musty shack beside the wharf.

A puzzled frown furrowed Kyle's brow when he halted the carriage in front of the chapel. Before he could assist Rebecca from the coach, a shot rang out and Daniel let out a yelp. Young Daniel, who had been wandering around the grounds, had become the target of a sniper, and the bullet had penetrated his thigh.

With his heartbeat quickening Kyle darted around the corner of the church, searching for his howling son. Behind him trotted a procession of family and friends who had just filed into the church and quickly reversed direction when the fireworks began. Grant trotted along behind his father. Following closely on Grant's heels was Neil, who had a tight grip on Abi, who could barely see where she was going through the long, thick veil that covered her face. Shuffling along behind the bride and groom were Rebecca and Amos and a various assortment of family and friends — all of whom were anxious to determine what had happened to young Daniel.

It was at that moment that Jarred and Eli thundered up the hill to the church. Jarred's eyes were glued to the veiled bride, who had just veered around the corner of the chapel. She clung tightly to Neil with one hand and grasped his medical bag in the other. Without reining his winded steed to a halt, Jarred vaulted to the ground and dashed off after the bride-to-be, who he erroneously presumed to be Chelsie.

"You can't marry Neil," Jarred declared breathlessly.

Abi was struck dumb when Jarred yanked her loose from Neil, who was making a beeline toward his injured brother. She stared apprehensively at the hand that was clamped on her elbow and set her feet when Jarred tried to uproot her from her spot. For what seemed forever, Abi struggled to formulate her thoughts. She stood there studying Jarred's haggard appearance through her concealing veil. Abi knew it was her place to explain why she was marrying Neil, but she was so apprehensive that her tongue was frozen to her palate. When she opened her mouth to apologize for breaking their engagement, nothing but inarticulate squeaks tripped from her lips.

"Did you hear me?" Jarred growled impatiently, giving the bride a hard shake. "You are not marrying my brother until we have a chance to talk!"

Neil knelt down beside Daniel, inspecting the bloody wound on his thigh. Frantically he glanced around him, wondering what had become of Abi, who had snatched up his medical bag on her way out of the church. Seeing Jarred shaking the stuffing out of Abi had Neil muttering under his breath.

"Jarred, get over here!" he commanded urgently. "Daniel has been shot. I need my supplies."

Hearing the distraught call, Jarred ripped the leather bag from the bride's fingertips and charged toward his fallen brother, leaving Abi to massage her aching arm.

When Daniel tried to prop himself up, a hiss of pain burst from his lips. Another whimper tumbled free when Neil hurriedly tore away the leg of his breeches to examine the seeping gash.

"What the hell happened?" Jarred wanted to know.

Blanching visibly, Daniel stared up at his disheveled brother, who was sorely in need of a shave. "I was just wandering around the church, waiting for the ceremony to begin, and someone ambushed me," he reported, grimacing. Weakly he gestured toward the skirting of trees that lay behind the whitewashed church. "It must have come from over there."

When Kyle, Amos, and the guests closed in around Daniel, he could barely draw a breath. His leg throbbed in rhythm with his accelerated heart, and his stomach pitched at the sight of his own blood. To complicate matters, well-meaning guests were bearing down on him, and he wasn't sure he wanted an audience when nausea overcame him.

"Back off and give him room to breathe," Jarred ordered, only to be cut off by the bark of a musket.

This time it was Grant who grabbed his shoulder and growled in pain. Rebecca screeched in horror when she saw her second nephew double over. While the crowd dashed for safety, Jarred scooped up Daniel and Neil offered Grant a supporting arm. Murmurs undulated through the crowd that stampeded toward the church. There was much speculating on who would dare to ambush a wedding party. No one wanted to be around when the sniper had the chance to reload and cut down another unsuspecting victim.

Jarred muttered irritably when he saw Chelsie (at least he assumed it was Chelsie) leaning on Neil like a clinging vine. Maybe he had spoken out of turn, Jarred thought as he eased Daniel onto the pew. Maybe Chelsie had truly fallen in love with Neil while Jarred wasn't around to complicate her life.

Kyle had counted heads to ensure his family had safely huddled inside the protective walls of the chapel. "Where's Chelsie?" he questioned worriedly.

"There," Jarred grumbled, hitching his thumb in the general direction of the heavily-veiled bride-to-be, who was now hovering behind Neil.

It struck Kyle just then that he hadn't had the chance to explain to Jarred why his fiancée was about to marry his older brother. This was a delicate situation, complicated by the recent chaos. Kyle struggled to compose himself and offered Jarred a hasty rendition of what had transpired during his absence.

"Well, you see, Jarred . . . a lot has . . . uh . . . happened since you left for Albany." Nervously he tugged at his cravat. "I should have waited until you returned, but . . . a . . . we . . . uh, that is, I decided to announce the engagement immediately. And, well . . . you know how anxious I've been to have a daughter-in-law."

Jarred glared at the bride-to-be. "I'm sure she will be everything you hoped she would," he replied, his tone lacking sincerity. Of course, Jarred thought they were discussing Chelsie instead of Abi, and Kyle assumed Jarred knew who was behind the veil.

"I only hope she knows what she's doing," Jarred growled, glaring resentfully at the camouflaged face.

"She loves Neil," Kyle said gently. "I know you are probably surprised and perhaps bitter about this unexpected change of plans. But you will accept the way of things in time. If you truly wanted to marry Abi, you should have done it before now. Two years is a long time to keep a woman waiting. . . ."

"*Abi*?" Jarred's head swiveled around to peer incredulously at the couple who had bandaged Daniel and had moved on to examine Grant's bleeding shoulder. "*Neil* is marrying *Abi*?" he croaked in astonishment.

"Well, of course he is. Who did you *think* he was marrying?" Kyle blinked bewilderedly. "I thought that was why you were upset."

Jarred was greatly relieved by the news, yet gravely concerned. "If Abi is the bride-to-be, where in blazes is Chelsie?"

The booming question caught the attention of the entire congregation and they glanced curiously around the chapel. But Chelsie was nowhere to be found.

"I thought the duchess was coming with you." Neil glanced up from his task of tending Grant's arm to peer gravely at his father.

"She wasn't in her room when I went to fetch her. I assumed she'd decided to come to the church with you," Kyle replied. "I haven't seen her since early this morning, when she joined us for breakfast."

A sickening dread swept over Jarred. He wasn't sure what the devil was going on, but he had the feeling Chelsie was in worse trouble than his two injured brothers. Muttering disgustedly, he stormed toward the door.

"Where are you going?" Kyle called after him. "We are not postponing this wedding."

"To find Chelsie," Jarred growled. "You can have your ceremony with your wounded wedding party if you wish, but I'm not coming back to the church until I know what has become of the duchess!"

Kyle lifted and then dropped his hands in a gesture of futility. "I'll never get any of my sons married," he breathed defeatedly. "We may as well load up our wounded and haul them back to the hotel."

Jarred didn't wait for the rest of the family to catch up with him. Time was of the essence. Unless he missed his guess, someone was up to no good, and it seemed Chelsie and his family were the target of some sinister scheme. Jarred didn't have the faintest notion who was behind the ambush. But he wasn't going to breathe easy until he knew what had become of that green-eyed leprechaun.

Chelsie grimaced when the door of the shack creaked open to reveal Isaac's parrot-like features. The smug smile that was plastered on his face worried Chelsie more than a mite. From the moment she'd had the misfortune to meet this vile ogre, his demented pleasures had inevitably come at her expense.

Setting his musket beside the door, Isaac limped across the damp room to loom over his captive. "Two down and three to go," he chuckled sardonically.

"What devilish scheme are you planning now?" Chelsie asked bitterly.

"I'm repayin' you and that uppity aristocrat who left me with this bum leg," Isaac snorted disdainfully. "I saw you come ashore yesterday. I was in the tavern last night when them highfalutin' McAlisters strutted in to boast of the upcomin' weddin'. They were braggin' about havin' a duchess in their midst and about the fancy ceremony they was holdin' today." His satanic grin revealed missing teeth. "Well, I damn sure messed up *their* plans. I ambushed two of 'em, and I'll bring you and the rest of 'em down a notch before I'm through. You and Jarred McAlister are goin' to wish you hadn't tangled with Isaac Latham!"

Chelsie stared at the homely sailor. He had planned to cut down the entire McAlister family just to get even with her and Jarred? He was a lunatic, that's what he was! But then, Chelsie had always known that. After all her hellish dealings with this vermin, she knew how sadistic and resentful he could be. But never in her wildest nightmare did she anticipate Isaac would carry his vindictiveness to such ruthless extremes.

An icy shiver ran up Chelsie's spine. She had placed a deadly curse on the McAlister family by associating with them. There was no telling who Isaac had victimized during his shooting spree or how badly the unsuspecting family had been injured. Which ones had been the recipient of a sniper's bullet? Rebecca? Kyle? Two of his sons? Neil's wedding day had evolved into disaster!

A diabolical snicker gushed from Isaac's lips and he scoffed at the concerned expression that puckered Chelsie's brow. "Don't fret, bitch, you'll be there when I put a hole through Jarred and the doctor," he assured her. "I left a note in yer room tellin' the McAlisters you'd been injured and needed first aid. When the doctor comes to yer assistance, he'll be the one who needs to be patched up."

Chelsie gulped hard. Her fingers clenched. She wished she could curl her hands around Isaac's bony throat. Willfully she fought to control her temper and attempt to reason with this maniac. "The McAlisters have nothing to do with this grudge between you and me," she reminded him through gritted teeth. "My father will pay handsomely to have me back. I should think money would compensate for your crippled leg."

"Aye, it will." Another devilish smile split his whiskered face. "But first I intend to make Jarred McAlister regret crossin' me. Yer the bait, duchess. And when I've brought the McAlisters down and disposed of Jarred, you'll be wedged in the hull with the cargo and shipped back to England. Cap'n Hutton is sailin' at first light. Once I git the ransom for you from the duke, I'll be one of them pompous aristocrats who swaggers around London in the fancy trappin's of a gentleman. And Meredith will be by my side, flauntin' the expensive jewels I'm goin' to give her. She won't be waitin' tables in that gloomy tavern in Annapolis, because I'm goin' to buy her indentureship and set her free." His eyes flickered maliciously over Chelsie. "Of course, you won't be around to see the two of us puttin' on airs. You and yer guard dragon will be roastin' in hell by then."

Chelsie growled in helpless frustration when Isaac lifted his foot and shoved her backward. "Yer goin' to regret spittin' in Meredith's face," he sneered vindictively. "We'll be livin' on yer ransom money, and you won't have any need of money where yer goin'."

Isaac was right about one thing: Chelsie did rue the day she had clashed with this poisonous viper. Isaac meant to seize an opportunity and make it work to his advantage. He was focusing his envy of aristocrats in general on the McAlister family. He was scheming to dispose of her and Jarred because he detested gentry and because he carried grudges to the most frightening extremes.

Well, at least Jarred would escape Isaac's wrath, Chelsie consoled herself. Jarred was miles away. And when he figured out who was responsible for the ambush and her mysterious disappearance, he would hunt Isaac down and slice him to bits. Of course, Chelsie wouldn't be around to see Isaac receive his just desserts for his bizarre brand of vengeance. But at least she would go to her grave knowing Isaac's days were numbered. Jarred would avenge his family's suffering, and it would be Isaac who regretted locking horns with Jarred McAlister. . . .

The clank of a bottle against the tin cup jolted Chelsie from her spiteful musings. She had heard that sound too many times before, and instinctively she strained against her confining ropes, praying they would snap and grant her her freedom. Isaac was pouring his concoction of whiskey, gin, and laudanum into the cup. It was the same potion he had forced down Chelsie's throat when he had spirited her away from England. Each time Chelsie caused trouble on board the ship, Isaac had demanded that she drink. The strong sedative left her oblivious to the world. And she wasn't the only one who had succumbed to this spiked drink. Spirits and crimps like Isaac employed the drug to daze their victims before dragging them to the docks to be sold.

When Chelsie clamped her mouth shut, Isaac snarled at her infuriating defiance. "Drink it, bitch, or I'll pour it down yer throat, just like I usually do."

True to form, Chelsie refused to obey. And Isaac did what he always did when the belligerent she-cat resisted him. Twisting her hair around his hand like a rope, he yanked her head backward and tugged on her tangled mane until Chelsie could no longer contain her cries of pain. Isaac slopped the potion down her throat and she sputtered and coughed to catch her breath. When she tried to gasp for air, Isaac poured another swig of the concoction into her mouth.

The drink took effect almost immediately, and Chelsie could feel her resistance ebbing. She fought the strong potion but knew she would buckle, especially when Isaac kept drowning her with it again and again. As the world faded into a haze Chelsie reminded herself that Jarred would avenge her death. Although she would go on suffering until only God knew when before Isaac disposed of her, Jarred would right this wrong. Not for her, of course, but for his family. At least Isaac would pay with his life. That was Chelsie's only consolation, hollow though it was.

If she had known Jarred was in Baltimore instead of enroute to Easthaven, she wouldn't have enjoyed a smidgen of satisfaction. But Isaac knew exactly where Jarred was. He had seen Jarred scoop Daniel into his arms after Isaac had shot him down.

And at that very moment Jarred was on his way to the hotel, frantically searching for Chelsie. If she had her way, Jarred would still be in Albany. But he wasn't, and Isaac was waiting like a hungry shark, anxious to make a feast of the McAlisters before he enjoyed the ultimate revenge on the man who had made him a cripple.

An explosive growl erupted from Jarred's lips when he barged into Chelsie's vacant room. His flaming blue eyes darted around the suite, searching for a clue that would lead him to that feisty elf who attracted more than her fair share of trouble. His smoldering gaze landed on the crumpled note on the nightstand. In two swift strides Jarred crossed the room to snatch up the message.

A lump of ice formed around his heart when the expensive locket tumbled to the floor. Jarred had the frustrating feeling he had been deliberately lied to twice, and sure enough, he had. When he opened the heart-shaped pendant etched with the Channing family crest, he found the inscription that lent credence to Chelsie's testimony—one he had refused to believe.

"To my beloved Chelsie on her sixteenth birthday. All my love, Evan," Jarred quoted for Eli, who stood a few steps behind him.

As if the gold locket embedded with priceless stones wasn't evidence enough, Isaac's letter testified to the fact that Chelsie was a real, live duchess. How long she would remain alive, Jarred did not know, and that tormenting thought had him suffering all the tortures of the damned.

Jarred scanned the scrawled message, then read it aloud for Eli's benefit. "The Duchess of Chessfield has been injured. Send the doctor posthaste. She waits in the cove north of Baltimore."

Jarred wheeled around to confront his grim-faced valet. "Go ahead, say it," Jarred muttered bitterly. "I know what you're thinking."

Eli accommodated him. "I told you so." He was too frustrated and concerned about Chelsie to be sympathetic to Jarred. "Maybe I should hurry down to the tavern and fetch you some food before you dash off to begin your search for the duchess."

Jarred could read his servant's mind like an open book. He knew exactly what Eli meant by that sarcastic remark. "No doubt the chef is serving crow for supper," he sniffed gruffly.

"Crow for the entrée, and humble pie for dessert," Eli grunted, glaring at Jarred as if this was all his fault.

"I'm not in the mood to eat, even if I deserve double rations," Jarred sighed as he raked his fingers through his tousled hair. "And with any luck at all, I'll get myself killed in the process of rescuing the duchess from deadly peril. Then I won't have to apologize for refusing to believe her."

While Jarred was standing there chewing himself up one side and down the other for believing Isaac and Cyrus, Eli retrieved the note. After reading it twice, he shook his head in dismay. "It sounds like a trap," he said bleakly.

"Don't you think I know that?" Jarred blurted out in exasperation.

Eli glanced up, his gray eyes teeming with ridicule. "Why should I expect you to figure that out when you couldn't figure out Chelsie was really a duchess, instead of a lowly peasant? You didn't want to believe her, did you?" he questioned scornfully. "You just wanted to use her to satisfy your lust without tormenting your conscience. You refused to accept the fact that you had deflowered a royal duchess—it was more convenient for you to denounce her claim to her title."

"This is not the time to list my faults," Jarred snapped. "Chelsie is missing and Isaac has taken her captive. That bastard will show no mercy to any of us. If I send Neil to aid Chelsie, Isaac will be waiting to cut him down the same way he bushwhacked Grant and Daniel."

Eli nodded grimly. "That scalawag is getting back at you by striking out at your family and at Chelsie. You made yourself a bitter enemy when you riled that vicious blackguard."

Jarred grumbled under his breath. He didn't appreciate having his troubled thoughts translated into words. But Eli was right . . . dealing with a vindictive man like Isaac Latham was dangerous. He wouldn't think twice about striking out at innocent victims in order to get back at Jarred.

"What the devil do you suppose Isaac is doing in Baltimore, anyway?" Eli mused aloud. "And how did he find Chelsie?"

Jarred shrugged, too concerned about her to speculate on how or why Isaac was in town. "He'll be lying in wait for us," Jarred predicted gloomily.

"Aye," Eli concurred. "And with an assortment of weaponry at his disposal, no doubt. He'll make sure you don't walk away unscathed."

When Kyle and Neil breezed through the open door, they knew instantly that more bad news awaited them. Eli's bleak expression and Jarred's black scowl were worth a thousand words.

"Who are these madmen trying to dispose of our family?" Kyle asked in frustration.

"One madman," Jarred corrected with a disdainful snort. "Isaac Latham and I have clashed once too often. Now he has decided to punish me by cutting down everyone associated with me." He handed Kyle the barely legible note and waited for his father to expel a string of resentful curses, which he did.

After Neil had read the message he pivoted on his heel. "I'll fetch my bag."

"This is your wedding day," Kyle blustered. "If you rush off to aid Chelsie, it could well be your own funeral."

"If not for Chelsie, I wouldn't even have a wedding day," Neil contended without breaking stride. "I owe her."

Kyle sat down before he fell down. He had been soaring in pleasure, anticipating the wedding. Now he was plummeting into the depths of despair. Two of his sons had been shot and the other two were considering becoming sitting ducks for a trigger-happy madman.

"Don't you worry, squire," Eli comforted Kyle as Jarred followed his older brother out of the room. "Jarred won't let anything happen to Neil. Isaac Latham can't be as difficult to deal with as those sneaky renegade Indians Jarred battled in the wilderness. He is a seasoned fighter, with years of experience to his credit."

"Aye, you are right," Kyle agreed, mustering his confidence. "Jarred will take care of everything, just as he always does."

Eli frowned. He had comforted Kyle, but who was going to console him? A man like Isaac Latham was a formidable foe—the worst kind of all. Isaac didn't care who he hurt during his vengeful crusade to destroy Jarred. If Chelsie, Neil, and Jarred were going to walk out of this trap alive, it might require a miracle. Eli hoped Jarred had one stashed in his pocket. He was certainly going to need it!

Struggling with Chelsie's limp body, Isaac situated her in the skiff he had anchored in the cove north of Baltimore. Although Chelsie had balked at drinking the concoction, Isaac had ensured she had taken a potent dose. It was all that had ever subdued this sassy bitch. If not for the mixture of whiskey, gin, and laudanum, Isaac wasn't sure he could have tolerated this daring minx on board the ship without strangling her. She was defiance and spirit personified. But thanks to the drugging potion, she was as lifeless as a rag doll and easy to manipulate.

After propping Chelsie's head against the bow of the skiff, Isaac draped her arms over each side so Jarred and Neil could see her while she lay adrift in the cove. Her silver-blond hair fluttered about her like a banner in the breeze. The glint of sunshine that sprayed through the trees framed her pale face, making her look like a vulnerable sleeping beauty who was in desperate need of saving.

A wicked chuckle rattled in Isaac's throat as he stepped into the second skiff he had towed behind him. What a genius he was, he congratulated himself. He knew Jarred would come, bringing his doctor brother with him. They would arrive to see the drugged duchess bobbing in the skiff. In their haste to revive her, the brothers would employ the pungey Isaac planned to leave for them. Before the McAlisters could row halfway into the bay, their skiff would sink beneath them, and Isaac would pick them off like pesky flies.

Dragging the skiff ashore, Isaac stripped the tar from the hull to ensure that the vessel would spring a leak. Cradling his assortment of weapons in his arms, he hobbled over to make his nest in the overhanging trees. From his camouflaged vantage point, he could monitor Jarred's every move. And this would be the end of that haughty aristocrat, Isaac promised himself. Jarred was about to embark on his one-way journey to hell, and very soon the duchess would join him! Isaac smiled satanically at the thought. Nothing would make him happier than to better his station in life at Jarred and Chelsie's expense.

Chapter 24

Jarred reined the mahogany bay stallion to a halt on the hill overlooking the cove. The late afternoon sun sparkled on the water and the skiff in which Chelsie lay like a corpse dipped and rose with the swells that tumbled toward shore.

A muffled growl tripped off Jarred's lips. He hadn't known what kind of trap Isaac had set for them until this moment, but he didn't like what he saw. Not knowing if Chelsie was dead or alive turned Jarred wrong-side-out and threatened to distort his logic. In frustration, he reminded himself that he had to keep his wits about him, instead of charging off half-cocked. That was what Isaac was counting on. The malicious fiend played to his enemy's weakness. Damn that vicious bastard, Jarred fumed, struggling for composure. What had he done to Chelsie?

When Neil nudged his steed forward, Jarred's hand snaked out to grab his reins. Astutely he surveyed their surroundings, searching for Isaac, who lay in wait. Gesturing for Neil to dismount, Jarred swung from his saddle. Using the horses as their shields, they proceeded down the slope while Jarred scrutinized every shadow, well aware that Isaac was waiting for them to make a crucial mistake.

"Where do you suppose he is?" Neil whispered, glancing around.

"Where would *you* be if you wanted to pick off your prey?" Jarred grunted disgustedly. "I suspect he is either up in a tree or scrunched down in the boat beside Chelsie."

When they reached the skiff in the reeds, Jarred cocked his

musket, wishing he could blow that wily bastard off the face of the earth this very instant. Pensively he peered at the semicircle of trees that lined the cove, trying to calculate which side would offer Isaac the best view and most protection. If Isaac was on the southeast side of the estuary, the sun's glare would reflect in his eyes. Cautiously Jarred glanced to the north, scouting the towering trees. But Isaac had selected clothes that blended into the background, and he was impossible to detect. Lord, what Jarred wouldn't give for helmets and two suits of armor!

"Now what?" Neil murmured uneasily.

Jarred's mind raced. His eyes dropped to the skiff set all too conveniently in the reeds. No doubt Isaac expected them to clamber into the pungey, and Jarred was prepared to bet his right arm that the varmint had sabotaged it. That thought inspired another speculation: Jarred was certain Isaac was perched in a tree. Otherwise, he wouldn't have rowed this skiff ashore.

"We'll use the horses," Jarred whispered.

"But the skiff would be . . ." Neil protested, only to be interrupted by Jarred's derisive snort.

"I'll wager the pungey isn't seaworthy. Isaac probably has in mind for this skiff to sink with us in it."

Neil didn't argue with his brother. Jarred was far more experienced in the tactics of warfare. Uncaring that he was ruining his wedding clothes, Neil hooked his medical bag over the pommel of the saddle and walked his steed into the water alongside Jarred.

While the McAlisters were clinging to their horses, Isaac was cursing profusely. It was difficult to take aim when the horses' head kept bobbing back and forth like rocking chairs. But time was running out, and Isaac couldn't wait, in hopes of taking the perfect shot. He had to strike before the McAlisters reached Chelsie. Like a war party of one, Isaac opened fire with his three muskets and the two pistols he had tucked in his belt.

The spray of buckshot pelleted the water. Wild-eyed, the horses thrashed, attempting to reverse direction. Muttering irritably, Jarred yanked on the reins when his stallion refused to continue on. The smoke from Isaac's musket alerted Jarred to the precise location of their sniper. Barking a sharp order to his steed, Jarred laid his musket over the saddle and braced himself on the stallion's back.

"Hold onto your horse," Jarred advised his brother. "He'll become skittish when I fire over his head."

Sure enough, both horses reeled sideways when Jarred pulled the trigger. Jarred's shot provoked results: the buckshot splattered around Isaac and zinged off the tree bark. A pained squawk erupted from Isaac's lips when he was hit in the face. Instinctively he tried to dodge the pellets from the second shot that ricocheted off his own pistols and muskets. Wiping the blood from his face, Isaac groped to grab hold of a weapon, but all he succeeded in doing was knocking his muskets from the crotch of the tree.

Jarred's gaze narrowed when he heard the falling rifles plunk in the bay and saw Isaac's legs dangling from the overhanging tree. Swiftly he pulled into the saddle and swung his flighty steed toward the oversized figure who was clinging to a tree limb. While Jarred aimed himself toward Isaac, Neil swam toward Chelsie without having to fear being bushwhacked.

Isaac glanced frantically about him when he spied Jarred approaching. His weapons were gone, and his only recourse was to drop to the water or climb higher into the tree. Isaac chose to climb. With any luck at all, he could scurry across the entangled limbs of the clumped trees the way he scuttled over the beams of the sails on board the schooner.

Dragging himself onto a higher branch, Isaac crawled toward the main trunk, then out onto another limb that would grant him access to the branch of another nearby tree. While Neil was swimming toward the skiff where Chelsie lay sedated, Jarred rode his stallion through the water. Employing his mount as a stepladder, Jarred reached up a sinewy arm to pull himself into the tree.

Looking like black thunder, Jarred swung onto the limb to pursue his fleeing assailant. Jarred moved like a panther, gobbling up the distance that separated him from Isaac. Although fear had put wings on Isaac's feet, his crippled leg slowed him down enough for Jarred to lessen the space between them. One glance over his shoulder was enough to scare the living daylights out of Isaac and send him scrambling at an even faster clip. Jarred was motivated by a killing fury, and it was written on the severe lines in his face. Never in his life had Jarred been so bloodthirsty. He was so hungry for revenge, he could almost taste it.

Isaac gulped the lump of fear that collected in his throat. He knew he was staring death in the face — a hard, unyielding face that promised no mercy. Gritting his teeth, Isaac sprang toward a higher limb that would lead him to the next tree. Although his leg pained him and trickles of blood blurred his vision, Isaac never paused for even a second. Although his pace was slow, he fought his way through the tangled branches. He had performed aerial maneuvers while he was checking the sails and riggings. The only difference was that now he was pursued by a vengeful giant who also had the agility of a monkey. Isaac could never get far enough ahead of Jarred to breathe even a sigh of relief. The growling avenger kept narrowing the distance between them.

Panicky, Isaac wheeled about to lash out at Jarred the second he reached for another limb. Isaac's foot caught Jarred in the chin, but it seemed to do more to incite his fury than inspire fear. An inhuman growl exploded from Jarred's lips as he steadied himself with one hand and grasped Isaac's kicking foot with the other.

A shocked squeal tripped off Isaac's tongue when he found himself stretched out. His fingers were clenched in the limb above him and Jarred was tugging on his outstretched legs, trying to jar him loose. Rough bark dug into Isaac's hands, but he held on for dear life and kicked for all he was worth.

Jarred braced himself when Isaac tried to knock him backward. The instant Isaac recoiled, Jarred pounced. Isaac was no match for Jarred's lightning quickness and superior strength. A shriek of terror flew from his lips when Jarred literally snatched him from his death grip on the tree branch. For a tense moment Isaac hung in midair, supported only by the hand Jarred had clenched on the shoulder of his shirt. Terrified, Isaac clawed at his challenger, trying to find something stable to which to cling before he fell to his death. But his wild thrashing caused Jarred to lose his grip on Isaac, who was left suspended in air. For a split second Isaac and Jarred glared poisonously at each other before Isaac fell backward on the limb below. Another horrified screech pierced the air when Isaac failed to grab hold of the branch and slammed against every branch on his way to the ground—twenty feet below.

Jarred peered down through the dense foliage at Isaac's broken, mangled form. Sucking in a harsh breath, Jarred made his way to the bough of the tree and dropped agilely to the ground. The rustle of grass and leaves behind him caused Jarred to glance over his shoulder. The expectant expression on Neil's face eased considerably when he realized his brother had survived. Neil had heard the screams and the dull thud as he dashed through the maze of underbrush. Only now did he know which man had taken the fatal fall.

Without the slightest bit of remorse, Jarred shoved his boot heel against Isaac's shoulder, rolling him to his back. Jarred didn't need his brother the doctor to determine Isaac's condition. "Dead," he diagnosed, his voice devoid of any emotion. He didn't look up . . . his eyes were riveted on Isaac's battered face. "What about Chelsie?" Jarred asked. He had to know.

"Alive," Neil reported. "I cut the anchor loose and rowed the skiff back to shore. Isaac must have given her a strong potion. I examined her, but found only a few scrapes and bruises. He must have laced her drink with laudanum."

Jarred's broad shoulders slumped in relief and he closed his eyes, offering a silent prayer of thanks. Without a backward glance at Isaac, Jarred aimed himself toward Chelsie. When he reached the shore, he sank down beside the sleeping beauty to trace his fingertips over her exquisite features. For several minutes Jarred savored the long-awaited sight of her, wondering what fiendish torment Isaac had subjected her to this time. No doubt her sleep would be interrupted with this new set of hideous nightmares. Well, at least this would be the last of them, Jarred mused as he tracked his forefinger over her petal-soft lips. Isaac was dead and he would never harm Chelsie again.

After allowing Jarred time to relish the sight of this lovely nymph, Neil ambled up behind him. "We have to rouse the duchess and get her on her feet," he insisted "We still have a wedding to attend." His brown eyes settled on Jarred. "And speaking of weddings, don't you think you should make this a double ceremony?"

After hoisting Chelsie onto legs that immediately buckled beneath her, Jarred flung Neil a wary glance.

"I know what has been going on between the two of you," Neil informed Jarred. Carefully he curled his arm around Chelsie's waist to lend additional support. "I was in her room, waiting to check her wound the night she crept back from your chamber." When Jarred glanced in the opposite direction, Neil chortled softly. "That wasn't the first time either, was it, Jarred?"

Jarred wisely chose to remain silent, not that it mattered one tittle. Neil was no one's fool.

"A man doesn't toy with an English duchess, Jarred," Neil reminded him sternly.

"Damn it, you don't understand," Jarred growled as he paced back and forth with Chelsie, trying to rouse her from her drugged sleep.

Blast it, he and this saucy minx were still at odds, and things weren't going to get better, either. She would never forgive him for treating her like his servant, for refusing to believe she was who she said she was.

"I understand plenty," Neil contradicted while he helped Jarred walk Chelsie in circles. "If you don't marry her, I'll tell Papa about your tête-a-tête, and he will escort you to the altar with the barrel of a musket tucked between your ribs. 'Tis bad enough that you were unfaithful to Abi for almost two years and that I kept silent when I wanted her for my wife. But to seduce a duchess without making her your bride?" Neil rolled

305

his eyes skyward. "Sometimes I wonder about your intelligence, Jarred. You were always a bit of a daredevil. I have come to expect that from you. But this is a different matter entirely. If the Duke of Chessfield is as powerful as Chelsie says, you could be barred from practicing law and booted out of the Assembly, not to mention shot, hanged, and stabbed for trifling with royalty. If I were her father, I certainly would be entertaining thoughts of ruining your life!"

Jarred peered down at the droopy beauty who was draped like wet laundry between him and Neil. Marry her? Hell, she probably wouldn't have him. Jarred had intended to court Chelsie properly and to woo her into forgiving him for treating her so abominally. But Neil was rushing things quite a bit! Chelsie would have to get over hating him before he could ever hope to be restored to her good graces. . . .

"*Today,* Jarred," Neil demanded as he shifted Chelsie's drooping head onto Jarred's shoulder. "I *refuse* to let you drag your feet. Either you speak the vows with Abi and me, or I tell Papa *who* has been sneaking back and forth between *whose* rooms. . . ."

Jarred's gaze dipped to the enchanting face that rested against his shoulder. It looked as if Neil meant for him to woo Chelsie *after* he married her. And in Chelsie's dazed condition, she wouldn't put up much protest. But later, when she roused . . . Jarred groaned at the thought. Chelsie would give him royal hell! He knew full well what she was going to think when he admitted his affection for her, knowing that he had finally discovered who she truly was. Lord, it was going to be difficult to convince that feisty sprite that what he felt for her had nothing to do with titles and fortunes. Chelsie was bound to think the worst of him, bound to be outraged that he hadn't believed her in the first place.

"I can't," Jarred breathed. "I once promised this sprite I wouldn't marry her if she was the last woman on earth."

"That was your first mistake," Neil declared with great conviction. "Don't make a second one. You will do each other a great favor if you marry. I won't have to tattle to Papa, and the

Duke of Chessfield might be more tolerant if you are his son-in-law." A wry grin pursed Neil's lips. "The Duke might simply be satisfied seeing you shot and hanged, without being stabbed first."

Finally Jarred nodded in compliance. What did he have to lose? Chelsie would probably despise him whether he married her or not. And Eli would be elated about the match, since he had been harping on the subject for over two months. Now that Neil had joined in the crusade, Jarred would never enjoy a moment's peace.

"Very well, Neil, we will have a double ceremony. You ride back to the hotel to inform the family of the change in plans. While you are checking on the dazed and wounded I'll see if I can bring Chelsie around enough to speak the vows before taking her back to town. I don't think it wise to force our injured brothers to travel back to the church. Send Eli to fetch the pastor, and we will have the ceremony in the hotel lobby."

"Done." Neil beamed like a lantern. "I'm glad you see things my way, little brother," he chuckled wryly.

Jarred regarded his brother's smug expression and frowned resentfully. "You have certainly turned over a new leaf since the last time I saw you."

"Some of Chelsie's spunk has rubbed off on me. And the world seems much brighter now that I'm marrying your fiancée," he teased. "Smile, Jarred, this is *your* wedding day, too."

Jarred cast Neil a withering glance and watched in silence as his older brother trotted off to fetch his horse. A change had overcome Neil: he was as bubbly as a schoolboy, now that he was going to marry Abi. It was a shame Neil hadn't stepped forward to confess his affection months ago. It would have saved Jarred and Abi from a long engagement that had been more of an obligation than romantic love.

The thought provoked Jarred to peer at the limp bundle of rumpled silk he was propping upright. Would he ever truly earn this wench's love? He had the uneasy feeling Chelsie would never let him live down the fact that he had taken Isaac and Cyrus's word over hers. She would probably hold his foolishness up to him for the rest of his natural life.

Maybe Neil did have an important point, Jarred mused as he visually sketched Chelsie's exquisite features. She wouldn't know what was going on until it was too late. She might hate him for marrying her, but she would be legally tied to him. And in time, he might be able to convince her that his intentions were sincere. Maybe one day (not anytime soon, of course, but someday), she might be able to forgive and forget. . . .

Chelsie's groggy moan roused Jarred from his reverie. Her tangled lashes swept up to see Jarred's blurred image swimming before her eyes. In her dazed state she assumed she had perished and was now drifting toward her eternal destination. Whether it be heaven or hell, Chelsie didn't know for certain. But one tormenting thought pierced her fuzzy mind: Jarred was drifting beside her and Isaac had obviously managed to dispose of him as well.

"Jarred?" Her wobbly voice cracked with disappointment. "You're dead, too?"

The comical expression on her smudged face caused Jarred to snicker uncontrollably. "We're both alive, little leprechaun," he assured her.

Chelsie nearly collapsed in a heap. Her feet felt as if they had anchors strapped to them. Lifting them was difficult. After Jarred had propped her upright once again, she peered up into his handsome face. One heavy arm lifted to limn his striking features, touching him as she had longed to do this past month while they were apart.

"I don't know *why* you have to be so blessedly attractive," she slurred out.

Jarred bit back a grin, but he had no time to retort because the liquor and laudanum had Chelsie jabbering like a magpie.

"I was so sure the devil had a ghastly face," she mumbled as Jarred forced her to march back and forth like a drill sergeant putting a lowly private through the paces. A hoarse bubble of amusement tripped from her lips, which dropped with a lopsided smile. "But 'tis the irony of hell, I suppose. Satan is the temptation no woman can resist. I could have loved you long and well," she murmured drowsily. "But now it can never be. . . ."

Her slurred remark had Jarred frowning bemusedly. "Why can't you love me, Chelsie?" he asked.

Her head rolled back and the tangled mane of silver-blond spilled over her sagging shoulders. Chelsie stared up at him as if she were pondering whether to dignify such a stupid question with an answer. "You know perfectly well why," she replied sluggishly.

"Nay, tell me," Jarred commanded as he pivoted to pace in the opposite direction.

In Chelsie's drugged condition she couldn't contemplate one thought very long before another one entangled itself in the hazy jungle of her mind. In a matter of seconds Chelsie forgot what topic they were discussing. Glancing up, she tried to focus on the foggy image that multiplied before her eyes.

"I really must sit down," she sighed weakly. "I'm not feeling very well. . . ."

Without further ado, her knees folded like an accordion and her head bobbed sideways. Grumbling, Jarred gave her a firm shake and steadied her on her shaky legs.

A silly smile dangled on the corner of Chelsie's mouth as she peered up at Jarred. "Are you dead, too?"

Jarred muttered under his breath. They were back to square one again. Every time Chelsie woke she couldn't remember where she was. "You are going to walk off this stupor," he commanded. "Just put one foot in front of the other and lean on me for support."

With tremendous effort Chelsie pried open both eyes and concentrated on walking. But suddenly it wasn't Jarred who was beside her; it was the same homely face that tormented her nightmares. Involuntarily Chelsie shrank from Jarred's touch. Her fumbling attempt to escape him caused Jarred to trip over her, knocking both of them flat.

While Chelsie sobbed hysterically—a prisoner of a recurring nightmare—Jarred muttered several ungentlemanly curses. After scraping himself off the ground, he hoisted Chelsie to her feet. She resisted every step, as if he were leading her to the guillotine.

"Take the money and leave me be!" Chelsie shrieked. "My father will pay to have me back. . . ."

Tears burned her flushed cheeks as she fought Jarred's restraining arms. As the thought fled to be replaced by another, Chelsie ceased struggling and allowed Jarred to march her back and forth. Sadly she shook her head and this time she thought she was conversing with Neil.

" 'Tis an ocean between us," she sighed disheartenedly. " 'Tis too wide and deep to cross."

Neil's voice echoed through her jumbled thoughts, assuring her that love would bridge the space between her and Jarred, no matter how many miles she put between them.

"It will never work," Chelsie murmured, looking up at Jarred through glazed eyes, seeing Neil's sympathetic smile.

Jarred expelled a frustrated sigh. He didn't have the foggiest notion what Chelsie was babbling about. Silently he trod across the lush grass, watching confused emotions flit through Chelsie's blurry eyes. She was in such a confused state of mind that her emotions were swinging back and forth like a pendulum. One minute she was shying away from him, the next she was mumbling about impassable oceans. For God's sake, how long did it take for that potion to wear off?

Chelsie's groggy giggle jostled Jarred from his pensive deliberations. When he glanced down, Chelsie was grinning like a Cheshire cat. One slender arm lifted to dangle off his shoulder when she pirouetted in front of him.

"Three wishes . . ." she murmured as her relaxed body molded itself to his masculine contours. "Ask and I will grant them once, twice, thrice. . . ."

Lord, she was so temptingly close, so vulnerable. Her alluring scent fogged Jarred's senses. He knew he should be walking Chelsie around in circles to clear her mind, but his feet refused to budge. And when she raised her parted lips to his, Jarred eagerly accepted the invitation. It had been eons since he had taken this beauty in his arms. Her memory had burned in his mind, constantly tormenting him. Now that he had her where he had always wanted her, he couldn't resist the addicting taste that had lingered on his lips for an agonizing month.

Jarred did have three wishes he would like to have granted to him. The first was that the potion would ebb and bring Chelsie back to her senses. The second was that Chelsie could return his raging passion that ached for release. The third was that he could spend the rest of the day making wild, sweet love to her each time the eternal flame blazed anew.

The impatient longings and sweet memories of days gone by converged on Chelsie. She gave herself up to the feel of Jarred's strong, protective arms . . . but only for a moment. The image that swam before her eyes changed again and Chelsie pulled away, aghast that she had embraced the man who had appeared in her hallucinations.

Blinking bewilderedly, Jarred stared down at Chelsie's stubborn chin. She was changing moods so quickly that Jarred's mind was in a whirl.

"Find yourself another meal ticket," she slurred out, glaring at one of the wily rakes who had courted her for her fortune. "I will not marry you when I'm in love with someone else."

Jarred did a double take. It had not occurred to him until now that there might have been another man in her life before she was whisked away to the colonies. He wasn't sure who Chelsie was addressing now—him, or one of the many images that flitted through her boggled thoughts. Jarred was so frustrated, he wanted to pull out his hair.

"Keep walking," he demanded tartly. "And don't stop until you remember who and where you are."

As Chelsie paced alongside Jarred's swift strides, a feeling of exhaustion overcame her. She wanted to lie down and sleep. In all the time Isaac had poured his potion down her throat, she had never been forced to walk off the drugging effects of the drink. Stifling a yawn, Chelsie concentrated in placing one foot in front of the other. Her attention focused on the tips of her stained slippers.

311

"Papa, why do you suppose the good Lord thought to give man five toes?" she questioned sluggishly. "Why not hooves, or webbed feet?"

As frustrated as Jarred was, he couldn't suppress a smile. "Probably because He created man last and he had already exhausted his supply of hooves and fins," he speculated.

The answer seemed to satisfy Chelsie . . . she nodded thoughtfully. "Aye, I suppose." Her attention shifted to her arm and she frowned as if she were engrossed in thought. "I wonder why He didn't give us elbows and knees that bent backwards."

Jarred burst out laughing at the comical expression on Chelsie's face. Her brain was like a saturated sponge and her thoughts were as tangled as twine. Her facial muscles were so sluggish that they seemed half-paralyzed. Although Chelsie's condition was pathetic, it was amusing to watch her wobble around like a newborn foal and blurt out ridiculous comments that sounded nothing like the keen-witted chit he had come to know.

"Come along, little nymph." Jarred propelled her to his steed and reached into his saddlebag for the bandages he had brought along in case of emergency. Wetting the cloth, Jarred smoothed the cool water over her brow. "Perhaps this will rouse you from your confused dreams."

The cool water was refreshing, but it would take more than a wet cloth to wash away the effects of Isaac's potion. Childishly Chelsie slapped away the cloth and the hand that held it.

"Just let me lie down and sleep . . ." she protested.

"Nay, we haven't time," Jarred grumbled, impatiently tossing the cloth aside. Gripping her shoulders with both hands, he peered down into those dull green pools. "Chelsie, I'm taking you back to the hotel and we are going to be married."

"That's nice." She yawned drowsily. "Then can I go to sleep?" After a moment the remark soaked into her pickled brain and she stared up at Jarred without the slightest hint of recognition. "Who are you?"

Jarred swore under his breath. "If I tell you, I doubt you'll remember in the next two minutes."

Deciding he was wasting his time trying to walk off Chelsie's drugged stupor, Jarred scooped her up and situated her atop his stallion. The moment he swung up behind her, Chelsie slumped back to use his body as her cushion. With her head tucked against his shoulder, Chelsie drifted off to sleep, lulled by the steady clip-clop of hooves.

As they rode toward town, Jarred tried to tell himself that Chelsie didn't know what she was saying while she was feeling the effects of Isaac's potion. He couldn't help but wonder if there was someone in England who had already won the heart of this feisty misfit. Then he reassured himself by recalling that Chelsie had murmured her affection for him the night before he'd left Easthaven.

Jarred expelled a heavy sigh. A man could not hold a woman responsible for what she said while she was drugged by potions or by passion. Whatever Chelsie truly felt was anybody's guess.

A rueful smile pursed his lips as he cuddled her shapely body ever closer. He'd decided to marry this sassy sprite, and that was exactly what he'd do. But wouldn't it be the crowning glory if this true-to-life duchess wanted nothing to do with him? She probably had more beaux awaiting her return to England than the King had royal jewels.

Aye, he had awakened Chelsie's slumbering passion and taught her the meaning of physical desire. But somewhere on the other side of that wide, deep ocean Chelsie had been babbling about, there was probably a man who had managed to earn her affection. No wonder Chelsie had been bitter after that first night he had seduced her. She was probably saving herself for the man of her dreams. She may have unwillingly succumbed to desires of the flesh, but she resented Jarred for spoiling her romantic fantasy with the Prince Charming who waited in England.

Well, he wasn't letting her go, no matter how many Prince Charmings were standing in line to beg for her hand. This would indeed become their wedding day, and Chelsie was in no condition to protest the ceremony. Hell, she didn't even know where she was! And somehow he would make her forget the man she had left behind when Isaac spirited her away from England. After Chelsie roused from her stupor, she would be greeted by her new husband. He may not be the one she wanted but he was the one she was going to get. Jarred would make her forget the other men in her life . . . and one day, maybe she might even come to love him as much as he loved her.

A melancholy smile hovered on Jarred's lips as he nuzzled against the silver-blond head that was tucked beneath his chin. If he never earned Chelsie's love, he would probably be getting what he deserved for taking women for granted all these years. But he wasn't going to give Chelsie up, and he wasn't going to keep a mistress, the way many of his friends did. He was going to be the devoted husband, and he would give Chelsie no reason to despise him more than she already did for his refusing to believe her. And if she thought to place obstacles between them, she would find them crumbling down around her like the walls of Jericho.

He and Chelsie were going to make a new beginning, Jarred promised himself. And if she ever forgave him enough to love him, he would want for nothing more. Jarred had been through hell, and he was anxious to resolve the differences between him and his bride-to-be. They had done enough fighting, and it was high time they got down to the loving. Now if he could only convince Chelsie of that when she came to her senses!

Chapter 25

Kyle's welcoming smile turned into a worried frown when Jarred guided Chelsie into the hotel lobby. "Is she all right?"

"She's still woozy from the potion Isaac forced down her," Jarred informed his father. "But she will be fine when the side effects wear off."

"A double wedding," Kyle sighed contentedly. "I've waited years for this day, and now two of my sons will tie the matrimonial knot." His twinkling gaze drifted back to Chelsie, who could barely keep her eyes open. "Are you sure the duchess understood when you proposed to her? She looks a mite confused to me."

"She's elated with the idea," Jarred insisted as he draped Chelsie over Neil's arm and hurried upstairs to change into his dry clothes.

Neil bit back an amused grin when Chelsie's glazed eyes fluttered open momentarily. "Feeling better, duchess?" he queried softly.

Chelsie stared at Neil as if she had never seen him before. Finally the visual image sparked a memory and she managed a sleepy smile. "Feeling better?" she repeated sluggishly. "Compared to what?" Her gaze circled the hotel lobby and her brow puckered in a frown. "Where are we, Papa?"

Neil shook his head forlornly. What a memorable wedding day this was going to be for Chelsie! She was walking around in a drugged-induced sleep while Rebecca was flitting about, organizing this makeshift wedding at the hotel. Kyle was strutting around like a peacock, displaying his colorful feathers and arguing with Eli about which one of them should give Chelsie away. Grant and Daniel were lounging in chairs, nursing their wounds, and Neil was anxious to make Abi his wife. For everyone else this was a monumental occasion, but Neil seriously doubted Chelsie would remember it at all. Well, it was still for the best, he consoled himself. This high-spirited pixie needed a man like Jarred, and Jarred needed her whether he admitted it or not.

When Jarred reappeared in clean clothes, he and Neil approached the clergyman. While Amos Shaw led his daughter down the aisle between the chairs that had been gathered for the guests, Kyle escorted the droopy-eyed beauty, who was mumbling bits and pieces of conversation to only God knew whom. Twice Eli had to come to Kyle's assistance when Chelsie's knees folded beneath her.

After Chelsie was delivered into Jarred's hands, he wrapped a supporting arm around her waist and clutched her tightly to him. Thrice Chelsie nodded off during the ritual and Jarred had to shake her awake, prompting her with her vows.

Chelsie, as Neil predicted, remembered none of what was supposed to be the happiest day of a woman's life. She slept through most of the ceremony and didn't even recall being scooped up in Jarred's arms and tucked into bed.

Smiling at his sleeping bride, Jarred strode off to fetch the sheriff while the rest of the family gathered downstairs to celebrate the wedding. Once Jarred had retrieved Isaac's mangled body, he saw to it that Captain Hutton was arrested and his ship impounded. After cross-examining the crew, Jarred discovered that the captain and Isaac had not only victimized unwilling citizens and sold them as indentured servants in the colonies, but they had also stolen the horses they'd auctioned off in Annapolis the past few years.

That bit of news had Jarred wondering if Chelsie had also been telling the truth about the copper dun colt and the mare Kyle had purchased at her insistence. From the sound of things, Cyrus and Isaac had not only kidnaped the Duke of

Chessfield's only daughter, but they had also made off with his prize stock. Lord, Kyle was going to be beside himself when he learned he had purchased stolen property. He had great visions for the colt Chelsie had been training. Damn. . . .

As Jarred rode back to the hotel, he retrieved the expensive heart-shaped locket from his vest pocket and stared pensively at it. He should send off a letter to the duke, assuring him that his daughter was safe. He should. . . . Jarred sighed tiredly. But if he did inform the duke, he might come to retrieve his daughter before Jarred had time to win her affection. The last thing Jarred needed right now was interference. Deciding to procrastinate, Jarred tabled the idea of sending a message to the duke. It was a pity he didn't know the duke was already on his way to Annapolis to hang Jarred from the tallest tree in Maryland. If he had, Jarred might have handled the situation differently. But Jarred was unaware that the duke had already been informed of his daughter's whereabouts. Jarred's thoughts centered solely on compensating for humiliating the Duchess of Chessfield by buying her redemption papers, treating her like his private concubine, and accusing her of thievery. And just wait until she learned he had dragged her through a wedding ceremony she didn't remember attending! Lord, Chelsie was going to be furious with him. He was going to have to do some fast talking to straighten things out between them!

Blast it, he should have believed her in the first place, Jarred scolded himself. But how was he to know that fiery vixen was truly of royal breeding? She didn't act like a dignified duchess. That had probably done more to convince Jarred that she was lying than both Cyrus and Isaac's testimonies put together!

Jarred expelled a sigh. If Chelsie ever forgave him, it would be a miracle. He didn't deserve her respect or devotion, and he reminded himself then and there that he shouldn't be too disappointed if he never won her love. He was asking a great deal after the shameless way he had treated that green-eyed leprechaun.

Chelsie moaned in agony when she finally fought her way through the laudanum haze. The hangovers she suffered after being forced to swallow Isaac's concoction were nothing short of hellish. After struggling up on one elbow, Chelsie tried to hold her pounding head in a position that didn't hurt. There was none. . . .

Suddenly the memory of Isaac looming over her with his vicious sneer crashed over her like a tidal wave. Her eyes popped open. Expecting to find herself closeted in the hull of the ship, she let a startled yelp burst from her lips when she glanced sideways to see Jarred sleeping peacefully beside her.

Chelsie's shocked squawk caused Jarred to come straight out of bed, glancing in every direction at once. When he got his bearings he peered over at Chelsie whose mouth was gaping wide.

"What are you doing here?" she croaked, frog-eyed.

Sporting an amused grin, Jarred bent over her, forcing her back to her pillow. And when Chelsie fell into those scintillating blue eyes, she didn't care how or when or why. Jarred was beside her after a long, tormenting absence.

"I came back for this . . ." he murmured as his raven head inched even closer. "Because I love you. . . ."

Chelsie didn't stop to reason why or to demand answers to the myriad questions that whizzed through the cobwebs of her mind. She allowed herself to believe Jarred truly cared about her. When he was beside her, sensitizing her skin with skillful caresses, she couldn't think past his encircling arms. It had been weeks since she had felt his hirsute flesh moving suggestively against hers. All the pent-up desires that had lain dormant for more than a month rose to enshroud her in a cloud of impatient need.

His body half-covered hers, crushing her into the sheets. His kiss was hot and hard and faintly forceful. His mouth moved expertly over hers and his tongue darted into the soft recesses, evoking erotic tremors that swelled out of proportion with each

318

passing second. There was not an ounce of feminine reserve in Chelsie's response. She merely reacted with wild abandon. And when she returned Jarred's ravishing kiss, sparks leaped between them like lightning bolts. There was nothing patient about Jarred's touch or Chelsie's caresses. They both bore evidence of the urgent needs that swept through them like a raging river tumbling from its banks. Their lips twisted and slanted, devouring each other's fervent response. Their hands wandered to and fro, rediscovering each sensitive point and igniting wildfires of passion.

Even Chelsie's throbbing headache yielded to the pulsating pleasure that channeled through every fiber of her being. She was on fire and Jarred was the flame upon which she fed. Her body instinctively arched upward as his fingertips swirled around the throbbing crests of her breasts. She adored the pleasure of his seeking hands. She needed his touch, craved his breathtaking kisses. And while his hands and lips migrated over her pliant flesh, Chelsie was returning his touch—kiss for ardent kiss, caress for bold caress.

Jarred's body shuddered as if it had been besieged by an earthquake. He could feel himself falling pell-mell through time and space. This emerald-eyed sprite made him glad he was a man when she responded so eagerly to him. She unveiled new dimensions of passion and sent him soaring over rainbows. Jarred was like a madman, wanting her so desperately that it left him teetering on the brink of insanity. Even when her supple body was pressed intimately to his, it wasn't enough to appease the monstrous craving that mushroomed inside him. Jarred couldn't be satisfied until he was a living, breathing part of this spirited beauty.

Groaning in unholy torment, Jarred crouched above her, seeing the hunger reflected in her passion-drugged gaze. "God, how I need you," he rasped as his swarthy body glided upon hers.

With each hard, demanding thrust, Chelsie was lifted higher and higher still. Dizzying rapture left her clinging to Jarred for dear life. She reveled in the feel of his masculine warmth. She absorbed his strength. As his body drove into hers, she arched toward him, unable to get enough of this tempting devil whose image formed the perimeters of her whimsical dreams.

And the fire blazed brighter as they spiraled toward a glorious horizon. Chelsie could feel herself letting go, feel the tumultuous sensations that took command of her quaking body. She had been here before, reveling in the wild breathless splendor Jarred created. And yet, it was like the very first time, had always been like the very first time. She wondered dazedly if she would ever grow accustomed to these soul-shattering sensations, even when she knew they would unfurl each time he lured her into his spell of desire. Each time Jarred made love to her, she found herself whirling in a paradox of emotions. Loving him was always the same, yet it was always incredibly unique. Jarred made passion a constantly changing kaleidoscope of sensations and emotions. He filled her world to overflowing and left her body throbbing with ineffable pleasure. . . .

The nerve-tingling sensations she had experienced one by one suddenly converged upon her, dragging a moan from her lips. Chelsie felt herself pulled down from her lofty pedestal and towed into the spinning whirlpool of ultimate rapture. Like a cat clinging to a floating log for safety, Chelsie dug her nails into Jarred's back, struggling to draw a breath to reactivate her stalled heart. And just when she swore she had depleted her last ounce of air, Jarred breathed life into her with a stirring kiss. Unbound pleasure streamed through her as Jarred's muscular body shuddered upon hers and he clutched her to him as if the world was about to end.

Tears of unparalleled pleasure trickled down her cheeks as she glided languidly back to the shores of reality. In the aftermath of passion, neither of them could speak. Their energies had been spent and every emotion had been drained. They nestled together in a blanket of contentment, drifting with the rolling tide of memories they had created.

320

It was much much later before Jarred mustered the strength and desire to roll away. He would have preferred to spend the entire day lounging in bed, feeding his insatiable craving for this delightful wench, recovering from his fast and furious ride and the hair-raising ordeal with Isaac Latham.

Jarred's pensive gaze dropped to the tangled spray of silver-gold hair that flowed across the pillow. Impulsively, he stretched out an arm to comb the silky tendrils away from Chelsie's enchanting face. The cryptic expression on her exquisite features caused Jarred to grin curiously.

"What mischievous thought provokes this impish smile, nymph?" Jarred questioned softly.

Her long lashes swept upward. Her eyes sparkled like polished emeralds. "I have just discovered a fascinating cure for the worst sort of hangover," she declared. Her smile evaporated when the tormenting memory of her encounter with Isaac shattered her pleasant thoughts. "Was any of your family hurt because of Isaac? I cannot remember anything except being forced to drink the potion. And how did you get here? I thought you were . . .

Jarred pressed his index finger to her lips to silence her. Gently he drew Chelsie's head against his shoulder and held her to him, reveling in these tender moments that came so seldom between them.

"I arrived in Baltimore just before the wedding was to take place. I thought you were going to marry Neil. I wanted to stop you because I cared too much to let you go. But instead, I found Abi was to become my older brother's bride. Before the ceremony could take place, all hell broke loose. Isaac was lying in wait and he bushwhacked Daniel in the thigh and Grant in the arm." When he felt Chelsie tense up, he ran his lean fingers down her spine in a comforting caress. "They both will be fine. But it was *you* I was most concerned about. I rode back to the hotel to find the note Isaac left in your room. He wanted me to bring Neil to the cove where he had left you adrift in a skiff, and he indicated that you had been injured and needed medical attention."

Chelsie grimaced, knowing what a nightmare the McAlisters had suffered because of her private feud with Isaac. But she spoke not a word and anxiously waited for Jarred to finish his account of the events of the previous day.

"Isaac left you draped in the skiff in the middle of the cove while he perched in the trees. He took potshots at Neil and me when we tried to retrieve you," Jarred reported. "When Isaac ran out of ammunition, I chased him through the overhanging trees. We struggled and he fell to his death."

Now Chelsie knew what had caused the scrapes on Jarred's hide, ones she had discovered with her exploring caresses. "I suspect Isaac's fiendish methods of revenge spoiled the wedding and disappointed Kyle." She sighed deflatedly. "He was so looking forward to a marriage in the family. . . ."

The rattle at the door sent Jarred and Chelsie diving for cover. To their utter amazement, Grant and Kyle swarmed inside without waiting for an invitation. Kyle was as radiant as the morning sun, and Grant, though his wounded arm was draped in a sling, was grinning in wry amusement.

"Forgive the interruption," Grant chuckled, his tone nowhere near apologetic. His eyes dipped to the hem of the sheet that barely concealed Chelsie's delectable figure and then he focused on her beet-red face that was surrounded by a tangled mass of blond hair. "Papa wanted to be the first to greet his new daughter-in-law, since she was too dazed to remember being congratulated yesterday."

Jarred scowled. He hadn't had time to offer Chelsie a full explanation of what had transpired the previous day. Now that Grant had blurted out his careless remarks, Jarred would be forced to rap out a hasty account of the wedding. For God's sake, wasn't a man permitted even a smidgen of privacy on the morning after his own wedding?

Chelsie peered incredulously at Kyle and Grant before turning her astonished gaze on Jarred. Before she could pose a single question, Kyle bounded toward her like a jackrabbit.

"I'm so pleased that you consented to marry Jarred," he enthused as he plopped down to give his thoroughly embarrassed daughter-in-law an affectionate squeeze. "Now I have a real, live duchess in the family." His brown eyes sparkled with mischief. "And you know how eager I am for grandchildren. . . ."

Chelsie felt another wave of color splash her cheeks—the fierce combination of anger, outrage and humiliation. Before she had time to compose herself, Kyle lifted her hand—the one that was clamped around the hem of the quilt tucked beneath her chin.

"Since Jarred was without a wedding ring for the ceremony, I gave him his mother's ring to present to you. I hope it will be as special to you as it was to my wife and to me."

Chelsie peered wide-eyed at the gold band inlaid with diamonds and rubies. She had often seen the ring on Kyle's little finger. He had worn it in memory of his love for his wife.

Although Kyle was doing all within his power to make her feel welcome, Chelsie was becoming more suspicious of Jarred by the second. Why had he suddenly decided to marry her? And why had he confessed his love for her before he worked his hypnotic spell of passion on her? Come to think of it, none of this sounded like the Jarred McAlister she had met in the bathhouse in Annapolis. Why was he being so nice to her? It was out of character. Jarred was usually growling at her for embroiling him in another of the many catastrophes that had plagued her since she had run aground in Maryland.

Instantly Chelsie's wary gaze swung back to Jarred, whose bronzed features were screwed up in an annoyed scowl. The answer to her befuddled questions came in visual form. To her amazement, Grant ambled over to drop her priceless locket in her hand.

"I believe this belongs to you, duchess," Grant remarked with a smile. "Jarred has been carrying it with him since he found it attached to the note from your abductor."

Chelsie murmured a quiet thank you, but on the inside she

was smoldering. The locket was obviously the reason Jarred had married her while she was besotted with the potion. That was also why he had murmured his affection to her before he made love to her. If Jarred had uttered his devotion to her a month ago, she might have believed him, but not now! He hadn't loved her when he thought she was a thief who had been deported from England and sold as a redemptioner. He had mocked her title and treated her like his private whore. He came to her to appease his lusts while he passively courted Abi and honored his noble obligation. Why, that lowdown, good-for-nothing hypocrite!

The past two months Chelsie had been hurt inside and out. But right now she hurt worse in places that didn't show—in her heart and soul. She loved Jarred and she had wanted him to care for her because of the woman she was, not for the title she held. Jarred had suddenly become one of the endless rabble of suitors who had courted her fortune, having little concern for the woman who held the purse strings. Anybody could love a duchess when she was fabulously wealthy, but no one loved a duchess who was presumed to be a pauper.

Chelsie's fist clenched around her locket, her mind racing with tormented thoughts. She didn't even remember what Grant and Kyle said before they exited the room. She was too busy seeing red and entertaining mutinous methods of repaying Jarred for this last round of humiliation. Damn that devil! The truth was he had married her to save face after Abi wed Neil. He had spoken the vows to satisfy his father's whim and to attach himself to a titled heiress. Jarred was trying to compensate for stealing the innocence of a duchess. But Chelsie didn't want to be just another obligation to a man who had an overactive sense of responsibility to his family, his country, and his reputation. Jarred had obviously mistaken obligation for love. And now he was trying to convince her that he really did care about her.

Love? Chelsie scoffed at the thought. Jarred didn't love her; he never had. If he truly cared about her, he would have said so long ago. He had used her . . . again! Curse his wicked soul! How could she love a man who made her feel like a fool?

So *that* was why Jarred was being so warm and attentive, Chelsie reasoned. He was trying to charm her by whispering his affection and making love to her. Then the silver-tongued fox had probably planned to offer his own version of why he had married her. But Grant and Kyle had foiled his devious scheme and the truth was out. Chelsie was never going to forgive Jarred for this, never in a million years! He wanted a female body to ease his lust, and Chelsie had always been convenient. But Jarred wouldn't have shamed his family by marrying a woman he presumed to be a lowly servant. Now that he had discovered she was who she'd said she was, he had everything to gain and nothing to lose by marrying her. His male pride had probably been smarting after his older brother stole Abi away from him. Naturally Jarred had rebounded off an engagement and into an impulsive marriage. He could swear he loved her until he was blue in the face, but Chelsie wasn't going to believe him. As always, she was convenient—a convenient paramour, a convenient scapegoat for his frustration, a convenient bride to marry when his fiancée exchanged vows with his brother. Damn him! Damn her for loving a man who would never truly care for her in all the ways she loved him. *Used to love him—past tense—*Chelsie assured herself resentfully. Aye, she had loved Jarred, but his deceit had spoiled that precious emotion that had blossomed in her heart.

And if Jarred McAlister thought he could sweet-talk her into groveling at his feet, that she would melt just because he said he loved her, he had damned well better think again! A month ago, when she was a nobody with a questionable background, she would have given most *anything* for this confession of affection. But certainly not now! Jarred had married a duchess just so he could *say* he had. But she didn't mean any more to him than she had when he trotted off to Albany to confer with the colonial bigwigs! Curse him! She would hate him to her dying day!

325

The moment the door slammed shut behind Kyle and Grant, Jarred knew he was in serious trouble. Chelsie's glare cut like a dagger. She was out of bed in a single bound, buzzing around the room like a hornet. Although Jarred knew she was furious, he couldn't restrain the smile that tugged at his lips. Chelsie was a sight to behold when she was in a snit. Her eyes blazed like torches, her face flushed hot pink.

"It isn't what you think it is," Jarred began calmly as he cushioned his head on his linked fingers. His gaze followed Chelsie while she stormed hither and yon, worming into her clothes and gathering her belongings.

Chelsie pulled up short and wheeled around. Her glower was meant to mutilate. "Do not presume to explain to me what I'm thinking," she hissed furiously. "You can save your eloquent speeches for the Assembly. I know why you did what you did." In two pouncing strides Chelsie was looming over him. Her breasts heaved with so much indignation she very nearly split the bodice of her chartreuse gown. Angrily she shook the gold locket in Jarred's handsome face. "You married my title for prestige and to save face because you lost Abi to Neil. And like so many of your disgusting gender, you will probably take a new mistress to replace the pauper who suddenly turned back into the princess you married on the rebound."

Inhaling a swift breath, Chelsie plunged on, eager to vent her frustration. "Did it occur to you that the reason I haven't married before now is that I wanted to be loved for *myself*, not for my title and fortune?"

"You are truly lovely," Jarred sighed, undaunted by her fuming tirade. His eyes wandered hungrily over the swells of her breasts, the luscious curves that he had pressed familiarly to himself the previous hour. "And I *do* love you, despite what you think of me and my motives."

Jarred had confessed his love, and Chelsie glowered at him as if he had committed an unforgivable crime.

Oh, how she wanted to clobber him! How dare he carry on this charade of masculine devotion? How stupid did he think

326

she was, anyway?

"Answer me, damn you!" she demanded. "Did it occur to you that I might not *want* to marry you? Don't you think I *know* what men want from a duchess whose father owns enough property to create his own country?"

"I'm not like the rest of the men you've met," Jarred insisted. "I loved you when I thought you were a peasant and I *still* love you, even though you are a duchess. You are a bit unorthodox in your behavior. You have a volatile temper, but my affection for you allows you to have a few flaws."

Chelsie stared at him in amazement. He really must think she was an imbecile not to know what he was trying to do. And how could he sprawl in bed, lying through his pearly white teeth? His colossal audacity was matched only by his arrogance!

"Do you honestly expect me to believe a man who has set a precedent with his two-year engagement to Abi Shaw was *so* swept away by all-encompassing love that he impulsively leaped into marriage to a woman who just *happened* to be a wealthy heiress?" Chelsie regarded him with mocking disdain. "How quickly the worm turns when this caterpillar transforms into a butterfly."

Jarred's sapphire gaze flooded over her voluptuous figure, not missing one detail. "If you weren't so busy being defensive, you would realize you are throwing obstacles between us that aren't really there. I loved the caterpillar as much as I adore the butterfly," he had the nerve to confess.

The man was incredible! How could he lie there so nonchalantly clinging to his ridiculous claim of devotion? If he *had* loved her a month ago, he should have said so. But he didn't. He hadn't loved her then; he didn't love her now.

"You aren't fooling me for a minute," Chelsie declared in a bitter tone. "Women have always been playthings to you, unless one of them can assist you in your climb up the ladder of success. Now you are pretending to be the picture of manly devotion because you have married a blueblood. You, the son of a one-time indentured servant who was down on his luck and who sold seven years of his life for a fresh new start in the colonies!"

Chelsie rose to her full stature and tilted her chin to a haughty angle. "Well, you aren't good enough for me, Jarred McAlister," she mocked. "And 'tis terribly out of character for you to portray the doting husband after being such an inconsiderate fiancé who bought himself a mistress to pleasure him whenever it met his whim. If I come across a young man who catches my eye, I will place him in my stable of studs. If a man can keep mistresses, a wife can stock her stable with lovers." Let him chew on that thought awhile and see how he liked it!

Jarred had been in complete control of his temper until Chelsie spitefully vowed to seek out affection wherever she pleased. Growling, Jarred yanked the sheet around his nude body and came off the bed like a bear emerging from hibernation. He was not in good humor, and when he loomed over Chelsie wearing nothing but a sheet and a poisonous scowl, she involuntarily retreated a step.

"I said I loved you and I meant it," he roared at her. "And there will be no bedhopping in this marriage. I intend to remain faithful to you, and you will return the same courtesy to me!"

If Jarred hadn't been in such a snit himself, he would have realized he had taken the wrong approach with Chelsie. Making demands on this stubborn firebrand was like issuing a declaration of war. She detested being told what to do, especially when she was madder than blue blazes.

"I will sleep where I please, with whom I please, and I will take as many lovers as meets my whim," she yelled back. "And when I've slept around as much as you have, I'll know for certain if you are below average or mediocre in bed."

Jarred was not accustomed to having his virility referred to as mediocre. Her taunting remark punctured his male pride just as she'd hoped it would. Chelsie had struck out in childish vindictiveness, wanting to hurt him the way he'd hurt her. She wanted

328

to share the company that misery loves so well, to compensate for the anger and frustration that boiled through her veins.

"It doesn't get any better than this," Jarred assured her tartly. "No other man can love you as well as I can."

Where he found the gall to utter such a pompous remark was beyond Chelsie. What did he think he was—God's gift to women? He was, but Chelsie would have cut out her tongue before she confessed the truth to this haughty galoot!

"When I have finished my experimentation, *I* will be the one to decide if your claim as an unparalleled lover is justified," Chelsie informed him hotly.

As Chelsie spun away, Jarred whisked her back around to breathe down her neck. "Don't defy me," he growled. "I can assure you that you won't like the vindictive side of my nature. Don't forget what happened to Isaac when he crossed me."

"Who said I liked even one facet of your personality?" Chelsie purred in sticky-sweet sarcasm. "And you *had* your chance to love me when I was poor. 'Tis a pity you employed such bad timing, my dear husband. I might have been foolish enough to believe you if you had confessed your affection the night before you left for Albany. Now it is too late."

Jarred grabbed her arm, yanking her against his swelled chest. "You said you loved me, remember? Now I ask you, duchess," he drawled out her title like a rumbling curse. "Who is trying to deceive whom? Admit it. You don't really love me. You never did."

"Aye, 'tis true. I didn't then, and I certainly don't now!" she lied to save face. " 'Twas all an act. You thought I was charading as a duchess, but the only charade I played was letting you think I cared one whit about you."

"That's just what I thought," Jarred grunted disgustedly. "Women are the world's *worst* about whispering words of love in the heat of passion. Being emotional, fickle creatures, they confuse desire with affection. But once the loving is over, they realize they don't care quite so much as they thought they did. You, witch, are the shining example of female hypocrisy!"

As if he detested their physical contact, Jarred flung Chelsie away from him and stomped over to fetch his clothes. "I think I liked you better when you were a peasant," he grumbled sourly.

"And I liked you better when you were honest about your physical needs and your shallow feelings toward me," Chelsie snapped, glaring poison arrows at the broad expanse of his back.

"There is nothing shallow about what I feel," Jarred bit off in such a hateful tone that it nullified his comment. Not that Chelsie believed him anyway. She was as certain that he didn't really love her as she was that the sun rose in the east.

"Considering the lack of depth in your character, 'tis extremely shallow, counselor," she countered caustically.

Jarred, his temper sorely put-upon already, came apart at the seams. Furiously he threw down the boot he held and glowered at Chelsie's smirk. "Damn it, woman, sometimes you make me so mad I wish I'd never met you! I was perfectly content with the way of things until you barged into my life and turned it topsy-turvy. It seems I have married Madame Attila. What is it with you women? Once you are wed, you think you have acquired a license to fight!"

So now his true feelings had poured out. Jarred felt as if he was stuck with her, just as he felt obliged to wed Abi after her husband had perished. That was all wedlock was to Jarred — institutionalized sex for the sake of posterity and a feather in his cap of success. He felt responsible for deflowering her, and once he learned she truly was a duchess, he was bound to do the honorable thing. But the truth was, Jarred regretted the day they met, and now their star-crossed affair had wound up in an impulsive marriage.

"I knew *one* day you would get around to uttering that wish," she said in a quieter tone that very nearly revealed the pain that stabbed at her heart. Proudly she raised her head to meet his flashing blue eyes. "You have one wish left. If it is that I walk out of your life forever, say so now and it will be done."

"Blast it, I'm not the one picking fights around here," Jarred fumed. "And don't try to put words in my mouth. I don't want you to go. . . . Come back here, for God's sake! You are *not* walking out in the middle of an argument!"

Oh, yes she was — and Jarred wasn't going to stop her. Chelsie clutched the doorknob and glanced back at Jarred's furious frown. "I can leave any time I choose. I may be your wife, but I do not, nor shall I ever, take orders from you," Chelsie all but shouted at him. "I will go where I wish, with whom I wish, and I will return if and when it pleases me!"

When she whipped open the door to breeze down the hall, Grant was poised to knock. An agitated frown knitted her brow. Men! They were as thick as mosquitoes. No matter which way she turned, there was another one staring her in the face. What she needed was time to wrestle with her tangled emotions. Before she could set one foot outside the door, she was greeted by Grant's cheerful smile, one that did nothing to sweeten her sour mood.

"I thought you were injured," Chelsie muttered as she slammed the door with such force that the woodwork rattled. "You should be in bed instead of parading up and down the hall." With that, she sailed past Grant like a flying carpet.

"I thought you were happy. You just got married!" Grant called after her. He frowned bemusedly when Chelsie shot off down the hall without ever looking back, as if the devil himself were hot on her heels.

"Happily married?" Jarred muttered as he reopened the door that had been slammed in his face. "That, dear brother, is a contradiction in terms." He whizzed past Grant like a cyclone.

"There looks to be trouble in paradise," Grant chuckled at his grumbling brother.

"There is when a man weds a woman who has a temper hot enough to start a forest fire," Jarred tossed over his shoulder.

"I wouldn't complain if I were given the chance to exchange places with you," Grant interjected with a roguish grin. "I have a soft spot in my heart for that lovely lady."

"Do yourself a favor, Grant," Jarred advised bitterly. "Don't *ever* get married. You wouldn't *believe* the change a woman undergoes when you slide a wedding ring on her finger. She might be everything you think you could ever want, but instead, you might wind up getting exactly what you deserve, just like I did."

When Jarred sped down the hall, Grant shook his head in bemusement. He swore there had been something fishy going on between Jarred and the duchess from the very beginning. They had been magnetically attracted to each other. And suddenly they were at each other's throats. But Jarred appeared to be right about one thing, Grant mused thoughtfully. Marriage seemed to bring out the worst, even in good-tempered individuals. Both Jarred and Chelsie were as unapproachable as rattlesnakes, and Grant would have dearly loved to know what had put them at each other's throats.

In frustration Jarred watched Chelsie saunter down the street, flinging smiles at everything in breeches. He was tempted to follow her, but he decided they both needed time to cool off. So much for charming the duchess out of her silk stockings, Jarred thought with an exasperated sigh. He had his work cut out for him. Chelsie had her heart set on hating him, and she had him convinced that she despised him thoroughly and completely.

Scowling in disgust, Jarred aimed himself toward the sheriff's office to make the necessary legal arrangements to have Captain Hutton delivered to Annapolis and bound over for trial. But Jarred couldn't keep his mind on business, not when Chelsie was roaming about unchaperoned. The thought of another man sampling her charms cut him to the quick. Jarred kept reminding himself that he had not come to Chelsie pure and innocent, and that as independent and rebellious as she was, she would demand the same privileges men enjoyed. . . .

Jarred swore under his breath. If he had known ten years ago that a blond-haired hellion with bright green eyes was going to steal his heart away, he would have saved himself for her. But how was he supposed to know things like that? He wasn't a seer! No other woman had ever bewitched him so much that he was willing and eager to contemplate and follow through with a wedding. *Willing and eager,* mind you! Jarred McAlister—the man who went through women like an elephant gobbling peanuts—was ready to put down roots. Unfortunately, the woman he wanted to spend the rest of his life with had every intention of spreading her wings and fluttering from one man to another like a damned butterfly! Chelsie was turning out to be as much of a rogue as *he* had been! How in the blazes was he going to convince her that he was sincere? What else could a man say, except that he was sorry he hadn't believed her, and that he loved her? Well, one thing was for sure—Jarred was going to have to devise an innovative way to prove his affection for that human hurricane or he was going to lose her forever! Oh, how he wished. . . .

"Three wishes? Bah," Jarred grumbled disdainfully. He wished he was stretched out on a medieval torture rack. It would be child's play compared to being torn apart on the inside by an emerald-eyed firebrand who wouldn't accept the offering of his heart, even if he cut it from his chest and served it to her on a silver platter. Women! They were placed on earth to drive men mad, and Chelsie Channing from Chessfield was making him crazy!

Chapter 26

The moment Chelsie stepped into her room at Easthaven, an annoyed frown puckered her brow. The servants, assuming she intended to share quarters with her new husband, had toted her belongings into Jarred's boudoir. After stamping her foot in frustration, Chelsie marched over to the adjoining door to retrieve her clothes. Before she could clutch the latch, Jarred appeared in the entrance, smiling that rakish smile that Chelsie itched to smear all over his handsome face.

"For appearance's sake, you will have to room with me," Jarred murmured.

That low, husky voice could send waves of goosebumps undulating under Chelsie's flesh. *Could, but didn't.* Chelsie mustered her defenses and fought against his magnetic charm. Jarred had married her title, and that was all he was going to get! She wasn't going to permit him to seduce her *ever again*.

Her chin tilted to a defiant angle as she whizzed past him, taking great care not to brush against his virile body. "Very well, for appearance's sake," she begrudingly concurred. "But nothing else." When Chelsie spied the carefully wrapped package that lay on his velvet bedspread, she eyed him warily. "What is this?"

"Why, it looks to be a gift," Jarred replied with mock innocence.

Leisurely he ambled up behind Chelsie, whose back was as stiff as a ramrod. Before her senses were fogged by the manly scent of the scoundrel who had married her for his own selfish purposes, Chelsie took two giant steps forward.

"I can see that for myself," she sniffed disdainfully. "Why is it there?"

Jarred swaggered over to retrieve the package in question and offered it to his reluctant wife. " 'Tis a wedding gift," he informed her. "When I saw it, I thought of you."

Chelsie stared at the package as if he was handing her a dead snake. "I don't want it."

Damn, but she was making this difficult. Jarred had resolved not to lose patience with her, no matter how furious she made him. He wanted her respect and affection. And from the looks of things, he was going to have to acquire them the hard way—by earning every bit. Chelsie wasn't going to generously give her love away.

"Perhaps you would like me to open it for you," Jarred suggested with his pleasant smile intact. But he swore his face would crack from trying to be nice to this brooding beauty.

Chelsie stood squarely in the middle of the room like a marble statue while Jarred unwrapped her gift. Carefully he lifted the gossamer negligee from its box. The garment was testimony to his expensive taste in clothes. But rather than admire the lacy white gown with its plunging neckline, Chelsie chose to speculate on how many women had received similar gifts from this seductive rake. The thought left her seething.

" 'Tis the only one of its kind," Jarred commented as he ran a ruddy hand over the fabric in a provocative caress. "While we were in Baltimore, I purchased it and had it altered just to suit you."

"To suit *you,* you mean," Chelsie corrected in a sarcastic tone. "If you are so fond of your creation, then *you* wear it. I have a dozen such garments in my wardrobe at Chessfield, all designed by renowned seamstresses."

Chelsie snatched up her own gown and stomped behind the dressing screen. Jarred expelled a wordless growl. *Damn that minx.* She wasn't making his crusade for her love difficult; she was making it downright impossible! Jarred grabbed the hem of the garment and popped it against his four-poster bed like a snapping whip—wishing his infuriating wife had been in it. But when Chelsie reappeared, Jarred was again the epitome of good humor and patience.

Chelsie plopped down in bed, wearing a prudish flannel gown that clung to her throat and extended to her ankles. Crossing her arms beneath her breasts, she silently dared Jarred to attempt another seductive technique. It would ultimately meet with defeat just as the first one had.

But Jarred wasn't giving up so easily. Meeting her challenging stare, he slowly unbuttoned his white linen shirt, baring his hirsute chest. Wearing an evocative grin that was difficult to resist, Jarred shrugged the gaping garment from his broad shoulders and tossed it aside with cavalier devilment. He saw Chelsie's eyes flicker with feminine admiration, even though she was trying like the devil not to let her emotions show. *Now* he was getting somewhere, he encouraged himself. She may have detested him, but her eyes assured him she still liked what she saw.

When Jarred curled his sinewy body forward to remove his boots, his whipcord muscles rippled and Chelsie's foolish heart leaped. She knew what he was trying to do, of course. But by damned, she wasn't going to melt into puddles just because this handsome, incredibly virile rake oozed with sensuality.

Again, Jarred met those beguiling green eyes. He unbuttoned his breeches, leaving them drooping provocatively on his hips. When he saw her gaze dip and linger longer on his anatomy than she intended, he smiled inwardly. Tucking his thumbs inside the waistband, Jarred slowly pushed the garment down until it dropped in a pool at his feet.

Chelsie swallowed hard. It was virtually impossible not to be aroused by the sight of this magnificently sculptured specimen. Although she had seen Jarred in the buff on a number of occasions, he was a feast she couldn't help but devour. The muscular planes of his body were awe-inspiring. Jarred McAlister, even though he was a deceitful womanizer, possessed a physique any Roman god would envy. It was perfectly natural for her to be aroused by the sight of this masculine specimen, she assured herself. Jarred would have the same effect on a ninety-year-old man-hater. And Chelsie was only twenty!

It was a test of her self-control to be satisfied with admiring his manly contours from a distance without buckling to the urge to run an exploring hand over that massive chest, tapered waist, and narrow hips. Jarred was visually tormenting her, accepting her challenge, daring her to deny she didn't want him in her bed for some other reason besides snuggling up to a warm body to sleep.

For one hopeful second, Jarred thought he had crumbled Chelsie's stubborn defenses, that she still wanted him in the same hungry way he wanted her. But to his frustration, she squirmed onto her right side and focused intently on the wall.

"Please snuff the lantern," she requested. Her voice disguised the desire he had aroused in her with his generous display of masculine flesh. " 'Tis been a long, tiresome day of traveling and I'm eager to sleep."

Jarred gnashed his teeth. Never in all his life had he shucked his clothes and purposely tried to arouse a woman with such dedicated tactics. Obviously he needed practice in the art of strip-tease! Chelsie didn't appear to be tempted past her resistance, not when she could stare at the wall while a naked man was poised at the foot of her bed!

Discouraged but far from defeated, Jarred resorted to a different technique. Scooping up the expensive silk negligee, Jarred wormed into the sleeveless garment and smoothed it over his hips. The gown barely reached his thighs, and if he dared to inhale a deep breath, he would split several seams. If he couldn't *seduce* Chelsie into forgiving him, he decided to try his luck at *amusing* her into forgetting how much she loathed him.

Jarred sashayed over to strike a ridiculously feminine pose in front of the wall at which Chelsie was staring. The lantern light streamed through the sheer garment, assuring anyone who cared to look that no matter how frilly the apparel, the body beneath it was one-hundred-percent male — perfectly formed,

337

willing and able to fulfill a woman's most erotic fantasies.

It was all Chelsie could do to keep from bursting into giggles. The ludicrous extremes to which this man would go to melt the wall of ice that encased her heart astounded her. And only a man who was confident of himself and his masculinity would have _wiggled into a garment that was so decidedly feminine.

Before Chelsie's deadpan expression cracked into a smile, she wormed to her left side, presenting her back to the would-be comic. Jarred walked right over her and the bed to place himself in front of the opposite wall, at which she was now staring.

"So? What do you think?" he questioned, batting his long black lashes.

Biting back a grin, Chelsie rolled over onto her back. Let him try to lie on the ceiling that she was presently staring at! "I think the swim you took in the cove near Baltimore warped your brain," she declared with a straight face. "I also think you should have stayed high atop the trees with the rest of the nuts. . . ."

Chelsie's voice trailed off when Jarred stepped onto the bed once again, causing the frame to creak and the mattress to sag from his weight. This time he straddled her to peer down at her from his towering height. It was obvious that Jarred hadn't employed this tactic of garbing himself in women's negligee's before. If he had, he would have known it was impossible not to look up his skirt while he was standing directly above her. Chelsie blushed deep crimson.

"No matter which way you turn, I'm going to be there," Jarred told her matter-of-factly. "I want you because I love you. I'm not going to be satisfied with anything less than your love. It doesn't matter to what extremes I have to go to acquire your affection. No challenge is too great when I consider what I shall gain for my efforts."

Chelsie pushed herself up against the headboard and then bounded off the bed like a mountain goat. In three swift strides she crossed the room to fetch an extra quilt. After she had rolled the blanket in the shape of a python, she placed it right in the middle of the bed, forming two equal sides—his and hers.

"And I am *not* giving my love away to a man who never had enough faith in me or respect for me to cover the head of a pin . . . until he discovered I had blue blood flowing through my veins," Chelsie hurled at him. "You can pull your best punch, Jarred McAlister, but nothing is going to change my attitude toward you. You showed your true colors the moment you learned Isaac and Cyrus had lied and that I was the one who was telling the truth all along. You wouldn't have broken your engagement with Abi to marry a lowly peasant, but you married a duchess for your own selfish reasons. We cannot go back to the way we were. You have spoiled *any* chance of that."

"For God's sake, Chel," Jarred muttered as he plunked down on his half of the bed. "I'm trying to make a fresh new start, trying to compensate for wronging you. You could make an effort to be receptive!"

"I don't want your charity *or* your insincere apologies," she insisted as she yanked the sheet over her shoulder and turned her back on him once more. "I just want to be left alone!"

"I can't leave you alone," Jarred admitted as he flipped the rolled quilt out of his way and loomed over her. "You're in my blood and you always have been. I want you—body, heart, and soul."

Chelsie twisted around to replace the improvised boundary line between her side of the bed and his. "Kindly remove your arm from my property," she demanded crisply. When Jarred didn't budge, Chelsie glared at the offending appendage. "Remove it, or risk losing the use of it for an indefinite period of time. . . ."

Jarred met her fuming glower. His gaze dipped to her pouting lips, sketching them in a visual caress. "I love you," he murmured with seductive huskiness. Defying her threat, Jarred bent to place the slightest breath of a kiss upon her soft mouth. Slowly he lifted his raven head. His liquid blue eyes locked with those defiant pools of green. "I'm calling it a night, but I'm not calling it quits. You can erect brick walls between us, but you can't stop me from caring, from longing to share a true marriage. Sooner or later you are going to want the love and passion I so freely offer."

"The Sahara will sooner be besieged by flood waters," she sniffed caustically. "I want nothing from you except your absence from my life."

His index finger traced the stubborn set of her jaw. The faintest hint of a smile rippled across his sensuous lips as he continued in that utterly provocative tone that Chelsie suspected he had practiced on so many women that he had managed to transform a whisper into a successful seduction. "I will wait until you come to me, until you are ready to rediscover the splendor of having your exquisite body molded intimately to mine, until you ache to feel my caresses gliding over your silken flesh. . . ."

Chelsie wished Jarred hadn't gone into such scintillating details. He set her heart to beating so loudly that she could barely hear herself think. And she definitely needed to be in full command of her mental capacities when dealing with this charismatic rake. She didn't need to be reminded of his masterful lovemaking. His suggestive descriptions left her to burn. But Chelsie vowed to let herself burn alive *long* before she succumbed to her wanton desires as she had so shamelessly done in the past.

She wasn't Jarred's consolation prize. Jarred was trying to make her feel like a quarrelsome shrew. He was preying on her passions and her sympathy, attempting to evoke feelings of guilt within her. He was being incredibly tender, making her look the culprit when she rejected his advances.

Aye, she loved him to distraction, but she refused to be at his beck and call just because he wanted a female body to make love to when the mood struck. She was not going to change her life to suit his. He expected her to do all the giving and forgiving, while he did all the taking and reaped the benefits of this marriage. Blast it, Jarred McAlister didn't need a wife, and he never had. He needed a lapdog. And that was one thing Chelsie would never be! Jarred had virtually rejected her when she confessed her love for him that night more than six weeks ago. He had his chance, and he had thrown it away. . . .

Her contemplative musings evaporated when Jarred brushed his fingertips over her clenched fist and drew her hand against him. "I yearn to feel your fingertips roaming over my chest — the way they did the night before I left for Albany and the morning after our wedding," he murmured. "I long for the warm, fervent sensations you arouse in me when you trace those sweet, tempting caresses over my belly, when your hands enfold — "

As if she were touching live coals, she jerked her hand away. "Enough!" Chelsie squeaked, her voice octaves higher than normal, her face flushed with intimate memories of passion. "And take that nightgown off! You look ridiculous in it. . . ." In a frustrated flurry, Chelsie flounced onto her stomach to spew curses into her pillow. "I want to forget I was your whore in another lifetime."

"Never my whore," Jarred contradicted. His soothing voice whispered against her ear. Unwanted sensations of pleasure played a forbidden melody on her soul. "You are the sweetest temptation. You are my only love. I tried to uphold my obligations to Abi, but even wild horses couldn't drag me away from you, little leprechaun. I fought what I felt for you, but nothing could make the wanting go away. I love you. . . ."

Chelsie pulled the pillow from beneath her face and clobbered him with it. This done, she flashed him a contemptuous glare. "Nay, you have mistaken your fierce sense of obligation and propriety for love, and you will never convince me otherwise."

Having said her piece, Chelsie wrapped her pillow around her head to drown out all sound. She didn't want to hear those huskily whispered lies. She didn't want to soften her defenses.

341

A man could say anything he wished in retrospect. But nothing could change the fact that Jarred hadn't offered a confession of love when Chelsie bared her heart to him.

If he had loved the pauper, she might have believed he also loved the princess. That was all she had wanted then—to know that Jarred cared about her. She wanted to be special to him, to know beyond all doubt that he cherished her, despite what he thought of her background and breeding. But Jarred had been influenced by who he *thought* she was then and by who he *knew* her to be now. Nothing he could say could dissolve her suspicions. A dozen verbal "I love you"s wasn't going to change Chelsie's low opinion of him. She wanted proof—the kind that spoke for itself.

Sighing heavily, Jarred scooted over to his half of the bed and snuffed the lantern. He was going to have to devise another way to penetrate that hard shell Chelsie had grown to protect her emotions. He could understand that she was wary and mistrusting of him. And he really couldn't blame her for being so cynical. He had given her very little reason to trust him *or* his motives. He had kept his feelings to himself too long, and now Chelsie was suspicious. No matter how honorable his intentions, he looked the devious scoundrel in her eyes.

If not for Isaac Latham, Jarred would have arrived in Baltimore to voice his affection long before he learned the truth about this unconventional duchess. If not for Isaac, Chelsie might have believed in Jarred instead of becoming even more skeptical of him. Jarred scolded himself for playing the if-only game. It was getting him nowhere fast.

Yet it was safe to say that circumstances beyond his control had soured Chelsie's belief in his commitment to her. Now he was just another of the endless rabble of men who had courted a wealthy duchess, hoping to marry themselves to a fortune and a title. Her past experiences with fortune hunters had made her skeptical of men in general, and Jarred's poor sense of timing had spoiled his chance of convincing Chelsie that he was sincere.

Would she ever reopen those tender memories they shared and stop to consider what had attracted them to each other in the first place? Jarred wished he knew. He would have been happier. But knowing how stubborn and determined Chelsie was, Jarred wondered if he would live long enough to convince her that he wanted her for herself. From all indications, he could expect to persuade this belligerent minx of his devotion around the turn of the century . . . if all went well. . . .

Chelsie lay there like a corpse, afraid to move, battling her betraying body and her feminine yearnings. It would have been so easy to reach out to Jarred, knowing he would weave his web of passion around her and make her forget why she was so annoyed with him. *Why* did he expect her to believe him, when he had openly admitted he didn't believe she had ever loved him? And he considered her to be skeptical! Ha! The pot was calling the kettle black.

Lord, if only her father would come to rescue her before she broke down and settled for less than Jarred's love. She could sail home with her father to visit Chessfield and never come back. Jarred had too many obligations in the colonies to accompany her. And Chelsie might be able to forget that handsome blue-eyed devil if she was on one continent and he was on another, with an ocean between them.

And while Chelsie was contemplating the thought of being rescued by her father, her wish was coming true. Evan Channing was somewhere between England and the colonies, itching to get his hands on the vile man who had the audacity to treat an heiress like a common peasant. Jarred knew his relationship with Chelsie was stormy, but he didn't have the foggiest notion what stormy was. The word had been invented to describe the Duke of Chessfield. When his notorious temper was billowing, he was lightning and thunder in the flesh—a cloudburst of churning fury and revenge that was searching for an exact location to strike.

It was an ill wind that blew the Duke of Chessfield toward Jarred's doorstep. It was most fortunate for Jarerd that Hurricane Evan was still out to sea. But he wouldn't be there for long. And when he hit landfall, there wasn't a shelter sturdy enough to protect Jarred from Hurricane Evan's wrath!

Chapter 27

Inhaling a deep breath, Chelsie pivoted to face the striking figure of the man who lounged leisurely beside the bedroom door. Without allowing Chelsie to accept or reject his suggestion, Jarred had planned an elaborate reception to show off his new bride to the neighbors and his friends and associates from Annapolis. It was killing Chelsie to know she was going to have to be nice to Jarred all evening. He had done this on purpose, damn him!

Reluctantly Chelsie admired the expensive cut of Jarred's clothes, the way the fabric strained over his muscular flesh when he moved with panther-like grace . . . Jarred, curse his handsome hide, was what female dreams were made of. Every time Chelsie peered overly long at his masculine physique and those rugged bronzed features, she felt her resistance slip another notch.

Jarred's black velvet waistcoat and matching breeches complimented his good looks. But then, everything did, no matter if he wore nothing but a seductive smile or fringed buckskin. There was a wild, earthy quality about him. Even his sophisticated manner couldn't restrain that rough underlying sensuality that naturally appealed to women young and old alike. And when Jarred was purposely trying to be charming, he was a lady-killer. And the lady he was presently killing was Chelsie! Lord, she wished to be struck deaf, dumb, and blind so she wouldn't be so vividly aware of how attractive he was.

Jarred pushed away from the wall and ambled over in front of his enchanting wife. His eyes roamed over her in total possession, and Chelsie jumped at the sheer impact of his potent stare. For a long moment Jarred simply drank in the bewitching sight that stood before him. And Chelsie stood watching him like a gunshy rabbit who expected to be attacked from all directions at once.

Chelsie had donned a pale pink silk gown for the occasion. The daring decolletage was bound to cause his male guests to lick their lips in anticipation, Jarred thought. A string of pearls encircled her swanlike throat and lay enticingly against the luscious swells of her partially exposed breasts. White corset bows were inset in the silk bodice that clung to her curves like a glove. The trim-fitting sleeves of the gown fanned out at the elbow in wide lace ruffles that rippled when she moved. The full skirt, which was surrounded by lacy ruffles, tapered inward to call attention to her tiny waist. Dressed as she was, Chelsie could send a man's heart leapfrogging around his chest and cause his blood pressure to rise. God, she was gorgeous!

Jarred felt the stirring of desire in his loins as his eyes made yet another thorough sweep of this picture of loveliness. If Chelsie hadn't made it clear that she was opposed to the idea, Jarred would have forgone the elegant ball so he could spend the evening in his chamber, making wild, passionate love to his wife. As much as he admired Chelsie's stunning gown, he would have preferred to see it draped over a chair while she was lying naked in his arms . . .

"Don't you think we should be on hand to greet all the guests you invited?" Chelsie questioned when Jarred's transparent gaze betrayed his lusty thoughts.

Displaying his courtly manners and the most masculine grace imaginable, Jarred swung into a bow, then lifted her gloved hand to his lips. A provocative smile hovered on his mouth as he met her impatient frown. "I think I would prefer to ignore our guests and keep you all to myself," he murmured suggestively. "It has been two weeks since the morning after our wedding. I can still see you lying abed with the sunlight caressing your silken skin. Although it has been a fortnight

346

since I made love to you, I can still taste your eager responses to my kisses and recall the way your satiny flesh quivered beneath my exploring touch. I can hear you whispering my name and your need as I came to you. . . ."

Chelsie was rudely unappreciative of his remarks and his undivided attention. With a distasteful sniff, she wormed her hand free and made a beeline for the door. Fighting down the blush that flooded to the roots of her silver-blond hair, Chelsie inhaled a steadying breath. "You can stay here and wallow in your erotic fantasies, if you wish, but I have hosted enough parties at Chessfield to know 'tis impolite to keep one's guests waiting."

"You remember every splendor-filled moment, don't you, Chel?" Jarred taunted. He bridged the gap between them in two long strides.

Chelsie flinched as if she had been stung by a wasp when Jarred purposely brushed his muscular body against her back and hips. "I wake up in a new world every day," she replied in contradiction. "I remember nothing. You must have me confused with that peasant who was once your unwilling mistress." Stiff-backed, Chelsie stepped forward to grasp the doorknob. "I am your wife, the Duchess of Chessfield. Ladies of breeding do not stoop to animal lust with the husbands who married them to fulfill their obligations after stealing their virginity. A lady who finds herself in my predicament gives as good as she gets. She seeks out men worthy and equal to her noble breeding and distinction and makes them her secret lovers."

Chelsie didn't see Jarred's fingers curl as if he meant to strangle her from behind. And by the time she glanced over her partially bare shoulder, he had regained some degree of composure. His annoyance was masked behind a carefully blank stare. Politely he offered the spiteful imp his arm, even though he would have preferred for her to run her turned-up nose into his doubled fist a couple of times.

"As you said, m'lady," he managed to say without barking out the words like a rabid dog, " 'tis time for us to greet our guests. I cannot wait for them to get a look at my lovely bride. I'm sure I will be the envy of every man in attendance."

"I'm sure you will," Chelsie agreed, just to infuriate him. She did, but Jarred's well-disciplined expression gave away none of his agitation. "With so many dignified statesmen in attendance, perhaps I can single out one or two men who meet my expectations as suitable lovers. Surely there are a few colonials hereabout who are descended from royal ancestry."

Without accepting his proffered arm, Chelsie breezed down the hall like a whirlwind to catch up with Abi and Neil, who stood at the top of the spiral staircase.

For a few seconds Jarred toyed with the wicked thought of giving Chelsie a swift kick in her shapely derriere and watching in devilish glee as she tumbled pell-mell down the steps. That witch knew how to get his goat. She delighted in flaunting the threat of taking lovers, then darting off, leaving him to fry in his own grease. Keeping a tight grip on his temper, Jarred marched down the hall, vowing to act the perfect husband. It wasn't going to be easy, he realized. Not when he was overwhelmed by the urge to yank that feisty sprite up by the neck and shake her until her teeth fell out!

Within an hour Jarred realized his attempt to prove his devotion had fallen flat. He had done little more than nod a greeting to his female guests. He hadn't lingered in conversation with even one woman, and he hadn't asked anyone to dance. But Chelsie hadn't had time to notice how Jarred had spent the past hour. She was too busy wearing out her silk slippers, dancing with every man who begged her companionship. There were several times when Jarred had to restrain himself from tearing some of his male guests limb from limb. When her dance partners held Chelsie closer than necessary and bent to whisper confidentially in her ear, Jarred chomped at the bit. Each time Chelsie nodded agreeably to whatever had been secretly whispered to her and then graced her dance partner

348

with a radiant smile, Jarred swore they were planning a romantic rendezvous.

After two more hours of torment, Jarred had endured all he could. Chelsie was going to pay for her mischievous flirting.

Signaling to the orchestra to pause before they struck up another song, Jarred aimed himself toward his wife—the social butterfly who had been in so many arms. Clasping her limp-wristed hand, Jarred led the vision in pink to the middle of the sprawling ballroom. Lifting his glass, Jarred made a toast in a ringing voice that caught everyone's attention.

"To my stunning bride," he announced before downing his drink in one swallow and tossing his empty glass to Grant. "The duchess has graced Easthaven with her beauty and enriched my life with her love."

To Chelsie's stupefied amazement, Jarred's arm stole around her waist. With a romantic flair, Jarred bent Chelsie over backward. To the delight and amusement of his guests, Jarred kissed her on the lips, right in the middle of the dance floor. The kiss he bestowed on her carried enough heat to melt the moon.

Chelsie was forced to cling to Jarred's shoulders or risk winding up in an unladylike heap on the floor. She couldn't reject his amorous display without making a scene. She was left with no recourse but to endure the maelstrom of sensations that rippled through her when Jarred kissed her blind and molded his muscular contours into her flesh. Had she not been made of sturdy stuff, she would have swooned. Jarred stripped the breath from her lungs and mashed her breasts against his chest. Chelsie hung there, bent backwards, certain her smoldering body would drip into a puddle at his feet.

When Jarred had the decency to prop her upright, Chelsie was forced to clutch at him to maintain her balance. While their guests applauded, Chelsie plastered a smile on her face. But oh, what she wouldn't have given for the chance to poke her fist in his triumphant grin. That sneaky lout!

After Jarred gestured to the orchestra, they burst into a love song. Chelsie found herself pressed familiarly against Jarred's warm, hard flesh. While they danced before their captive audience, Chelsie leaned back as far as his encircling arms would allow.

"I hate you," she murmured with a smile that was as brittle as eggshells.

"I love you," Jarred replied as he pressed a quick kiss to her lips—lips that were frozen in a pleasant expression that displayed the exact opposite of what she really felt.

"Nay, you don't," Chelsie denied.

"Aye, I do," he confirmed with great conviction.

The instant the dance ended, Chelsie swept toward the terrace doors, resisting the urge to break into a run. Jarred's mischievous tactics were playing havoc with her emotions. He forced her to be cruel and insulting in order to counter his unique attempts at crumbling her bulwark of defense. He tormented her with his visual image. He constantly reminded her of the passion they had once shared. He plied her with confessions she wanted to believe but couldn't, for fear he would break her heart again. The wounds had yet to heal. If he left her heart to bleed a second time, Chelsie swore she would never recover. . . .

"Chelsie . . ."

Jarred's soft, haunting voice reached out, and she had to clutch the railing to prevent her feet from involuntarily moving toward the compelling sound. No one could put such inflection in his voice and make her name sound so seductive.

"What, for God's sake?" she gritted out, staring into the darkness, seeing nothing but sapphire eyes and an inviting smile. Chelsie was so flustered, she didn't even realize she had resorted to voicing Jarred's favorite expression. Had she been aware of her slip, she would have been annoyed no end.

Jarred expelled a long sigh as his footsteps took him across the terrace to linger beside his defiant wife. Tenderly his hand glided up her tensed arm to massage her stiff neck.

"How much longer do you plan to keep this up?" he questioned as his forefinger traced the loose curls that dangled beside her temple.

"How much patience do you have left?" she countered crossly.

Jarred stepped around to lean against the railing to which she clung as if it were her lifeline. "As much as it takes," he replied. "I'm not giving up on you until. . . ."

"Jarred! There you are, you handsome devil."

"Oh, for crying out loud, not now," Jarred muttered half-aloud. The comely redhead who sailed onto the terrace was a woman from his past — one who hadn't been the least bit discouraged by his engagement to Abi. Obviously she was just as unconcerned about his marriage to Chelsie.

Carla Dayton was undaunted by the shapely blonde in pink silk. She had been widowed for more than five years, and she had enough money to keep her in the manner to which she had grown accustomed. Jarred had always been one of her favorite lovers, and she wanted it known that his marriage hadn't curbed her interest in him.

"Come dance with me," Carla cooed sweetly, ignoring Chelsie as if she were a stick of furniture. "I've been waiting all night to get my hands on you."

Composing herself, Chelsie turned to face the top-heavy widow who had sidled close enough to Jarred to plaster her voluptuous breasts against his arm. Chelsie well remembered meeting Carla in the receiving line and at Neil and Abi's reception. And she also recalled Eli mentioning this brazen lady the day Chelsie had been dragged to Jarred's hotel suite in Annapolis. Carla was the promiscuous neighbor who provided Jarred with sexual favors when he wasn't in the mood to roam far. Since she owned the property directly north of Easthaven, Jarred was indeed a hop, skip, and a jump away from a willing woman.

"Do grant our guest her wish," Chelsie purred in a tone that was as sticky-sweet as syrup.

Deciding to turn the tables on her ornery husband, Chelsie

wrapped her arms around his neck while he was still half-propped on the rail. The kiss she delivered was just as potent as the one Jarred had bestowed on her in the middle of the ballroom. Her lips slanted over his, teasing him with her darting tongue, promising intimacies she had withheld from him for more than two tormenting weeks. Her thigh pressed suggestively between his legs and her breasts brushed wantonly against his massive chest. Jarred groaned silently, wishing there were no hindering garments between them and that they were in bed instead of on the terrace with Carla hovering beside them.

When Chelsie finally came up for air, she traced his moist lips with her fingertips. "We can take up where we left off later . . . after our guests have gone home . . . when we are in the privacy of our room and our own bed. . . ."

Clasping Jarred's hand, she placed it in Carla's eager one. "He's all yours, for the time being," Chelsie said generously. "But don't forget where you got him. And please don't wear him out. I am a very demanding woman."

As Chelsie fluttered through the terrace doors to be swamped by a half-dozen eager dance partners, Carla stared bewilderedly after her. "I thought duchesses were straitlaced," she mused aloud. "It seems you have as much as you can handle at home."

Well, at least Chelsie's remarks had given Jarred some encouragement. She didn't think she wanted him, but she didn't want any other woman to have him, either. That was a step in the right direction. Jarred broke into a wry smile, then glanced down at Carla. "Aye, I need no more than the duchess can give," he admitted with a wry wink.

Carla caught his intended meaning and flashed him a saucy grin. "We can still have one last dance together for old times' sake. But I guess you won't be dropping by anymore. . . ."

"Nay, I don't suppose I shall," Jarred chuckled as he led the vivacious redhead into the ballroom.

Carla, eager though she was, knew she and Jarred were a thing of the past. Abi Shaw hadn't captivated this swarthy rake, but Chelsie certainly had. Carla could tell by the way Jarred's eyes followed his wife around the dance floor that he was hopelessly bewitched by her. It was a pity Chelsie hadn't intercepted those longing glances. She might have realized Jarred truly *did* care for her. But Chelsie was purposely ignoring her handsome husband and mustering her defenses in preparation for his next devastating assault on her heart.

The instant Jarred opened the bedroom door, Chelsie propelled herself toward the dressing table to pull the pins from her long mane of hair. As was his custom, Jarred strolled up behind her to suffocate her senses.

"That parting kiss you gave me before you left me in Carla's clutches told me what I wanted to know," Jarred commented softly, meeting her startled reflection in the mirror. "The fire is still there, banked beneath your cynicism and contrariness."

Chelsie combed out her hair so vigorously that she practically pulled the bristles off the brush. "You have an incredibly active imagination," she declared. " 'Twas all an act designed to cool your mistress's lust."

A wry smile pursed his lips. "No one can kiss like that without meaning it," he insisted. "Even a woman with your phenomenal theatrical ability."

Chelsie was in just the perfect frame of mind to accept that dare, even though she was unknowingly playing right into Jarred's hands. Wearing a smug smile, she rose and turned to shatter this ornery rake with an embrace that would long be branded on his one-track mind.

Although Chelsie wasn't strong enough to bend him over backwards, she could knock him off his feet — figuratively speaking. Her mouth slanted across his and she nibbled provocatively at his lips. Her tongue darted into the warm, soft recesses of his eager mouth to titillate and explore. Her supple body glided against his and then receded like a stirring breeze caressing the trees. Her hand skied over his shoulders, feeling

353

the bunching muscles tense in eager anticipation.

Chelsie told herself she was only toying with him, arousing him without their embrace having the slightest effect on her whatsoever. But the truth was that she felt the potent shock waves of her own amorous ploy. She had become as much the victim of the fiery kiss as Jarred was.

When Jarred groaned low in his throat and clutched her to him, his body shuddering with passion, Chelsie gulped down her pounding heart. Determined to conceal her spontaneous reaction to this blue-eyed demon, Chelsie pried herself loose and floundered to retrieve her discarded hairbrush. Fearing her knees were about to fold beneath her, Chelsie plopped down in her chair to take up her chore of tending her hair.

"Was that proof enough?" she managed to say without her voice cracking completely.

"Aye, the fire is still there," Jarred teased, monitoring her jerky movements.

"Ice," Chelsie retorted as she bounded to her feet and marched over to the dressing screen to shrug on her flannel gown. "I didn't feel a thing."

When she emerged from the screen, Jarred was stripping from his clothes in the same seductive manner he'd employed every night for the past two weeks—a slow, deliberate assault on her senses.

"I think we are ready for a change of habit," Jarred growled huskily, his eyes roaming heatedly over her as he shucked every stitch of clothes.

"Aye, we are," Chelsie enthused, focusing on the bed instead of the incredibly masculine chest and dark hair that trickled down his lean belly to the. . . .

Willfully, she squelched the thought. She refused to become a prisoner of her own hungry needs. She would starve from lack of affection long before she accepted what Jarred so blatantly offered!

"A change is definitely in order," she agreed. "For the next two weeks, you sleep on this side of the bed and I'll sleep over there." She indicated the half of the bed on which Jarred had sprawled for the past fortnight.

In a single bound, Chelsie plopped onto the opposite side of the bed and placed the rolled blanket squarely in the middle. Jarred stared at her defiantly tilted chin and heaved a frustrated sigh. This minx was incredibly hard on his male pride. It left him wondering if he could still entice a woman. *Not this woman,* Jarred thought resentfully. He would need a sledge-hammer to crack her firm resolve!

"At least this will ensure you don't get up on the wrong side of bed," he grumbled as he sank—stark-naked—onto the mattress.

Chelsie chose to count the flowers on the wallpaper rather than torment herself for the hundredth time by admiring Jarred's well-carved contours. Since the lantern was now on her side of the bed, Chelsie quickly doused it. But even the darkness couldn't conceal the strong, vital image implanted in her brain. She could still see that arresting physique and recall the tingles of pleasure that rippled through her when her body was pressed to his.

When Jarred performed his tormenting ritual of kissing her goodnight, Chelsie turned her head. There would be no more kissing on the lips! Three times in one night had done enough damage to her eroding willpower!

"I love you." Jarred breathed the words on her skin.

"You are wasting your breath," Chelsie bit off, fighting like hell for her composure. But all the while, her pent-up desires were wreaking havoc.

"Nay," he chortled as he sank back on his side of the bed. "You're wasting a perfectly good night of loving . . . I'm ready and willing. . . ."

"Not interested," she ground out in frustration, wishing she meant what she said.

Chelsie clenched her fists so tightly that her nails dug into her palms. Every predatory glance, every touch she had endured this evening had intensified her craving. Chelsie wasn't sure how much more she could stand before she lost her self-control or her sanity, or both! All that saved her were Jarred's overnight jaunts to oversee the other plantations. When he was gone for a few days, she could give herself pep talks and harden her heart before he returned to torment her again. Thank the Lord, Jarred was to leave the following morning to confer with Washington on the construction of the wilderness road that joined the seaboard to Ohio country. The Virginia militia was presently hacking a path in preparation for General Braddock's troops to march westward for their campaign against the French. With any luck at all, Jarred would be gone a full week. After the frustrating chain of events of this night, Chelsie was certain she would require a full seven days to forget how much she wanted this seductive devil, even when she swore up and down she didn't!

Chapter 28

Chelsie chose to refer to those long weeks following her wedding as the civilized war between her and her new husband. Well, at least it was war on her part, she amended as she saddled Trumpeter for his daily exercise. When the rest of the family was underfoot or when they entertained guests, Chelsie was courteous and polite to Jarred. When they were alone, she continued to give him the cold shoulder. Chelsie refused to dispense with the ritual of rolling a quilt and dividing the bed into two equal halves—his and hers.

Although Chelsie made it clear time and time again that she wanted nothing to do with Jarred and that she was merely tolerating him, he was the epitome of attentiveness. He persisted in employing his sense of humor and his courtly manners in an attempt to charm Chelsie out of the cold war she was waging. He tried to kill her with kindness, but she was wise to his technique. She knew he was attempting to soften her defenses with flattery and persuasion, and he had suddenly acquired the legendary patience of Job.

Even though Chelsie avoided Jarred like the plague, he showed up at the most unexpected moments to offer her a disarming smile and whisper his affection. There had been times this past month when Chelsie had very nearly buckled to her yearnings, almost yielded to a love that refused to die, no matter how valiantly she fought it. Jarred had told her so many times that he loved her that he almost had her believing it. But she couldn't quite trust his motives.

She had lost some of her self-confidence when she tried in

vain to convince Jarred she was a duchess and when she admitted to caring for him. She had accepted the fact that she had nothing but money to offer a man. And just when she had learned to cope with being chased because of her title and not because of the woman she was, Jarred turned up in Baltimore to say he loved her. Oh, why couldn't he have uttered that confession one month sooner, so she could have known for certain he was telling the truth?

Chelsie heaved a tormented sigh. She had no more faith in Jarred than he had in her. She had criticized him a zillion times because he wouldn't believe she was telling the truth about her identity. So she had turned right around and become guilty of the very crime she detested Jarred for committing. She had no faith, no trust, and far less self-assurance than she'd had when she was snatched from her estate and taken to Maryland. Now she was a miser with her affection, but blast it, how could she be sure Jarred wasn't using her the same as he always had? How was a woman supposed to know for certain when a man was telling her the truth?

Even though Chelsie had spitefully insisted she would go searching for another man to appease her passions, it was only a childish threat voiced in a fit of temper. No other man stirred her the way Jarred did, and she didn't expect to find another man who moved her in ways this raven-haired rake did. That was too much for a woman to expect. And so Chelsie kept her frustrated love bottled up inside her, refusing to buckle each night when Jarred stripped naked, allowing her to devour him with her eyes, tempting her until she wanted to pull out her hair in exasperation. And like clockwork, she would snuff the lantern and Jarred would lean over to press a kiss to her cheek and murmur his love. . . .

Chelsie blinked back the tears as she swung onto Trumpeter's back. Empty words from lying lips, she reminded herself sensibly. Jarred could say the words so easily because he had practiced them on every woman he'd met in an effort to get him where he wanted to be—in her bed. And that was all he wanted from Chelsie — a physical release for his lust. The only difference was that now he was treating her with respect because he knew she was descended from royalty. But Chelsie guarded her wounded heart like a dragon, refusing to put stock in a man who had said nothing about love when he thought she was a thieving peasant. And how the devil did she know he was being faithful to her each time he trotted off to oversee the other three family plantations? He was gone several days at a time. He was a man who probably had a mistress at every port and this mock marriage probably wasn't cramping his style one bit. . . .

"Do you mind if I join you while you put Trump through his paces?"

Chelsie flinched at the tormenting sound of Jarred's voice. It was soft and velvety and altogether seductive. She hated the way she melted like snow each time Jarred spoke in that sexy baritone. He was the shining example of kindness and patience, and it was driving her mad. She was constantly rebuilding her defenses — the ones this blue-eyed devil crumbled when he assaulted her with that suave, sensual charm. Thunderation, how long would it be before she could hear his voice or see his swarthy physique without being bombarded by so many bittersweet memories?

"Suit yourself," Chelsie replied coolly. Sitting upright in the saddle, she squared her shoulders and elevated her stubborn chin. " 'Tis a relatively free country. You can come and go as you please without asking my permission."

Jarred broke into an amused grin as he stared at Chelsie's back, rigid as a flagpole. If he didn't know better, he'd have sworn Chelsie was so rigid with stubbornness that she slept standing up.

After four weeks of employing every ounce of self-reserve and charisma he possessed, Jarred found Chelsie as unapproachable and unreceptive as ever. When he spoke to her in private, she always looked the other way and barely acknowledge his presence. Either he was losing his touch with women, or he had confronted the exception to every rule he had ever observed about those of the female persuasion. Damnation, this celibacy couldn't last much longer or Jarred was going to explode!

When Chelsie nudged Trumpeter, he took off like a cannonball, leaving Jarred and his stallion choking in the dust. Jarred trotted in Chelsie's wake, waiting until the copper dun colt had raced at full speed for a quarter of a mile. When Chelsie brought the steed to a walk, Jarred eased up beside her.

"I received a letter from Annapolis this morning," he commented. He may as well have tried to converse with a stone wall. As usual, Chelsie didn't appear to be paying one tittle of attention. "Cyrus Hutton is to receive his day in court, and I am to represent Maryland as the counselor for the prosecution."

Chelsie breathed a relieved sigh. With Jarred as the prosecuting attorney, Cyrus would pay full penance for his thievery and kidnaping. "I'm sure you will see him severely punished for his crimes," she murmured.

"Shall I punish him as severely for his crimes as you are punishing me for mine?" Jarred questioned in a casual tone. "I have grown tired of playing these cat-and-mouse games, Chel. When I come in, you go out. When I invite you to travel with me to attend business elsewhere, you decline. I was hoping for more from this marriage of ours. Indeed, I am willing to meet you more than halfway," he added in that notoriously provocative voice.

Chelsie marshalled her sagging defenses. "To quote a famous Maryland lawyer, politician and soldier, " 'This is as good as it gets,' " she reminded him flippantly.

"Come to Annapolis with me," he requested softly. "Give love a chance to grow. Give me the chance to earn your trust."

"Nay," Chelsie replied, refusing to glance in his direction, refusing to fall victim to those baby blue eyes that could tear a woman's heart in two.

Jarred reached over to grasp Trumpeter's reins, bringing him to a halt. "Chel, look at me and tell me you don't love me, not even a little. After all we've been through together, can you honestly say that what we shared, that all the sweet memories we've made were in vain? That our marriage is a tragic mistake?"

When the stubborn minx refused to comply, Jarred heaved a frustrated sigh. "I have told you dozens of times that I'm not going to be satisfied with anything less than your love."

"And I warned you that you were in for a bitter disappointment. You may have married my money, but my heart is not part of the bargain," Chelsie flung at him.

Every time Jarred plied her with soft persuasion, he made her feel like a heel for snapping back at him. But how else was a woman supposed to stick to her guns? And where would she be if she broke down and admitted she *did* want a true marriage and that she loved him beyond rhyme or reason? Jarred would enjoy the ultimate victory over her. When *he* said he loved her he lied. When *she* said it, she *meant* it, even if she had later denied it to salvage her wounded pride. And she would never utter those three little words again. She was going to hold out until her father arrived, and then she was going to bury these tormenting memories so deep they would never again rise to haunt her.

Jarred had had enough. He had been kind and patient and understanding for four long weeks, and he had received very little for his efforts. He hadn't forced himself on this obstinate wench, nor had he demanded his husbandly rights when he most certainly could have. He had waited for Chelsie to come to him. He kept hoping his soft confessions of love would finally penetrate that stubborn mind of hers and she would begin to believe that he truly meant what he said. But Chelsie had countered every tactic, never giving an inch, and Jarred was at his wit's end.

His patience depleted, Jarred snaked out a hand to pluck Chelsie off Trumpeter's back and deposit her on his lap. "I have had my fill of your icy routine and those frigid smiles," he growled into her furious glare. "I am leaving for Annapolis this afternoon, and I am not going until you send me on my way with a kiss, instead of your usual sneer!"

"Put me down this instant!" Chelsie sputtered, squirming to free herself from his imprisoning arms.

"Not until you kiss me good-bye," Jarred stipulated gruffly.

"I'd rather be whipped," Chelsie spewed indignantly.

"That's exactly what you need," Jarred uttered. "If the duke hadn't spared the rod, you wouldn't be such a spoiled, feisty misfit!"

Although Chelsie put up a terrible fuss, Jarred mashed her against his thighs and soundly whacked her shapely derriere. Her furious squawks sent Trumpeter lunging off, and the bay stallion pranced uneasily beneath his master and the outraged Chelsie, who continued to kick and curse and scream bloody murder.

When Jarred had given her the thrashing he thought she deserved, he sat her upright in his lap. His lips swooped down on hers before she could protest. (And she most certainly would have if Jarred hadn't stolen her breath with his ravishing kiss.)

The forbidden memories pummeled against her body like a sledgehammer. Chelsie's defenses cracked. She didn't want to enjoy the taste of his skillful kiss. She didn't want her senses to be swarmed by his musky scent. She didn't want to crave the feel of his sinewy body pressed so close and yet so maddeningly far away. But confound it, she did want all those wondrous things they had shared before Jarred discovered she was a duchess instead of a peasant. Oh, why did he have to say he loved her when she knew he didn't? She had learned to accept the limitations of his affection—the physical attraction he felt for her. She had wanted more, but had settled for those precious scraps he offered when he had sneaked into her room to teach her even more about the powers of passion. She would much prefer his honesty to these empty phrases of love. And try as she may, even when she knew she was every kind of fool,

Chelsie couldn't pull away from this raven-haired rogue. It had been two weeks since she had felt those full, sensuous lips moving possessively over hers, and it was impossible to follow logic when her heart and body ached for his masterful touch. He was a hopeless addiction, and she needed him as much as she needed air to breathe. Two weeks seemed to be her limit. After fourteen days of willful restraint, she gave in to those heart-stopping kisses and nerve-tingling caresses. And later, when her brain began to function properly, she would curse herself a thousand times over for surrendering to this dark-haired demon.

Jarred was on fire. His need for Chelsie was frying him alive. He was like a desperate traveler who had been stranded on a desert for weeks on end. One kiss demanded another. One caress led to a dozen more. And even while the stallion stamped in circles, protesting the amorous assault that was taking place on his back, Jarred was caring less and less about where they were and more and more about appeasing this insatiable craving he had denied himself for too many tormenting weeks. He wanted to lie down and love this fiery sprite for all the times he'd longed to gather her close and had instead refused to force himself on her.

Oh, what the hell, his male desires whispered to him. *She can't hate you more than she already does.* Jarred gave way to that hushed voice of temptation. He would be gone for at least a week, and he needed one memory to sustain him. He had to have Chelsie in his arms. It was as simple as that.

With agile grace, Jarred stepped from the stirrup, pulling Chelsie along with him. They tumbled in the grass, still clinging together as if the world was about to end. Chelsie scolded herself when she responded in wild abandon. She didn't want to feel these splendid sensations that spilled over her. But Jarred was a magical wizard who could lure her into his spell before Chelsie knew she was there, and then it was too late to escape the web of pleasure he wove around her.

His bold caress glided beneath the hem of her riding habit to map the silky flesh of her thighs, and Chelsie moaned in tormented pleasure. She had managed to restrict this blue-eyed devil to a few kisses for almost a month . , . but oh, at what tremendous cost to her self-restraint! When she denied him, she denied herself. And now there was no holding back the crumbling dam of passion. She was a creature of need who had been deprived of rapture beyond compare. When she returned Jarred's tantalizing caresses, her pride was forgotten. Suddenly it didn't matter that Jarred had used her and that he was still using her. She needed to be loved, if only in the physical sense, if only for this one fleeting moment.

Hungrily, her fingertips delved beneath his shirt to make stimulating contact with his flesh. He was strength personified — the beating, breathing essence of vitality. Chelsie needed to be one with him, to replenish her supply of energy, to satisfy these maddening longings. And when she drank her fill of passion's intoxicating brew, she would climb back inside her protective shell and resume her cold war against the one man who couldn't love her as completely as she wanted and needed to be loved.

With Chelsie it had to be all or nothing. She wanted to enjoy the strong bond her mother and father had shared — a love neither of them had expected to find in their contracted marriage, a love so enduring that even death had not severed the ties. She was too much like her father. He hadn't gotten over loving his departed wife. He had simply transferred his affection to his one and only daughter. Chelsie had been blessed with a great capacity for love, but cynicism and mistrust often restricted her. She needed that same emotional bond with Jarred, but she was afraid to give her heart a second time, afraid she would only be hurt and disillusioned once more.

And yet, knowing what she needed for her love to thrive, she was still a prisoner of her own wild longings. Her betraying body arched up to meet Jarred's skillful caresses and her restless hands made their way across his muscled flesh, cherishing the feel of his rough skin beneath her palm. A tiny whimper escaped her lips when his warm mouth covered the tip of her breast, leaving her throbbing with a need that drove her mad with wanting. She was going to yield to this fierce passion that flared between them, and later she would scold herself for her lack of willpower. But for now. . . .

The thunder of hooves tore Chelsie's thoughts from her fogged mind. She was forced to withdraw from Jarred's embrace when she ached to share the intimacy they had once enjoyed before he lied and said he loved her. Stumbling to her feet to rearrange her clothes, Chelsie waited for the groom to draw his mount and the riderless copper dun colt to a halt.

"I was afraid this high-spirited thoroughbred had thrown you, duchess," the trainer murmured. His eyes made short shrift of assessing Chelsie's ruffled appearance and Jarred's thunderous scowl. Hesitantly he handed the reins to Chelsie and then tipped his hat. "Excuse the interruption, but I was worried about you."

When the trainer had trotted away, Chelsie clasped the pommel of the saddle to climb on Trumpeter's back. Before she could get her foot in the stirrup, Jarred handcuffed her wrist. Since she refused to meet his gaze, Jarred cupped her chin in his hand. Her eyes were sprinkled with a mist of unshed tears and her kiss-swollen lips quivered as she struggled to compose her shattered emotions. Even while they stood there staring at each other, Jarred could feel the invisible wall go up between them as it had so many times the past month.

He was fighting a hopeless battle, he realized dismally. Chelsie was never going to love him. They were never going to enjoy a true marriage. She was stubborn and proud from the tip of her toes to the top of her silver-blond head. It was easy to understand why no man had tamed this feisty duchess. She was too much woman for any normal man to handle.

Jarred had begun to doubt there was a man in England who held the key to her heart. He still didn't know what she meant that day at the cove while she was under the influence of the strong drugging potion. She had mumbled that she couldn't fall in love because she was in love with someone else. Perhaps it was all nonsensical gibberish and she truly *didn't* know what she was babbling about. But if there really was such a man awaiting her in England he obviously had more power over this sassy sprite than Jarred ever would.

Most likely there wasn't, Jarred told himself as he peered into those eyes that sparkled with living fire. Ruefully he recalled the adage that suggested there were some horses that weren't meant to be broken and some women who were never meant to be tamed. Chelsie Channing from Chessfield was one of those women, and Jarred was an arrogant fool if he thought he could ever win her wild heart. He might as well try and catch the wind. He would meet with the same amount of success.

Expelling a frustrated sigh, Jarred dropped his hand to his side. He had employed every tactic he could invent to woo Chelsie back into his arms, to gain her trust. But nothing worked effectively. Even now he could see the resentment clouding her eyes. She hadn't wanted to succumb to him, but he had forced her by unleashing her feminine desires. But that wasn't enough for Jarred these days. He wanted her heart and soul as much as he craved this delicious body of hers.

"I have only one wish left, little leprechaun," Jarred said in a deflated tone. He peered up at her through a veil of thick velvet lashes and broke into a wistful smile. " 'Tis a love wish, Chelsie. I do not desire the wealth a duchess can provide, nor the prestige of royal blood in my family. I want you because I need you, and I need you because I want you." Gently he reached up to trace her trembling lips, memorizing their exquisite texture, remembering her petal-soft kisses. "My last wish is that you love me the way I love you. There has been something wildly unique between us since the very beginning. We ignite fires in each other, Chel. The flames have always fed upon themselves, blazing hotter each time we touch. Even your skepticism hasn't changed the way we respond to each other.

"I want to watch love blossom and grow, but you seek to smother that precious bloom. You would destroy what I yearn to create, and before long you are going to spoil our last chance at happiness. I'm sorry I didn't believe you when twice I was told you were but a servant for sale. I can't change the past, but I can offer you a future and a love for all times. Yet, to win your love, I must first earn your trust. But it seems your faith in me is as slow in coming as my trust in you." Bitter laughter tripped from his lips. "Not that I can blame you, duchess. I know I'm getting exactly what I deserve instead of what I truly want."

Jarred pivoted away to grab the stallion's reins. "If you deny my love wish, then I will no longer hold you to the vows you don't remember speaking." He swung into the saddle and reined his steed up beside Chelsie. His somber gaze fell upon the shapely beauty who was the cause and cure of four months of torment. "If you have packed up and left while I'm seeing to business in Annapolis, I won't come searching for you. If you need money for your journey to London, Neil will see that you have it. And if this is good-bye . . ." His blue eyes penetrated hers, searching for some sign that he had finally gotten through to this stubborn spitfire. "I love you, Chel. The miles you place between us aren't going to change what I feel. You won't let yourself believe it, but 'tis the truth. Maybe I can't find a way to earn your love, but you can't stop my heart from loving you, nor my soul from reaching out to you. . . ."

Tears scalded her cheeks as Jarred galloped away, leaving her throbbing with a need no other man could fulfill. She desperately wanted to believe him. She wanted to grant him love's wish. But . . .

Chelsie slapped Trumpeter on the rump, sending him lunging at breakneck speed, allowing the wind to rush past her face and dry her tears. What if Jarred really *was* telling the truth? What if he *did* love her and she walked out of his life forever? She would suffer through a meaningless existence. Yet how could she be sure this wasn't just a last effort to get her in his bed for passion's sake?

Well, there was one way to test Jarred's loyalty, Chelsie

reminded herself. The true test of a man's character was what he did when he didn't think he would get caught. She would follow him to Annapolis to keep an eye on his activities. Kyle had planned to journey to the capital at the first of the week, and Chelsie had agreed to join him to race Trumpeter. She would simply make up some excuse as to why she was leaving earlier than she had originally planned.

Determined of purpose, Chelsie aimed herself toward the mansion. She would garb herself in men's clothes and follow the road to Annapolis while Jarred traveled by schooner. What that handsome rake did with his spare time while he thought his wife was miles away would provide her with the answer she needed. And if Jarred went in search of sexual favors . . .

Chelsie gritted her teeth. He had better not seduce another woman. For if he did, she would be on the first ship back to England. If she missed her father, he would simply have to catch up to her. But no matter what, Chelsie wasn't going to remain on the same continent with a man who had lied and cheated while she was carrying an inextinguishable torch for him.

Ah, what a frustrating emotion love was, Chelsie thought dispiritedly. There was nothing simple about it. Doubts clouded her thinking and desire kept her longing for something she feared wasn't really there. If Jarred disappointed her, she wasn't sure she could cope with another rejection. These past months already had her tied in knots. She couldn't eat, or sleep, or think straight these days.

Chelsie had gone to Neil to vent her frustrations, but he couldn't offer the consolation she so desperately needed. Her life had become so complicated! She harbored the inescapable feeling that she would never be able to forget Jarred, no matter how hard she tried, no matter how much time and distance she put between them.

This jaunt to Annapolis was to be the final test. If things went badly, she was going to gather the shattered pieces of her heart and sail home to seek refuge at Chessfield. Knowing this was either the beginning or the end of her rocky affair with Jarred kept Chelsie's nerves as tangled as yarn.

Oh, how she wanted to restore her faith in Jarred! But if she clung to foolish hopes, she could wind up hurting worse than she ever had before. Even Isaac's abuse couldn't hold a candle to wounds of the heart! Jarred could do far more damage than Isaac ever had. He had only one chance to prove himself. And if he botched it, Chelsie would be long gone and she would never *ever* let herself fall in love again. It was too painful, too frustrating! And blast it, there were times when she wished she could exchange places with Trumpeter. The colt didn't know how lucky he was! He wouldn't have it quite so good if he was human and was forced to deal with this maiming emotion called love!

Part Four

What is love? 't not hereafter;
Present mirth hath present laughter;
What's to come is still unsure:
In delay there lies no plenty.
Then come kiss me, Sweet-and-twenty.
William Shakespeare

Chapter 29

After the first day of the proceedings in Cyrus Hutton's trial, Jarred ambled from the courthouse with his associates. When his friends trotted off to unwind with their mistresses, Jarred lingered on the steps, glancing in one direction, then the other. He was sorely tempted to seek consolation in a willing pair of arms. But he had employed that technique in Albany, and Chelsie's enchanting face had risen from out of nowhere to haunt him.

Perhaps a drink would cool his need for a woman, he thought hopefully. It might require an entire bottle, but he had all night to drown his frustration. As Jarred aimed himself toward the pub, he didn't notice the "caped gentleman" who was following an inconspicuous distance behind him. But Chelsie was there, her figure concealed beneath a full cloak, and her face disguised by the shadows cast by her wide-brimmed hat.

To her relief, Jarred swerved toward the tavern instead of the brothel beside it. Once inside the smoke-filled pub, Chelsie parked herself in the corner to keep a watchful eye on Jarred. Amid the ale that flowed freely and the fog of smoke that drifted across the tavern, a congregation of men gathered around Jarred. While he sipped one mug of ale after another, he was interrogated by interested citizens who wanted to hear all the details of the Albany Assembly and the progress of the wilderness trail that was being prepared for General Braddock's arrival.

Curious, Chelsie pricked up her ears to learn what policies the colonists had devised when their top politicians put their heads together. Unwillingly Chelsie admired the rapport Jarred had with the citizens of Annapolis. He was well-respected, and his opinions were important to those who surrounded him, whether they be paupers, laborers, or aristocrats.

"We have taken a gigantic step toward uniting the colonies and planning for our own defense against the French invasion," Jarred announced before taking another gulp of ale. "In the Plan of Union there will be a president appointed by the Crown and a Grand Council appointed by each colonial assembly. The president and council will have the authority to levy and collect taxes for our defense. We will also have the right to declare war and negotiate treaties with the Indians who have taken sides with the French. If we can come to terms with the Indians, we will have won half the battle."

"What about the western territory?" one man asked. "Are we conceding the rights to that land to France?"

"On the contrary," Jarred replied, then guzzled another swig of ale. "The president and council were given the power to offer land grants to adventurous settlers and to construct forts to protect them. We have staked our claim on the disputed lands, and reinforcements should be arriving very soon to drive the French back to Canada. General Braddock and his well-disciplined troops will travel into the Ohio Valley on the road that is nearing construction."

While Jarred drank fast and furiously the other men in the pub proposed toasts to the upcoming victory over the pesky French and their sneaky Indian allies. Chelsie, however, was not so optimistic about the English's chances in the backwoods on the outposts of civilization. In her opinion, King George the Second had sent the wrong man to quell troubles on the western frontier. General Braddock would have to be replaced if the colonists were to push the French from their strongholds. . . .

Chelsie's eyes narrowed in grim recognition when a buxom waitress positioned herself in Jarred's lap to whisper sweet nothings in his ear. The fact that the wench was none other than Meredith Holt, the spiteful harlot she had encountered on board the ship, made it doubly difficult for Chelsie to sit still and hold her tongue.

Meredith used her body to gain favors, and she didn't have enough scruples to fill the eye of a needle. She had constantly played up to Isaac and Cyrus Hutton for privileges and extra rations. Chelsie had locked horns with this devious bitch so many times in the past that it made her blood boil just thinking of all the hell Meredith had put her through. Isaac may have intended to fetch Meredith after he retrieved the ransom from the Duke of Chessfield, but he would have been wasting money if he planned to buy this wench's indentureship. From the look of things, Meredith was making money on the side. The tavern owner who bought her redemption papers didn't seem to mind that Meredith was playing up to everything in breeches. And Chelsie wouldn't have been the least bit surprised if the proprietor was receiving a few favors of his own from this wench of indiscriminate tastes.

When Meredith began slobbering all over Jarred, Chelsie shrank back in the shadows, anxious to see how her husband handled this amorous assault. Jarred had more than enough ale to take the edge off his conscience, but not nearly enough to make him forget the blond-haired leprechaun who tormented his days and haunted his nights. Each time Meredith put her hand where it didn't belong, Jarred removed it and Chelsie silently seethed at this bitch's audacity. She had seen Meredith paw at men in the dark hull of the ship, but now she was in a lighted pub!

Sluggishly Jarred clamped his hands around Meredith's waist and set her to her feet. "I'm a married man," he slurred out as he unfolded himself from his chair and wobbled on unstable legs.

"Are ye now, gov'nor?" Meredith smirked in offended dignity.

"Aye," Jarred confirmed in a sluggish tone. "And I have vowed to be faithful to the duchess."

"A duchess?" she parroted in a mocking tone. "The only duchess I ever knew wouldn't have been woman enough to appease a virile man like you." Meredith sashayed closer to run her index finger over the buttons of his linen shirt. "What you

375

need is a female who knows how to please a man. . . ."

"Chelsie pleases me very much, even if she doesn't think so," Jarred mumbled before weaving unsteadily toward the door.

Chelsie? Meredith's face flushed with irritation and disbelief. Chelsie was supposed to be dead! Damn that she-cat. She had obviously been blessed with nine lives and she had managed to marry this handsome aristocrat. That bitch had all the luck. Meredith had detested and envied Chelsie since the moment she saw her in her elegant gown and her expensive jewels. Although she had persuaded Isaac to steal Chelsie's emerald ring—the very same that now encircled Meredith's finger—she had truly wanted to get her hands on the heart-shaped locket that was worth a fortune. But Isaac had kept it for himself.

"You'll get none of what you need from an uppity heiress, gov'nor," Meredith taunted spitefully as Jarred wobbled across the tavern. "And when yer ready for a full-fledged woman, you come look me up."

Chelsie ground her teeth. It was difficult to sit idly by while Meredith belittled her. But it certainly wasn't the first time Chelsie had been forced to endure Meredith's degrading sarcasm. If she didn't fear that Jarred might recognize her, Chelsie would have bounded to her feet to tear that haughty, deceptive bitch limb from limb.

Jarred purchased a full bottle of rum and then propped himself against the door. Absently he glanced at the voluptuous maid who stood with hands on hips, her chest thrown forward to draw attention to her full bosom. "Thank you for the invitation, but I'm satisfied with what I have," he insisted before tucking the bottle under his arm and ambling out into the darkness.

While Meredith silently smoldered with envy, Chelsie smiled quietly to herself. Perhaps it was true that Jarred loved her. *Her!* Not her title or her fortune, but *her!* Her eyes misted with happiness as she came to her feet to follow her besotted husband. If she hadn't been so anxious to trail after Jarred, she might have taken time to smash a chair over Meredith's head. But having her revenge on Meredith wasn't nearly so important as catching up with her faithful husband and telling him how much she adored him.

Jarred didn't wait until he reached his room to uncork his bottle of liquor. He felt like drinking until he couldn't think, until he couldn't see the tormentingly lovely image of a blond-haired, green-eyed pixie who swam before his eyes. He knew Chelsie would be long gone when he returned to Easthaven. And like a noble fool, he had vowed not to come searching for her. He should never have made that promise. He was going to regret it, sure as hell.

After chugging another drink, Jarred peered at the blurry gas lamp that split in two and then converged into one when he blinked. "I hope you're happy, Chelsie Channing from Chessfield," he slurred out. "It would please you to no end to discover I'm miserable. . . ."

Chelsie bit back a giggle while Jarred carried on his conversation with the lamppost. She had never seen Jarred inebriated before. His agile movements were now slow and sluggish, and his step clumsy. The deep, rich timbre of his voice now resembled the croaking of a bullfrog that was having difficulty untangling its long tongue. His power-packed body was so uncoordinated that he weaved to and fro like a wind-tossed sailboat. When Jarred rammed into two lampposts, Chelsie was tempted to grasp his arm and lead him to the hotel. But she wanted to make certain that that was where Jarred was headed. In his condition, he might revert to his old habits and veer toward one of the many brothels, instead of retiring to his room alone.

By the time Jarred reached the hotel his bottle was empty and the mountain of steps which confronted him seemed insurmountable. Inhaling a deep breath, Jarred clutched the banister and pulled himself up. Lord, he was drunk. He had sworn off drinking after his last binge in Albany, yet here he was again, trying to drown Chelsie's memory and failing pitifully. Each time he swiveled his head on his shoulders, it took a minute for his soggy eyes to catch up with him. His feet felt like blocks of wood that clanked against the steps, and his nose was so numb,

377

he wasn't sure he still had one.

When Jarred reached the top of the staircase, he smiled triumphantly. He had been so busy guarding his step that he hadn't thought about Chelsie for a full two minutes. He was making progress, he complimented himself. At this rate he could expect to have forgotten all about that spitfire in about a hundred years. Falling in love with Chelsie Channing from Chessfield when he hadn't meant to had been the easy part. Forgetting her was going to take forever.

"Why couldn't you have loved me back?" Jarred asked the walls, which were superimposed with Chelsie's bewitching image. "I've never been in love before. I have never said the words to anyone but you. And the one time I did, my confession fell on deaf ears. . . ."

Jarred stumbled and caught himself before he sideswiped the wall. "Confounded witch," he muttered bitterly. "You were sent up from hell to make me pay for every sin I've committed, plus a few dozen I hadn't even conthithered . . . considered," he corrected himself.

Pausing in front of the door, Jarred squinted to be sure it was room thirteen. In his besotted condition, he couldn't risk stumbling into the wrong suite. It was thirteen, all right, he decided as he traced the numbers with his forefinger.

When Jarred fumbled his way across the dark room, tripping over the maze of furniture, Chelsie lingered beside the door. Quietly she slipped into the room to watch Jarred fight his way out of his clothes. Once he had fallen into bed, Chelsie approached him. For a long moment she stared down at his sleeping form and chortled softly to herself. There was nothing more pathetic than a fallen giant. Yet there was nothing so endearing as learning the man she loved *did* need her for all the right reasons. Jarred must care about her, or he wouldn't have been tormented because she had withheld her love from him.

But not anymore, Chelsie promised herself as she untied her cape and shrugged it from her shoulders. Jarred had proved himself tonight . . . he wanted her for the woman she was, faults and all. He didn't care if she was a princess or a peasant.

378

And Chelsie didn't care if Jarred had backslid as far as a man could slide. He had never impressed her more than when he allowed his vulnerability to show. She knew of his courage in the face of danger, of his strength and ingenuity. But at long last she was permitted to see that this remarkable man was also human. She adored the sensitive man who was usually suppressed by the strong, dynamic side of his personality. Jarred had earned a place of honor and respect with his peers and with the Crown, and he had won Chelsie's heart. They had traveled a long and rocky road, but from now on they were going to tread the path together, instead of pulling in opposite directions.

Chelsie eased down on the edge of the bed to spear her fingers through the tousled mane of raven hair that capped his head. Lovingly, she traced his shadowed features.

"I did love you before," she admitted softly. "But not as much as I do tonight. . . ."

Tenderly, she bent over to press a soft whisper of a kiss to his lips. Chelsie longed to express all the love she had kept locked inside her. She yearned to convey her devotion in worshipping caresses and reverent kisses. It felt so good to touch this powerful mass of masculinity, to rediscover the muscular terrain of his body.

Exploring hands lifted Jarred from the dense fog of liquor that engulfed him. He could feel a haze of pleasure settling over him, but he couldn't quite drag himself from the dark depths of whiskey-induced sleep. He was left suspended somewhere between dreams and reality, experiencing the most incredible sensations imaginable.

Streams of rapture flowed over him like an incoming tide lazily caressing the shore. Butterfly kisses fluttered over his cheeks, eyelids and lips. Jarred melted into the featherbed as if it were a fluffy cloud. A shuddering sigh escaped him when Chelsie's gentle hands swam over his bare flesh, rediscovering each sensitive place and bringing his slumbering passions to life.

Jarred didn't really want to rouse from this exquisite fantasy, because he knew he was imagining it all. He was reliving the forbidden dreams of a love that could never be, and he wanted to cling to each pleasure-filled moment, enjoying it as long as it lasted. This was paradise, and he didn't dare spoil it by waking up.

Chelsie had never been so deliberate, so patient. There had been times in the past when passion swept her up in the vortex of an ardent storm and she could do nothing but respond to the wild tempest of desire. But tonight she was in full command of their lovemaking, and she wanted to return each moment of pleasure Jarred had given her. Caressing Jarred's magnificent body was pleasure in itself. She couldn't seem to get enough of him, and she savored each wondrous touch, each feather-light kiss. She sought out every inch of his virile body, mapping the sinewy contours, committing each masculine curve and muscled plane to memory. Each caress and kiss was laced with her love for him. Chelsie reveled in the satisfaction of arousing him, hearing him moan quietly in response to her brazen touch.

Jarred groaned again when one tantalizing sensation piled atop another. He could feel himself hovering over a flame that warmed him by degrees. He could feel the fire burning over him, through him. And from somewhere near the end of the long, winding tunnel he heard an angel whisper his name. Jarred moved instinctively toward the enchanting sound, envisioning an exquisite face that was dominated by green eyes and framed with silky hair that was spun from strands of silver and gold.

Jarred was so far into his cups that he couldn't determine who had come to him, offering passion. The fog that dazed his eyes and his brain was too thick and the pleasure too wonderful to question. He merely responded to the feel of satiny flesh gliding upon his and skillful hands boldly caressing him. His body throbbed with a need which intensified with every accelerated beat of his heart. Over and over again, soft womanly flesh surged upon his, dragging another tormented groan from his lips.

His tingling body burst with the flame of passion, and Jarred became a creature of need, driven by his innate desires. His arms, though they felt as if they were weighted down with lead, enfolded the shapely angel who molded herself intimately against him. The fuzzy haze was infiltrated by the sweet, feminine fragrance that clouded his senses. Jarred was being possessed by a haunting spirit—the spirit of the one woman who would never be his. He clung to each soul-shattering sensation as the hypnotic cadence of lovemaking lifted him from one lofty plateau to another.

What had begun as a slow, languid hunger for rapture became a swift, ravenous craving that had sneaked up and captured Jarred before he realized it. He was ablaze with passion, and tremors of rapture rippled through his body. He was soaring through time and space, sailing past the sparkling stars to circle the dark side of the moon. Sensations of ecstasy toppled over him like an avalanche of searing flames. His body shuddered in sweet release and he clutched his angel to him, seeing Chelsie's lovely face above his, even though he knew this was only an illusive dream.

Chelsie was engulfed in splendor. When Jarred instinctively crushed her to him, he had squeezed the last ounce of restraint out of her. The tumultuous feelings of love burst like an overinflated balloon. As her body surged upon his, Jarred's name tumbled from her lips. And for what seemed eternity, Chelsie lay in his encircling arms, waiting for the erotic feelings to ebb. But by the time the numbing pleasures of lovemaking delivered her back to reality, Jarred's muscular body had slumped back into a deep sleep and she had no opportunity to assure him that she loved him with every fiber of her being.

A wry smile pursed Chelsie's lips as she laid her head on Jarred's shoulder. She couldn't help but wonder if Jarred would even remember the passion they had shared. But she would never forget the dreamy ecstasy. When the dawn streamed into the room, she would be here to relive the intimate pleasures and grant Jarred his love wish. Never again would she bottle her emotions inside her. She loved Jarred with every beat of her heart, and she would express her affection with words as well as deeds. . . .

The quiet rap at the door caused Chelsie to frown bemusedly. Who the devil could that be at this hour? Eli hadn't accompanied Jarred on this trip to Annapolis, and the McAlister family wasn't due until the following day.

The second tap forced Chelsie to scramble into her men's garb. But before she could tug on her boots, a woman's whispering voice wafted around the crack of the door.

"Gov'nor? Are you in there?" Meredith Holt called softly.

The moment Meredith was relieved from her chores of tending the bar and waiting tables, she had made a beeline for the hotel to seek out Jarred. She had a personal vendetta against Chelsie Channing—a feud that had begun the moment the comely duchess was shepherded onto the ship. Nothing would delight Meredith more than to seduce the man who that persnickety bitch had managed to marry. After all the trouble Chelsie had caused her, Meredith swore she would have the last laugh.

While Meredith was on the outside of the door, Chelsie was on the inside, silently fuming. She didn't have to be a genius to determine what a slatternly wench like Meredith wanted with Jarred. Meredith had come to spread herself beneath him for a handful of coins, jewelry, or whatever else she could steal while her victim was in a drunken stupor. Chelsie had seen Meredith employ such techniques on more than one inebriated sailor during their voyage to America. Meredith had slept with a dozen men on the ship, but each time Isaac appeared below deck, one would have thought the wench had eyes for only him. Meredith was one of those disgusting females who would sleep with anyone if she thought there was something to gain by it.

Well, Meredith wasn't getting her filthy hands on Jarred! Indeed, what that female wastrel needed was to be cleansed of her numerous sins. Wearing a devilish smile, Chelsie poured water from the pitcher into the basin and tiptoed to the door. After all the jeering and harassment Chelsie had suffered at Meredith's hands, she was finally going to have her revenge.

When the door eased open Meredith struck her most provocative pose and pasted on a seductive smile. To her amazement she was met with a basin of water that slopped over her painted face and drenched her skin-tight blouse. Meredith flew into an instant rage when she recognized the mocking smile that was illuminated by the lantern in the hall.

Four times during the course of their voyage, Chelsie and Meredith had gone for each other's throats. And four times the other passengers and sailors had pried them apart. Fool that he was, Isaac had come along to listen to Meredith's rendition of the incident that put them at odds and to punish Chelsie for a fight she didn't start. But now there was only Jarred to break them apart, and he was so far into his cups, he didn't even know he was sleeping on a battlefield. This was one time Chelsie didn't need Jarred's assistance. She intended to compensate for all the times Meredith had weasled out of their encounters without suffering so much as a tongue-lashing.

Hissing furiously, Meredith pounced on Chelsie, employing her familiar tactics of biting and pulling hair. But Chelsie had been in enough scraps with this vicious wench to know what to expect. Before Meredith could yank her hair out by the roots, Chelsie countered the clawing hand and bared teeth by stuffing a doubled fist in her opponent's midsection. Unfortunately, Chelsie was governed by a sense of fair play, unlike Meredith, who followed no rules whatsoever. She had no qualms about leveling blows to the face or anywhere else that might increase her chances of victory.

Meredith's doubled fist targeted her left eye, and Chelsie immediately discarded the laws of civilized warfare. Although her eye throbbed from the punishing blow, Chelsie came un-coiled like a rattlesnake. In a burst of fury, Chelsie launched herself forward, becoming a blur of flying fists, sharp nails, and clenched teeth. When Meredith leaped at her to take advantage with her superior size, Chelsie bit chunks from the hide of her nemesis. They rolled and tumbled on the floor like two tigresses defending their dens. Growls and hisses erupted from their lips as they satisfied their craving to tear each other to pieces.

The loud commotion and the jarring of his bed finally roused Jarred from his drugged sleep. He had just propped himself up on one elbow when an unidentified body came flying across his chest. Just who the body belonged to, Jarred didn't know. His eyes were blurred and the room was as black as pitch. With all

383

the hissing and caterwauling going on, Jarred had the strange feeling he had awakened in the middle of a cat fight.

When another body bounded across his lap, Jarred winced uncomfortably. Clumsily he grasped the foot that was squashing his privates. A flying elbow slammed against his jaw, knocking him back against the headboard. In Jarred's inebriated condition, he had very little control over his reactions and his reflexes. But he was suddenly reminded of the months he had spent in the wild, fending off marauding Indians. His instincts for self-preservation immediately came to life as they had so often in the backwoods (sluggish and misdirected though they were).

Since Jarred's reflexes weren't what they should have been, he was a half-second too slow in recovering from the first two blows. Before he could recoil and strike, a knee jabbed him in the groin, causing him to let out a roar. His pained howl was muffled by the two writhing bodies that plopped down on top of him.

While Jarred was mashed flat, Chelsie managed to roll onto Meredith, gaining the advantageous position. Her fingers were clutched at her opponent's throat and she sank down on Meredith's belly to hold the squirming bitch in place. Once and for all, Chelsie intended to repay Meredith for the nightmares she had forced her to endure and for Isaac's brutal abuse. At long last Chelsie was going to see justice served . . . or so she thought.

Since Jarred didn't have the foggiest notion who was waging war on top of him, he struck out to discourage both brawling females from making his bed their personal battlefield. The blow he delivered would have been even more painful if he hadn't had to cock his arm around the tangled mass of hair and the head that was wedged against his shoulder.

As fate would have it, the flying fist connected with his wife's jaw—the wife he presumed to be sleeping peacefully in her bed at Easthaven. Chelsie was sleeping, all right, but not in her own bed. Jarred's right cross knocked her senseless and she wilted backward like an unwatered flower buckling beneath the intense summer sun. With a dazed groan Chelsie toppled off the edge

384

of the bed to land in a crumpled heap on the floor.

With one down and one to go, Jarred reared up to clutch at the trailing hair that whipped past his face. Meredith squealed like a stuck pig when Jarred very nearly twisted her head off her shoulders. She was towed back against Jarred, who had again doubled his fist, prepared to cold-cock the other intruder. Although Meredith frantically struggled for escape, she knew she was about to be on the receiving end of the same meaty fist that had decked Chelsie. Her only consolation was that the haughty duchess had been knocked silly by her own husband. It was small consolation. Meredith gritted her teeth, waiting in agonized torment for Jarred's knuckles to crack against her cheek. . . .

Chapter 30

Hurricane Evan had blown ashore in Annapolis just before dusk. For six weeks the Duke of Chessfield had been planning to exact his own brand of justice on the odious man who had taken his precious daughter as a bondswoman. Although Evan was fit to be tied, no one had dared to throw a rope around the brooding duke. He had paced the decks of the schooner, chewing the sailors up one side and down the other because the vessel hadn't sprouted wings to fly him to the colonies.

Upon arriving in Annapolis, Evan had stormed to the sheriff's office to demand a warrant for Jarred McAlister's immediate arrest, as well as that of the two men Chelsie had named as her abductors. Although Sheriff Grimes reported that Isaac Latham was no longer among the living and Cyrus Hutton was presently standing trial for his crimes, Evan was only partially satisfied. He wanted Jarred's head on a silver platter, his body strung out on a torture rack, his remains sprinkled over the fiery pits of hell!

Firing questions like bullets, Evan had interrogated the sheriff, who was so intimidated by the duke's ominous stature, not to mention his irascible temper, that he answered each growled question without hesitation. Evan had learned that the perverted lecher who had bought his daughter resided on a plantation north of the city. He also discovered that Jarred was at that very moment sojourning in Annapolis.

Like Satan on a crusade of revenge, Evan stalked from the office to tear the town upside down. With the colonial official slinking at his heels, Evan had barged into first one pub, then another, to learn the whereabouts of Jarred McAlister. His persistent search led him to the tavern where Jarred had conversed with friends only two hours earlier. From there Evan was directed to one of the hotels where Jarred was reported to be staying.

For weeks now Evan had harbored a vendetta against a man he had never even met. His imagination had run rampant, speculating on what the fiendish scoundrel had done to a lovely woman like Chelsie. He shuddered to think of the humiliation to which she had been subjected, the emotional scars she suffered because of this heartless blackguard. Evan had warned the sheriff at the outset that he was taking the law into his own hands and that the colonial official would lose his position of authority if he dared interfere with an influential member of Parliament. When Evan finally got his hands on Jarred, he vowed to make mincemeat of the scurrilous brute.

With eyes blazing like a forest fire, Evan plowed through the hotel lobby. The ferocious snarl that was stamped on Evan's face caused the color to seep from the innkeeper's features. Evan employed his threatening size to intimidate those who stood in his way, and he knew how to throw his weight around. One murderous glance from Evan, and crowds of people parted to let him pass. He had the knack of cowing the most courageous of individuals. And when Evan Channing wanted something, no one prevented him from getting it. Right now he wanted Jarred.

"Where is Jarred McAlister?" Evan growled.

"Room 13," the innkeeper bleated.

"His unlucky number," Evan snorted derisively. Wheeling about, Evan bowed his neck and propelled himself toward the staircase.

The hissing noises and the sound of furniture crashing against walls and floors caused Evan to quicken his stride. The racket in one of the upstairs rooms left Evan speculating on what sort of perverted orgy was going on. With his pistol in one hand and the lantern from the hall in the other, Evan stormed toward room 13. Shoving his shoulder against the door, he barreled inside, startling the occupants of the suite.

The light from the lantern sprayed across the ransacked room. There, poised with a doubled fist in midair and one hand clenched in Meredith's damp hair, sat Jarred—bare-chested and bare-bodied beneath the tangled sheet. Upended furniture formed a maze in the room and clothing was strewn hither and yon. Meredith's face and arms were a mass of bloody scratches, and her wet blouse had been partially ripped from her heaving breasts during her tussle with Chelsie.

The scene before Evan's eyes had him scowling mutinously. From the look of things, Jarred McAlister was a sadistic rapist who chose to beat his lovers before and after he sexually abused them. Evan's black frown cut harsh lines in his leathery face as he scrutinized the man whose raven hair looked as if it had been styled by a windstorm. Jarred's eyes were as streaked as a road map, and the smell of colonial rum and Meredith's cheap perfume hung in the room like a poignant cloud.

The unexpected intrusion caused Jarred to slacken his grasp on Meredith's hair. With a mortified squawk, she vaulted off the bed, clutching her sagging bodice. Like a bullet she shot toward the door, but Evan barricaded the exit with his sturdy frame.

Disgustedly, Evan glowered over Meredith's head to sneer at the man who had clutched the sheet around his bare hips. "Are you Jarred McAlister?"

"Aye."

"Then prepare to die, you bastard." Evan's booming voice circled the room in echoing vibrations that ricocheted off the walls.

Bloodshot blue eyes widened in stupefied astonishment when the burly red-headed gorilla cocked his flintlock and aimed it at Jarred's chest. Moving in slow motion, Jarred hurled himself off the opposite side of the bed, just as the bullet whizzed past him to embed itself in the headboard.

"You miserable son-of-a-bitch," Evan snarled as he stomped around to the side of the bed where Jarred had dived for cover. "Where is . . ." His voice trailed off when he spied Jarred scraping himself off the unconscious body he had inadvertently landed on.

"Chelsie!" Jarred and Evan croaked in unison.

"Shoot him where he sits!" Meredith spluttered. "That scoundrel seduced me after he beat the chit and knocked her cold. He

388

was planning to beat me to a pulp, and he would have if you hadn't barged in. He's the most perverted heathen I've ever met!"

Jarred was stunned when he rolled Chelsie's limp body over to see her black eye and swollen jaw. What the devil was going on here? Chelsie was supposed to be in Easthaven. And where did she get those ridiculous clothes? She was dressed like a bandit, for God's sake!

Before Jarred could stumble through his thoughts to find answers for these baffling questions, Evan's doubled fist slammed against his jaw. Jarred, unprepared for the teeth-rattling blow, was knocked into the corner and left to check for loose teeth. Damn, this raving lunatic packed a mighty whallop. Who the hell was he, and what was he doing here? Jarred had never seen him before in his life . . . at least not while he was sober.

"Don't you ever touch my daughter again, you bastard!" Evan flared furiously.

"Daughter?" Jarred peeped, inspecting his tender jaw.

If first impressions were important, Jarred was in serious trouble. The scene into which the Duke of Chessfield had walked was incriminating in itself. And Meredith's testimony left Jarred highly suspect. For a silver-tongued lawyer, Jarred found himself fumbling for an explanation, facing a man who had appointed himself the judge, jury, and executioner. Lord, how many times had Jarred heard Chelsie threaten him by saying, "Just wait until my father gets here?" Well, the duke was here, all right, and he was as ominous and foreboding as the Prince of Darkness himself!

Grimly Jarred glanced from Chelsie's limp form to Meredith's mutinous glare. Sweet mercy, had he really seduced Meredith? He remembered the strange, erotic fantasy of passion, but . . . Christ! Had he been in bed with this wench when Chelsie had found them together? Was that what that cat fight was all about? From the look of things, Chelsie had followed him to Annapolis to determine if he could be faithful to her when he confronted temptation. And Jarred had failed the test. He had bedded another woman during his drinking spree, and Chelsie had been there to catch him red-handed.

"I want this man locked behind bars until I can have him placed before a firing squad," Evan hissed as he knelt down to scoop his lifeless daughter into his arms.

Chelsie's garments were tattered. Evan was left to wonder if this demented pervert had forced her to garb herself in men's clothes to perform in another of his fiendish orgies.

"I want McAlister charged with every crime he has committed, as well as the half-dozen he probably got away with because he supposedly holds a respectable position. By God, no man abuses my daughter and lives to boast about it!"

The sheriff would have objected to the fierce demand if he could have mustered his nerve. But after watching Evan knock Jarred for a loop, the sheriff thought it wiser to hold his tongue than to lose his position and a few of his teeth. The duke was in no mood to hear anyone list Jarred's noble credentials or offer a character reference. Evan wanted Jarred hanged and then propped up in front of the firing squad to be shot a couple dozen times. Jarred would have to do some fast talking if he intended to explain this incriminating predicament. At the moment, Jarred did look to be the perverted scoundrel Evan seemed to think he was.

While Sheriff Grimes was gathering Jarred's scattered clothes and Evan was cuddling his bruised and battered daughter in his arms, Meredith lit out like a house afire. She had no intention of being on hand when Chelsie roused to give her rendition of the incident. After witnessing the duke's vicious assault on Jarred, she wanted to be miles away when the swarthy brute came gunning for the woman who had instigated the fisticuffs with Chelsie and antagonized her during the voyage to the colonies.

Meredith's mind raced as she sailed down the hall. She desperately needed assistance if she hoped to escape unscathed. And she knew just where to find a man who was as anxious to shake the dust of Annapolis off his heels as she was. Cyrus Hutton would be indebted to her if she freed him from jail. Meredith crossed her fingers, hoping Sheriff Grimes had left the jail unattended when that red-haired Goliath stormed into town to locate his daughter.

Cyrus would be eager to accompany her out of town, Meredith

assured herself. Besides, she and Cyrus had been on the friendliest of terms while she was aboard his ship. She had granted him sexual favors for extra rations. Aye, he would accompany her. Chewing on that positive thought, Meredith scuttled toward the sheriff's office. Cyrus and Meredith needed each other if they were to survive!

Evan expelled a shuddering breath and tried to compose himself. In anguish, he stared down at the discolored face that he cradled against his heaving chest. His precious daughter had endured a dozen kinds of hell these past months, but he would compensate for all the physical and emotional abuse she had suffered. As soon as Chelsie was resting comfortably on board the schooner, he would file the necessary papers to have Jarred McAlister tried for his crimes and sentenced to death.

The moment Evan shouldered his way into Doris Wycoff's cabin on board the ship, she gasped in dismay. "My God, what happened to her?"

"That cussed Jarred McAlister is what happened to her," Evan scowled as he carefully laid Chelsie on the cot.

While Evan explained what he had seen in the hotel room, Doris cleansed Chelsie's scratched face and pressed a cold cloth to her swollen jaw and bruised eye. During the voyage, Doris had tried to control the duke's raging temper, but now she was as eager to see Jarred crucified as Evan was. Chelsie was like Doris's own child. She had raised the rambunctious sprite since her mother's untimely death, and Doris had become far more than a housekeeper at Chessfield. Indeed, she was like a member of the family, and she was outraged by Chelsie's brutal treatment.

Pacing the confines of the cabin, Evan slammed his fist into his palm and cursed vehemently. "I swear by all that's holy, I'll see justice served to that miserable bastard." Apprehensively he glanced over to see if Doris's gentle ministrations had roused Chelsie. They hadn't, and that made him all the madder.

"You'll have to stand in line to get at him," Doris muttered furiously. "I cannot imagine how any man could mistreat this lovely lass. Just look at her! What kind of animal would lay a hand on this bewitching face?"

"A perverted madman," Evan snarled contemptuously.

Doris vaulted off the edge of the bed and toward the door. Evan frowned at her unexpected exit.

"Where are you going?"

"To the jail, to read that vicious scoundrel the riot act," Doris seethed. "Then I'm going to blacken *his* eye. We'll see how he likes it when someone pounds him flat!"

Evan crossed the room in two quick strides to catch her before she breezed down the companionway. "Nay, you are staying with Chelsie," he insisted. "I'll go post the charges, and finish what I started with McAlister."

"You had better punch him twice for me," Doris growled vindictively. "I'm itching to get my hands on him!"

With his jaw set in grim determination, Evan stamped out the door. As he bounded off down the gangplank, the shrill whinny of a horse caught his attention. When he glanced toward the other sailing vessel that had eased into port the same time his schooner had arrived, his eyes popped from their sockets. There, poised on the plank of the nearby ship, was none other than Trumpeter. As usual, the copper dun colt balked at traipsing across the plank, and a group of men were scurrying about trying to persuade the flighty colt to walk over the water.

Evan didn't have the slightest idea how his prize colt had gotten to the colonies or who had stolen him. Chelsie's letter had requested that he bring along Moonraker, his expensive silver-gray stud. (And only God knew why Chelsie had made that peculiar request.) Yet, she had said nothing about the where-abouts of the two horses stolen from Chessfield.

Demons of curiosity caused Evan to detour from his intended route to the sheriff's office. He fully intended to get to the bottom of this horse theft business before his valuable steed disappeared from sight.

"That is *my* horse," Evan bellowed as he strode toward the plank.

Kyle McAlister blinked in disbelief when the oversized aristo-crat came storming toward him. What the blazes was this bulky giant ranting about? " 'Tis my horse," Kyle contradicted in his own booming tone.

Trumpeter wasn't helping matters one whit. He did not like boarding or unloading from ships. Without Chelsie around to soothe him, he was practically unmanageable. He was flighty by nature. His instinct to bolt and run warred with his fear of walking over the water which flashed like silver when it reflected the moonlight.

Evan's lightning voice and Kyle's thundering tone, compounded with being tugged across the gangplank in the dark, caused Trumpeter to rear in fright. His trainer yelped when he was yanked backward and knocked off balance. The shrieking trainer rammed Trumpeter broadside and the colt bolted backward, knocking Kyle off the plank. Kyle expelled a loud squawk as he plummeted into the water alongside the trainer who had been unable to steady himself on the plank.

Wild-eyed and free from restraint, the fidgety colt lunged forward. Since there was barely room for himself on the plank, Trumpeter made no attempt to swerve to miss Evan, who stood in front of him with feet apart. Expelling a pained grunt, Evan found himself run down by his own colt. With his arms flapping like a windmill, Evan sailed through the air and landed with a splash in the water below.

Cursing in fluent profanity, Kyle, Evan, and the trainer thrashed toward shore. Grant and Daniel immediately gave chase to the runaway colt, leaving Neil and the servants to fish the men from the bay.

All hell had broken loose and the darkness was ablaze with torches, salty curses and Trumpeter's shrill whinnies. While Chelsie was dragging herself from the throbbing pit of darkness, her father and her father-in-law were spouting threats and promising to have each other arrested. Evan and Kyle had only met and they didn't know each other from Adam. But they were already bickering over who owned the valuable steed that was being chased down by the two youngest McAlister brothers.

Chapter 31

When Chelsie managed to pry open one eye, she was assaulted by a hellish headache. She felt as if she had been trampled by a herd of stampeding horses and then stuffed into a meat grinder. Her entire body complained when she tried to prop herself upright. A muddled frown knitted her brow when her blurred vision cleared enough to recognize Doris Wycoff bending over her.

"Where am I?" Chelsie chirped.

Relief washed over Doris's wrinkled features. Lovingly she smoothed the wild silver-blond tendrils from Chelsie's bruised face. "You are safe now, my darling. You will never again have to suffer that horrible brute's mistreatment. Your father has gone to the jail to box that lout's ears once more for good measure."

"Jail?" Chelsie swallowed with a gulp. She well-remembered the frame of mind she had been in when she jotted the condemning note to her father. At the time she had been furious with Jarred and humiliated no end.

Having been unconscious when her father arrived, Chelsie didn't have the foggiest notion what had transpired in the hotel room. But judging from the housekeeper's mutinous tone and the spiteful remarks about Jarred, both Doris and Evan detested Jarred on sight.

Spurred into action by her fear for Jarred's safety, Chelsie swung her legs over the edge of the cot. Although stars spun around her head, Chelsie felt the urgent need to stop her father before he pulverized Jarred. Before Chelsie could gain her feet, Doris pushed Chelsie back to her pillow.

"You are going nowhere, young lady," Doris declared. "What you need is rest, and rest you shall have. Your father will see to it that Jarred McAlister suffers for the horrible way he abused you."

Chelsie was frantic. She didn't have time to explain what had happened, and she knew how irrationally her father behaved when he was in a fit of temper. If Evan was on his way to jail to carve out Jarred's heart, Chelsie had not one second to waste! She bounded off the bed like a mountain goat. Her abrupt movement startled Doris, who tumbled from the cot to become entangled in her petticoats.

Scraping herself off the floor, Doris darted after Chelsie, whose blow to the jaw had obviously addled her brain. "Come back here!" she demanded. "Chelsie Renee Channing, you are not well enough to be on your feet!"

It was a mad dash down the companionway. Chelsie darted up the stairwell with Doris scurrying five paces behind her. The booming voices that rolled across the wharf were easy to recognize, but Chelsie didn't linger to determine why her father was raving at Kyle and why Kyle had arrived in Annapolis a day earlier than he'd originally planned. Whatever had caused their shouting match was the least of Chelsie's concerns. She had to reach Jarred before her father tore him to shreds. Evan's argument with Kyle bought her precious time. Once Jarred was safe from her father's wrath, she could set Evan down and calmly explain. But not while the duke was in a towering rage. He wouldn't listen to reason!

When Chelsie trotted up the path that led to town, Doris came to a skidding halt. She, too, had recognized the duke's bellowing voice. Determined to seek his assistance, Doris scurried across the wharf to inform Evan that his befuddled daughter had spirited off into the night, destination unknown.

Desperate, Doris thrust herself between the two men who stood barely a foot apart, spouting curses that burned her ears. Accusations were flying like sparks, but Doris was too concerned about Chelsie to wait until these two scowling men finished biting each other's heads off.

"Your daughter just flew off up the road," Doris reported

breathlessly, tugging at Evan's arm. "I don't think she knows *who* she is, much less *where* she is. We've got to find her, and quickly."

The frantic comment drew Evan's immediate attention. With a parting glower to Kyle, Evan spun on his heels. "After I see about my daughter, I'll have you arrested for horse theft," he vowed spitefully. "So don't think to leave town, because I'll hunt you down."

"And I'll have a warrant for your arrest, you old buzzard!" Kyle fumed, brandishing his clenched fist. "If my prized steed suffered any injuries because of you, I'll see you pay the full price of replacing him!"

While Doris and Evan jogged up the road, Kyle darted off to see if his sons had rounded up Trumpeter. And while Chelsie's family and in-laws were giving chase in opposite directions, she was dashing toward the sheriff's office as fast as her feet would carry her.

In the meantime, Meredith Holt had confiscated the pistol she had once before stolen from her master's office at the tavern, and she had planned Cyrus's jailbreak. As she had anticipated, the jail was quiet and the sheriff had left his prisoner without taking time to appoint a deputy to stand guard. She made short shrift of rummaging through the desk to locate the key to Cyrus's cell. Within a few minutes, Cyrus and Meredith were mounted on two stolen horses and had pointed themselves toward Baltimore, where the schooner remained impounded until after the trial.

A wordless scowl erupted from Jarred's lips when he reached the jail. Cyrus Hutton's cell stood empty, and Jarred was reluctantly ordered to park himself in it. Grumbling, the sheriff retrieved the set of keys Meredith had left dangling from the lock.

"For God's sake, Horace, let me give chase," Jarred requested. "There is a criminal on the loose!"

Horace Grimes heaved a frustrated sigh. "If I let you go, the duke will have my head. The man is a walking keg of blasting powder. If he comes back and you're gone, there is no telling what he might do." Reluctantly, he shut the door to the cell in which Jarred stood—half-drunk, guilt-ridden, and tormented as hell. "You and I both know you have an upstanding reputation. But the Duke of Chessfield seems to think you are the lowest form of life, and he is out for blood. He won't think rationally until he calms down."

When Jarred sent the sheriff a pleading glance, Horace threw up his hands in a gesture of futility. "Blast it, Jarred, he's a duke! He not only has friends in high places, but he occupies a lofty pedestal himself! If I cross him, I'll lose my job and we'll both be drawn and quartered before you can explain. . . .

The sound of the office door crashing against the wall caused Horace to grimace in apprehension. No doubt it was the duke, come to stretch Jarred's neck out like a giraffe's. Timidly Horace stepped from the hall that led to the cells. His eyes bulged from their sockets when Chelsie, toting the flintlock he had laid on his desk, grimly approached him.

"Let him out," she ordered impatiently.

"Confound it, I can't," Horace muttered sourly. "Your father is on the rampage. . . ." His voice trailed off when Chelsie cocked the trigger and took careful aim.

"Perhaps you didn't hear me. I said let him out . . . now!"

Horace sorely wished he could find a hole to crawl into until Hurricane Evan blew over. He dreaded being in the office when that red-headed cyclone breezed in. Like a prisoner marching to the gallows, Horace reversed direction to unlock the cell. The moment Jarred stepped out, Horace stepped inside. Reaching through the bars, he locked his cell, then tucked the key in his pocket.

"One nice thing about a prison cell is that a man is protected from being torn limb from limb." A bleak smile pursed Horace's lips. "Evan Channing will have to rip the bars off the walls to get to me. That should take him a couple of minutes."

Hardly daring to look into Chelsie's bruised face, Jarred grasped her hand and propelled her out the door. "Cyrus escaped," he informed her.

"And my father will be only a few minutes behind me," Chelsie reported, matching Jarred stride for stride as he darted down the alley. Her eyes drifted over the red welt on Jarred's jaw, one that was as puffy and swollen as her own. Without asking, she knew who had delivered that brain-scrambling blow. "I'm sorry," she murmured apologetically.

"Not half as sorry as I am," Jarred muttered as he aimed himself toward the blacksmith's barn to fetch two horses. "Cyrus is probably headed back to his ship."

Jarred was groping for conversation. He hated the silence that stretched between them. It allowed him too much time to curse himself for what he thought he had done a few hours earlier. Chelsie must surely hate him for falling into bed with a wench he had only met. Chelsie had followed him to test his loyalty, and he had slept with Meredith! God, he wished he could contort his body to become the donor and recipient of a well-deserved kick in the seat of the pants.

When the foggy memories clouded his brain once again, Jarred winced. He may have bedded Meredith while he was drunk, but it was Chelsie he had made love to. It was still *her* face he had seen in the shadows of his mind, even if she really hadn't been there. It had been Chelsie he truly wanted, had always wanted since the moment he'd met her.

Jarred could imagine himself offering an explanation to Chelsie. He would draw himself up in front of the cynical beauty. Then he would look her straight in the eye and confess that he had bedded another woman, but that he had pretended it was Chelsie.

A rueful smile hovered on Jarred's lips. The story sounded ridiculous even to him. Chelsie would never believe it. She would be so outraged that he had the audacity to voice such a stupid excuse that her legendary temper would explode. After she threw a few things at him and ran him through with a dagger a couple of times, she would finally get around to laughing in his face.

Bleakly Jarred accepted the cold, hard realization that he had committed an unpardonable sin. He had to bear his guilt, shame, and regret without voicing any explanation. And because of his reckless indiscretion he could never have this feisty green-eyed leprechaun. Once he apprehended Cyrus and put him behind bars where he belonged, Jarred may as well turn himself over to the Duke of Chessfield and let the towering giant beat him to a pulp, just the way he deserved.

"Meredith is probably the one who freed Cyrus," Chelsie speculated and then inhaled a quick breath. "She was the vicious bitch I confronted several times on the schooner. Isaac was foolish enough to think the wench had eyes for only him. But Meredith has more past lovers than the queen has jewels. The truth is, she never met a man she didn't sleep with . . . even Cyrus."

Jarred muttered several epithets to his own name when Chelsie uttered that particular remark. He had the unshakable feeling it was directed toward him.

"Knowing Meredith, she used her charms to persuade Cyrus to take her with him," she added on a sour note, unaware of the guilt Jarred was erroneously suffering. Chelsie had been unconscious when Meredith pointed an accusing finger at Jarred, who remembered nothing of what he had done while he was drinking. Had Chelsie known he thought he had bedded Meredith, she'd have set him straight. But she didn't, and Jarred was suffering all the torments of the damned.

Once Jarred retrieved the horses, they rode hell-for-leather. While they were chasing Meredith and Cyrus, Doris and Evan were on their way to the sheriff's office to form a search party to hunt for Chelsie.

The moment Evan marched into the office, he scowled a number of curses. "Where is he?" Evan demanded of the sheriff, who had locked himself in jail for safekeeping.

Horace smiled bleakly at the raging giant. "Your daughter broke McAlister out of jail . . ." He barely got the words out before Evan exploded like a volcano.

"My God, she *is* out of her mind!" Evan growled. "That bastard knocked her senseless, and now she thinks she's supposed to protect *him* from *me*." His fiery green eyes seared Horace. "Where did they go?"

"They were chasing Cyrus Hutton, the prisoner who escaped while we were hunting down McAlister," Horace informed the fuming duke.

Evan swung about to buzz out the door and aimed himself

toward the blacksmith's barn. While he and Doris were trotting down the street, he spied Chelsie's long mane of hair glowing in the moonlight. The sight of the man who was riding beside Chelsie as they galloped out of town had Evan sputtering every obscenity in his vocabulary.

Within a few minutes Evan had secured two horses, but Doris put up a fuss about being deposited on the four-legged creature. She had never climbed on a horse, and she insisted she was too old to do so now. Unfortunately, Evan refused a more comfortable mode of transportation and Doris found herself plucked off the ground and stuffed into the saddle. Praying nonstop, Doris held on for dear life as she bounced up and down on her galloping steed. She was sure Evan would eventually catch up with his runaway daughter and the ruthless Jarred McAlister. But Doris doubted she would be around to witness the scene. She would be lying in a broken heap on the side of the road, to be buried in these cursed colonies where heathens and renegades ran rampant!

Horace rolled his eyes in disbelief when he heard the office door bang against the wall for the third time in less than half an hour. "Now what?" he muttered sourly.

Intent on pointing an accusing finger at the red-haired gorilla who claimed to own Trumpeter, Kyle came to register a complaint. Neil, Grant, and Daniel stood aside while Kyle ranted and raved about the brute who had frightened off his racehorse and subsequently caused him to take an unexpected swim in the bay. Trumpeter had been captured, but the trainer had his hands full trying to calm down the flighty colt. Kyle was determined to have that growling giant behind bars for slandering the McAlisters' good name, among other things!

"I wish to issue a warrant for a man's immediate arrest and an even quicker hanging," Kyle insisted in a spiteful tone. Drawing himself up in his dripping wet clothes, he stared down at the sheriff who had let himself out of his cell after Hurricane Evan whizzed off in search of Jarred. "The man stands at least six-foot-two inches tall and weighs about two hundred and fifty pounds. His flaming red hair matches his explosive temper. I swear he is a raving lunatic, and he—"

"And he is presently chasing your son," Horace interrupted, hitching his thumb toward the door. "If you want to see Jarred in one piece again, I suggest you find yourself a fast horse. You may have to glue Jarred back together after that bellowing maniac tears him apart."

Why Jarred was being pursued by that vengeful ape, Kyle didn't know. He and Evan hadn't gotten past name-calling to bother with the formality of introducing themselves to each other.

Knowing what a hothead the big brute was, Kyle wheeled around and shot out the door. With Neil clutching his medical bag and Grant and Daniel on his heels, Kyle dashed off to fetch four horses.

The McAlisters rode off like the four musketeers, intent on saving the day. Meredith and Cyrus were trying to outrun Chelsie and Jarred, who were attempting to keep one step ahead of Evan and Doris. Although Evan and Doris didn't know they were being followed, the McAlister clan was only a few minutes behind them, hoping to rescue one of their kin from the one-man war party who had turned his wrath on Jarred for only God knew what demented reason.

Chapter 32

Jarred's keen eyes sought out the silhouettes that emerged and disappeared into the shadows on the road ahead of them. Swerving his steed toward Chelsie's mount, he yanked back on her reins. Before she could inquire what he thought he was doing, Jarred gestured for her to follow him along the winding trail that veered off to the right. Without explaining his purpose, Jarred picked his way along the path that ran parallel the marsh—the shortcut he hoped would permit them to intercept Meredith and Cyrus at the bend in the road.

Although Chelsie considered herself made of sturdy stuff, their moonlit ride beside the marsh had her fidgeting at all unidentified sounds. Reeds thrashed in the darkness as the horses brushed past. The splash of creatures taking cover to avoid the intruders who invaded their domain and the soft slithering of predators in the swamps set her nerves to tingling. Her imagination ran wild with speculation. It was only when she heard the pounding of hooves around the bend that she put aside her apprehension about her surroundings to concentrate on the moon-dappled figures who approached. The sight of Meredith riding beside Cyrus set Chelsie's blood to boiling. She couldn't wait to get her hands on that worthless bitch and finish what they had begun in Jarred's hotel room.

Chelsie's gaze swung to Jarred, who crouched on his steed like a tiger poised to pounce. And with a growl that would have put a jungle cat to shame, Jarred sprang from his horse, launching himself at Cyrus as he thundered past. Startled, Cyrus let out a yelp that could have raised the dead when two hundred twenty pounds of iron-hard muscle slammed against him. His horse kicked up its heels in fright, catapulting both of them into the swamp.

While Jarred was pounding Cyrus flat, Chelsie gouged her mount to catch up with Meredith, who had decided to leave Cyrus to fend for himself. Chelsie's hand snaked out to grab a handful of the tangled black hair that trailed behind her nemesis. Meredith squealed in pain when Chelsie very nearly ripped her scalp off her head. The abrupt jerk caused Meredith to somersault off the back of her horse. She had only hit the ground when Chelsie bounded from the saddle to charge like a provoked bull.

"No one will rescue you this time," Chelsie sneered as she buried her fist in Meredith's belly.

"I wish my aim had been more accurate the day I saw you parading around at the fair in your fancy clothes," Meredith hissed as she struck back at Chelsie. "You would have been dead long ago!"

The comment caught Chelsie by surprise. From the sound of things, it wasn't Isaac who had come ashore to dispose of her, but rather Meredith whose aim with a dagger and knife wasn't as good as it should have been, thank the Lord!

Although Chelsie was startled by the revelation of learning who'd tried to kill her, she didn't allow Meredith to catch her off guard. Meredith's arm circled through the air to land a painful blow, but Chelsie was poised and waiting. Using her forearm as a shield, Chelsie deflected the flying fist and landed a painful blow of her own. The well-directed punch smashed the air from Meredith's lungs with a whoosh and mashed her stomach into her spine. The forceful impact sent her stumbling backward, tripping over the trailing hem of her skirt. With a splat, Meredith plopped down in the boggy marsh and shrieked in pain when Chelsie pounced on top of her.

While Chelsie was beating Meredith to a pulp, Jarred was taking out every ounce of his frustration on Cyrus. The poor man didn't have a prayer of defending himself against Jarred's fighting abilities and superior strength. Cyrus had become a human punching bag, and he swore his vengeful challenger had broken every bone in his body.

Chelsie and Jarred were still pounding their opponents into the

403

ground when Evan and Doris rode upon the scene. The sight of Jarred poised with his arm cocked, prepared to deliver a bone-jarring blow, had become a familiar one to Evan Channing. Seeing the muddy bastard poised in the marsh ignited Evan's fury. He had lost his temper three months earlier, and he hadn't found it since. The opportunity of making a meal of the scoundrel who had abused his daughter was incentive enough for Evan to attack Jarred.

Evan swung from his steed, lowered his head, and charged at Jarred like a battering ram. Mud splattered everywhere. Jarred went skidding through the slime with Evan's bulky body mashing him down. Although Jarred knew he should have lain there and taken the beating he so richly deserved, he instinctively fought back. The duke had been allowed one unanswered punch in the jaw at the hotel. That was all he was going to get. Like a bucking horse, Jarred threw Evan sideways, then rolled over to deliver a slimy fist to the cheek. The sting of pain infuriated Evan even more.

Seeing her father and husband wallowing in the mud, pelleting each other with blows, reminded Chelsie of two monsters rising from the swamp to lay claim to their domain. Their growls and sneers, intermingling with the crack of flesh against flesh, spurred Chelsie into action. Hurriedly she dragged Meredith's limp body from the marsh, retrieved her emerald ring, and ordered Doris to fetch a rope to bind the spiteful wench before she made another attempt to escape. Gladly, Doris swung down from the saddle. While she tied Meredith's ankles and wrists, Chelsie dashed over to pull Evan and Jarred apart.

It was at that moment that the McAlisters arrived upon the scene. Neil, Grant, and Daniel leaped from their horses, dashing off to rescue their older brother from the maniac trying to tear him apart. Kyle was one step behind his sons, cheering them on.

For years Jarred had assumed all the duties of managing and overseeing the estates, leaving Kyle to pursue his hobbies of hunting and racing. Although Kyle doubted his second son needed much help in beating the tar out of the red-headed gorilla, he decided to lend his assistance. Kyle wanted to take a shot at the big galoot for his ridiculous accusations. The buffoon had accused Kyle of horse theft. Him! A man who had never stolen anything from anyone in all his life!

Like a regiment of soldiers rushing into battle, the four McAlisters waded into the bog to assist Jarred, whose youth and pantherlike agility had already brought the oversized duke down a notch. And of course there was Chelsie, who was valiantly trying to pry Jarred loose from her father. She had been shoved backward twice and was covered with slime, just like the two enraged stags who were slinging mud and doubled fists at each other. By the time Chelsie thrashed to her feet, waist-deep in the marsh, all four McAlisters had thrown themselves on Evan and were holding his face down in the muck.

"Enough!" Chelsie shouted at the top of her lungs.

"Not until this madman has been properly subdued," Kyle spluttered, giving Evan another shove when he tried to raise his head to grasp a much-needed breath of air. "He accused me of horse theft and declared Trumpeter was his colt!"

"Of course Trumpeter is his," Chelsie yelled over the drone of growls and hisses. "This is my father, and the colt is not only from his stock, but Trumpeter was stolen from our estate."

Kyle stared at Chelsie and his hands dropped away from Evan's neck. "This is your *father?*" he croaked. "This is the Duke of Chessfield?"

The other McAlisters released Evan so quickly that he plopped back in the slime, swearing a blue streak. Neil latched onto Chelsie, pulling her from the marsh to ensure that she hadn't suffered unnecessarily from her wild escapade.

"Are you all right?" Neil questioned. His expression lent testimony to the extent of his concern for Chelsie.

"Aside from the fact that I'm bruised, scratched, and covered with slime, I'm in splendid shape," Chelsie replied, impatiently worming away from Neil, who was checking her for cracked ribs and whatever else might have been injured during the brawl.

Jarred, who had been knocked out of the way by his own brothers, waded forward to assist the growling duke to his feet. He found his hand immediately slapped away.

"Don't touch me, you perverted lecher!" Evan spat poisonously.

"That is my son you are addressing," Kyle snapped, taking quick offense. "And what kind of thanks is this?" His derisive snort hung over the swamp like a fog. "My son graciously came to

Chelsie's aid when she was stranded in the colonies. I myself have made her welcome in my home."

Evan expelled a snarl. "My daughter was kidnaped by spirits and crimps and sold to this . . ." He pointed a blunt-ended finger at Jarred. ". . . This rapscallion who has used her in his disgusting orgies. I witnessed one of them earlier this evening in his hotel room. He knocked my daughter senseless. There is no telling what else he'd have done if I hadn't arrived just in the nick of time. England has its pervert in the form of Sir Francis Dashwood, but the colonies have their own version in Jarred McAlister!"

While Kyle gaped in outrage, Grant bit back an amused grin and Daniel frowned bemusedly at the reference to Dashwood. Worming free of Neil's supporting arms, Chelsie waded back into the bog to assist her father to his feet.

"You didn't see what you thought you saw, Papa," Chelsie insisted.

"Nay?" Evan scoffed. "Then who put that welt on your jaw and bruised your eye?"

"Meredith is responsible for my bruised eye, and I am responsible for the scratches and welts she sustained while we were fighting," Chelsie explained. "Jarred was sleeping off whiskey when Meredith . . ."

"What were you doing in his room?" Evan wanted to know that very second. "And who hit you in the jaw?"

Chelsie's head dropped when all eyes turned toward her. "I was spying on Jarred, and he struck me when Meredith and I were battling on top of his bed."

The confession infuriated Evan, who wheeled around to pounce on Jarred. Before he could initiate another battle, Kyle and Grant grabbed both arms to halt him.

"I didn't mean to hurt Chelsie," Jarred declared with sincerity. "It was dark and I woke to find two bodies flying across my lap. I would never have struck her if I'd known. I thought she was safely tucked away at our plantation."

Kyle frowned in confusion. "But Chelsie told us she was going to Annapolis with you instead of making the trip with us."

"I lied," Chelsie admitted quietly. "Jarred and I were at odds and I wanted to know if he truly meant what he had said about . . ." Her voice trailed off.

"What about all the things you said about McAlister in your letter?" Evan growled while he glared at Jarred. "You said he was a . . ."

"I know what I said," Chelsie interrupted before her father quoted her degrading description of Jarred. "But that was *then*. This is *now*."

"Chelsie heaved a frustrated sigh and glanced at each muddy face in the congregation. Blast it, this was a difficult explanation. Evan knew only a third of what was going on, the McAlisters knew another third. In order to make everyone fully understand what had happened, Chelsie would have to start at the beginning. And judging by the sneer on her father's face, he was in no mood for a lengthy explanation.

"Jarred is my husband, Papa," Chelsie blurted out in exasperation. "And you can't have him hanged, because I don't want him to die."

"Husband?" Evan's legs folded up beneath him and he plunked down right in the middle of the swamp.

"Hanged?" Kyle sat down before he fell down—right beside Evan.

"The marriage will be annulled posthaste," Evan growled, glaring daggers at Jarred. "I will not have you forced into matrimony with a man who bought you as his indentured servant and kept you at the home of the very man who stole our prized steeds!"

That spiteful outburst brought Kyle to his feet. "If you call me a horse thief one more time, I'm going to punch you in the mouth!" he threatened. "I know nothing about Jarred buying Chelsie. We have treated her like a duchess since the moment we met her. Jarred happens to be an influential lawyer and politician, and he will have you behind bars for making such slanderous remarks."

Kyle plunged on, still gathering steam. "Chelsie is going to give me the grandchildren I have waited decades to enjoy, and no one is going to deprive me of having toddlers underfoot." His snapping brown eyes riveted on Evan's inflated chest. "You can crawl back to England where you belong, Duke." Spinning about, he glared at Jarred. "And you are going to apologize to Chelsie this instant for whatever put the two of you at odds. Chelsie is like my own daughter, and I am not giving her up. Besides that, she promised to race Trumpeter at the meeting tomorrow afternoon. I've waited five years to defeat that ornery Amos Shaw on the track."

"Chelsie is going home where she belongs . . . with me," Evan insisted, his voice booming like thunder.

"She stays!" Kyle bellowed.

"Goes!"

"Stays!"

"Nay, Chelsie will do as she pleases," Jarred inserted in a more reasonable tone than either his father or father-in-law had employed. "Since the moment she was whisked onto Cyrus Hutton's ship against her will, she has been deprived of choices." His gaze swung to the muddied beauty, and he winced inwardly, thinking he had betrayed her, still unaware that Meredith had lied. "No one will make any demands on the duchess. For the first time in four months, she is going to consider her options and select one that suits her. Chelsie is her own woman. I will not make her decisions for her, and neither will anyone else. Chelsie can do as she pleases," he repeated sternly.

When Chelsie lifted her smeared face, Jarred looked the other way. He still couldn't meet her gaze without being hounded by guilt and regret. God, if he could turn back the hands of time, he wouldn't have drunk himself blind and permitted Meredith to fall into his bed. But he had, and he deserved to lose Chelsie because of his reckless indiscretion. He had confirmed her suspicions that he was a philanderer, even when he hadn't meant to touch another woman. He was all the rotten things Chelsie said he was. And if he declared he thought he was making love to Chelsie while Meredith was in his arms, she would laugh him out of the swamp. But Jarred didn't dare bring the subject up for discussion. There was no need to reopen a bleeding wound. He had betrayed Chelsie even though he hadn't meant to, and nothing he could say would right that unforgivable wrong.

"If I am to be granted my whim, my first wish is for all of you to stop arguing. My second wish is for a warm bath in my private room at the hotel," Chelsie declared. Bemusedly, she watched Jarred turn away from her as if the sight of her repelled him. What was the matter with him? He was acting a mite strange. "And as for the matter of the race, I intend to ride Trumpeter, because I gave Kyle my promise that I would."

Kyle beamed and Evan scowled.

"And my third and final wish is . . ." Her curious gaze drifted back to Jarred, who was suddenly avoiding her like the plague. "I suppose I should save it. I wouldn't want to waste it, knowing it will be my last. . . ."

The remark caused Jarred to flinch, as if he had been stabbed in the back. He knew what Chelsie implied . . . or at least he thought he did. He had stood before her that day in the meadow at Easthaven, requesting his final wish—his love wish. And like an idiot, he had traipsed off to Annapolis, gotten himself rip-roaring drunk, and bedded another woman. Now he had wasted his last wish and spoiled his only chance at happiness. He would have to satisfy his insatiable longing by wandering back and forth between the wilderness and civilization, just as he had before Chelsie had come into his life.

He would be a lost spirit who could never find his resting place. Until Chelsie had come along, Jarred hadn't been able to stay in one spot for any length of time. It was as if he'd been in search of some missing part of himself. And when he'd found the one woman who gave his life new meaning, he'd botched it left and right. First he'd bought her indentureship, refusing to believe her story. He'd married her while she was incapable of rejecting his proposal. And to make matters worse, he'd slept with a woman he barely knew while Chelsie was there to spy on him. Damnation, if he had his pistol, he would turn it on himself and end this torment. That would ensure that he stayed in one place—permanently—instead of roaming around, looking for something he'd lost and would never find again.

When the captives were tied to their horses, the entourage left for town. Although the McAlisters and Channings shared the same road, there was an invisible wall between them. Evan continually glared at Kyle and Jarred. Kyle shot Evan sizzling glowers that would have burned a lesser man to a crisp. All the while, Meredith rattled on about how she had been unduly used and made to perform deeds against her will ever since the moment she'd been herded on board Cyrus's schooner in England. When Chelsie had her fill of the lies, she stuffed a gag in Meredith's mouth. The wench was chattering like a magpie, and Chelsie preferred the stilted silence to Meredith's prefabricated chit chat.

By the time they returned to the sheriff's office, the hour was late. Chelsie couldn't wait to enjoy a moment of privacy and a much-needed bath. Her first order of business was to formulate a concise, detailed explanation to present to her father the following morning. She hoped the fact that she was alive and well would soothe his legendary Irish temper. She wasn't eager to explain everything over Evan's roaring growls.

To Chelsie's disappointment, Jarred didn't come to her in the shadows of darkness. Had she known he was laden with guilt because of his careless affair with Meredith (one he hadn't truly had), Chelsie would have set the matter straight. But she didn't know of Jarred's torment because she lay in a senseless heap while Meredith was spinning her lies to the duke and to Jarred, who had been too drunk to know what he was doing.

Early the following morning, Evan returned to the hotel to see his daughter. He had just climbed the steps when he spied Jarred ambling down the hall toward Chelsie's room. Gritting his teeth, Evan approached the raven-haired rake. Extracting a purse of coins from his pocket, Evan forced the money into Jarred's hand.

"This is compensation for what you paid for Chelsie's indentureship and for food and clothing," Evan said stiffly.

Jarred lifted the heavy purse, calculating its worth by its weight. " 'Tis a mite too generous," he insisted. One thick brow climbed to a mocking angle. "Or am I to assume the extra compensation is bribe money, and that you expect me to permanently remove myself from your daughter's life?"

Evan's expression left no doubt as to his feelings toward Jarred. There was no love lost between them, and Evan made no attempt to be anything but civil. "You are very astute, McAlister," he replied crisply. "If you want what is best for Chelsie, you will back away without trying to influence her. She belongs with me, and I will not give her up." His piercing green eyes probed Jarred like a scalpel. "My daughter is the product of generations of blue blood. She has been educated by the finest tutors and given the best of everything that money could buy. She is destined to marry a man who matches her status. And from what I have seen, you are nowhere near worthy enough to claim a duchess as a wife."

"And you, sir, are a pompous snob," Jarred had the nerve to say

410

right to the duke's face!

Evan puffed up like a balloon. "At least I know my place!" he hissed.

Jarred heaved a sigh. He had only a few moments to spare before he reported to the courthouse to resume Cyrus's trial and file criminal proceedings against Meredith for theft and attempted murder. He had hoped to spend his time apologizing to Chelsie. But from all indications, Evan Channing wasn't going to let Jarred near her without a fight. If Jarred hadn't been so plagued with guilt, he might have disputed Evan's remark. But he was no longer worthy of attempting to win Chelsie's love. The previous night he had sacrificed all rights to her and wasted his last wish.

With an unblinking stare, Jarred dropped the pouch back in Evan's hands. "You have my word that I will not try to influence your daughter, but I will not take your money."

"And I will not be feeling the least bit indebted to you," Evan said with chilling tolerance. Although Evan attempted to shove the purse back into Jarred's hand, he refused to take it.

Sporting a nonchalant smile that disguised his true emotions, Jarred stepped away to bow mockingly before the oversized duke. "You may have your daughter back, if that is her wish," he stated. "I won't stand in the way of what she wants. Keep your money, sir. I have no need of it. Despite what you think of me, I love your daughter."

"Well, you certainly have a strange way of showing it," Evan snorted disdainfully.

Doing an about-face, Jarred pivoted and walked away, leaving Evan muttering under his breath. There was something annoying about that self-assured rake, something that really got under Evan's skin. Most individuals shrank away when Evan leveled one of his murderous glares. But Jarred blatantly defied him. His smiles held a taunt, and the sooner that rascal was out of Chelsie's life, the better. Love, indeed! Jarred wanted Chelsie to better his station in life. She would be a feather in that colonial bumpkin's cap, but Evan would never permit the marriage to last. It was doomed!

Inhaling a deep breath, Evan tried to compose himself before confronting his daughter. When he had control of his temper, he rapped at the door. After a brief greeting, Chelsie sat her father down to give him a detailed explanation of what had transpired the past few months. Although Evan showed his disapproval, Chelsie was determined to present a connected narrative without unnecessary interruption.

When Chelsie explained that Jarred had been more than generous to her and had saved her from the brutal man who had mistreated her on the ship, Evan began to regret behaving so harshly toward his son-in-law. He still didn't like Jarred, of course, but Evan might have attempted to be more congenial. The duke was blind, protective, and most unforgiving where his daughter was concerned. And he still intended to return Chelsie to Chessfield, where she belonged.

How Jarred could have denounced the fact that Chelsie was a full-fledged heiress of royal breeding was beyond Evan's comprehension. Since he and Jarred had gotten crosswise of each other the moment they met, nothing could completely smooth over their differences. And the fact that Meredith claimed to have been seduced by that blue-eyed devil was another strike that kept Jarred from entering Evan's good graces. Although Chelsie was concise in her explanation, she was vague about the incident in the hotel room. She found it difficult to confess to her father that she had sneaked into the room to seduce her drunken husband. That wasn't something she could easily discuss with her father. Had she known what Evan thought Jarred had done, she'd have forgone her embarrassment. She had no idea that Jarred thought he'd betrayed her and that Evan believed his unwanted son-in-law had bedded another woman while Chelsie was lying unconscious.

Although Evan considered Jarred the black sheep of the family, he was more forgiving of Kyle McAlister after Chelsie's explanation. She had informed her father of Kyle's generosity, his penchant for quality horses, and his craving to defeat his rival on the track. Chelsie also confessed that she encouraged Kyle to buy their stolen horses and that it was her fault the squire was laboring under the misconception that the horses were truly his. Chelsie knew her father wanted his prize mare and colt back; that was why she requested that Evan bring the high-bred stud along with him. The silver-gray stallion bore English thoroughbred and Arabian blood, and he had produced his fair share of nationally acclaimed champions. Kyle would be allowed to cross his mares with the

412

thoroughbred without paying any stud fees. He would then have his own line of steeds, sired by Moonraker—one of England's most noted studs.

Once Chelsie finished her account of the past four months, she and Evan proceeded to Kyle's room to clear up all his misconceptions and reassure the squire that he would be compensated when he returned Trumpeter and the brood mare to their rightful owner—the Duke of Chessfield. Kyle grumbled, until Chelsie explained that Moonraker would stand at stud at Easthaven until Daniel sailed to England to begin his studies at Middle Temple.

When both families had offered rounds of apologies, they ambled off to enjoy the goings-on at the fair and to exercise Trumpeter for his upcoming race. While Evan and Doris delighted in comparing the English fair to its colonial counterpart, Kyle was wandering about wishing the race would begin. For months he had thrived on the anticipation of enjoying a victory over his rival. And when Amos appeared to do what he usually did before a race—heckle Kyle no end—Kyle gritted his teeth and prayed he would finally get even. Indeed, Kyle was counting on Chelsie to put wings on Trumpeter's hooves so he could give that ornery Amos Shaw a taste of his own medicine!

Chapter 33

Jarred sighed as he strolled from the courthouse. He looked as bad as he felt. One eye was still partly swollen shut, thanks to Evan's powerful fist, and his jaw was tender. Presenting his case against Cyrus had been torment, and Jarred suffered each time he opened his jaw. But justice had won out, and Cyrus had been sent to prison. Meredith was to appear in court the following week, and Jarred had no doubt that she would be convicted of horse theft, abandoning her master, and attempted murder.

Jarred's consolation was that those who had made Chelsie's life a living hell were to be put behind bars and kept there until they mildewed. Well, at least some of them, he amended. He was still running around loose. But he may as well have been shot and stabbed and tossed in a musty dungeon. Jarred knew he was going to lose that green-eyed leprechaun and would never see his last wish come true. That was to be his private hell. Chelsie would prefer to return to Chessfield with her father. Jarred was as sure of that as he was of his own name. And as much as he wanted Chelsie to stay, he wasn't going to stop her. . . .

"Colonel McAlister?" A young man's voice seeped into Jarred's pensive musings. Extending his hand, the corporal presented the dispatch. "Benjamin Franklin requests your presence in Williamsburg. General Braddock has arrived, and he wishes to confer with you and Colonel Washington before he begins his campaign against Fort Duquesne. Franklin asks that you lead the Maryland militia once again."

Jarred unfolded the message and quickly scanned its contents. If he intended to make the conference with Braddock, he didn't have a minute to spare. That thought had him grumbling irritably.

"I'm sorry this is given on such short notice," the corporal apologized. "I rode to your plantation first and found you gone. It took me more than a day to locate you in Annapolis."

With the young corporal striding behind him, Jarred hurried back to the hotel to leave a note for his father and collect his baggage. Swinging onto his mount Jarred stared at the tents that dotted the fairgrounds. He regretted not having the chance to say goodbye to Chelsie. But giving the matter second consideration, he decided he would be better off if he made an uneventful departure. Seeing her again would only remind him of what he'd lost. Besides, he was never *ever* going to forget that beguiling pixie's face, those dancing green eyes. There was no sense in tormenting himself with her image—one that was marred by the swollen jaw he had inadvertently punched. Jarred carried her picture in his memory, and he always would. He had only to close his eyes and he could reach out and touch that lovely elf. She was there, just beyond reality.

And there she would stay, Jarred thought dispiritedly. There would be miles between them, an ocean, in fact. But that wasn't going to stop Jarred from loving that saucy minx.

It was far better for Jarred to preoccupy himself at the conference than to wallow about Annapolis, watching Chelsie sweep onto the England-bound schooner, taking his heart with her when she went. As Jarred and the corporal rode past the throng of people who were attending the fair, Jarred spied the copper dun colt exercising on the track. On Trumpeter's back, with her silver-blond hair undulating behind her like a flag, was Chelsie.

A rueful smile hovered on Jarred's lips as he watched the spirited elf put her colt through the paces with experienced ease. The colt and his mistress were teeming with energy and spirit. Chelsie was wild and free, and Trumpeter was her winged steed. As always, Chelsie was flying off in the opposite direction and Jarred would never catch her. She had sneaked up on him, and he had fallen in love with her without planning to. By the time Jarred got around to expressing his affection, Chelsie thought he wanted her just because she was a wealthy heiress. And when she followed him to Annapolis to test his fidelity, he had wound up in bed with the very woman who had caused Chelsie grief during her voyage to the colonies. He had added insult to injury and he would never forgive himself.

If the situation had been reversed, Jarred wouldn't have forgiven Chelsie. He had gotten what he deserved, and he was going to have to learn to accept his enormous loss.

As Chelsie disappeared into the crowd on the far side of the track, Jarred focused on the road ahead of him. Even the laughter and gay voices that wafted their way from the fairgrounds didn't lift his sagging spirits. Jarred had never expected to fall in love. Now that he had, he didn't expect to fall out of love any time soon. He had the dismal feeling that scouting for General Braddock wouldn't be distraction enough. It would take a full-scale war to preoccupy him, and even then Jarred wondered if Chelsie would rise like a genie to torment him in the heat of battle.

For God's sake, Jarred mused. He was moping around like a man who'd lost his only friend. Love wasn't all it was cracked up to be. It wasn't a glorious state of suspended existence illuminated by sunshine and rainbows. It was hell, pure and simple. What *might* have been could never be. By the time he returned to Annapolis, Chelsie would be in England, and he would never again peer at that impish smile or fall into the sparkling depths of those emerald eyes . . . except in his tormented dreams. . . .

Chelsie sat upon Trumpeter's back, her fingers clenched around the reins. Although Kyle was hopping up and down in eager anticipation of the race, Chelsie was raw on the inside. She had returned to the hotel to change into her riding clothes, hoping to have a private conversation with Jarred. Instead, she found the message he had left for his father. When she read the note, her legs very nearly folded beneath her. The last thing she expected was for Jarred to go marching off to battle, especially without so much as a good-bye.

Even while Chelsie waited for the discharge of the pistol signaling the beginning of the race, she was distracted by the words Jarred had written to his father. He had informed his family that he had been called to Williamsburg to meet with General Braddock and would serve as an aide in the campaign. Chelsie was horrified to hear Jarred was planning to engage the French and

Indians in Ohio country. But what tore her to pieces, bit by excruciating bit, was Jarred's last farewell—one so impersonal that she nearly burst into tears.

Give my best regards to the duchess. I have posted the bands for the annulment of our marriage. They await only her signature to be made final.
Jarred

Chelsie was crushed, Evan was delighted, and Kyle was sorely disappointed. And if Chelsie hadn't promised Kyle that she would ride in this race for him, she would have . . .

Blinking back tears, Chelsie coiled atop the prancing colt. To be honest, she wasn't sure what she would have done—run after Jarred or away from him. The fact that Jarred had given her up without a fight made her wonder if he thought she was worth keeping as a wife. And this damned war with France wasn't helping matters one whit! What she and Jarred needed was time to evaluate their feelings without outside interference from his family, her family, or the call of duty. But they had been granted no time for privacy, not even a minute!

And just whose fault was that? It was *her* fault. She felt like climbing down and letting Trumpeter tromp all over her, but there wasn't time. She should have gone to Jarred later that night after they apprehended Cyrus and Meredith. But like a fool she had waited for Jarred to come to her, and he hadn't. They had needed to discuss their future together . . . or the lack of it. Now it was too late. Jarred was gone and Chelsie didn't know if he truly wanted her to be there when he returned. Perhaps he loved her, but apparently not enough to make another attempt to see her before he left. He was obviously content to let her return to Chessfield, if that was her wont. What sort of love prompted a man to let his wife go so easily? It certainly didn't sound like the lasting kind Chelsie needed to make her life complete.

Blast it all! Chelsie didn't know what to do or how to proceed from here. She had never been in love before, and she didn't have the faintest notion what the proper procedure should be when the light of her life walked away without so much as a good-bye. Someone needed to write a book which listed the rules for falling in love so that inexperienced novices could follow a few guidelines. Well, Chelsie could write a book on how *not* to fall in love! Because of her stubborn pride and her cynicism, she had lost Jarred. He didn't know how she felt about him, and now it was too late to tell him. . . .

The bark of the starting pistol scattered Chelsie's thoughts. Although she felt as if her throat were full of thorns and her eyes were full of sand, Chelsie concentrated on the race, employing it as a release for her frustrations. When Trumpeter bolted forward, Chelsie lifted her hips, keeping her body poised above him so she wouldn't inhibit his up-and-down movements. She didn't want Trumpeter to waste unnecessary energy lifting her weight while he raced at his swiftest speed.

It was mere seconds before Trumpeter stretched out to take over with a free-flowing, elegant gait. Trumpeter had grown into a tall, handsome creature who possessed phenomenal grace. He moved without wasting a single motion. His sleek coat was smooth, with bold muscles rippling beneath it. He looked every inch the champion thoroughbred who boasted English and Arabian ancestry. After months of careful feeding, training, and grooming, he was a mountain of finely tuned muscles, spirit, and speed. He was lithe and sinewy and lean, and he could run like the wind. . . .

Amos Shaw's thoroughbred was only a half a length behind them, but Chelsie paid no attention to the other horses and riders. She was determined to let the colt set his fastest gait in his own time. And once he reached his stride there was no need to employ the whip as the other riders were doing. The sound of her voice was incentive enough for Trumpeter to give Chelsie all he had. Although Trump was high-strung, he was generous of spirit. For Chelsie he would run until he dropped. For his male trainers he tossed his head and constantly changed his lead. But not today, not with Chelsie on his back. Trumpeter never broke stride. He took to his wings and soared.

The wild, pounding excitement of the run echoed in Trumpeter's ears. He did not possess the herding instinct and never had. He had never been satisfied to cling with other horses and follow the speed they set. He was bred to run, born to lead, trained to fly. And fly he did.

Kyle stood beside Evan Channing and Amos Shaw. By the time

the race was halfway over, Kyle had already lost his voice from screaming encouragements to Chelsie. Evan, caught up in the excitement, was shouting and cheering for his daughter and the copper dun colt. Although Amos Shaw had resorted to contesting the fact that a woman was to ride Trumpeter, the duke threw his weight around and Amos's complaint was quickly overruled by the racing committee. If Chelsie decided she wanted to ride at the meeting, Evan was prone to let her. Even though the duke had no use for Jarred, he did agree with the young lawyer's statement that after all Chelsie had been through, she deserved to have her whims met without resistance. And being the proud father, Evan rooted enthusiastically for his daughter.

As the horses thundered toward the finish line, Amos Shaw cursed profusely. It was no contest, much to his dismay. The copper dun colt had left his competition in his dust, outrunning Amos's prize stallion by a full two lengths. He was rankled to no end that he hadn't been beaten out by a little more than a nose. If he had, he could have harbored the satisfaction of thinking the long-legged Trumpeter had been blessed by a stroke of luck. But the duchess and the colt had won hands down. Amos was forced to shell out a fortune to repay his bet.

"Well, well," Kyle gloated as Amos slapped the money into his hand. "It seems the worm has turned."

Amos gnashed his teeth when Kyle chuckled triumphantly.

"At long last the king of the Annapolis racetrack has been dethroned, and I reign supreme," Kyle goaded Amos, relishing every moment of his victory.

While Evan and Kyle (who had found they had a good many interests in common) were slapping each other on the back and rubbing Amos's nose in his defeat, Abi and Neil McAlister were making their way through the crowd to reach Chelsie.

"Are you all right?" Neil questioned as he pulled Chelsie from Trumpeter's back.

"I'm better than all right," Chelsie insisted, forcing a smile that didn't quite reach her eyes. "All those long hours of training paid off. We won. I imagine Kyle is dancing on air."

Neil's shoulders slumped in relief. "I'm sure he is, but you are not racing that flighty colt for my father anymore. Papa has had his taste of victory, and I will not have you risking your life. . . .

"Oh, Neil, I was riding long before I could walk," Chelsie bit off, casting him a silencing frown.

"Perhaps," Neil mumbled, for the sake of argument. "But you have already endured a rough-and-tumble week. Need I remind you that you are. . . ."

"We are not having this discussion!" Chelsie snapped irritably.

"Did you tell him?" Neil demanded to know.

"Him who?" Chelsie questioned in mock innocence.

"You know perfectly well who we are discussing," Neil grumbled.

"We are discussing no one, because we are not having this conversation," Chelsie reminded him tartly.

Abi, who glanced from one grim face to the other, threw her hands up in frustration. "What is it we are not debating? The two of you are talking in riddles."

"We are referring to Chelsie's—" Neil tried to explain to his bemused wife, but Chelsie's dagger-sharp voice cut him off in midsentence.

"Confound it, Neil, you promised!"

"That was before I read Jarred's message," he snapped back.

"Neil, what on *earth* has gotten into you?" Abi chirped incredulously. She had never heard her mild-mannered husband address anyone in such a harsh tone. And why he was reading Chelsie the riot act was anybody's guess!

Before Neil could respond to his wife's question, Evan and Kyle came bounding toward them like excited children. Chelsie allowed herself to be congratulated and led away from Neil. She did not need to be reminded of the private conversation they had before she followed Jarred to Annapolis to spy on him. Neil had been her confidant, sharing secrets that had gone no farther than their own ears. She had confessed her feelings toward Jarred and begged his silence in this matter, as well as one or two others.

After Jarred had married her, Chelsie had sought out Neil to interrogate him about what had really happened that afternoon when Isaac drugged her. Neil had reluctantly admitted that he had urged Jarred to speak the vows, even while Chelsie was too dazed to know what had transpired. And now, the mild-mannered doctor was trying to influence Chelsie. Although Neil wasn't as overt and forceful as Jarred, he still had an uncanny knack of getting his way in matters. Except in this one, Chelsie reminded herself stubbornly.

The choice was still hers, and she had to do what she considered best without any outside interference. Grappling with that thought, Chelsie glanced over her shoulder to see Neil standing in the same spot, his arms crossed over his chest, his feet askance. The expression on his refined features was worth a thousand words, none of which Chelsie wanted to hear. Eli had ambled up beside Neil and was staring at her with that same probing expression that made her uncomfortable. She knew what both men expected her to do and why.

Refusing to be influenced by Neil and Eli's unspoken requests, Chelsie focused straight ahead and nodded graciously when Kyle and her father plied her with praise. Neil and Eli were not going to torment her, Chelsie vowed. She had seen to it that Neil was able to marry the light and love of his life and her thanks was his silence. And he had better not interfere! He owed her a debt, and she was determined that he pay it by keeping a tight rein on his tongue.

Chelsie had her fill of circumstances beyond her control. Where she decided to go from here was her business. And for once, Jarred wasn't around to influence her, either. He had left without saying good-bye, granting her freedom. She thought she meant something to him, but obviously she didn't mean enough for him to fight for her. Since she had freed him from jail, he had been distant and remote, treating her with nothing more than polite respect. Was that the behavior of a man who was truly in love? Had she truly become just another obligation in his life? And now that her father had arrived, had Jarred decided to give up his responsibility for her? Maybe she had been right all along. Maybe Jarred had mistaken love for obligation and Evan's arrival had given him the chance to gracefully bow out.

She was so confused by Jarred's actions and his absence that she honestly didn't know what to think. Chelsie needed time to analyze her feelings, to sort them out one at a time. And that was what she was going to do — find someplace to sit herself down and evaluate her wants and needs. Maybe she had expected too much from Jarred. At the first opportunity to return to the wilderness, he was gone. Maybe she was being too selfish in expecting more than a casual note of good-bye. *Give my best to the duchess,* he had said. Chelsie let out her breath in an exasperated rush. If Jarred cared as much as he said he did, he would have left her a private letter . . . wouldn't he?

Frustrated, Chelsie aimed herself toward the hotel, but she had one hell of a time outrunning Jarred's memory. She couldn't forget all they had shared—the storm and the splendor. And she couldn't stop fretting about his upcoming battle with the French. There was trouble brewing on the western outposts of civilization, and Chelsie feared Jarred would soon be in the thick of things. And she was absolutely right.

While Evan Channing was making plans to sail home with his daughter in tow, Neil and Eli were on hand to plead with Chelsie to stay. Quite honestly, Chelsie didn't know whether to stay or go. All she had to do was put her signature on the annulment papers, as her father insisted she do, and her marriage would be over.

Aye, the marriage would be over, Chelsie mused as she wrestled with her dilemma. But signing her name to a piece of paper wouldn't make the memories go away. She would live with them forever. But if she stayed, would Jarred be eager to see her if and when he returned from the wilderness?

Chelsie was so frustrated, she wanted to pull out her hair strand by strand. On one hand, her father was listing all the reasons why she should return to Chessfield, and all his arguments made sense. And on the other, Neil kept reminding her of her obligation to marriage vows she didn't remember taking. She knew why Neil wanted her to stay, but it was still her life and she had to live it her own way. If only Jarred had. . . .

Chelsie squelched the whimsical thought. She had always claimed she was her own woman. Now she was going to have to make her own decision, difficult though it was.

Chapter 34

Staring bleakly ahead, Jarred hunkered down on his haunches. Although it was unseasonably hot and swarms of mosquitoes constantly harassed him, Jarred found it necessary to ward off the chill of doom that formed icicles on his spine. After what seemed forever, the regular army and colonial militias had reached the bend of the Monongahela River. During the months that had inched along at a snail's pace, Jarred had repeatedly heard Chelsie's foreboding speculation ringing in his ears.

The stout, sixty-year-old General Edward Braddock was polished brass who went strictly by the military regulation handbook, just as Chelsie predicted he would. For all Braddock's pomp and circumstance, he was out of his element in the backwoods. The general had dismissed half the colonial militia because he considered them undisciplined and unruly. He had discarded all but ten of their Indian allies who had agreed to scout and fight with the English.

Jarred and George Washington advised Braddock to rely on the techniques employed by the Virginia and Maryland militias when they confronted the French and Indians at Great Meadows. But Braddock had quickly replied, "These savages may indeed be a formidable enemy to your raw American militia, but upon the King's regular and disciplined troops, it is impossible they should make any impression."

And clinging to that arrogant attitude, Braddock had proceeded to the battlefield in the same custom he employed when engaging in European wars—in a royal coach. Finally, when the slow-moving procession was within a hundred miles of Fort Duquesne,

Braddock realized his army was the product of too much excess baggage — considering the barely passable roads and the tangled timbers that slowed their progress. The staunch general called out fifteen hundred of his best men and tossed only the most necessary equipment on horses and wagons.

On a roadbed that was only twelve feet wide, he had his soldiers marching four abreast and the columns of infantrymen stretched out four miles behind him. Like a brightly colored snake winding its way into the wilderness, the British army trod over piles of leaves, wound around insurmountable hills, crawled over perilous ridges and plodded through muddy gorges.

Grumbling, Jarred slapped away one of the oversized mosquitoes that was trying to make a meal of him. Wearily, he glanced over the upreaching flames of the campfire to stare at the grave-faced George Washington, who looked as dispirited as Jarred felt.

"We could lay siege to the fort and anticipate victory if the general would lower himself to fighting like the Indians," Jarred muttered quietly. "I have the inescapable feeling this campaign is on a collision course with catastrophe."

George nodded in grim agreement. "The scouting reports counted but eight hundred Frenchmen at the garrison and an additional eight hundred warriors camped beside it. If we prepared a sneak attack, our chances would greatly increase."

"I think the general expected the French to be intimidated by his flashy army, but they have no intention of retreating," Jarred sighed before lifting a cup of coffee to his lips. "Come this time tomorrow, I fear we are going to have a bloodbath on our hands. But Braddock still plans to make a parade of it even when I advised him to reconsider his strategy."

"I voiced the same reservations to him this afternoon," George muttered. "I met with no more luck at changing his mind than you did."

By the next morning, Jarred's dismal prediction proved correct. Marching to the beat of drums and fifes that announced their approach, the well-drilled army swung down the riverbank. Red coats, blue coats, and brass-peaked helmets splashed through the water. Jarred cursed the pageantry of war and sorely wished

424

Braddock would have taken to the woods to fight Indian-style . . . but no such luck.

Focusing intently on his surroundings, Jarred felt a gloomy anticipation. He glanced speculatively ahead at the area where the underbrush thinned and the woods opened to form a natural path to Fort Duquesne. And suddenly the sound of impending doom echoed in his ears. War whoops erupted from the forest that flanked the narrow meadow.

The leading regiment of infantrymen formed their traditional line of battle across the improvised trail. The first rank knelt to fire, and the band of whooping Indians scattered. The thunder of concentrated fire staggered the French and their Indian allies. For one brief moment Jarred thought the British regulars might enjoy victory. But when the French and Indians darted into the forest like wild animals returning to their natural habitat, Jarred's hopes were dashed. The English regulars became rattled. There was no enemy to charge nor targets at which to fire. There was only the howling war whoops that seemed to come from all directions at once.

The first flank became entangled with the second flank that was still marching in military procession. Jarred cursed sourly when the unseen enemy opened fire from the trees and underbrush. The English countered, but hit nothing. They tried to form battle lines as they had been taught to do, but they had become sitting ducks for the French and Indians. Suddenly the disciplined army that Braddock so highly praised became a milling mob that clung together in confusion.

Sweeping onto the side of his steed, using the mount as his shield, Jarred wove through the crowd of confused soldiers to reach Braddock, who sat like a proud, invincible warrior on his fourth steed. (The first three had been shot out from under him.)

"Permission to take my militia and infiltrate the woods," Jarred bellowed over the whistling bullets and piercing cries of the wounded. "Your men are being slaughtered!"

Jarred had just voiced the request when Washington rode up to plead with the general to let his men fight Indian-style.

"Permission denied," Braddock growled. "We will fight as we have always fought — in close order."

Jarred's frustrated gaze met George's, but neither of them had

425

time to make another plea. Braddock, seeing some of his regulars breaking for cover behind the trees, charged furiously after them.

"Cowards!" Braddock yelled in outrage. Riding up beside the fleeing soldiers, Braddock whacked them with the flat of his sword.

A wordless scowl erupted from Jarred's lips as he watched the general berate his men for following their instincts of self-preservation. If Braddock had dispensed with his military handbook and allowed his men to take the battle into the woods, they might have saved the day. But after four grueling hours of useless slaughter, Braddock still refused to admit that his military strategy in this situation was worthless.

When Braddock's fourth mount fell beneath him, he shouted to one of his men to fetch him another. Just as he swung into the saddle, a bullet pierced his lung. Jarred and George sprang from their horses to assist the fallen general and ordered the drums to beat in retreat. The regulars, seeing their general buckle, threw down their weapons and darted toward the river to avoid the Indians who swarmed from their hiding places in the forest to scalp and plunder.

When Jarred and George had placed Braddock in a cart, he glanced up at his aides through pained eyes. "Had I been governed by your advice, we never should have come to this," he breathed weakly. A bitter smile traced his ashen lips. "Who would have thought I would be struck down in such a place as this?"

While Jarred and George kept their militias in the forest to provide cover for the retreating regulars, Braddock was carted away from the bloody battle. Pitifully, Braddock glanced at his men who trudged defeatedly behind his cart. Of the fifteen hundred regulars he had brought with him to the valley of doom, only five hundred had survived.

"Who would have thought it?" he kept muttering over and over again as he bumped along in the procession of humiliating retreat.

For two days, the general lay in his cart, regretting his foolish mistake. And when he breathed his last breath, Jarred and George buried him in the middle of the trail so the tramping soldiers and wagon wheels would cover his grave, preventing the marauding

Indians from dishonoring the general a second time.

Jarred could not remember experiencing such deep regret in all his life. He had been helpless to stop an expedition that was doomed to disaster. And he had gone into a futile battle knowing he had already lost that special part of him that time and distance could not erase. Chelsie . . . Her name echoed through his mind, triggering memories of a love that had come and gone.

He was suffering all the torments of hell, and the British colonists would have to tolerate the intrusion of the French and Indians who terrorized the frontier. Only when Parliament and the colonial Grand Council declared full-scale war against the French would the colonists be able to retaliate with any hope of success.

Jarred detested the defeat they had endured. He wasn't accustomed to it, and it left him frustrated. It was the same sort of frustration Chelsie must have felt, he imagined. She had found herself dragged off to unfamiliar surroundings and dictated to by others who would not listen to her pleas. Jarred had spent months enduring the same upheaval of emotion she had been subjected to. At long last he could fully sympathize with what she had endured and experienced.

Grimacing, Jarred squeezed his eyes shut. He had handled Chelsie as poorly as Braddock had managed the Battle of the Wilderness. And though he had survived, he had died a little inside when other men fell beside him. In retrospect, Jarred could understand why Chelsie had reacted to him the way she had. She had been fighting, just as Jarred had been in battle. It had been a maddening experience. God, if only Chelsie was there waiting at Easthaven when he returned, if only he hadn't betrayed her by bedding Meredith while he was besotted with rum . . .

Lord, how he loathed his indiscretion. Chelsie meant the world to him and he had lost every chance of winning her heart and her respect.

Through the weeks that followed, Jarred tried to rally from the depths of depression. But it was difficult after the ordeal he had endured. Defeat was hard to accept, especially when there was no one to turn to for consolation, no one awaiting him with open arms. Oh, how he needed to be loved and cherished just now. How he ached to return home to gaze into those twinkling emerald eyes that sparkled with living fire. How he longed to enfold that high-spirited leprechaun in his arms, to let her breathe the life back into him.

Jarred found himself needing Chelsie in ways he had never needed her before. Now he knew the full extent of his love for her. When the smell of death fogged his senses in battle, her image had been his lifeline, his inspiration. Even though he had lost her, he vowed to survive to see her again—someday, somewhere, somehow.

"I love you, little leprechaun, even if you cannot grant me love's wish," Jarred whispered to the sparkling stars that graced the black velvet sky. "You are a part of me that time and trouble can never erase. Having survived this last raging battle, having lost you, makes me realize just how precious your memory is to me. And these same stars that glow like beacons in the night are watching over you from across the sea. Each one is a treasured memory of the moments I spent with you. They will shine on until the end of time as a symbol of my affection for you. . . ."

Although Jarred hadn't spoken the words to the blond-haired enchantress who held the key to his heart, he felt better having vocalized his innermost thoughts. And if he was asked to become an ambassador to England to consult with the English prime minister, he would detour to Chessfield, even if he wasn't particularly welcome there. He had to see Chelsie again, if only from a distance, to ensure that she was well. . . .

Heaving a heavy-hearted sigh, Jarred shifted uncomfortably upon his steed. What a fool he had been. He hadn't known just how priceless Chelsie was to him until he was forced to do without her. Now she was gone and his world seemed bleak and dreary. God, if only he could relive those months he had spent fighting his attraction for Chelsie! He wouldn't have wasted his time denying his affection. He would have held her in his arms, knowing that his true happiness was in the horizon of her emerald green eyes and the spectrum of her radiant smile . . .

Chapter 35

To Jarred and George Washington's surprise they reached Williamsburg to give their report to Governor Dinwiddie and found themselves laden down with medals of honor. The dispatchers who had preceded them to Virginia had boasted of their bravery under fire, of their attempt to save the day and provide cover for the British regulars who were forced to retreat. Suddenly they were famous for their acts of valor. They were labeled as "charmed" because they had both managed to dodge a dozen bullets. Several bullets had passed through their clothes without embedding themselves in flesh. Jarred didn't consider himself charmed, only swift of foot. He decided it just wasn't his time to die. He was to live and go on enduring the torment of losing the only woman he had ever loved.

The colonists designated the battle as Braddock's defeat, not that of the militias who could have taught the British a thing or two about warfare in the wilderness if their staunch general had listened to the voices of experience. Being hailed as a hero lifted Jarred's low spirits, but the love and respect he really wanted could come from only one woman. Jarred would gladly have sacrificed his medals if he could have wished himself to England to catch a glimpse of the green-eyed leprechaun who had captured his heart and had stolen the sunshine from his days.

Leaving Washington in Williamsburg, Jarred aimed himself toward Annapolis to give his report and recommendations to the governor and the Assembly. Again his heroic deeds preceded him and he found himself the toast of the town. When he completed his obligations in Annapolis, Jarred pointed himself toward Easthaven and then inwardly groaned: he could imagine the avalanche of paperwork that awaited him. He had left Grant to oversee the workings of the four plantations and his young brother capably filled his shoes—except in one aspect. Grant had no desire to log bills-of-sale and receipts into the business ledgers. Each time Jarred returned, he was forced to spend endless hours shuffling through mounds of tedious paperwork. . . .

His thoughts dispersed when he rode upon the rise of ground to view the serene surroundings of Easthaven. It was Sunday morning and all was quiet. The world lay at peace, and Jarred breathed a contented sigh. He had heard enough pistols and booming cannons to last him a lifetime.

His keen blue eyes drifted to the front door of the mansion. If only Chelsie would breeze onto the porch to welcome him, his homecoming would be complete! But she wasn't there. Jarred was met with silence as he nudged his mount along the path.

Before he could grasp the latch and let himself in, Neil swung open the door to greet him with a beaming smile. And suddenly Jarred found himself the recipient of a bear hug. Neil had never been one to openly display affection. Apparently his marriage to Abi had changed him considerably. Jarred nearly had the stuffing squeezed out of him by his older brother.

When Neil finally let go, Jarred was assaulted by servants who congratulated him on his valiant deeds in battle, but that was where the glowing accolades ceased. The rest of the family was nowhere to be seen.

Accepting a warm cup of tea, Jarred plunked down on the sofa and cast Neil a curious glance. "Why aren't you at church with the rest of the family?" he questioned.

A pleased smile pursed Neil's lips as he sipped his steaming tea. "I was needed at home. Abi is enduring the first stages of labor. And you should be an uncle before the day is out."

Jarred smiled for the first time in months. "I'm sure Papa is delighted beyond words," he chuckled.

"Aye," Neil concurred. "Suddenly he has found everything going his way. This morning he dashed off to church in anticipation of winning another race against Amos after prayer meeting."

A muddled frown knitted Jarred's brow and Neil snickered at his bemused expression. "Ah, I forgot—you have been out of

430

touch with the family for ten months. Chelsie rode Trumpeter to victory at the meeting last spring, and Papa has been floating on a cloud since his first monumental victory on the Annapolis track.

"The Duke of Chessfield took an immediate liking to Papa after all their misunderstandings were resolved. Since Papa was as avid a fan of racing as the duke, he decided to leave Trumpeter in Maryland when he sailed home. The duke claimed he had never seen a man enjoy victory as much as Kyle McAlister. Besides, he didn't relish dragging that contrary horse back on board ship since the colt has such distaste for boarding and unloading from schooners. These days Trumpeter is referred to as the king of the colonial turf. He is transported to races in a wagon with his own padded stall and he has finally permitted a male jockey to ride upon his back during the races."

"I'm sure Papa will be so proud of his winnings that I will hear of nothing else for a week," Jarred groaned.

"I'm sure you will," Neil agreed. His expression sobered. "But racing helped Papa cope when he was hounded by the fear that he would never see you again. It was a long, agonizing wait before he finally received word about you." Neil sank back in his chair to take another sip of tea. "The house seemed empty without you and Daniel around. Our little brother accepted the duke's invitation to reside at Chessfield while studying at Middle Temple. And Papa desperately needed a distraction while you were off to battle and his youngest offspring was studying in England."

Ah, but Daniel was the lucky one, Jarred mused, staring into his cup. Young Daniel could feast his eyes on Chelsie whenever it met his whim. He appreciated the fact that Neil had only made one reference to Chelsie since he began filling Jarred in on what had transpired during the ten months he was away. Although Jarred wanted to know everything Neil could tell him about the emerald-eyed nymph, he hesitated to ask. Jarred was still raw on the inside and lonely as hell. Chelsie's name and her beguiling vision constantly gnawed at the empty pit of his belly.

Had Chelsie asked Neil to say good-bye for her? Had she cared that he was tramping around in the backwoods, dodging French bullets and Indian spears? The fear that Chelsie hadn't mentioned Jarred at all prevented him from posing questions Neil would have to tactfully answer, making both of them uncomfortable.

"Neil! Abi is calling for you," one of the servants summoned from the top of the staircase.

"If you will excuse me, I had better console my wife," Neil commented as he unfolded himself from the chair. "Abi doesn't withstand pain as well as . . ." His voice trailed off and he broke into a smile. "Let's just say I have had far better patients than my own wife."

When Neil strode away, Jarred gulped down his tea and ambled into the hall to request a bath. Heaving a melancholy sigh, he trudged up the steps to his room. His homecoming should have been enough to brighten his spirits, but it wasn't. He hadn't enjoyed a pleasant day or a happy thought since he'd ridden away from Annapolis ten months ago. The sun had eclipsed when the duke took Chelsie away from him. . . .

The rustle of skirts on the landing caused Jarred to force a smile and uplift his head to greet whichever servant stood before him. His heavy heart leapt in disbelief when the bewitching face from his dreams materialized before him. There, looking more lovely than ever, was Chelsie. She reminded him of a luscious lemon drop when she was garbed in that exquisite yellow velvet gown. Her long blond hair was swirled atop her head, and wispy curls brushed against her forehead and temples.

Had he died during his climb up the steps? He had somehow wound up in heaven. Chelsie couldn't be at Easthaven. Why would she be?

God had labored long and lovingly over this handsome face, Chelsie mused as she grasped the banister before her knees buckled beneath her. Although Jarred looked thinner and his features were tired and drawn, he was still the most attractive, dynamic man she had ever met. He was garbed in buckskin clothes that fit his muscular physique like a second skin. There was something arousing about the way his raven hair swept recklessly across his forehead, about the rugged clothes that complemented the appearance, temperament, and personality of this lion of a man. Chelsie could have spent the day standing there staring at him. Indeed, if Neil had told her Jarred had arrived, she wouldn't have wasted a second in seeking him out, even if he didn't care if she had awaited his return.

For several moments they simply peered at one another, resisting

432

the urge to fly into each other's arms, wondering if the doubts and misconceptions that drove wedges between them still clouded one another's mind. Their eyes remained locked, and the eternal spark that time couldn't dim or smother leaped between them.

Jarred could endure no more. Even if he wasn't welcome in Chelsie's arms, he needed her in his. He cast pride and doubt aside and walked deliberately toward her. He needed to wrap this curvaceous sprite in his embrace and hold her for all the times he had wanted to love her and couldn't.

All it took was Jarred's initial step toward her. Chelsie was set to flight by her own wild needs. She was in Jarred's sinewy arms in less than a heartbeat. They clung together like two long-lost lovers who had been separated throughout eternity.

"God, I've missed you," Jarred breathed as he sought out her inviting lips.

Like a starving man he devoured her, drowning in the intoxicating taste of her kiss. And Chelsie responded without an ounce of feminine reserve. The musky fragrance of Jarred's cologne fogged her senses. The feel of his brawny arms encircling her provoked sensations that had tormented her for months. Being meshed against his muscled contours kindled flames of gone but not forgotten memories. They were all lying dormant, waiting to erupt at first touch. Emotion boiled forth, putting tears in Chelsie's eyes, sending a raft of goosebumps racing over her tingling flesh.

Chelsie reached up on tiptoe. Her trembling hand limned the craggy features that she feared she would never see again. Kissing and touching him wasn't enough, would never be enough, not ever again. She was only whole and alive when Jarred was a living, breathing part of her. The thought provoked her to press closer, reveling in the feel of his masculine flesh moving familiarly against her.

The creak of the door didn't break the distracted couple apart, so Neil relied upon the technique of loudly clearing his throat. Finally, Jarred and Chelsie broke their embrace long enough to glance in Neil's direction.

"I *wondered* how long it would take for you to find each other," he snickered as he propped himself against the wall and crossed his arms and legs in front of him. "I'll have you know I needled this stubborn duchess for two long weeks before she was to set sail for

Chessfield with Daniel and the duke. In fact, she was packed and standing on the deck of the schooner before she finally came to her senses. Her father put up a terrible fuss, but Chelsie informed him that she had to see you when you returned, that she could not get on with the rest of her life until she did."

Curiously, Jarred peered down into the enormous green eyes that rippled like dew-covered grass waving in the breeze. "Why did you stay, Chel?" he murmured, his voice wobbling with an overflow of emotion. "I didn't think you would ever want to see me again."

"Not want to see you?" she parroted, then giggled giddily as she threw her arms around him. "That was what ultimately stopped me from sailing to England. The thought of never seeing you again outweighed all my reasons for going, even if you weren't particularly pleased to find me here when you returned."

"Not pleased?" Jarred croaked in astonishment. "I never wanted you to leave. *I love you.* I always have. But after what I did in Annapolis, I didn't think you could ever forgive me, much less love me. I couldn't ask you to wait for me after what happened."

Neither Jarred nor Chelsie heard Neil slip back into his room to comfort Abi. They were so intent on what each other was saying that nothing else fazed them.

A puzzled frown puckered Chelsie's brow. "What you did? You did nothing that needed my forgiveness. Indeed, the very fact that you *didn't* was proof enough for me. But then you left without a word, leaving me to sign the annulment papers. I thought you had decided what we felt for each other wasn't worth fighting for, that it wasn't meant to last."

Jarred stared at her as if she had grapevines growing out her ears. "You didn't care that Meredith wound up in my bed while I was too drunk to know what I was doing?" he chirped incredulously.

Now it was Chelsie's turn to peer at Jarred. "What makes you think you bedded Meredith?"

"She said so," Jarred muttered.

And all of a sudden Chelsie understood why Jarred had refused to glance in her direction that night they pursued Cyrus and Meredith, why he hadn't come to say good-bye. He was hounded by guilt and he thought she wanted him out of her life.

" 'Twas *I* who followed you to your room and to your bed that night," she informed him. "Meredith *lied* to you. Had I known, I would have set the matter straight. Meredith Holt never told the truth in her life when a lie would suffice."

The light of understanding dawned in Jarred's eyes. No wonder he had felt as if he had made love to the only woman who had made passion a rare, unique experience that encompassed all his emotions. It had been Chelsie. He hadn't fantasized, after all! And thank the Lord he didn't have to carry that frustrating guilt around with him the rest of his life!

"Meredith swore to both your father and to me that I had seduced her. She spat out the lie after I had knocked you senseless," Jarred grumbled resentfully.

"So that is why Papa holds this grudge against you," Chelsie surmised. "He kept insisting that I could never trust you. He insisted I sign the annulment papers, but I wouldn't, because . . ." Her voice trailed off. She decided it wasn't the time to delve into that particular matter. When her gaze dropped to monitor her wandering fingertips, ones that toyed with the lacings on his buckskin shirt, Chelsie became distracted. Lord, she would love to spear her hand inside those garments to touch his steel-honed muscles and his hirsute flesh.

"When you drew up those annulment papers and left them for me to sign, I thought you didn't care enough to give our love another chance. I remained at Easthaven, awaiting your return so you could answer that question for me," she murmured, afraid to meet his gaze.

A rakish smile pursed Jarred's lips as he cupped her chin in his hand, lifting her eyes to his. He couldn't wait to get Chelsie alone in his room. Standing here touching her was driving him to distraction. He was on a slow burn, and nothing could extinguish this arousing flame until he had made wild, passionate love to her at least a dozen times before the day was out.

"If you don't know the answer to that question, duchess, I suppose I will just have to show you how much you mean to me, how long I have waited to have you by my side . . ." His voice dropped to a low, seductive growl. "And in my bed. When I finally get you there, I may never let you up again."

The front door couldn't have swung open at a more inopportune moment. Although Jarred was pleased to see his father and Aunt Rebecca again, he wasn't at all thrilled to see the burly, red-headed gorilla who towered behind Kyle.

Kyle beamed with pleasure. First he had trotted off to church and then handed Amos another sound defeat in their after-prayer-meeting horserace. And lo and behold, on his way home he had met the duke, Daniel, and Doris Wycoff, who had just arrived from England to pay the McAlisters a long-awaited visit. And there on the landing stood his second son, cuddling Chelsie to him as if he never meant to let her go.

Kyle wasn't the only one who took note of the couple who clung to each other. There had been dozens of times these past months when Evan swore his daughter had made a crucial mistake by remaining at Easthaven. He had returned to check on her once since he reluctantly left her in the colonies. Again he had urged her to sail to Chessfield with him, but Chelsie wouldn't budge from her spot.

And now Evan knew why. He had never seen such an adoring expression on Chelsie's animated features, nor a more tender, loving expression on Jarred's. Evan could almost feel the aura that hovered about his daughter and his unwanted son-in-law. Jarred's indiscretions ten months ago seemed a dim memory in the glow of affection that lit up both their faces.

A nostalgic smile pursed Evan's lips. Suddenly he could see himself as he had been twenty-five years earlier. He had peered down at Chelsie's mother with the same rapt attention. He never thought Cheslie would find herself hopelessly enamored, since she had been so fickle and particular about the endless rabble of beaux who had courted her.

But from all indication, here stood the man who had tamed Chelsie's restless heart—this raven-haired rogue who had made a name for himself in the Battle of the Wilderness. Aye, Evan had heard the reports in Annapolis. General Braddock had failed his colonial cousins, but George Washington and Jarred McAlister had defied death in the throes of battle and led their troops from the valley of doom. They had proved more about themselves in defeat than the French had proved in victory.

Suddenly Evan's head jerked up. He had been so lost in thought that he had neglected the foremost reason for making this special

436

trip to Easthaven. "Where is he?" Evan demanded as he pushed his way to the front of the congregation that stood at the foot of the steps.

The question put a bemused frown on Jarred's rugged features. Puzzled, he watched Evan fly up the steps with Doris Wycoff bounding sprightly behind him. When Jarred glanced at Chelsie she was smiling cryptically at him.

"In here, Papa," Chelsie murmured as she pivoted to press a greeting kiss to the duke's cheek and then led him to her room.

Curious, Jarred followed in Chelsie's wake. When she eased open the door, Jarred's jaw fell off its hinges and he half-collapsed against the wall. Immobilized by astonishment, Jarred watched the oversized duke tiptoe across the room to peer down into the cradle. Wide blue eyes blinked once and then twice as Jarred swiveled his head around to meet Chelsie's proud smile.

"His name is Lucas Evan Kyle McAlister." Chelsie's loving gaze remained fixed on Jarred's stupefied expression. "He is two months old and the image of his father."

"But he is showing signs of developing his mother's green eyes, even if he has a thick crop of dark hair," Kyle contended as he edged up beside the duke.

Jarred was jostled to his senses when he realized he was the father of the sleeping child Evan had just scooped up into his brawny arms. Before the duke could cuddle his grandson close, Jarred stole his son away. Lucas opened his droopy eyes and Jarred caught his breath when the sunlight sparkled in his son's bluish-green eyes. There was something in Lucas's cherubic face that gave a fierce tug on Jarred's heartstrings.

Even the grim battle Jarred had endured in the wilderness hadn't brought tears to his eyes. But meeting the son he didn't even know he had for the very first time certainly did! A mist of sentimentality clouded his gaze as he admired his son, who bore his mother's mystical quality.

"You are the evidence of your father's everlasting love for your mother," he whispered as he pressed a kiss to Lucas's forehead. "And you will grow up, basking in the warmth of our love. . . ." His shimmering stare shifted to the duke, whose penetrating gaze was focused on his son-in-law. "Make no mistake, sir." Jarred's voice wavered with heartfelt emotion. "I love your daughter more than life itself. I did not betray her as you believe. 'Twas Meredith's spiteful lie that put us at odds. There has been no one else, and there will never be."

For the first time ever, Evan stared at Jarred without the slightest hint of resentment. "I asked no more than that you love her as dearly as I do," he murmured with genuine sincerity. "And if you could see your way clear to visit me on occasion, I would like to show you around *our* property."

Shaking off his sentimentality, Evan retrieved the infant from Jarred's arms. "You have the rest of your life to fuss over my grandson. I have to settle for semiannual visits." The rocking chair groaned when Evan stuffed his gigantic body into it. "Now, if you will excuse us, Lucas and I would like to become better acquainted."

As the congregation filed into the hall, Neil approached Chelsie before Jarred could get her all to himself. "Abi requests your presence, for moral support," he informed his sister-in-law. "The baby is going to arrive sooner than I expected."

His remark sent everyone rushing off to make preparations for the arrival of Lucas's new cousin. Jarred was abandoned in the hall. He ached to have a few moments of privacy with Chelsie, but he was forced to put his raging desires on hold. Well, if his wife was to be preoccupied until she became an aunt, the duke was going to have to compromise and allow Jarred the chance to cuddle his son.

Drawing himself up, Jarred breezed into the nursery, where Evan sat scrunched up in the rocking chair. "I need to hold my *son*," Jarred declared.

Evan cuddled Lucas protectively against him. "And I need to hold my *grandson*," he grumbled acrimoniously. "You'll get your turn later."

"A compromise is in order," Jarred announced. Retrieving Lucas from his grandfather's sinewy arms, Jarred strode over to place the infant in the middle of Chelsie's bed. While Jarred clasped one of Lucas's tiny hands in his own, Evan plunked down on the opposite side of the bed to enfold the other. Together the two men peered down at the lively bundle of energy who exercised his legs and cooed conversationally with the two men who hovered over him.

"Isn't he the cutest baby you ever laid eyes on?" Jarred questioned with fatherly pride.

"Aye," Evan agreed. "Though Chelsie was a sight to behold when she was this size."

"She still is," Jarred insisted, flashing Evan a wry smile. "And I'm crazy about her."

Evan nodded and chuckled. "I'm just beginning to realize that. Luckily, Chelsie married a man who can keep up with her. She is and always will be a handful." His gaze locked with Jarred's. "My daughter has married well, and I am satisfied."

Jarred spoke not a word. He simply smiled at his father-in-law. The dissension between them dissolved into mutual admiration. Contentedly both men played with Lucas until he was so exhausted from all the attention he received that he fell fast asleep, much to his father and grandfather's chagrin. . . .

Chapter 36

My, what a busy day it had been! Jarred found himself dragged from one conversation into another. He was encouraged to relate the accounts of the expedition in the West and his speculations about another confrontation with the French. He then listened to Kyle spout off about his victories on various tracks in Maryland, Virginia, and New York. Grant assumed control of the conversation to rattle off an extensive list of duties that needed Jarred's attention and Daniel had oodles of stories to convey about his life in England. Not to be left out, Evan passed on information he had received in Parliament.

Upstairs, Neil monitored his wife's progress. Chelsie remained at Abi's side, intermittently taking time out to feed and tend Lucas. The only problem arose in the never-ending power struggle between Rebecca and Doris. Rebecca saw her chance to become the social director of this houseful of guests. And Doris (who was accustomed to ruling her own roost) had her own ideas about how these family gatherings should be handled. Each time Doris expelled a disgusted sniff and declared, "Well, that is the way it is done in England," Rebecca put out her chin and promptly replied. "This is the way it is done in the colonies!" The two women couldn't even arrange the silverware on the table to suit each other.

By mid-afternoon, Jarred was so restless he couldn't sit still. He had trotted up and down the steps a dozen times to admire his son and catch a glimpse of the shapely nymph who remained just out of his reach and was as busy as a bumblebee. But each time they crossed paths, Jarred flung Chelsie a rakish smile that held intimate promises of what she could expect when they were finally

440

granted a few minutes of privacy. And Chelsie countered with seductive grins that made Jarred ache up to his eyebrows.

Early in the evening the family swarmed upstairs to hover around the newest addition to the McAlister family. The father-doctor was bursting with pride and his wife beamed with contentment as they presented Elissa McAlister to her two grandfathers. Amos Shaw was on hand to fight over the first rights to hold the precious little girl who carried a strong family resemblance to her two-month-old cousin Lucas.

While Chelsie was standing there admiring Elissa, Jarred grasped her hand and drew her away from the clump of eager onlookers. Chelsie didn't put up an ounce of resistance. She had waited all day to have Jarred all to herself. Hand-in-hand, they ambled down the hall to Jarred's room and quietly locked the door behind them.

Chelsie had just emitted a relieved sigh when Jarred pulled her into his arms to kiss the last remaining breath out of her. And Chelsie reveled in the feel of his encircling arms and those warm, sensuous lips. Lord, it seemed it had been forever since she had inhaled Jarred's masculine fragrance and snuggled against his hard, muscular contours.

"I can see right now that we are going to have to take up residence at one of the other plantations," Jarred whispered when he finally came up for air. "If we stay here, I'll never have you to myself."

Her thick lashes swept up and she peeked up at him with those sparkling emerald eyes that could so easily entrance him. "And now that we are alone, what do you want to do, my dear husband?" she purred provocatively.

"Hundreds of things that have nothing to do with conversation, but everything to do with expressing my love for you," Jarred growled hungrily, and then proceeded to help Chelsie from the gown that deprived him of seeing what he longed to devour.

As he peeled away the yellow velvet dress, his eyes swam possessively over every inch of her exposed flesh. Like a man who was viewing a portrait that had been hidden from his sight for years, Jarred stood back to absorb the visual image of exquisite loveliness.

"Do you know how very beautiful you are?" he breathed in awe.

Chelsie sashayed toward him wearing nothing but an elfin smile. Impatiently she tugged at the shirt that concealed what she yearned to see and touch. "Do you know how terribly overdressed you are? I cannot tell you how long I have waited to do this," she whispered, her tone thick with unfulfilled passion. "I've wanted to make love to you every night while you were away. And tonight I fully intend to compensate for the times I've wanted to reach for you and you weren't there. . . ."

That did it! Jarred had been doing a superb job of holding the reins on his raging passion. In fact, he deserved another medal for his self-restraint . . . until Chelsie tantalized him with her words and her appreciative stares. She made him feel every inch a man — a man who was cherished, loved, and desired. There was no containing the wildfire that sizzled through his blood when Chelsie's exploring fingertips skied down his shoulder and ribs to trace the band of his breeches.

Like a pouncing cougar, Jarred uplifted her into his arms and pivoted toward the bed. But he was too busy thinking about what he was going to do when he got there to pay attention to getting there. With a startled squawk, he tripped over the discarded clothes and boots that lay before him like an obstacle course. Unceremoniously he fell upon the plush fur rug that lay halfway between the bed and the door.

To prevent injuring Chelsie, Jarred braced his left arm and cushioned her fall. A pained groan erupted from his lips when his weight and Chelsie's collapsed on his arm — the same arm they had fallen upon when they'd crashed into the shrubs with the broken trellis on them.

"Jarred, are you hurt?" Chelsie questioned, her worried expression showing the extent of her concern. "Shall I summon Neil?"

"Don't do that, for God's sake!" Jarred grimaced as he levered himself up on his good elbow. "I can't wait another hour while my brother examines me. I'll have burned myself into a pile of frustrated ashes by then!"

"Then perhaps I can kiss the pain away," she suggested throatily.

And she did. When Chelsie's butterfly kisses floated over his flesh and her inquiring hands sought out each ultrasensitive point, Jarred felt no pain whatsoever. *Aches,* yes, but no pain. His male body burned from the spell of splendor Chelsie cast upon him.

Jarred didn't think it possible to forget how potent this green-eyed leprechaun's magic was. But she could do even more incredible things to his mind and body than he had remembered. He couldn't imagine that he had forgotten even one sensation provoked by those soul-shattering kisses and heart-stopping caresses. But even the potent memories were dim flames in comparison to the holocaust of pleasure Chelsie bestowed on him.

Suddenly each of those twinkling stars he had wished upon while he stood gazing skyward in the wilderness were sprinkling their fire upon him. He could reach up to touch the flames that flickered from those diamonds in the night. They shined only for him and Chelsie. Each one symbolized a sweet memory from the past and signified all the future memories of love that lay ahead of them.

"Your third wish has been granted," Chelsie murmured softly. Jarred not only heard her words, but he felt them whispering over his sensitized skin. "Long ago you wished for my love, and now 'tis yours for the taking. It has always been kept for you, and I have waited for just the right moment to offer it to you. Now I give it freely to you to keep forever. . . ."

Jarred rolled above her, favoring his injured arm. But there was no pain in his eyes as he stared down at the pixie-like face that peered adoringly up at him. His sapphire gaze rippled with love—the kind that knew no beginning or end. Chelsie's bewitching features formed the dimensions of his world, and Jarred couldn't see past the wide horizon of green eyes that were rimmed with thick curly lashes.

There was so much emotion churning inside him that he couldn't begin to translate his feelings into words. And so he communicated his boundless love with his body, soul, and heart. If Chelsie had any lingering doubts that Jarred wasn't exactly where he wanted to be, he intended to chase her skepticism away once and for all. When he fell in love it was forever. He had found the one woman who was strong enough to match his wild spirit and who was gentle enough to earn his devotion without requesting it. This feisty leprechaun had the power to hold him when no other woman had come remotely close to accomplishing the feat. Chelsie made him believe in forever, because to him, her name had become synonymous with love.

His ardent needs had lain dormant for ten agonizing months. But now he could delight in what had once been just an elusive dream. His caress was embroidered with love and his kisses were laced with passion. He savored each miraculous sensation that swept over his body like waves of fire. His passion blazed like a thousand suns, and a love to endure for all time was all that could contain the bursting flames. Jarred came to her, seeking ultimate depths of intimacy, groaning in tormented splendor, loving her so completely that he swore there was no room left inside him to harbor any other emotion.

And just when he feared he would die from the breathless ecstasy of loving Chelsie with every ounce of his being, he was catapulted through the flames and set into motionless flight. And he soared higher and higher—scraping rainbows and tiptoeing across the stars that sparkled like diamonds in the night—following the twinkling stepping stones to paradise. And then he found himself drifting in a sea of silver-lined clouds that paraded toward a golden sunset. A kaleidoscope of glorious feelings assaulted him, leaving him swirling in a tempest of mounting pleasure that exploded like an erupting volcano.

Jarred clutched Chelsie to him as he spun in dizzying circles—tumbling, falling, shuddering convulsively with the intense rapture that converged upon him. Passion mingled with love poured forth like an eternal spring, and Jarred drowned in the sublime satisfaction of being held in the never-ending circle of Chelsie's arms.

Having come so close to death in the wilderness had given Jarred a new lease on life. His tormenting experiences had made him realize that every second was precious. It was for this moment that Jarred had willed himself to survive against all odds. It was his lingering hope that Chelsie had not forgotten those priceless memories they had created together that had brought him safely from the jaws of hell. Now he was in paradise, clinging to a green-eyed angel. . . .

"Shall I fetch Neil to tend your arm now?" Chelsie questioned when the veil of sublime pleasure finally fell away and allowed her to return to her senses.

Jarred gave his tousled raven head a negative shake and smiled that roguish smile that melted Chelsie into mindless mush. "I'm not through loving you yet, minx," he purred like a panther.

Chelsie grinned up at the ruggedly handsome face that was enhanced by lantern light and skipping shadows. Reverently, she sketched his swarthy features, marveling at the myriad of emotions she experienced when she looked up at this mountain of a man to see her whole world in the scope of his sapphire blue eyes.

"In that case . . . we really should do something about the fact that Lucas doesn't have a sister," she teased playfully.

Jarred returned her impish smile. "And let's not forget that Papa requested a houseful of grandchildren. The duke privately confessed that he would like at least a half-dozen babies to spoil," Jarred tittered, his eyes flickering with eager anticipation.

Chelsie studied Jarred in mock deliberation. "A houseful and a half-dozen? If my calculations are correct, it will take us twenty years to fill that order."

Another utterly roguish smile displayed Jarred's pearly white teeth. "Maybe longer," he enthused. "And we will have to schedule plenty of time for practice in between, to ensure that all our children turn out to be as perfect as Lucas."

Chelsie's lighthearted laughter was sweet music to Jarred's ears. "Ah, I love you madly," she admitted, giving him a zealous squeeze.

The smile that cut crinkles in his bronzed face slowly evaporated. His unblinking gaze worshipped the dazzling beauty who lay contentedly in his arms. "You are my love wish, Chelsie Channing from Chessfield. All I'll ever need is you. . . ."

And Jarred proceeded to express the full extent of his affection once again, just in case Chelsie wasn't paying close attention the first time. If his arm was paining him in the slightest, it didn't show. Indeed, it didn't appear to inconvenience him at all, Chelsie mused as she surrendered to the titillating caresses and kisses Jarred spread upon her flesh. His hands and lips roamed everywhere, whispering his need and his love. Once again they set sail on the most intimate of journeys across the sea of stars to explore the far-reaching perimeters of the universe.

It was the best homecoming Jarred ever had. But with Chelsie in his arms, Jarred wasn't sure he would ever return again. He was dangling in time and space, watching his wish come true—a love wish granted by a feisty leprechaun whose supernatural powers exceeded his wildest imagination!

LOVE'S BRIGHTEST STARS SHINE
WITH ZEBRA BOOKS!

CATALINA'S CARESS   (2202, $3.95)
by Sylvie F. Sommerfield

Catalina Carrington was determined to buy her riverboat back from the handsome gambler who'd beaten her brother at cards. But when dashing Marc Copeland named his price — three days as his mistress — Catalina swore she'd never meet his terms . . . even as she imagined the rapture a night in his arms would bring!

BELOVED EMBRACE   (2135, $3.95)
by Cassie Edwards

Leana Rutherford was terrified when the ship carrying her family from New York to Texas was attacked by savage pirates. But when she gazed upon the bold sea-bandit Brandon Seton, Leana longed to share the ecstasy she was sure sure his passionate caress would ignite!

ELUSIVE SWAN   (2061, $3.95)
by Sylvie F. Sommerfield

Just one glance from the handsome stranger in the dockside tavern in boisterous St. Augustine made Arianne tremble with excitement. But the innocent young woman was already running from one man . . . and no matter how fiercely the flames of desire burned within her, Arianne dared not submit to another!

SAVAGE PARADISE   (1985, $3.95)
by Cassie Edwards

Marianna Fowler detested the desolate wilderness of the unsettled Montana Territory. But once the hot-blooded Chippewa brave Lone Hawk saved her life, the spirited young beauty wished never to leave, longing to experience the fire of the handsome warrior's passionate embrace!

MOONLIT MAGIC   (1941, $3.95)
by Sylvie F. Sommerfield

When she found the slick railroad negotiator Trace Cord trespassing on her property and bathing in her river, innocent Jenny Graham could barely contain her rage. But when she saw how the setting sun gilded Trace's magnificent physique, Jenny's seething fury was transformed into burning desire!

Available wherever paperbacks are sold, or order direct from the Publisher. Send cover price plus 50¢ per copy for mailing and handling to Zebra Books, Dept. 2678, 475 Park Avenue South, New York, N.Y. 10016. Residents of New York, New Jersey and Pennsylvania must include sales tax. DO NOT SEND CASH.

SURRENDER YOUR HEART
TO CONSTANCE O'BANYON!

MOONTIDE EMBRACE (2182, $3.95)
When Liberty Boudreaux's sister framed Judah Slaughter for murder, the notorious privateer swore revenge. But when he abducted the unsuspecting Liberty from a New Orleans masquerade ball, the brazen pirate had no idea he'd kidnapped the wrong Boudreaux—unaware who it really was writhing beneath him, first in protest, then in ecstasy.

GOLDEN PARADISE (2007, $3.95)
Beautiful Valentina Barrett knew she could never trust wealthy Marquis Vincente as a husband. But in the guise of "Jordanna", a veiled dancer at San Francisco's notorious Crystal Palace, Valentina couldn't resist making the handsome Marquis her lover!

SAVAGE SUMMER (1922, $3.95)
When Morgan Prescott saw Sky Dancer standing out on a balcony, his first thought was to climb up and carry the sultry vixen to his bed. But even as her violet eyes flashed defiance, repulsing his every advance, Morgan knew that nothing would stop him from branding the high-spirited beauty as his own!

SEPTEMBER MOON (1838;, $3.95)
Petite Cameron Madrid would never consent to allow arrogant Hunter Kingston to share her ranch's water supply. But the handsome landowner had decided to get his way through Cameron's weakness for romance—winning her with searing kisses and slow caresses, until she willingly gave in to anything Hunter wanted.

SAVAGE SPRING (1715, $3.95)
Being pursued for a murder she did not commit, Alexandria disguised herself as a boy, convincing handsome Taggert James to help her escape to Philadelphia. But even with danger dogging their every step, the young woman could not ignore the raging desire that her virile Indian protector ignited in her blood!

Available wherever paperbacks are sold, or order direct from the Publisher. Send cover price plus 50¢ per copy for mailing and handling to Zebra Books, Dept. 2678, 475 Park Avenue South, New York, N.Y. 10016. Residents of New York, New Jersey and Pennsylvania must include sales tax. DO NOT SEND CASH.

DISCOVER THE MAGIC
OF ZEBRA'S REGENCY ROMANCES!

THE DUCHESS AND THE DEVIL   (2264, $2.95)
by Sydney Ann Clary
Though forced to wed Deveril St. John, the notorious "Devil
Duke," lovely Byrony Balmaine swore never to be mastered by the
irrepressible libertine. But she was soon to discover that the human
heart — and Satan — move in very mysterious ways!

AN OFFICER'S ALLIANCE   (2239, $3.95)
by Violet Hamilton
Virginal Ariel Frazier's only comfort in marrying Captain Ian
Montague was that it put her in a superb position to spy for the
British. But the rakish officer was a proven master at melting a
woman's reserve and breaking down her every defense!

BLUESTOCKING BRIDE   (2215, $2.95)
by Elizabeth Thornton
In the Marquis of Rutherson's narrow view, a woman's only place
was in a man's bed. Well, beautiful Catherine Harland may have
been just a sheltered country girl, but the astonished Marquis was
about to discover that she was the equal of any man — and could
give as good as she got!

BELOVED AVENGER   (2192, $3.95)
by Mary Brendan
Sir Clifford Moore could never forget what Emily's family had
done to him. How ironic that the family that had stolen his inheri-
tance now offered him the perfect means to exact his vengeance —
by stealing the heart of their beloved daughter!

A NOBLE MISTRESS   (2169, $3.95)
by Janis Laden
When her father lost the family estate in a game of piquet, practi-
cal Moriah Lanson did not hesitate to pay a visit to the winner, the
notorious Viscount Roane. Struck by her beauty, Roane suggested
a scandalous way for Moriah to pay off her father's debt — by becoming the Viscount's mistress!